PRAISE FOR *PEEPSHOW*

'*Peepshow* is a triumph . . . Stripping with irony, all bundled up into a ripping crime novel! I can't wait for more.'
—*Stiletto Magazine*

'With *Peepshow*, Redhead announces herself as the bright new kid on the crime block.'—*Sydney Morning Herald*

'Witty, quite brilliant first novel.'—*Weekend Australian*

'A wonderful debut.'—*NW Magazine*

'Redhead has created a true original.'—*Daily Examiner*

'Tarts with hearts are always winners.'—*Sunday Times*

PRAISE FOR *RUBDOWN*

'The best Australian crime novel this year has been Leigh Redhead's *Rubdown*.'—*Weekend Australian*

'Leigh Redhead offers a flute of refreshing bubbles in *Rubdown*.'—*Spectrum*

'*Rubdown* is a criminally witty romp on the sexy side of the mean streets.'—*Australian Book Review*

'Redhead announced herself as the bright new kid on the crime block, less shabby chic than tart noir.'
—*Sydney Morning Herald*

'Robust, good natured and enjoyable thriller. Who needs imports like Evanovich when there's a Redhead in St Kilda?'—*The Age Review*

PRAISE FOR *CHERRY PIE*

'Like a literary striptease, the plot is revealed little by little, just enough to keep the reader engrossed.'—*Sun Herald*

'*Cherry Pie* should come with a series of warnings. Do not read this book if you have led a sheltered life and plan to keep it that way . . . Do not, under any circumstances, read this book in public, while eating or drinking, as you may splutter with laughter and embarrass yourself.'—*Sydney Morning Herald*

'Reckless and easily riled, full of sass and spirit, Simone has a sharp eye and smart mouth, and her wry world view infuses these books with a kind of wisecracking tone that will be welcome and familiar to readers of Sue Grafton or Janet Evanovich—although Redhead's books can be a lot sexier.'—*The Age*

'*Cherry Pie* unfolds an intriguing story, full of twists and turns you don't see coming, all underpinned by a great sense of humour.' —*Sisters in Crime*

LEIGH REDHEAD's first novel, *Peepshow*, burst onto the crime scene introducing PI Simone Kirsch to readers. Simone made her next appearance in *Rubdown*, followed by *Cherry Pie* and now *Thrill City*, Leigh's fourth crime novel.

This is a work of fiction. Names, characters, places and incidents either are the product of the author's imagination or are used fictitiously, and any resemblance to actual persons, living or dead, business establishments, events or locales is entirely coincidental.

First published in 2010

Allen & Unwin
83 Alexander Street
Crows Nest NSW 2065
Australia
Phone: (61 2) 8425 0100
Fax: (61 2) 9906 2218
Email: info@allenandunwin.com
Web: www.allenandunwin.com

Cataloguing-in-Publication details are available
from the National Library of Australia
www.librariesaustralia.nla.gov.au

ISBN 978 1 74114 737 7

Set in 11.5/14 pt Bembo by Bookhouse, Sydney
Printed in Australia by McPherson's Printing Group

10 9 8 7 6 5 4 3 2 1

thrill city

LEIGH REDHEAD

For Michael Lynch—A boy as beautiful as you shouldn't be buying his own drinks

prologue

'I need to pee.' Kate crossed her legs and squirmed, pulling the bottom strap of her seatbelt away from her lower abdomen.

Jeremy kept his eyes on the road and his hands tight on the steering wheel.

They were on their way from Melbourne to Daylesford and the countryside had changed from parched fields to swelling hills dotted with giant boulders and small scrubby trees. Soon there would be forest. She couldn't wait. It had been so long since they'd had a weekend away, and they wouldn't even be here now if it hadn't been for that horrible argument after Carl's barbecue. At least something good had come out of it, because now they were headed for forests, lakes and country cottages, cherry-hued pinot noirs and exotic, washed rind, handcrafted cheeses. Proper forests, too. Birches and spruce and maple and pine.

She felt vaguely unpatriotic preferring European trees, but the Australian bush was so coarse and prickly and such a washed-out khaki colour that it made her mouth dry just thinking about it. She wanted deep lush greens and rich mahoganies, and fields of grass as soft and verdant as billiard table felt. She wasn't sure why. She'd only been to the UK and Europe once, as a backpacker, fifteen years ago. Perhaps it was a collective, Anglo-Saxon, unconscious thing?

Pain spiked up her urethra like hot wire. She pressed her thighs together. 'Jeremy, I *really* need to pee.'

He glanced at her, irritated. It seemed to be his default setting these days. When had he changed? They'd been together for seven years, married for three. Was it after the wedding? Or since they'd bought the house? She'd been so excited to own a home at first, but now it loomed over them like a money sucking monster, an insatiable demon demanding to be fed. No holidays away, no bottles of French champagne, definitely no all-night benders like they used to go on—lots of booze, the occasional pill or line of coke if they were feeling particularly naughty. Definitely no crazy sex in hotel rooms till way past dawn. They only had sex about once a month now anyway. He was fixated on having a baby, not that they could afford it, and only wanted to do it when she was ovulating. How the hell was she supposed to know when she was ovulating? It wasn't like you could feel the egg pop out of the fallopian tube.

'Jeremy.'

'We're almost there.' His receding brown hair fluttered in the air-conditioner's updraft. 'Twenty, thirty minutes, tops. Just hang on.'

'I can't.'

'Fuck's sake, it's not even a two hour drive. Didn't you go before we left?'

'Of course. But I've drunk a litre and a half of water since then.' She kicked at the empty plastic bottle rolling around in the foot-well.

'What the hell for?'

'They say you have to drink at least four litres a day. Not counting coffee and alcohol.'

'Who's they?'

'I don't know. Experts.'

'I thought it was six glasses.'

'That was in the eighties. It keeps going up. It was two litres in the nineties and now it's four.'

'Jesus.'

'Look.' She pointed as they whizzed past a green metal road sign. 'Turnoff for Castlemaine. Eight kilometres. There's a sign for a public toilet.'

'I am not going sixteen k's out of our way.'

'Then I'll wee on the seat.'

Jeremy abruptly hit the brakes and jerked the steering wheel so that the hatchback swerved onto the shoulder, crunching gravel and spitting up dust. The sudden inertia woke their labrador, Charlie, who gave a whiny yawn, stretched, and stuck his head in the gap between the seats. Kate smelled his hot, meaty breath and felt his tongue slobber affectionately over her ear. She reached back, hooked her fingers under his collar and rubbed his thick fur. Jeremy stared at her.

'Well, you going?'

'Not here.'

'What?'

'People driving by will see me.'

'You'll be sheltered by the car, and the open door.'

'Not sheltered enough. Anyone driving south will be able to see my bum sticking out from underneath.'

'They won't know it's *your* bum.'

She crossed her arms and looked straight ahead.

'Fuck.' Jeremy slapped the indicator, pulled out and turned off at the next laneway, driving fifty metres until they were out of sight of the main road. The landscape had become more densely forested and he stopped the car beside a sagging wire fence, beyond which there was a patch of grassland, then a plantation of mature pines. Charlie was agitated, whining and scrabbling about in the back seat.

'Don't let the dog out,' Jeremy warned, so Kate held the door open just a fraction of a second too long and Charlie slithered through even as Jeremy was making a grab for his collar. He ran straight through a gap in the wire and bounded off, floppy eared and delighted. Kate suppressed a smile, shrugged and followed the dog into the grove.

It was hot outside the car but not humid, and the air was sweet and smelled like pine needles and earth. A soft breeze ruffled the knee-high grass and she felt like she was actually living in one of those tourism ads on the TV, the forties-style black and white ones that made rural Victoria look like the Umbrian countryside: chock-full of lavender fields, vineyards and stone trattorias. All she needed now was for the hatchback to morph into an old Jag, and Jeremy into a spunky Italian guy with dark eyes and thick hair named Giorgio—no, wait, Paolo.

She ducked behind the first tree she came to, bunched her skirt around her hips, wiggled her knickers down to her knees and squatted, resting one hand on the rough bark to steady herself. Charlie trotted over and sniffed around her bum for a bit until she shooed him away and finally she could let go. A small fart escaped and then a fierce stream of sweet relief, shooting down on the pine needles. The force of the cascade made a small pond which quickly broke its banks and splintered into tiny, fast-moving tributaries that all seemed hell-bent on flooding her sandals so she inched her feet further apart, feeling the burn in her thighs, the hot urine scent reminding her of horses, and stables and hay. Then another odour hit her nostrils, a vaguely rotten smell, like someone had been dumping rubbish, or maybe a dead roo was lying belly-up at the side of the road. Craning her neck, she saw Charlie rooting around in a pile of old sticks and branches and she hoped he wouldn't roll in anything nasty and stink out the Corolla. Christ, Jeremy would hit the roof.

'Charlie. Here, boy. Come on,' she called as she forced out the last of the pee and started bouncing on her haunches to dislodge the final drips. 'Charlie!'

The dog backed out of the woodpile and came running towards her at speed, ears flying back, eyes shining and something clamped between his jaws, a lump of mud and shoots by the looks of things. A nest? Before she had time to get to her feet and pull her knickers up he was there, scratching her bare bum with his find, and she got a stronger whiff of the decaying garbage smell. Disgusting. What on earth did he have in his mouth?

'Get. Go on, get.' She tried to shoo Charlie away once more but he dropped the filthy object in her lap before leaping sideways with glee. Her skirt was stretched tight between her knees so that the object nestled there like a baby in a bassinette, and even before she was completely aware of what it was she gasped in revulsion at the leathery brown and red centre and the yellow pointy-tipped twigs sticking out the edges. A claw, she thought, and then it hit her. It wasn't a claw but a hand, a severed, decayed hand, bones spiking from withered fingertips of shredded flesh. She screamed as she tumbled backwards onto the damp, prickly ground.

chapterone

It was a hot November day when I first met Nick Austin. Venetian blinds slapped the glass as he pushed open my office door, strolled in and looked around the waiting room, taking in the blue Freedom Furniture couch, wilting rubber plant and faux-timber coffee table fanned with second-hand magazines. Sitting in the office proper, I saw him through the door and freaked. I'd forgotten to lock up when I came in from the shops, and clients never just fronted up. They called or emailed first, or texted if they were young and annoying.

He wasn't young, mid forties maybe, and he was handsome in a rugged, slightly asymmetrical way. His light brown hair, longer at the front than the back, was still thick and his height—nearly six feet—helped to disguise the beginnings of middle-aged spread. He wore an expensive grey shirt with rolled-up sleeves, a jacket slung over one shoulder, and could have passed for an ageing catalogue model—or a hitman, I thought, panic prickling my bare arms. There were any number of people who'd pay good money to have me bumped off, and there I was, idiot, leaving the office unlocked so they could waltz on in. If I couldn't get to the back door and sprint to my car, I was dead.

Then I came to my senses. Surely contract killers were only suave looking in the movies, or overseas, say Paris or Milan. The Australian version would probably show up in stubbies and a blue singlet, sporting jail tatts and supermarket thongs. Not strolling bare-faced past my security camera in the middle of the day.

The guy wasn't acting particularly hitmannishly, once I thought about it. In fact, he was looking around in almost wide-eyed wonder, as though my waiting room was the coolest thing he'd ever seen. I'd seen similar expressions on trippers late at night at the 7-Eleven, delighted the store stocked something so hilarious as canned tongue.

'Can I help you?' I leaned back on my desk and crossed my arms, trying to sound stern and professional because I sure didn't look it. I was wearing cut-off denim shorts and a 'Damn Right I'm a Cowgirl' t-shirt, and my long dark hair was in a ponytail, wispy bits escaping and sticking to my lip-gloss. Normally I went for a pantsuit-and-white-shirt combo at work—made me look like a plain-clothes copper and seemed to inspire respect and confidence in clients—but that day I wasn't expecting anyone and had been washing my car out back with a bucket.

My PI business was in a narrow street-level shop-front that had housed a shoe store before I took over and partitioned the space with a cheap plasterboard wall. Sunlight shafted through half-open venetians, brightening up the waiting room, but the office at the back was dim. He wandered over to the doorway and peered into the gloom.

'I'm looking for Simone Kirsch.' His voice was deep and he was well-spoken. Educated with just a hint of ocker.

'And now you're looking *at* her.' I pushed off from the

desk and walked over, switching on the overheads. His eyes adjusted, pupils pinning then enlarging as he spotted my outfit. He smiled as though it confirmed something, or amused him, I wasn't sure which. In the fluorescent light I noticed his cheeks were marred with faint, pitted acne scars—although marred was probably the wrong word. The scars added character, gave him a Richard Burton kind of vibe, and without them he would have looked handsome but bland. He stuck out his hand and I shook it.

'I'm Nick Austin,' he announced, as though it meant something.

It didn't, so I just nodded. Up close my finely honed detective skills allowed me to notice something else. He held it well, but he'd been drinking. The glassy eyes and the faint reek of whiskey on his breath and in his sweat gave it away. Pretty hardcore for a summery weekday afternoon, but it explained the kind of bright-eyed way he'd been looking around.

'I'm a writer,' he continued when I didn't respond. That got a reaction. I snatched my hand away.

'Journalist?' I'd had enough of them after all the crap I'd gone through. When would they get it into their heads I wasn't going to do any interviews?

'No. Crime.'

'True crime?' Just as bad. Journos with stamina.

'False crime. I mean, crime fiction. I write the Zack Houston private detective books. They turned the first one into a telemovie. Aired last month? Cameron Davies played Zack.'

'Oh yeah . . .' I retreated behind my desk to the fake-leather recliner and gestured for Nick to sit on the blue armchair that had come as a set with the couch. 'I mighta read the first one.'

'*Dead Reckoning*? What'd you think?'

'It was good. I liked the character of Zack . . .'

'But?'

I squirmed in my seat, torn between wanting to be honest and possibly offending a potential client. 'Well, it was a bit unrealistic . . .'

'How so?' He leaned forward and didn't seem offended, just interested, so I relaxed a bit and grabbed the bottle of whiskey from my bottom drawer. What the hell, it was almost four and if it was good enough for Ernest Hemingway over there . . .

The corners of Nick's mouth tugged up as I poured a couple of fingers each into some cheap tumblers I kept at hand. We clinked and sipped and the whiskey lit up my gullet, burning and medicinal. He finished half in one go so I topped him up, then myself. He relaxed back into his chair. That was me, always putting people at ease.

'What did I get wrong?' he asked.

'Jeez, where do I start?' I said, feeling immediately fortified by booze. 'Like, Zack always gets a park right outside of wherever he's going, even St Kilda or Fitzroy or the CBD. He must have a bladder of cast iron, since he never pees during surveillance—in fact, he never hangs a leak ever, despite sinking copious quantities of Coopers Pale. And the chicks . . .' A little snort escaped my nose.

Nick frowned. 'What *about* the chicks?'

'They're always throwing themselves at him.'

'Zack's a tough, good-looking guy.'

'I don't care how tough and good-looking he is, no one's gonna be . . . you know . . . within seconds of meeting him. Girls don't do that.' Then I thought of my boyfriend, Sean, who was getting back from an Asia-Link police exchange in Vietnam any day. But that had been different. I'd known him for at least twenty-four hours, we'd been shot at, I'd been drunk . . .

'You sure? What if the character was a femme fatale, trying to manipulate him?'

'Dude, in my experience the best way to manipulate men is to *not* root them.'

Nick laughed, clapped his hands and sat back, looking satisfied. 'See, this is why I need to hire you. Curtis was right.'

'Curtis Malone?' Curtis was an acquaintance of mine, a titty-mag hack who'd gone to the dark side and started reporting crime. He'd got me fired from my last job, knocked up my best friend and was writing a book about a case I'd been involved in. He was a pest.

'Yeah. We were just having lunch at the Stokehouse with our mutual publisher and a couple of other writers from Wet Ink Press. I mentioned I wanted to introduce a female PI in my next Zack book and he suggested I talk to you.'

'So that's why you're here, to speak with me?'

'More than that. I'd like to spend a bit of time with you, maybe tag along on a couple of jobs, really get an understanding of what it's like, being a woman *and* a private detective.'

'I'd imagine it's much like being a man, only we have to stick a funnel into the juice bottle before we piss in it. Look, I'm happy to answer a few questions but I don't want any more publicity and I usually work on my own.'

'You don't have to worry about being identified and the thing is, I don't have any specific questions to ask. I just wanted to soak up the atmosphere, see how you go about things. It's the little details that add veracity. Like the whiskey bottle. I wouldn't have expected that from a female PI.'

'What *did* you expect?'

'In my rough draft I have her drinking green tea.'

I stuck my fingers in my mouth and pretended to gag.

'You have to admit, the whiskey's a bit of a cliché. Along with the chrome desk fan.' He nodded in its direction. Cheeky bastard.

'I'd pay you for your time,' he went on.

'Yeah?' I tried not to look too interested, but the truth was I was desperate for money. I'd gone into the red to get myself started and the paying jobs were only just starting to dribble in. I wasted a lot of time talking to window shoppers and freaks who'd seen me in the paper, knew I'd worked as a stripper and wanted to gawk or, worse, ask me on a date. I had debts coming out my arse and the combined rent on my office and one-bedroom flat in Elwood was nearly five hundred bucks a week.

'Yeah. I'm pretty flush after the TV adaptation. I'll pay your going rate just to be able to ride around with you. Say, a couple of days, sixteen hours or so? You'll be doubling your money for the same amount of work. What *is* your hourly rate?'

I briefly considered lying, but it was advertised on my website and in my newspaper ads. 'Fifty.'

'That's ridiculously cheap.'

I shrugged. He was right, but being a relatively inexperienced one-woman operation who'd gotten herself very publicly in trouble more than once, it was the only way I could get work. It was my unique point of difference, to use small-business parlance.

'The only stuff I have coming up is pretty boring,' I said. 'There's a WorkCover job, following some guy who reckons he's got a crook back.'

'Sounds great. When's it start?'

'Tomorrow morning.'

'Count me in.'

'I'll need the money upfront.' Sixteen hours was eight hundred bucks and I was determined to get paid before he sobered up.

'I don't actually have any cash on me.' He patted his pockets.

'I have EFTPOS.' I waved towards the card-swipe machine with a gameshow-model flourish. 'Credit, cheque or savings?'

chaptertwo

Nick showed up at six the next morning looking relatively chipper and I wondered if he'd quit drinking and crashed out early, or woken up and consumed a heart-starter.

The job, though boring, was a great success. Tooling around in my work car, an innocuous nineties-model white Ford Laser, we tracked the target from his home in East St Kilda to a lumberyard in Moorabbin and eventually to a house site in Carrum where I got plenty of photos and video of him lugging timber, bending, stretching and even clambering about on a roof with the agility of a spider monkey. He knocked off at three, drove to an industrial area in Cheltenham and parked around the back of what looked like an old factory. We stayed on the street.

'More building stuff?' Nick squinted and scrutinised the facade.

'Brothel.'

His eyes opened wide. 'How do you know?'

'No name on the building, street number so big it's probably visible from space, windows blacked out.' I'd spent a lot of time skulking around knocking shops on a case six months before.

Nick pointed to a smaller sign underneath the bright yellow numbers.

'*Rear Entrance.* That a pun?'

'Unintentional. I've got more than enough here to keep the insurers happy. Want to knock off and go to the pub?'

'I thought you'd never ask.'

The Balaclava Hotel sat half a block down from my office and was one of the last watering holes left in the area that actually looked like a pub. The place was the size of a large lounge room, crammed with chipped tables and covered with well-worn carpet patterned in hieroglyphs of orange, brown and green. The bar in the back left-hand corner was just a metre and a half across and completely devoid of mirrors or fancy downlights. The only adornments on the beige walls were an old footy tipping chart and two posters, one for Fosters and the other advertising Carlton Draught. Half the patrons were over sixty and wheeling vinyl shopping trolleys. The other half sported faded tattoos on their arms, necks and, in one case, shaven scalp.

The Balaclava was my kind of place. Unpretentious, with cheap booze, and the regulars were friendly, regardless of the rough-looking tatts. Nick mustn't have minded it either because despite his flash clothes, which got a few looks from the locals, he seemed quite at home as he sauntered off to the bar. I'd have bet money he was mentally rewriting his book though, removing his female PI from the juice bar and substituting her wheatgrass frappé for something a little more substantial.

I grabbed a seat at the window facing Carlisle Street, watching trams, traffic and pedestrians go by. Balaclava had been sprucing itself up, but still wasn't as trendy as nearby St Kilda and Elwood. Old ladies trundled past, dodgy dudes in shiny tracksuits, mums with prams and the occasional hipster who hadn't been able to afford the soaring real estate prices over on the leafier, prettier side of Brighton Road. The shopping strip was dotted with discount stores, delis and bagel shops, and orthodox Jews strolled by in full regalia. The suburb had character, and if I tried really hard and squinted I could almost imagine I was living in some borough of New York.

Nick returned with a pot of Coopers for himself, champagne for me, and a whiskey for both of us. What with the warm day and the cheap champagne it wasn't long before a fuzzy, pleasant sensation washed over me, and it took a second or two to distinguish the unfamiliar feeling as contentment. Winter had been harsh, and not just because of the temperature. Summer was going to be different. Sean would be back, work would trickle in and life would be calm and cruisy for once. I clinked my glass against Nick's and grinned.

'Getting your money's worth?'

'Oh yeah.' He slid his notebook out of his breast pocket and flipped it open. 'I learned that female PIs drive like maniacs, swear like wharfies, urinate frequently and dress dog-ugly when they're trailing a guy.'

'You didn't like my tracksuit?'

Nick just shuddered and I couldn't really blame him. It was no sexy, low-slung velour number but a cheap grey fleece that ballooned out in the middle and came in tight around the wrists and ankles. The set had cost twenty bucks at a discount store and made me look like a pregnant rhinoceros. I'd teamed it with no makeup and my hair tucked into a cap. Not even a builder was gonna look twice. Soon as we'd got back to the office I'd ripped the vile thing off, changed into jeans and a Willie Nelson t-shirt and slapped on a little powder, mascara and lip-gloss. Not that I was trying to flirt with Nick. Sure, he was hot for an older bloke, but I had a boyfriend and I didn't do that anymore. Although there was no guarantee it would work out with Sean and me, if it did go to hell, I wasn't going to be the one who'd screwed it up.

I had pretty much spilled my guts in the day spent in the car. You did when you were sitting around bored and it had made the day go faster. I'd rambled on about my hippy childhood, half-finished uni degree and all the stupid jobs along the way. Deckie on a prawn trawler, waitress, checkout chick, and finally stripper when I'd had enough of bitchy supermarket customers giving me the shits. He'd asked how I got into the inquiry agent racket and I'd explained the circuitous route, how I'd always wanted to be a cop—partly rebellion, partly because a policewoman had once saved my mum from a violent boyfriend—only I'd been ridiculously, scrupulously honest about my background on the application form and they'd decided it was best not to let me join.

I'd told him about the PI course, which had seemed the next best thing, my best friend Chloe getting kidnapped and my short-lived job with an agency. A case I'd gotten involved with degenerated into an absolute shit-fight when the lawyer who'd hired me ended up trying to kill me, and I'd been fired after the media splashed my mug across the television and newspapers. The stripper angle thrilled them to bits and allowed tabloids and broadsheets alike to print pictures of poles and girls bursting out of tiny bikinis. My boobs were on the modest side, which is why they usually supplemented the articles with pictures of Chloe: a bottle-blonde with far more impressive assets. I'd been approached to tell my story more times than I could count, and could have made a lot of money, but I was enough of a joke as it was. I didn't want to go on *A Current Affair* and lose what last shreds of professional dignity I had left.

For all my raving I hadn't said a word to Nick about what had happened to my mother, even though I was sure he knew.

Three months earlier a missing person job had turned ugly and gotten too close to home. Mum survived, just, but her partner Steve had been killed. I was still pretty fucked up about it and the last thing I wanted was sympathy or, god forbid, a hippy-style back-rub. I'd seen a counsellor for a while but she'd had such a hard time getting me to talk that she actually suggested we quit the sessions until I thought I was ready.

'How'd you become a writer?' I asked. Nick had more than enough background on my life. Now we'd clocked off it was my turn to interrogate him.

He grimaced and ran his fingers through his thick hair. 'God,' he said, 'where do I start? Wanted to be one since I was a kid. Soon as I could pick up a pen I'd be jotting down stories about cowboys and aliens and monsters. I was sick a lot when I was little so I spent a lot of time propped up on pillows, writing from my bed. Then as a teenager I had a rather unfortunate case of acne.' He gestured towards his face. 'I didn't socialise much. There's all the time in the world to write if you're not burdened with the responsibilities of partying and picking up girls. What can I say? I was a nerd.'

'I was kind of nerdy too,' I admitted, and Nick rolled his eyes like he didn't believe me.

'Anyway, I went to uni, studied English lit, did a Dip Ed, met my first ex-wife, Jenny, and started teaching. I was always writing and finally finished a semi-autobiographical novel based on my childhood growing up in Sale. A small press offered to publish and I was thrilled—my lifelong dream was coming true. They warned me it would be a small print run, two thousand copies, and I wouldn't make any money out of it, but I was stupidly optimistic. In my heart I just knew it would take off, get published overseas, and someone would turn it into an award-winning movie.' He smirked at himself, shook his head, drained his beer and moved on to the whiskey.

'I'm guessing it didn't work out like that.'

'Book got some good reviews, but pretty much sank without a trace. I kept teaching and continued writing. Beavering away on my next manuscript in the evenings after school. Damn thing was giving me grief though. Classic second-novel syndrome. I couldn't make it work, so I started penning this hard-boiled detective novel. I'd always loved crime. Read it to escape from all the dense, literary stuff I studied at uni. I created this character Zack, bit of an alter ego, and he took over and the book seemed to write itself. I was way behind schedule with the serious novel, and in a meeting with my publisher I told them, just joking, that I had a PI manuscript in the bottom drawer. They wanted to see it, and the rest is history. My crime series sold ten times better than my literary novel, and is really taking off now the first one's come out as a telemovie. The others are in preproduction as we speak.'

'Wow, congratulations.'

He shrugged, then looked at me and asked something weird. 'Why are you a private detective?'

'I already told you about the cops saving my mum and stuff.'

'That's the how. I want to know the why.'

I'd asked myself the same question but had never come up with a definitive answer. I liked being my own boss. I got a kick out of spying on people. I was easily bored and addicted to adrenaline. Sticking it to the Victoria police by proving I was better than them was part of it, but mostly I hated when rich, powerful people tried to become even richer and more powerful by screwing with people who couldn't defend themselves. I didn't tell Nick any of those things, though.

'I dunno.' I shrugged.

'What about your dad? Is he on the scene?'

'Haven't seen him for fifteen years.'

'How does that make you feel?'

'It doesn't make me feel anything. Why?'

'Sorry, I can't help myself. I'm always trying to figure out motivation.'

'Let me guess—I became a stripper because I needed the male attention and I became a PI because, shit, you tell me.'

Nick shook his head and blushed a bit. It made him look like a teenager. 'I shouldn't have . . .'

I chucked him on the shoulder. 'Don't stress. I'm just messing with you, not pissed off.' It was half true.

Nick changed the subject. 'When's our next session?'

I pulled my diary out of my bag and flipped through. 'How about Monday? I've got something a bit different from the WorkCover case. Guy thinks his wife is having an affair, little lunchtime liaison, so I'm gonna follow her around the CBD. No trackie-daks either, we'll have to go corporate on this one.'

'Monday's great. Meet at your office?'

'Nah, I'm gonna follow from her home. Lives in Collingwood.'

'I'm in Abbotsford.'

'Great. I'll pick you up.'

We shook hands and Nick got up to leave. 'Oh, almost forgot.' He patted his jacket, withdrew a couple of laminated passes and handed them to me.

'Yarra Bend Summer Sessions,' I read out. 'Sounds like a dance party.'

'It's a mini arts and writers' festival at Yarra Bend Park in Clifton Hill this Saturday. Come along if you're not busy, bring a friend. I'm on a panel with Shane Maloney and Peter

Temple, so should be a good one. Pass includes entry into everything and a couple of free drinks.'

'I'll see what I can do. May have some work coming up . . .'

God I was a liar.

chapter three

After the pub I decided to drop in on my best friend, Chloe. She held the lease on the building that housed my office and sublet to me while she ran her agency, Chloe's Elite Strippers, from her flat upstairs.

The Carlisle Street entrance, a glass door next to mine, was locked, so I entered my office intending on scooting out back, before hesitating. I don't know whether it was the champagne, or Nick's amateur psychology, but I booted up my computer and composed an email to my dad, care of the IT company he'd worked for the last time I'd seen him. I kept it simple—*Hi Mark, it's your prodigal daughter, Simone. Long time no see. What's up?*—and pressed send before I could chicken out. I turned off the computer, left my office, jogged across the small rear car park, and took the back stairs up to the deck at Chloe's.

Her place was pretty basic, a couple of bedrooms facing Carlisle Street and a small formica kitchen she never cooked in. The huge lounge in the middle was her command centre: vast corner desk, practice pole in the middle of the room, feather boas hanging from hooks and body-glitter ground into the carpet. Publicity pictures of the girls decorated the walls, along with posters of Marilyn Monroe and prints of old-time dancers like Blaze Fury and Gypsy Rose Lee. Opposite the desk sat Chloe's pride and joy, a recently purchased red couch shaped like a pair of lips. French doors opened from the lounge room onto the best thing about the place: a concrete deck at the back of the building that looked out over the rooftops and train line. Chloe had set it up with outdoor furniture, potted plants and lurid green astroturf.

That's where I found her, lying topless on a yellow striped banana lounge, simultaneously eating chicken-in-a-biskit, flicking through *Picture* magazine, and talking to prospective clients on the phone. She was just over six months pregnant, belly stretched taut and boobs so enormous they were terrifying. She'd always been on the busty side, but now her nipples were the size of saucers and her breasts practically blocked out the sun. She looked so rampantly fecund she reminded me of an ancient fertility symbol, although I doubted the Venus of Willendorf had ever been depicted slick with coconut oil, wearing a pink G-string and clear perspex stripper heels.

I pulled up a matching pink lounge and lay back, a pleasant little buzz on after the drinks at the pub. It was five o'clock and the sun was still quite high in the sky but the worst of the heat was gone. The smell of coconut oil made me think of cocktails and tropical holidays, and I wondered if, when Sean came back, we could take some sort of break at the beach, just for a few days. I closed my eyes, imagining salty, sweaty sex in a hotel room under a slow-moving fan. Meanwhile Chloe was on the phone, reciting the spiel she knew off by heart.

'G-string strip's a hundred, full nude a hundred and twenty, and raunchy—that's open leg work, darl—hundred and seventy-five. Any extras, say, strawberries and cream, vibes, pearls, or fruit and veggies? That's two fifty. What's a fruit and veg strip? Use your imagination, hon. Bi twin's three fifty, five hundred if you want the whole lezzo shebang. You got internet access? Check out the girls on our website. We also run Chloe's Boob Cruises—very popular for a work do—and we have state-of-the-art jelly-wrestling facilities. You'll have to book early though. Coming up to Christmas is a very busy time of year.' She hung up and had just drawn a breath to talk to me when the phone rang again. She rolled her eyes and answered.

'Chloe's Elite Strippers, Chloe speaking. Hi, Tiara, what's up?' A pause, then: 'You're fucking kidding me. Listen, if you don't wanna work, I can just take you off the books.'

Soon as she'd said that I heard tinny shrieking, and Chloe winced and held the handset away from her ear. I didn't envy her having to organise a bunch of strippers, most of whom were even crazier than she was.

'Fuck's sake, Tiara. Call back when you've straightened out. Yes you are, you're off your tits. Wake up to yourself. Take a fucking Valium and take the next week off. I've had it. This is your last chance.'

She hung up and I raised my eyebrows. '*Tiara*? Is it just me or are the names getting stupider?'

'The names and the fucking girls.' A midge adhered itself to one oil-basted breast and she flicked it off. 'This one started out okay until she got a new boyfriend and got into ice. Lost a ton of weight and now she's losing the plot. I'd fire her but she's good, when she actually shows up.'

'Isn't ice just like speed?'

'No, mate, it's ten times as strong. I mean, we always did a bit of coke or Louie to keep us awake and give us a bit of energy for the shows, but this stuff's fucked up. They smoke the shit through crack pipes, don't sleep for three days, and it sends them mental. You don't wanna do her show, do you?'

'What is it?'

'Just raunchy. You won't have to stick anything up your clacker.'

'Sure.' I was trying to wean myself off stripping, but with all my debts I needed every cent I could get.

Chloe made a note in her Hello Kitty diary and looked pleased. 'Thanks, Simone. You may not be the best stripper in the world, but you are the most reliable.'

I gave her a look.

'Hey,' she said. 'How'd the thing with the crime writer go? I checked out his website. You never let on he was hot. Gonna shag him?'

'Chloe. Sean's coming back in a couple of days.'

'You haven't seen him for six months. How do you know you still like him? How do you know he still likes you and hasn't been boffing some Asian chick?'

'I don't. I guess I'll find out. I guess we'll both find out.'

'And what about Alex?'

Alex Christakos was in the Fraud Squad and he was gorgeous: tall and broad-shouldered with black hair, dark chocolate eyes, and big hands with veins on the back that roped all the way up his forearms. He favoured expensive shirts and wore this woody, earthy aftershave that did strange things to me when I smelled it up close.

I'd always fancied Alex and had worked closely with him on a few occasions, but despite the obvious chemistry between us, getting involved would have been disastrous. He was a hell of a lot straighter than me, disapproved of pretty much everything I did, had a fiancée he was marrying in two days and, worst of all, was Sean's best friend.

Alex had been on leave from the service for the past few months because of an injury he'd sustained working on a case with me. He'd been in a coma and nearly died, and he still hadn't completely recovered. He was getting physical therapy to regain full use of his right arm, and the docs suspected a slight brain injury may have affected his impulse control. Not real swell when your job involves packing a loaded weapon. The police service was his life, and every time I thought of what had happened to him I felt like crying because I knew it was all my fault. Him, my mum, my mum's partner Steve . . . *Don't think about it.* That was my mantra. Nothing wrong with a bit of repression.

'What about him?' I asked, as casually as I could.

'Ever since you came back from his buck's night you've been acting strange.'

I'd unwittingly turned up at Alex's bachelor party because some arsehole cousin of his had thought it would be funny to hire me to do a cop-themed strip. I strode into the room, came up from behind, and it wasn't until I'd straddled his lap that I realised it was Alex. Soon as I clocked him I ran out of the function room and locked myself in a disabled toilet, mortified. Then he'd come into the cubicle with me, drunk, and—

'See, you're doing it now,' Chloe said. 'You've got this weird, faraway look in your eyes. Did something happen between the two of you at the party?'

'I told you. Soon as I found out whose buck's it was I left.'

'Took you a long time to get back here.'

'Waited ages for a cab.'

She looked like she was going to keep hassling, and all I wanted was to put everything behind me and never think of Alex Christakos again. Desperate to change the subject, I plucked the passes out of my jeans pocket and dangled them in front of her. She squinted, examining the laminated cardboard.

'Backstage pass?'

'To a writers' festival. Nick gave them to me.'

She plucked one from me and read it closely. 'The Summer Sessions!' She sat up straight. 'We have to go.'

'Wow. Nice to see you're so excited. And there I was thinking your idea of literature was *Penthouse Forum*.' Mean, but I owed her for the 'not the best stripper' crack.

'I read, sometimes. But that's not why I wanna go. Curtis is doing a true crime panel there and I have to check up on him.'

I did a double take. Far as I knew, Chloe didn't particularly like Curtis. They'd dated for five months, then she'd got knocked up and decided to have the baby and ditch the boyfriend. He'd been hopelessly devoted, but she'd been rather cruel, using him for sex when she felt like it then berating him for continually hanging around.

'Why?'

'He didn't answer my last booty call. It got me suspicious. I think he has a girlfriend.'

'So what? You've had about five boyfriends since you two broke up.'

Pregnancy hadn't taken the edge off her libido, or her ability to attract anything with a pulse.

'Not boyfriends. Roots. Big difference.'

'Either way, why do you care?'

Her hand fluttered to her chest and her voice went all breathy. 'Simone, he's the father of my unborn child!'

What bullshit. She just loved having him at her beck and call. It was an ego trip and I told her so. 'Chloe, you don't want him, but you don't want anyone else to have him.'

She opened her mouth wide, trying for shocked and hurt, but there was a sly look in her eye and I knew I'd hit the mark.

chapter**four**

Chloe and I headed off to the writers' festival in my pale blue '67 Ford Futura. It was good to be driving The Beast again, zebra-patterned seat covers, dangling mirror ball and all, much more fun than the boring, innocuous Laser I used for work. I'd even added a new sticker to the bumper that read, in Western-style script, *Country Music Is Not a Crime.*

It was another hot day and I was wearing my usual summer uniform of faded, ripped hipster jeans and a top with the sleeves cut off. My 'Damn Right I'm a Cowgirl' t-shirt was in the wash so I'd gone with 'Save Water—Drink More Champagne'.

Chloe, however, was a different story. A hint of competition and she'd pulled out the big guns. Platinum hair boofed at the roots and curled at the ends, two hours of makeup including individually applied false eyelashes, a double session at the solarium and even a new dress: a pink gingham baby-doll number cut so low you didn't notice the belly because you couldn't tear your eyes away from the cleavage. As usual she was tripping along on high heels, but in deference to the location had gone for cork platforms to minimise her chance of getting bogged.

Yarra Bend was a huge swathe of parkland on the northern edge of the inner city right next to Clifton Hill, made up of grass ovals, bushy slopes and scenic bike paths. A broad, muddy stretch of the Yarra River twisted through it, lined with ghost gums and overhanging willows.

I squeezed The Beast into a car park and we made our way across a sports field towards a cluster of canvas marquees. Melbourne folk loved festivals; there was about a dozen taking place at any given moment, and the ground was packed with people and dogs and kids. I smelled barbecued meat and heard amplified voices and the occasional burst of laughter and applause.

I resolved to get out of the office more and into, like, nature and shit. Sean was back in less than twenty-four hours and, if everything went well, we could do stuff like this all the time. Like normal people. Speaking of normal, all the ordinary citizens were staring at Chloe like she'd just beamed down from the mother ship, but that was okay. She'd always been a rampant exhibitionist and got seriously perturbed when folks *didn't* gawk. The one time she passed a building site and no one whistled she'd turned feral and screamed abuse at the construction workers.

Nick's session wasn't scheduled to start for twenty-five minutes so we headed straight for the bar tent to take advantage of our VIP passes. Lord knew I was going to need some liquid encouragement if I had to sit still for an hour while three middle-aged blokes nattered on about the writing process, and also I had a feeling we'd find Nick there. I was right. He was at a white plastic table in a corner, sitting with Curtis Malone and two women I didn't recognise. I waved, Chloe pretended she hadn't seen Curtis, and we headed to the bar where she flirted with the waiter, waving around her laminated card, declaring it was her 'back-door' pass and that she was with the band.

Nick pulled across a couple of chairs as we approached with our champagnes, and when I introduced him to Chloe I witnessed a massive triumph of will as he managed to keep his eyes on her face.

'It's *so* great to meet you, Nick,' she said, jiggling as she talked, laying it on thick for Curtis' benefit. 'Simone's told me all about you and I *love* your books.'

Nick raised his eyebrows and looked pleased. 'You've read them?'

'No, but I saw them on TV! Cameron Davies was *so* hot as Zack.'

Nick gave me a look and all I could do was shrug. He pointed to a woman on his left with shoulder-length, flicked-out blonde hair streaked with silver. 'Simone and Chloe, meet Liz. She's not only my publisher, she's also my twin sister.'

'Twins?' Chloe squawked. 'Get fucked.'

'It's true,' said Nick.

'Not identical.'

'No.' Liz pursed her mouth.

'Keeping it all in the family.' I laughed, trying to lighten the mood.

'My publishing Nick's books has nothing to do with nepotism and everything to do with the quality of the work.'

Yikes. The sharp tone and stern look made me feel like I was fourteen and back in the principal's office.

'Curtis you know,' Nick said quickly, 'and this is Desiree. She's another author.'

Chloe usually stared out other blondes, kind of a territorial thing, but that day she only had eyes for Desiree or, more specifically, the hand Desiree had just proprietarily placed on Curtis' thigh.

Desiree looked strangely familiar; she was about ten years older than Chloe and me, late thirties perhaps, and my first thought was that I wanted to be like her when I grew up. She wasn't exactly pretty, but she was stunning, tall and slim with burgundy hair blunt-cut at her shoulders and a thick fringe that skimmed her black eyebrows. Her skin was tanned and her face angular, with sharp cheekbones, a long nose, feline eyes winged with liquid liner, and a wide mouth painted red. She wore a tight black knee-length skirt, a sleeveless, dark red cheongsam top and exotic-looking jet earrings. She seemed sleek and predatory, a red-haired Cleopatra, and made my friend, in her flouncy gingham, look like a kewpie doll in comparison.

As Desiree stared back evenly at Chloe I suddenly realised who she was: the former high-class callgirl who'd penned a book about her exploits, naming no names but providing just enough information so you could make a fair guess who her rich and powerful clients had been. After the memoir she'd written a book of sex tips and now had regular spots on various television and radio shows as their resident 'sexpert'.

I had to hand it to Curtis, he had a lot of luck with the ladies considering he wasn't the hottest tamale in the bain-marie. He wasn't ugly exactly—in fact, with his sandy, slightly curly hair, boyish face and putty nose some people might have called him cute—but he'd always seemed like an annoying younger brother to me, even though he was thirty-three. When we'd first met, Curtis had worked for *Picture* magazine and had been the proud owner of a mullet-style haircut, a host of flannelette shirts and Dunlop Volley tennis shoes. After moving to Melbourne, becoming a crime journo and dating Chloe, he'd changed his style, going to the other extreme: natty shoes, slicked-back hair and shiny ties that made him resemble an extra from *The Sopranos*, albeit an albino one. Now that he was an actual true-crime author his sartorial style had settled: khaki chinos, Adidas slip-ons and a short-sleeved, red-checked, tastefully retro Wrangler shirt.

'Hey, Curtis, how you going?'

'Great.' He stretched out the word and slouched into his chair, one arm slung over the back. Mr Cool, these days. 'Book about the Wade case is all but done, just waiting for the trial and soon as that's over, bam, we rush the release. Couple of other writers are covering it too but I'll blow them out of the water, seeing as how I was personally involved in the situation. You know there's still time for you to give me an interview, let me know exactly what was going through your head when you thought you were gonna die.'

'No thanks.'

Curtis shrugged. 'No probs. I'll just make it up.'

I tried to like him, god help me I did.

'Any word on the trial date?' Nick's sister asked.

'Early next year,' I said. 'Late January, early Feb.' I didn't want to think about it because every time I did my stomach flipped.

Emery Wade was one of those rich, powerful people I couldn't stand: a high-profile criminal lawyer who'd knocked off members of his own family to protect his reputation and get ahead. His favourite hobby had been to visit prostitutes, find out what they wouldn't do, and try to force them into doing these things by using money, drugs or violence. Most crims were dumb or on drugs or both; Wade scared me because he was as intelligent as he was sadistic. I kept worrying he'd exploit his wealth and connections to worm his way out of the murder and manslaughter charges, and I couldn't relax until he'd been found guilty.

'See you there.' Curtis pointed a pen at me, studiously ignoring Chloe just as she was ignoring him. She was pretty focused on the woman next to him, though.

'Desiree, like, that's your real name?'

I couldn't believe that after five whole minutes that was the best she could come up with. Maybe pregnancy really did melt your brain.

Desiree just smirked. 'It's more real than your hair colour, honey.'

Curtis sputtered with laughter, Chloe gasped, and I was sure she was going to leap across the table and go her when suddenly a festival volunteer, a plump young woman wearing an oversized 'Summer Sessions' t-shirt and carrying a walkie talkie, ran up and said, 'Nick Austin?'

'Uh-huh.'

'Oh, thank god I found you.' She was breathless and sweating, and wisps of light brown hair were plastered to her forehead. 'There have been a couple of last-minute changes to your panel. Shane and Peter have had to drop out. It's unbelievable. Shane's plane was delayed and Peter's come down with the flu and—'

'You're kidding,' Nick said, but he sounded sympathetic, not mad. 'So, what—it's just me up there?'

'Oh no.' She was still gasping, sucking in air. 'We've been really lucky and got a couple of fantastic authors on short notice. Rod Thurlow you'd have to know, he's the best-selling action writer, and we also have Isabella Bishop.'

The indulgent smile slipped right off Nick's face and the plastic cup of beer he was holding indented with a sharp crack. 'Is this some kind of joke?'

She frowned, confused. 'Uh, no. Is something the matter?'

I glanced around the table. Desiree arched her brows and exchanged a look with Curtis, and Liz frowned and put her hand on Nick's shoulder. 'You don't have to do the panel. You agreed on the proviso it was with Temple and Maloney, not—'

'I have to do it. If I don't I look like I'm chucking a tantrum.' Nick stormed out of the tent, chucking what looked very much like a tantrum. He stopped next to a large gum tree by the river, took out a cigarette and smoked furiously.

'What is it? What did I say?' The hapless volunteer was literally wringing her hands.

Liz crossed her arms and shook her head. 'It's not your fault. You weren't to know.'

'Know what?'

Desiree sipped her red wine and piped up. 'Isabella is Nick's ex-wife. They had a rather rough break-up. She left him for Rod Thurlow nine months ago.'

chapterfive

A hundred or so people were crammed into the large marquee, sitting in rows on white plastic chairs. It was hot, and the stifling air inside the tent smelled of river water, mown grass, canvas and takeaway lattes.

Four armchairs had been arranged in a shallow semicircle on the low stage at the rear, each with its own microphone, angled on a stand. Nick sat at the far right, and a guy in his sixties with a beard and a tweed jacket with elbow patches sat on the left of the stage, chatting to a sound technician. The two seats in between were empty. Water bottles stood on side tables between the chairs, but Nick clutched a tall glass of clear liquid and his small grimacing sips suggested it was straight vodka or gin rather than H_20.

Chloe and I were sitting in the middle of the tent, Liz was in the front row and Curtis and Desiree somewhere up the back, getting smoochy. The session had been due to start five minutes earlier, so Chloe'd had plenty of time to bitch furiously to me under her breath.

'Can you believe what she said about my hair?'

'Come on, babe.' I sighed. 'You started it. And anyway,

what's it got to do with her? He's a single guy. Why shouldn't she be rubbing his leg? All's fair and all that . . .'

Chloe huffed. 'You're supposed to be my friend.'

'I am. Did you know Desiree's the famous sexpert? Must be a real wildcat in the sack. Maybe we should buy her book, pick up a few tips.'

Chloe got so frustrated that she actually pinched me, so I slapped at her hand then turned away and studied the crowd. Apart from a small contingent of high school kids they were mostly female, middle-aged and middle class, some with husbands in tow. A few uni student types sat close to the front, probably wannabe writers judging from the way they clutched notepads and stared at Nick as though the secret to getting published hovered about him like a hippy aura.

People were getting restless, checking the time and looking around and murmuring, when the growl of an engine reached the spectators. Everyone twisted in their seats in time to see a Hummer, one of those boxy half-car, half-tank things that all the Hollywood celebs were fond of, bouncing across the field. It barrelled straight for the tent and skidded side-on at the last moment, churning up clods of dirt and grass. The vehicle had been painted with a camouflage pattern, and the cover image from Rod Thurlow's latest book—*Lethal Force: A Chase Macallister Adventure*—had been airbrushed onto the side of the truck; it depicted a soldier with an assault rifle slung over his shoulder, standing on a sand dune, silhouetted by an enormous orange setting sun. The tag-line read, nonsensically: *How far would a man go to save his country and rescue the woman he loves? The only way he knows how. With Force. Lethal Force.*

The driver's side door opened and out leapt a fit-looking guy in army fatigues, his ginger hair shorn into a buzz cut. He wasn't much taller than me, maybe five eight, but he was built like a brick shithouse. His tight sleeveless tee showed off an inflated chest, and his bi's and tri's were so pumped his arms appeared to have contracted until they were a little too short for his body. He slammed the door, jogged around to the passenger side and gallantly lifted a woman to the ground.

After action man I was expecting a latter-day GI Jane, but Isabella Bishop was tiny, delicate and pale, and with her jet-black bob, flowing silk dress and cloche hat, she looked like she'd come straight from the bohemian quarter of Paris in the nineteen thirties. Rod linked his arm in hers and they walked down the aisle towards the stage, him strutting like a bantam rooster, her gliding on vintage Mary-Janes. As they passed I saw she was beautiful, with exquisite doll-like features. Chloe noticed too, let out a low whistle and leaned towards me, the Desiree situation temporarily forgotten.

'What the hell's a gorgeous chick like her doing with him? She's so hot she'd make me turn.'

'Don't you already swing both ways?'

'Yeah, but I'm talking about switching teams.'

'If you're so bisexual, how come you've never tried to root me?'

'Mate, you're my best friend,' Chloe scoffed. 'You don't shit in your own nest.'

I turned my attention back to Nick. He didn't take his eyes off Isabella as she walked onto the stage. She nodded and sat down next to him. Rod offered his hand but Nick ignored him. The guy in the tweed looked slightly panicked, and as soon as Rod had sat down he leaned forward and spoke rapidly into the mike.

'Welcome, everybody, to our "Scene of the Crime" session. For those of you who don't know me, I'm Phillip Cummings, host of *Sunday Afternoon Book Talk* on the ABC, and despite some last-minute program changes we have three truly fabulous crime writers with us this afternoon. At my far left we have the author Nick Austin, whose first Zack Houston book has recently been made into a very successful telemovie.

'We also have the lovely Isabella Bishop. Isabella is probably best known for her exquisite poetic novella *The Liquidity of Desire*, and she's just made her first foray into the mystery genre with her new book, *Thrill City*, described as a literary crime novel. And right next to me is Rod Thurlow, a man who needs no introduction. Rod is one of Australia's best-loved and best-selling authors. He's an ex-SAS soldier whose thrilling tales of adventure have been translated into fifteen languages and optioned by a major Hollywood studio. His latest Chase Macallister book, *Lethal Force*, sold four hundred thousand copies in Australia alone. Please put your hands together to welcome all our guests.'

As the applause died down Rod leaned in to talk into the microphone. He had a deep voice and sounded a little like Russell Crowe. 'Actually, Phillip, it's *eighteen* different languages, including Swahili, and according to the latest Nielsen Bookscan figures I've sold four hundred and fifty thousand in Australia.'

He leaned back, elbows splayed, legs wide apart, and flicked Nick a look. Nick ignored him, staring straight ahead and sipping his 'special' water. Although his expression was relatively relaxed and neutral, his eyes were like slivers of stone. Isabella sat between them, hands folded in her lap, head tilted and ankles elegantly crossed.

'Thanks for that, Rod,' Cummings said. 'Well, I guess the first question I want to ask our panellists is: why crime fiction? Nick?'

Nick lost the flinty look and turned on the charm, recounting the difficult-second-novel story with just enough self-deprecation to get a few sympathetic laughs. 'My theory about the genre is that it's cathartic,' he said. 'It forces you to confront your fears, and finally resolves anxieties when the baddies get their just deserts. It's also a terrific way for a writer to explore personal and even social issues. I think it was Ian Rankin who said, "If you want to know what's going on in a society, read its crime fiction."'

A few people in front of me nodded, and one or two took notes. Nick went on to tell the audience he'd been inspired by the pulp fiction of the forties and fifties and by the greats: Chandler, Hammett, Jim Thompson, James M. Cain.

'My protagonist, Zack, is definitely part of that anti-hero tradition. I think it's important to have a flawed character rather than a superman who can take on a bar-room full of henchmen with one hand tied behind his back.' The crowd tittered and Nick finally looked over at Rod. 'And by flawed I mean morally, as well as physically and psychologically. I can't stand goody-two-shoes characters, the kind who always do the right thing and never hit the bottle or get led astray.'

'Led astray by one of those pesky femmes fatales?' asked Phillip, and everyone laughed.

'You know, I'd have to disagree with Nick,' said Rod.

'How so?' Phillip crossed his legs and leaned forward again, holding his chin.

'People don't want a flawed character, they want a hero—someone larger than life who can act as a role model, show them the difference between right and wrong, and inspire them to be the best they can be. I don't want to read about a weak man. And I doubt the general public do either.'

As Rod talked Nick shook his head and threw back the last of the liquid in his glass, spilling a little down the front of his shirt.

'Bullshit.' He wiped his face with the back of his hand.

An old duck tutted somewhere behind me.

'I think Rod's sales speak for themselves, Nick,' Isabella said.

'Then the general public are idiots.'

There were more tuts and even a hiss from the back of the tent.

'Awww, not you guys, of course.' Nick rustled up a charming smile, but he was just a little too pissed to get the measure of the crowd, and I could sense them starting to turn.

Cummings leapt in before Nick dug himself further into the shit. 'So, Isabella. Why did you choose crime? Why did you change midstream, so to speak?'

'I'm glad you asked me that, Phillip.' Her voice was soft, cultured. 'I was really intrigued with the possibility of playing around with such a rigid and, let's face it, clichéd genre. I wanted to ignore the conventions and experiment with the—'

'Crime fiction *is* the conventions,' Nick said. 'You can twist them but you can't ignore them. And since when did you decide to write a bloody crime book? Last I knew you were trying your hand at erotica.' He pulled a silver hip flask out of his briefcase-style bag and started refilling his glass. The tuts grew louder. No hiding what was in there now.

Isabella smiled in a humble, friendly way that put the crowd on her side and made Nick look bad. 'I actually worked on my book, *Thrill City*, for a year as part of my master's thesis. The title itself suggests a trashy, hard-boiled pulp novel, but that's intentionally misleading. There are no anxieties resolved in my work because I challenged the detective hermeneutic and broke the rules. I mean, why do you need an investigative figure? Why must the crime be solved? I'm very proud of *Thrill City* and feel I've really experimented with the form.'

Nick gulped his drink and rolled his eyes. 'Experimented yourself into the remainder bin, most likely.'

More tuts, a couple of gasps, and one 'well I never' emanated from the crowd, and Cummings dabbed sweat from his forehead with a handkerchief. Rod gave Nick a squinty look and flexed the tendons in his fingers like he was about to spring up out of his chair, but Isabella put one dainty hand on his forearm and shook her head sweetly. Her nail polish was a deep red-wine with a hint of brown, a shade that I'd been trying to get hold of for ages. I glanced over to the front row and saw Liz pinch the bridge of her nose.

Rod's jaw worked, but he stayed put and defended his lady's honour with praise. 'I've read *Thrill City*, and although it was a bit deep for a regular guy like me, I can tell you this: it's a masterpiece. I like to think of myself as a wordsmith, but Bella . . . Who would imagine that such a beautiful princess could also write like an angel?'

Nick snorted and gave Isabella a look that seemed to say, 'Where did you find this chump?'

Cummings jumped in. 'Well, certainly some heated debate and a lot of food for thought. I'd like to finish off the panel with a short reading from each of the panellists, then open up the floor for questions. Nick, if you'd like to start?'

Nick fumbled in his bag for his latest novel and read out a scene in which his hero got drunk, ended up in bed with one of the aforementioned femmes fatales, then got knocked unconscious by some bad guys right in the middle of the act. After meeting Nick, I couldn't help but imagine Zack Houston as looking exactly like him.

When Nick was finished, Rod recited a tale of incredible derring-do that involved Chase Macallister jumping from a helicopter onto a skyscraper to save his girlfriend—a perky part-time model and full-time astrophysicist—from a group of Muslim separatists.

Nick didn't try to hide his contempt, shaking his head, swigging from his glass, and occasionally snorting. When Thurlow finished, Nick mimed a yawn, laying it on so thick that Isabella couldn't pretend to ignore him any longer.

'He's just jealous,' she told Rod and the rest of the crowd. 'I think the passage has a wonderful, exuberant energy.'

'Thank you, darling. Some critics have called my plots a bit far-fetched, but I don't think so if you look at what's happening in the world today. The terrorist threat we all face is terrifyingly real. I have to say that I draw a lot on my experiences as a soldier—although I can't tell you the precise details. That's classified information.'

Cummings opened his mouth to say something, but Nick butted in: 'You know, I wasn't actually surprised that you slept around on me.' He slouched sideways to face Isabella. 'But I can't believe you'd let Mr Axis of Evil here stick his shrivelled, right-wing dick inside you.'

'That's it.' Rod stood up, but Isabella and Cummings lunged and grabbed a wrist each to keep him in place. A woman down the front madly scribbled in a notepad, while a guy with a big camera snapped off shots. A grey-haired lady was so appalled that she actually stood up and shouted, 'You ought to be ashamed of yourself!'

Nick nodded in mock wide-eyed innocence, slurring slightly. 'You're right, madam, she should be. Izzy looks pure as the driven slush but don't let that fool you. Got a real mouth on her—one time she called me a cockless cunt. Wasn't so much the insult bothered me but the fact a so-called professional writer would use such an obvious tautology.'

Cummings could bear it no longer and tried to wrest back a modicum of control. 'Mr Austin! There are schoolchildren in the audience.'

'Oh, I'm sorry.' He turned to them. 'Tautology: the redundant repetition of meaning in a sentence. I mean, a vagina, by its very definition—'

'Would you like to take this outside?' Rod was red-faced and sweating.

'Not particularly.' Nick shrugged.

I looked at Isabella, sure she'd be mortified by the turn of events. I was; it was so cringe-worthy I was wincing and digging my fingernails into my palms. Chloe seemed to be enjoying herself, though. She'd been watching back and forth like she was at the tennis. But Isabella didn't even look embarrassed. She had a glint in her eyes and a small smile on her lips and looked almost . . . triumphant.

Cummings checked his watch. 'I know it's a little early but we might have to wrap it up here. My apologies to the audience, but if guests turn up intoxicated and then refuse to act in a civilised manner—'

'No, Phillip,' Isabella said. 'I'd still like to do my reading. That is, if Nick can control himself for five minutes and refrain from interrupting.'

Nick held up his hands, palms out.

Cummings said, 'If you're sure . . .'

She nodded. Cummings held up Isabella's book and read from the blurb at the back: 'Atmospheric, evocative, elusive and erudite, this literary crime novel transcends the genre—'

'Transcends the plot,' Nick snorted. 'This I gotta hear.'

Isabella gave him a look. 'I did send you a signed copy, Nick.'

'Must have chucked it in the trash.'

'Well, you'll have to buy a new one with your own money.'

It suddenly occurred to me that they were flirting with each other. The eye contact, the insults; it was nasty and brutal, but it was flirting nonetheless. Rod finally caught on too, because he stared at them, a deep crevice indenting the skin between his bushy ginger eyebrows.

Isabella started reading, talking soft and low into the microphone, her velvety voice lulling the crowd.

'It is a house of mirrors, you know that now. Sleek-surfaced, burnished and brittle as the man's crystalline consciousness. A leather lounge reflects light, the slippery cushions where he pushed you down . . .'

Nick went pale and stared at Isabella with an expression I couldn't quite read. Was he angry? Scared? Had she plagiarised something he'd written? His fingers clenched around his glass.

'You glimpse yourself, for a moment, in the television's vast, dead screen: dress torn, breasts exposed; clutching the statue high above your head. Fingers twined in chrome veins, you sweep it towards his ruined skull and as it hooks the scalp you look, finally, and laugh at the banality of the object which—'

Bang! The audience jumped as Nick's glass shattered in his fist. He sat there and stared as blood poured out of his palm. Cummings jumped up, brandishing his handkerchief and trying to help, but Nick just stumbled down the steps and lurched out of the tent.

chaptersix

As the crowd shuffled out of the marquee, I turned to Chloe. 'I'm going to find Nick,' I said, 'see if he's okay and still up for the ride-along on Monday.'

'Cool. Meet you at the signing.' Chloe didn't look at me. She was tracking Curtis and Desiree, not letting them out of her sight.

I finally spotted him half-hidden behind a willow tree on the banks of the Yarra, smoking another cigarette, his injured hand held up to his chest. Liz was talking to him and it looked like she was imploring him to do something, probably go to hospital for stitches, but he shook his head and waved her away. Just as I was about to approach, Isabella appeared from the port-a-loos and swept straight for him. I hung back, peeking out from behind a gum tree, too far away to hear exactly what they were saying.

First they shouted, then appeared to calm down. Isabella took the cigarette out of Nick's mouth and had a couple of drags before grinding it out under one dainty Mary-Jane. In no time they were shouting again until suddenly Nick leaned in and kissed her. She pulled away and slapped him, then took his face in both her hands, pushed him against the tree and kissed him back, hard. Writers. I gave up trying to figure them out, went to look for Chloe and found her in the book-signing tent, in front of Rod Thurlow, the line behind her stretching out across the oval. He signed her copy of *Lethal Force* with a flourish and a smile, but she didn't move on.

'Now do my boobs!' She leaned over the table and hung her cleavage in his face like she was a groupie and he was Tommy Lee.

Rod looked bemused. 'Whoa. I'm not sure I have enough ink in my pen.'

'Oh, come on, Mr Thurlow.' She licked her lips and winked. 'You look like the sort of guy who's *always* got enough ink in his pen . . .'

Looking around I immediately found the reason for the display—Curtis and Desiree, perusing the true crime section, her hand wedged into his back pocket. I'd had just about enough; this wasn't so much a writers' festival as an expo for jealous lovers. I went over to them, and Chloe, who had just finished getting her tits autographed, glowered at me like I was Judas Iscariot, before pretending to browse the book stacks.

'You weren't kidding about the rough break-up,' I said to Desiree, low enough so Rod wouldn't hear. 'That panel was a fucking fiasco. How long since they've been divorced?'

'Oh, they haven't quite untied the knot yet,' Desiree said smoothly. 'You have to be separated a year. Isabella wanted to fudge the date on the papers but he wouldn't have it. Isabella wants to marry Rod on Christmas Day so it's all a bit . . . fraught.'

She wasn't wrong. Isabella came in and sat at the signing table next to Rod. Her cloche hat was on straight and she'd reapplied her lipstick.

'Where have you been, darling?' he asked. 'People have been waiting to get their books signed.'

'Sorry, got caught up talking to some of the audience members. They all agreed that Nick behaved appallingly.'

Suddenly there was a commotion at the entrance to the book-signing tent as a tall blonde swanned in. She had the figure and sweetly pretty features of a Miss Australia contestant and was trailed by a cameraman and a guy with a boom mike.

'Isabella!' said the blonde.

'Victoria!' Isabella stood and the two hugged, lightly. 'What's with the camera?'

'Oh, it's for a documentary. A year in the life of best-selling writer Victoria Hitchens.' Victoria rolled her eyes.

Rod was giving Victoria a dirty look. Victoria put her arm around Isabella and spoke direct to camera. 'This is Isabella Bishop, a terrific author and my best friend from high school. I don't think I could have become a writer without her. She really inspired me.'

Isabella smiled graciously, if somewhat tightly, towards the camera.

'Oh shoot.' Victoria looked at her watch. 'I'm late for my panel. So great to see you again.'

'Mmm-hmm,' Isabella murmured as Victoria swanned off.

Curtis' phone emitted a jangly version of the *Mission Impossible* theme, and he pulled it from his back pocket. 'Malone,' he said. 'Speak.'

It was another thing he did that irritated the hell out of me, and I wondered how a sophisticated woman like Desiree could stick him. Chloe I could understand. She could be almost as annoying as he was.

'Hey, Andi, what's happening?' Curtis said.

Andi was a friend from my childhood, now a journalism student. Three months earlier she'd gone missing; her disappearance was the case that had led to my mum getting shot. Andi hadn't gotten off lightly either: she'd nearly died, and had to have the lower half of her right leg amputated. She'd sold her story, not for money but for an opportunity to work on the newspaper who'd published it, and was now actually working as a journo while she finished her degree.

Curtis turned away from me and Desiree, dug his notebook out of his shirt pocket and started scribbling on it. 'Uh-huh. Yep. No kidding? Shit yeah, I'd be into it. Now? Pick you up in twenty.'

'What's going on?' I asked.

'A body's been found just outside of Daylesford. Word on the street is it's Lachlan Elliot.'

'Who?'

'Investment banker who disappeared eighteen months ago. Toorak guy. Had links to bikies and organised crime.'

I vaguely remembered seeing the story in the papers and on the news. There'd been rumours he owed money and had faked his own disappearance.

'It's gonna be a big one, so me and Andi are teaming up. Malone and Fowler. Has a ring to it, don'tcha reckon? Andrew Rule and John Silvester have had it too good for too damn long. They better get wise there's a new true-crime team in town.'

Chloe was lurking behind a pile of books, pretending not to listen, and Curtis did a hair flick to cover his glance back to check she was there.

'Hey, babe,' he told Desiree. 'Gotta blow this popsicle stand.'

She slid her arm around his waist and they performed an ostentatious kiss with rather a bit too much porn-star tongue. Curtis smacked his new girlfriend on the arse, slid on a pair of those mirrored sunnies favoured by American highway patrolmen, and swaggered off into the day.

I'd had enough of the freak fest and went to find Chloe so we could go home. She was flipping through a book, but when she saw me she hurriedly stuffed it back onto a shelf. I could have sworn it had *Sex Secrets of a Thousand Dollar an Hour Callgirl* in the title.

chapterseven

The next morning I woke with a start, heart beating fast, and it was a few seconds before I realised why. Shit. It was Sunday, November the eighth; Alex was getting married and Sean was arriving back from Vietnam. He was going straight to Alex's from the airport so I wouldn't see him until late that night, but I still had a lot to do before then. Hair cut and dyed, nails painted, eyebrows shaped, solarium, Brazilian. Amazing how feral you could turn when no one was getting up close and personal.

I had a couple of hours to kill before my first appointment, so I got up and drank a plungerful of coffee, pulled on terry-towelling short-shorts and a faded Mickey Mouse t-shirt, threaded the house key into the laces of my ancient, worn-out runners, and headed out for a jog. The path beside the canal ran all the way to the ocean, behind houses where flowering vines curled around fences and indolent cats snoozed in the sun.

As I ran I thought about the debacle at the festival the day before. It was funny, I'd always thought strippers were the most fucked-up profession, but those writers were sure giving them a run for their money. Perhaps they spent too much time ferreting away in their garrets, living inside their own heads, slowly going mad. It was supposed to be healthy to engage in artistic pursuits, but honestly, sitting on my arse all day writing stories about characters who didn't exist would have driven me bonkers. Stripping was my creative outlet, even though people scoffed when I tried to explain that, and I knew I'd have to give it up completely, soon enough. At twenty-nine I was getting too old, and it didn't exactly do wonders for my PI reputation either, but I knew I'd miss it. Not to mention the fact that I was hopeless at painting and sure as shit couldn't play guitar. Maybe I could write a book about my adventures, seeing as how everyone else seemed to be. Although they weren't so much adventures as an embarrassing list of fuck-ups.

At Ormond Esplanade I jogged on the spot as I waited for the walk sign, dashed across the road, and then I was running south along the bay, dodging bike riders, roller-bladers, dog walkers and young mums with high-priced prams. Grey-green water lapped the sand of Elwood Beach and a soft, salty wind cooled the sweat on my face. I sprinted all the way to the lifesaving club and stopped for a drink at the bubbler before turning and running back. At the public toilets I veered onto the grass and pounded up the hamstring- and lung-punishing Elwood Hill. Leaning against the white wooden lookout I stretched my quads and tried to get my breath back. Up there I could see the palm trees of St Kilda, the arc of the Westgate Bridge and the skyscrapers of the CBD. On a clear day Geelong was visible across the vast curve of Port Phillip Bay, but that morning a hot haze hung in the air, smelling of ozone, reminding me of the one occasion I'd visited Los Angeles.

I was fourteen, and it was the last time I'd seen my dad, who lived there with his new, American family. We'd never been close—he and my mum had split when I was tiny—but after that last visit we'd never spoken again.

My email from last week hadn't worked either—just bounced back with the message 'delivery failure'. I debated with myself whether it was worth tracking him down, and wondered why I wanted to contact him anyway. Because Mum wouldn't talk to me? And what did I hope to get out of it? Money? Fatherly advice? A tearful reunion?

Yeah, right. He'd never tried to get in touch with me.

I ran down the other side of the hill past the dense scrub, which, combined with the public toilet, made the area such an attractive gay beat, sprinted across the park then up Glenhuntly Road past the Elwood Lounge, video store and cafés. Left on Broadway, then I slowed to a shuffle. I'd almost finished my loop when one of my shoes finally carked it, flopping open like the mouth of a panting dog. Rivulets of sweat ran down my back, seeping into the waistband of my shorts, and I was just nearing my unit-block, mentally planning my day, when I got the creepy feeling I was being followed. I whirled around and saw a stretch limo with tinted windows come to a halt behind me. I didn't have to be a detective to put it together—white limo, Alex's wedding day. For half a second I had the idea he'd gone AWOL from his own nuptials and had come straight to my place to tell me so. Then the driver's door opened and out popped Sean.

He was wearing a tuxedo and a shit-eating grin and he leaned one arm on the roof of the vehicle. In the other hand he held a bouquet of orchids, filched from the wedding party by the look of things. I'd been so caught up being angst-ridden about Alex that I'd forgotten how goddamned gorgeous Sean was. He was a couple of inches taller than me, a young-looking thirty-five with a boyish face, and his perfectly formed lips had a pronounced rim that always caught the light. His short red-gold hair ruffled in the breeze, setting off his perpetually glinting, slate-blue eyes, and beneath the monkey suit I knew his body was lean and tightly muscled. My heart was beating fast and I couldn't remember how to breathe. Act casual, I told myself.

He tilted his head, inverted his eyebrows and put on his best Connery-inspired Bond drawl. He already had a Scottish accent, but he did have to lower the register a tad.

'Shields.' He smirked. 'Sean Shields.'

I put one hand on my hip and smirked back, trying for sultry although I probably resembled Forrest Gump after his trans-national marathon. 'Guess that makes me Pussy Galore.'

'Damn right it does.' He was trying hard to keep the suave expression, but his mouth kept lifting at one side. The smile was infectious. I'd also failed to remember how much fun he was, and his remarkable enthusiasm, and facility, for oral sex. I couldn't believe that just a few moments before I'd actually been disappointed he wasn't Alex.

I switched from Pussy G to Dr No. Or maybe it was Dr Evil. Either way, the German accent I spouted sounded pretty hammy. 'So, Mr Shields, we meet again. From where did you appropriate the limousine?'

'Commandeered it for my mission.'

'Which is?'

'Get in the back seat and you'll find out.' He clicked open the door.

chapter eight

Monday morning I was stuck in traffic on Punt Road, heading north to Nick's place in Abbotsford. I'd tried to call him to make sure he was still up for the ride-along, but he hadn't answered his phone that morning or the day before. I was pretty annoyed and could have just gone about my business without him, but he'd advanced me quite a large sum which I really didn't want to give back. I figured if I fronted up regardless, I'd have fulfilled my part of the bargain and the money was mine to keep.

To tell the truth I was hoping he wouldn't want to come. It would be awkward after witnessing his scene at the writers' festival, and I didn't want to dick around. My plan was to finish the job in record time, type the report, attach the photos, then hurry back to Sean. I kept remembering the day before and getting little aftershocks when I thought about his tongue on my clit and his cock in my pussy, the two of us tussling in the back of the limo among plastic-wrapped hire suits and boxed corsages. At first I'd protested—I hadn't had time to preen myself and I was too sweaty and hairy to fool around—but

Sean had insisted he'd take me any which way, and after a few seconds I wouldn't have cared if I had ten centimetres of regrowth and a bush down to my knees.

Later, after the wedding, he'd staggered back to my place and we'd done it all over again, my carefully blow-dried hair turning into a bird's nest once more. Being pissed, he spilled his guts, confessed how much he'd missed me and how bad he felt about not being there when all the hideous shit with my mum went down in Sydney. I'd told him to shut up, it wasn't his fault and he had nothing to feel guilty about. Then he'd asked if he could stay a few days. Curtis was still subletting his place and couldn't find anywhere else to rent, so I said sure. It was only for a little while, and he promised to cook and clean and provide sex on tap.

I'd also managed to get some goss on the wedding. Sean knew I'd unintentionally shown up at the bachelor party, but not about Alex following me into the toilets. I'd been worried Alex's scumbag cousin would spill the beans, but Sean's face hadn't betrayed any trace of suspicion as he told me about the day.

Apparently the ceremony had gone ahead without a hitch, but Alex had gotten really smashed at the reception, and Sean and some other groomsmen had to hustle him out of there and put him to bed. He couldn't have had much of a wedding night. The strange sense of disappointment I'd felt on hearing the ceremony had gone ahead turned into an evil kind of satisfaction. It was sick, but I couldn't help myself.

I drove my boring, sensible Ford Laser past Nick's place. The entrance wasn't much to look at, just a high wall with a garage and a door, but I guessed the rest would be pretty posh. The street was in an upmarket part of Abbotsford, and one side was crammed with renovated terraces and converted warehouses. The other, Nick's side, featured expensive homes perched on a slope overlooking the river. Unlike his fictional character Zack, I didn't get a park out front. A BMW, Toorak Tractor and rubbish skip were in my way, so I pulled in half a block up and doubled back.

The sun beat off the asphalt and I was hot in my Portman's skirt suit. If Nick was actually home, I was sure he'd get a kick out of my corporate look: court shoes, black-rimmed glasses and sleek ponytail. Four years of stripping costumes and characters had made me not only a master of disguise but a halfway decent actor. I wasn't going to be performing Shakespeare at the Globe in a hurry, but was pretty confident I could nail *Neighbours* or *Home and Away* if I had to.

I rapped on the steel door, bruising my knuckles, and waited. No answer. I found a bell to the side of the doorframe and pressed. Nothing. I tried again. Sweat was beading on my forehead and beneath my pantyhose, causing the gusset to sag. I tried to tug up the nylon through my skirt, thinking that although gusset was probably the most disgusting word in the English language, it'd make a good name for a female punk band.

With my ear to the metal I pushed the button again, heard the bell chime and something else—music, turned up pretty damn loud. At least that meant he was home. I tried the door, assuming it would be locked, but the handle depressed, the mechanism clicked, and it swung open a couple of inches. Not a good sign. No one left their doors unlocked in the big city, especially not in a fancy house a couple of k's from the housing commission towers.

A small kernel of fear cracked open in my stomach, my mouth dried up and very bad thoughts swirled around my mind. Nick on a bender since Saturday afternoon, falling over and hitting his head on the side of the coffee table. Nick pissed and choking on his own vomit; or worse, drunk and despondent over Isabella, he'd slit his wrists in the bath, hung himself or got hold of a gun . . . I knew from personal experience what a couple of those options looked and smelled like, and graphic images danced in front of my eyes. I thought of calling the cops so I wouldn't have to go in, but what the hell would I tell them? For all I knew he could be in there relaxing on a Jason recliner, wearing a Hawaiian shirt, drinking a piña colada and getting a blow job from a fan. Nick would be pissed off, the cops would have the shits and I'd be a laughing stock.

I glanced down at my hand on the door handle. It was trembling. You'd think the things I'd seen would have made me hard-edged but it was the opposite. I was turning into a sissy, a nancy, a goddamn girl. Toughen the fuck up, I told myself. Get your arse in there. Go.

I pushed on the heavy steel door, took a couple of steps and found myself in an entrance hall. Down the other end was a door, to my left the garage access, and in front of me, a little to the right, a suspended staircase made of polished blond wood. A shattered gin bottle lay on the floor, and as well as the solvent stench of cheap booze I smelled something underneath it, organic and nasty. Something like blood? My stomach spasmed and the bones in my ankles felt brittle all of a sudden. The music was coming from the top of the stairs so I took a deep, ragged breath, crunched through the broken glass and climbed, calling out all the way.

'Nick? Nick, it's Simone. Are you there?'

There was no reply. The music was very loud and I realised I knew the song, although I hadn't heard it for years. It was a duet by Kirsty MacColl and Shane MacGowan from The Pogues. 'Fairytale of New York'.

The landing at the top of the stairs turned into a large open-plan space. It was gloomy, with just a little ambient light filtering through tightly closed blinds at the other end of the room. I made out a stainless steel kitchen to my left, a red 'feature wall' next to it, and a long living area stretching out in front of me. The place looked like someone had just moved in and only made a half-arsed effort to unpack. Boxes littered the floor, some sealed, others splayed open and spewing crumpled newspaper. A bookcase had been assembled sans shelves, the couch was cushion-less, and an enormous rug leaned against the wall, still rolled up and secured with packing tape. The music came from a laptop perched on a tea-chest with a pair of iPod speakers attached. Empty bottles and saucers full of cigarette butts cluttered every available surface, and the place reeked of stale booze, smoke and dirty socks. At least it didn't smell like blood anymore, and I chalked that up to a sensory hallucination, brought on by fear and post-traumatic stress, most likely.

As I inched forward, heels clicking on the polished wood, I made out a pair of sock-clad feet sticking out from behind a packing crate over by the windows, soles pointing to the ceiling. Hurrying over, I found Nick. It was too dark to see if he was alive or dead so I grabbed the cord for the blinds, zipped them up and was momentarily blinded by brilliant sunlight. He lay completely still, wearing the same clothes he'd had on at the writers' festival, just filthier and more rumpled. I couldn't see him breathing and my heart trilled as I bent down to try to find a pulse. As soon as I touched his throat he jerked, and I jumped back and let out a girly little scream. He produced a snuffling, hog-like snore in return, and I was so relieved I coughed out air and started laughing and shaking my head.

'You arsehole, Nick.' I nudged his ribs with one pointy toe. He didn't wake up, just muttered and rolled his head to the other side. On the floor next to him I saw a bunch of photos. I bent and picked one up. Him and Isabella, arms around each other in front of one of those old country pubs with a big wraparound veranda on the first floor. Her hair was longer, he was a few kilos leaner and they looked happy. Nice, but for the fact the photo had been ripped in two, then stuck together again with clear tape. I'd certainly had my weird, obsessive moments, but I'd never done anything like that. Had I? I let the photo flutter from my hand and looked out the window. Hell of a view. Beyond a large sundeck made of sixties-looking crazy-paving, the muddy Yarra wound, trailed by bike paths and lined with oaks and willows. Pretty.

Nick was going to have one hell of a hangover when he finally woke up, so I went all Florence Nightingale and clip-clopped over to the kitchen, rinsed out a glass, filled it with water, took it back and placed it in his line of sight. I dug around in my handbag for some Nurofen Plus, my hangover cure of choice, and generously left the whole pack propped up on the glass. It was the least I could do since I was keeping his money.

The song finished, then immediately started again. How long had he been playing it, over and over? I unplugged the speakers from the laptop on my way out.

It was time for me to get to work, and I wanted to leave before he woke—it would just be embarrassing for both of us. I descended the stairs, feeling like a prize dickhead for freaking out over nothing, until I reached the ground floor and the meaty smell hit me again, even stronger than before. I looked towards the door at the end of the corridor and instinctively knew it was coming from there.

chapternine

I stood very still at the base of the stairs, looking down the polished wood hallway to the matt, dark blue door and feeling as though if I stared hard enough I might be able to figure out what lay behind it. Without music the house was quiet, the only sounds those that filtered in from outside: distant traffic, whirring cicadas and the faint, crunching chime of a bicycle bell.

I couldn't shake the feeling I was being watched, although it was impossible. There were no windows in the entrance foyer, no old-fashioned keyholes, no large gaps underneath the doors.

Skirting the broken bottle I walked to the blue door, barely breathing, head starting to spin. The odour became stronger the closer I got: coppery and visceral, sweet and slightly musty. I could practically see tendrils of scent winding cartoon-like through the air.

Remembering my training I depressed the door handle with my elbow, nudged it open with my foot, then wished to god I hadn't. My stomach shrivelled and I had to lean against the frame to stop my legs buckling beneath me.

I was staring into an office with a floor-to-ceiling window overlooking the river. More unpacked boxes were stacked against the walls, and between me and the massive desk sat a high-backed leather swivel chair, facing away.

And the whole room was covered in blood. Crimson streaks spattered the walls, the floor and the papers strewn across the desk. Directly under the chair the beige rug had turned burgundy and was so saturated it looked like it would squelch.

Someone sat in the chair, very still, and too short for me to see the top of their head. All I saw was one pale, slender limb hanging over the armrest. A languorous pose, except that the delicate hand at the end of it was missing two fingers. The index and middle fingers were bloody stumps, and the thumb was hanging on by only a slender ribbon of flesh. The ring and pinkie fingers were intact, though, the nails painted that deep claret colour I'd admired two days earlier.

I don't know why I acted as I did, because I must have known she was dead: the pool of blood, her stillness, the complete absence of the slightest electrical spark that signified the presence of another living human being. Maybe I desperately wanted to believe she was just wounded, however badly, because I called out, 'Isabella,' rushed over, and spun the chair around.

What happened next seemed more like a series of nightmare flashes than a sequence of real events. Cloudy eyes staring. A head lolling forward. Her silk dress torn open to the waist and instead of the expected white flesh, a jagged gash coloured purple, brown and red. A flash of yellow rib. Glistening organs. Blood in her lap. When the chair stopped, Isabella's corpse kept moving and she slumped towards me. I jumped back, but not far enough, and her torso landed on my foot with a sloshing, sucking sound. I felt warm wetness seep into my shoe. Horrified, I jerked it out from under her body and a loop of intestine came too, trailing after me like an enormous, misshapen worm.

The vomit came without warning. No nausea, no surge of saliva, just a sudden heave of scrambled eggs and bile.

And then I ran, back down the hall, foot sliding about in my shoe.

'Hey!' Nick had staggered halfway down the stairs, red-eyed, wild-haired, blood staining the front of his white t-shirt.

I gasped and ran onto the smashed bottle, skidded and went down, broken glass nipping my shins, knees and palms. He stumbled forward as I tried to clamber to my feet.

'Get away from me,' I yelled, hysterical. He was at the bottom of the stairs reaching out for me like a horror film zombie. I groped at the wall, dragged myself up, lurched for the door and yanked it open, but before I could escape he grabbed my arm and pulled me back into the house and around to face him. His eyes were mad looking, and up close he smelled like an alco, sour spirits and nicotine leaching from his pores.

'Hey,' he growled, fingers digging into my bicep like claws. 'Hey!'

I went crazy, slapping and scratching at him until I felt pain pierce the heel of my hand. At the same time Nick swore and swayed back, and I saw that a shard of broken glass from the bottle had transferred from my palm to his face, narrowly missing his eye. I bolted out the door, ignoring the sting in my legs and hands, straight for my car, but when I got there I realised I'd lost my bag and my keys somewhere inside Nick's.

I looked back. He was still coming, bloody, shuffling, blinking in the light and shouting something unintelligible. I kicked my shoes off and sprinted, faster than I thought possible, running like hell through the back streets of Abbotsford.

chapterten

It was four pm on Christmas Day, and I was lying on a striped banana lounge on Chloe's back deck a little away from the party, partly hidden behind a cocos palm. I was kitted up in a denim mini, off-the-shoulder embroidered peasant blouse and a sombrero, and drinking what might have been my sixth margarita—I couldn't be exactly sure.

Our 'orphans' Christmas' had a south-of-the-border theme which explained the papier-mâché chilli-peppers, giant inflatable cactus and donkey piñata dangling from the washing line. It was also the reason Ricky Martin was warbling through the speakers. Earlier, Sean had put on a disc of an obscure but highly respected authentic Tijuana mariachi band, but the majority of the party, Chloe and most of her strippers, had booed, rolled their eyes and made gagging sounds, so we were stuck with a vaguely Latino party mix: Ricky, J-Lo and whoever the bastards were who had inflicted 'The Macarena' and 'Mambo Number Five' upon the world.

Chloe, despite her advanced state of gestation, was shaking her bon-bon in a hot pink bikini and heels, and Curtis, assisted by a few of the dancers' boyfriends, manned the barbecue, beer in hand. Sean was over by the makeshift bar in faded jeans, Converse sneakers and a Speedy Gonzales t-shirt, simultaneously mixing margaritas and sharing a joint with my journalist friend Andi.

Andi was part Maori, small, dark and punky looking with a pixie crop, a wide, white-toothed grin and big brown eyes. Her cut-off shorts showed off her new prosthetic leg that attached at the knee. She'd got us all to scrawl lewd graffiti on it while telling us all about amputee-love websites she'd discovered on the internet.

A few other people I knew had drifted in and out during the day, on their way to and from family do's, including Tony Torcasio, my old boss and trainer from the Australian Security Academy, and Hannah, the hippy massage-parlour owner I'd helped out. Reg, a sixty-year-old sailing instructor who'd lent a hand taking down some bad guys what seemed an aeon ago, had turned up with shortbread in a tartan tin and a bewildered look on his face. We'd even had a visit from Trip Sibley, who looked and acted like a rock star but in reality was a celebrity chef. I couldn't actually recall Trip leaving and, knowing him, it was a fair bet he was holed up in Chloe's bedroom with a couple of strippers and a selection of Class A narcotics.

I lifted the paper plate up from the ground next to me and bit into a soft taco filled with barbecued prawns, coriander and spiced black beans. I'd been trying to resist pigging out but damn, it was just too good. If Sean and I hadn't been able to save the music at least we'd rescued the food. Chloe's idea of party catering was a couple of boxes of Mexican-flavoured Shapes, corn chips and dip, and an economy pack of supermarket sausages spiked with paprika and labelled Hot 'n' Spicy. Not to mention a bottle of cheap mescal with one of those worms that always put me in mind of a tiny severed penis bobbing around in formalin.

Sean and I had spent the previous day scouring The Essential Ingredient and the Prahran and South Melbourne markets for ripe avocados and obscure chillies, Monterey Jack cheddar, tins of tomatillos, bright green, hot as hell picante sauces, and overpriced limes. We'd spent the morning side by side in my little pink and grey kitchen, mashing, juicing and chopping, marinating chicken and beef strips for fajitas, and cutting up red, green and yellow capsicums. Necking Coronas wedged with lime, we'd performed abbreviated salsa moves, bumping hips and occasionally stopping to snog against the bench.

Seeing as how the couple of days he'd wanted to stay had somehow extended into six weeks, Sean knew his way around the kitchen better than I did. Curtis reckoned he was having trouble finding a place, although I doubted he was trying too hard and suspected that Sean was not exactly pushing him out. It had been years since I'd lived with a guy and normally I'd never have jumped in so quick, but it had been a godsend having him around. If he hadn't been there, the previous six weeks would have gone down as the worst of my life.

Since I'd stumbled upon Isabella's body, things had really turned to shit.

Several blocks from Nick's house, I'd finally stopped running, burst into a pub and screamed for the barmaid to call the police. I knew they'd take me in to interview me, but hadn't expected to be kept for over eight hours and questioned like they thought I'd killed her, either alone or in cahoots with Nick. It didn't help that by the time the cops got to his place he'd disappeared without a trace. I'd been worried that I might have had to deal with Detective Inspector Duval, the head honcho of Homicide who'd threatened to arrest me or take away my PI licence if I got involved in any more crap. Instead I was confronted with his offsider, Talbot, a whippet-thin forty-something broad with a straight brown bob, who smelled like instant coffee and strong cigarettes and had gone for me like a terrier, probably following Duval's orders to arrest me for whatever she could. She'd drilled me on my relationship with Nick, what I was doing at the house and even why I'd been at the writers' festival that weekend.

I'd been completely honest and told her everything I'd seen and heard, but she still insinuated I was guilty, that Nick and I had cooked up some sort of plan together. I couldn't wait for them to bring him in and was hoping he'd confess so I'd be off the hook, but they couldn't find him. Despite news bulletins, wanted posters, and Rod Thurlow going on TV, begging for information, Nick remained at large. Albeit with that many false sightings he could've been Elvis.

Of course, it was a huge story in the press. Famous writers, a love triangle, and me, the stripping detective. Once again I refused to talk to them—even Andi and Curtis, who attempted to guilt-trip me into it.

The media had always pissed me off in the past, but I hadn't realised they'd actually been giving me a fair trot until they turned. Articles appeared posing questions about why I'd been involved in so many deaths, stopping just short of actually accusing me of murder. Opinion pieces popped up questioning if I was morally capable of holding a PI licence, having worked as a stripper. I couldn't quite understand how taking off my clothes made me unethical, but it didn't stop the current affairs and radio talkback programs running pieces with such titles as 'Melbourne's Dodgiest Detective?' I'd kept my head down, waiting for it to blow over, but there was worse to come. The cops bowed to public pressure and suspended my licence, pending investigation. I wasn't the villain, I was the victim, but nobody else saw it that way, not even my mum. After weeks without contact she finally called to tell me I was seeking out violence and darkness, attracting negative energy into my life, and she didn't want anything to do with me until I saw the error of my ways and sought out some vigorous spiritual cleansing, preferably with a rebirthing component. Hippies.

I would have been completely screwed up if it hadn't been for Sean. He'd cooked and cleaned and made love to me, and for the first couple of weeks he was still off work so he took me down to a cottage on the Great Ocean Road where he dosed me up on sex and sauvignon blanc and kept me away from newspapers and TV.

When he was back at work he continued to keep me occupied whenever he had time off: movies, plays, art galleries, picnics in the park. Normal shit, like a normal couple. And on days when I couldn't face leaving the house he hunted and gathered, bringing me food and books and DVDs, and assuring me it would all blow over. He even paid my rent. I didn't deserve it. When I accidentally let slip that Sean was the sort of guy who would go down on you not only before sex but also after, Chloe, who was generally dirty on men, agreed that he was some kind of saint.

Sean was right, though: the frenzy did eventually wane. With no new information it ran out of steam: and there were new murders, politicians fooling around with showgirls, buildings collapsing, bikie shootouts, football drug scandals and terrorist bomb threats. My name gradually disappeared from the papers and the airwaves, and Sean said it was only a matter of time before I got my licence reinstated.

So as I lay there on the banana lounge I felt better than I had in weeks. It was Christmas, I was surrounded by a dysfunctional family of my own making, I wasn't in jail, dead or maimed, and I had the most perfect boyfriend in the world, not to be too smug about it. And even though my mum had told me I was evil, at least she'd called: that was something. Everything was going to be okay. And what with the margaritas and the positive thoughts I began to doze, warmed by the sun.

Until I heard the clanging footsteps of someone coming up the metal stairs just below me. I hoped it was a friend of Chloe's and not someone else from my past, and decided to keep my eyes closed until they passed by.

'Hola, señorita.'

I recognised the deep, slightly gravelly voice and the hint of aftershave at the same time. The cologne was mellow and woody and smelled like a combination of aged cognac and exotic bark; it must have contained some sort of pheromone because my afternoon drowsiness disappeared as effectively as if I'd just blasted a quarter gram of speed into my main vein. Blood pumped through my chest, and heat spread out from my cheeks and climbed my scalp, prickling like tiny needles. Why did I always have to react like that? I couldn't let him see the effect he had on me so I yawned, tipped the brim of my hat back a fraction and lazily opened one eye.

'Oh, hey, Alex,' I said.

chapter eleven

Alex stood a couple of stairs down from the landing and I noticed there was something different about him. He was thinner, for a start, and the dark brown hair he usually wore slicked back now hung over his forehead and curled slightly at the nape of his neck, as though it had been a long time between trims. His sideburns had grown unruly and roamed halfway to his jaw. The hair and the weight loss suited him and made him seem younger than his thirty-six years.

So did the outfit. Even on his days off I was used to him looking like a sleek detective-about-town in expensive suits and designer shirts, black brogues buffed to a high shine. I'd never seen him dressed like this, in jeans, scuffed trainers and a faded black Kiss t-shirt that looked like it'd been dragged out of a charity bin. He was as handsome as ever, but I couldn't say he was a picture of health. A few new lines traced his face, stubble peppered his chin, and underneath his eyes a blue tinge showed through the olive skin.

'What are you doing here?'

'Sean asked me.' He sat down a couple of steps below me, hidden from the rest of the party. 'Didn't think I'd be able to come, what with my rellos, then Suzy's.'

'Your wife let you leave family Christmas to attend a party with me and a whole bunch of strippers?' I hoisted myself up on my elbows so I could see him better.

'Got in an argument with her dad about preventative policing and stormed out during the fruit cake and sherry. He's another fucking cop. She doesn't know I'm here.'

As if on cue his phone started ringing. He looked at the display, then switched it off. I saw that his liquid chocolate eyes shone in the way a sober person's never do.

'You're pissed.' Like I could talk.

'It's Christmas.' He leaned up and grabbed my margarita, downed half in one gulp, then stared at my thighs so intently my skin buzzed.

'What are you looking at?'

'I can see right up your skirt. Black lace knickers. Nice.'

'Alex!' I hissed, crossing my legs, unsuccessfully attempting to pull down my mini and glancing over to see if Sean had noticed. He was still deep in stoned conversation with Andi, but Chloe had seen me talking to someone and she undulated over. Against her swollen breasts her bikini top looked no bigger than a pair of pasties.

'Who are you talking to?' She caught sight of Alex and her eyes widened. 'Oh. *Hello.*'

'Chloe, this is Alex.' I couldn't believe that after everything, they'd never actually met.

'The famous Alex, huh? Simone wasn't kidding when she said you were hot.'

I gave her a look. She ignored me.

'My god—' Alex was openly staring at her boobs—'your tits are huge.'

I winced but needn't have worried, she wasn't the least bit offended.

'Thanks.' She took one in each hand and appraised them like a fruiterer testing the quality of a couple of oversized cantaloupes. 'I am up the duff though.'

'No shit.'

Chloe looked from me to Alex and back again, a knowing smirk on her face.

'Well, nice to finally meet you, but I know when I'm in the way. Guess you two have a lot to talk about . . .'

I reached out to flick her leg but she was gone.

'A lot to talk about?' Alex raised his eyebrows as he took another swig of my margarita.

'Pregnancy,' I said. 'She's gone mental.'

'So, what's it like being public enemy number one?'

'Piss off.'

'Hey, did you hear the latest? Rod Thurlow, the writer, put up a million-dollar reward for info leading to Nick Austin's arrest.'

'Really? He's rung me a couple of times but I never called back. Maybe I should find the fucker. I could use the money.'

'Heard your licence got suspended. What *are* you doing for work? Back on the game?'

'Fuck you.' I kicked out at him.

He caught my bare foot and squeezed. I pulled it back.

'Stripping isn't prostitution—not that there's anything wrong with being a working lady.'

'If you say so.'

'And for your information I'm not dancing at all.'

'Why not?'

'Sean didn't reckon it was a good idea.'

'He's laid down the law? Told the irrepressible Ms Kirsch to keep her kit on? I didn't think it was possible.'

'No. He heard that a few of those current affairs shows were going to smuggle in cameras. Get footage. Thought it was best to say I wasn't stripping anymore, not add any more fuel to the fire.'

'Uh-huh.' He sounded like he didn't believe me.

'Sean's not the kind of guy to tell me what I can and can't do. Unlike some people . . .'

'You sure? No bloke wants to think of other men perving on his chick.'

I raised my eyebrows. It was fine for chicks to call each other chicks, but arrogant coppers . . .

Alex continued, on a roll: 'I'd never let my wife get her gear off for anyone but me.'

'Don't you sound like the unreconstructed Greek boy. Hard to believe you did your masters on gender equality in policing.'

He ignored me and kept on, snickering to himself. 'Hear you guys are living together, too. I can just see it, Simone the hausfrau, cooking breakfast, seeing her man off in the morning, darning his socks, polishing his handcuffs . . . ah, domestic bliss. Next thing you know you'll be popping out a mess of kids.'

'Who's talking? You're the one who just got married, and how long have you been off work? Must be a hell of a house husband by now.' I instantly regretted saying it, but hell, he'd been winding me up.

'And whose fucking fault is that?' he barked, eyes going flat and dark.

'Sorry,' I said quietly.

He looked away, out over the train lines, and when he turned back his eyes weren't flat anymore, they were glittering. 'Want to make it up to me?'

'How?'

'I was thinking something along the lines of what happened at the pub.'

'What happened at the pub?' Sean's voice.

I snapped my head around, saw him approaching with a margarita and hoped to hell he hadn't picked up the rest of the conversation.

'Hey, buddy, glad you could make it,' he said to Alex.

I guessed he hadn't heard, thank Christ.

Sean handed me a drink, and Alex sprang up and the two hugged in a blokey way with lots of back-slapping.

'We were just talking about Alex's prick of a cousin hiring me for his buck's.' I shook my head and did an amazed laugh which sounded pretty fake even to me. So much for my acting skills.

'Hey, mate, make one of those for me?' Alex asked Sean.

'Sure.'

'Good to see you, Simone.' He looked at my legs again. Jesus. He was Jekyll and Hyde after the head injury, and it was impossible to predict what he'd say next.

Alex and Sean repaired to the bar and I did the only thing that seemed sensible under the circumstances—started drinking heavily. Andi and a couple of the strippers were downing shots of cocksucking cowboys, so I joined in as the sun sank low over the train line and melted into a dazzling pink glob.

'How's your crime story going?' I asked Andi as a viscous mix of Baileys and butterscotch schnapps slid down my throat. It was fairly obvious how the drink got its name.

'Which one?'

'The new one you're writing with Curtis. Dead financial dude.'

'Fucking crap,' she said. 'Case has just died. Elliot went missing eighteen months ago. He was rumoured to have connections to bikie gangs and speed or ice or whatever they're calling it these days. But the cops haven't found any evidence to link him to them. Probably won't. They reckon he was hit over some sort of drug money—there was a contract out on him.'

The stripper to the left of us, a painfully thin blonde who'd been talking a hundred miles a minute to another girl, whipped her head around.

'You talking about that rich cunt, found his body up near Daylesford?'

'Yeah.' Andi downed another shot, keeping her eyes on the girl.

'Contract didn't go out on him till *after* he disappeared.'

'How do you know?' I asked. Drunk and nosy.

'My ex was with the Red Devils. That Lachlan bloke was always hanging around the clubhouse, doing go-ey, taking in the shows.'

I guessed this was Tiara, who Chloe had been arguing with on the phone weeks before. Judging by her glittering eyes, sharp features and inability to shut up, it didn't look like she'd given the amphetamines away.

'I heard he pissed off with a lot of cash and drugs,' Andi said.

'I heard that too. But the papers said he's been dead about a year and a half, right? He was killed by someone else. Bikies get blamed for everything, but they didn't do it.'

'The date of death's only an estimate. It could have been a contract job.'

''Cept the contract was never paid out.'

Andi suddenly looked very alert and sober. No mean feat, considering the joints and the booze. 'You willing to go on record and say that?' she asked Tiara.

'No fucking way. You think I've got a death wish? I'm not sayin' nothing.' Tiara slammed back another cocksucking cowboy, gave Andi a slit-eyed look and turned back to ear-bash her friend.

Andi got up, a little unsteady on her prosthetic leg, and limped into Chloe's office. I saw her through the French doors, sitting at the desk, grabbing a pen and scribbling on a piece of paper. I felt a hand on my shoulder, turned my head. It was Sean. Alone.

'Where's Alex?' I asked.

'Gone home.'

'Nice of him to say goodbye.' I felt offended.

'He was pretty smashed.'

'So am I.' The pink splotch had finally sunk and it was getting dark on the deck. 'If we tell Chloe we're going home she'll never let us out the door. Wanna do a runner?'

'What'll we do at home?'

'I'm sure we can think of something. Watch *King of Kings* on TV?'

'Thought you'd never ask.'

We snuck down the back stairs, fell into a cab on Carlisle Street and directed the driver to Elwood. Sean had his arm around my waist and I had my drunken head on his shoulder. He smelled good, too. His aftershave didn't have quite the effect of Alex's, but it was nice just the same. It suddenly struck me that I had a boyfriend, and a live-in one at that. It was weird, yet also kind of cosy. I remembered the shit Alex had given me about domesticity, intimating that Sean was controlling me and didn't want me to strip. What a crock.

I lifted my head off Sean's shoulder. 'Hey, I was talking to Chloe about New Year's. There's some big parties on, lots of shows. She reckons I can easily pull in a thousand bucks that night.'

When he didn't say anything I went on. 'Isn't that great? I won't have to keep sponging off you.'

I thought he'd agree but he stiffened and moved away a little. The cab turned left onto Brighton Road. The interior smelled like plastic seat covers, sweat, fried onions and barbecue sauce. Outside the windows everything rushed past in a blur. The Greyhound Hotel, traffic lights, big leafy trees.

'What's wrong? You have to work New Year's too. We can celebrate on the first instead, when I'm all cashed up.'

'I just don't think it's such a good idea.'

'But I'm old news, you said so yourself. There's been nothing in the papers for weeks.'

'You'll get your licence back soon.'

'Even if I do, I still have to supplement my pathetic income somehow.'

Sean didn't reply, just turned and looked out the window, like he was fascinated with the tram that was keeping pace with us.

I poked him in the shoulder. 'You're pissed off? You can't be. You knew what I did when you met me.'

Sean turned back, face serious, voice flat. 'Actually, when I met you you'd given up stripping and were working for Tony Torcasio as an inquiry agent. You went back to it when I left for Vietnam.'

'I had to. He fired me. And what do you mean, I'd *given up*? You make it sound like a vice.'

He stared at me for a couple of seconds, exhaled hard out of his nose, then turned to look out the window again. Righteous indignation welled up inside me.

'Let me get this straight, are you telling me I can't work as a stripper?'

'No. I'm telling you I don't like it.'

'I've got to make a living somehow.'

'There are other occupations.'

'None I'm any good at.'

'You've worked in restaurants, supermarkets . . .'

'I'm not going back to being a waitress or a checkout chick. I hated those jobs.'

'And you like stripping?' His tone was uncharacteristically sarcastic.

'Bet your arse I do. It's fun, good exercise, creative.'

He snorted.

'What?' I said.

'Creative? You're not choreographing a piece of innovative modern dance for the Victorian Ballet, Simone, you're shaking your tits in front of a bunch of drunken tradesmen in some scungy pub.'

The taxi driver flicked me a look in the rearview.

'Stop the cab,' I told him.

'Don't stop the cab,' said Sean.

The taxi driver looked confused.

'Stop the fucking cab.'

He stopped. We were on Glenhuntly Road, Elwood, just around the corner from my place, next to the darkened Turtle Café.

'I want my keys back.' I held out my hand to Sean.

'What?'

'You heard.'

He looked at me, mouth slightly open. 'Are you breaking up with me?'

'I don't know what I'm doing. All I know is I don't wanna spend the night with someone who thinks I'm a tragic slut.'

'I didn't say that.'

'Actually, you did.' I fumbled in my bag and pulled a twenty out of my wallet. I thrust it at Sean. 'Here.'

'I don't want your money.' He waved it away so I bunched it up and threw it at him. Plastic notes never crumple too well and it fluttered to the foot-well.

I opened the door, gathered my bag to my chest and shimmied across the seat, bare legs squeaking on the plastic seat cover.

Sean grabbed my bicep. 'Do you have the faintest idea why I don't want you to strip?'

I yanked my arm out of his grip and stepped unsteadily out of the cab.

'It's because I—'

I slammed the door so I didn't have to hear the rest. Alex had been right. The bastard had been right.

I staggered down Broadway, the wide, leafy street that snaked from Elwood to St Kilda. My flat was on the first floor of an ugly brick block, a one-bedder with a balcony that had last been renovated in the eighties. I climbed the concrete stairwell and let myself in. The walls were off-white, the carpet was old, and the lounge was furnished with mismatched, second-hand furniture. The only decorations consisted of tatty posters advertising kitsch sixties films and cool local country bands, like Doug Mansfield and the Dust Devils and the Red Hot Poker Dots. As a Christmas present, Sean had given the place a mini-makeover, framing the posters and covering the old couch and armchair with matching chocolate-coloured throws. He'd chucked out my brick and board bookcase and replaced it with a wooden entertainment unit that held the CD player and kept books and CDs neatly aligned. I stood in front of it, swaying slightly, and swept a row of books onto the floor, muttering like a petulant child about how nobody told *me* what to do.

Being ordered not to strip made me want to do it more than ever. Hell, it made me want to do it then and there, so I slid open the balcony door to let in some air, poured a glass of white I really didn't need, then ran to my room and rooted around in the closet for my red satin stripper heels. I blew off the dust, strapped them on, and tiptoed back into the lounge, spike stilettos catching in the carpet.

I crouched down unsteadily, already feeling the burn in my inner thighs, and tilted my head to scan the CDs, so drunk I had to squint to make out the titles. I noted that Sean's jazz discs were encroaching on my country, cheesy disco and cock-rock, then plucked out an old stripping mix and shoved it in the mouth of the player.

'Fastlove' by George Michael came thudding out of the speakers. The song was basically a homage to casual sex, the lyrics and low thrusty beat perfect for a bit of bump 'n' grind. I danced in front of the window so I could clock my reflection, and when I raised my arms my blouse rode up and I was alarmed to see a bit of belly overhanging the waistband of my skirt. Still, there was a week before New Year's and if I spent it running and eating chicken breasts I ought to be right for the shows. At least my thighs still looked alright in a short skirt.

Speaking of which, the burn was becoming pretty agonising, so I leaned back against the wall and gyrated my hips. When even that became exhausting I got down on the carpet on all fours. My knees were going to pay for it the next day, but I didn't give a shit.

Chris Isaak had replaced Georgie-boy and was growling out 'Baby Did a Bad, Bad Thing', and I was caterwauling along and pretty much humping the rug when I heard the knock on the door. Sean? Some arsehole neighbour complaining about the noise?

Whoever the hell it was, I was gonna tell them to go fuck themselves. It was Christmas: couldn't a girl have some fun? I crawled to the couch, held onto the backrest to hoist myself up, swilled more wine, then pulled my shoulders back and strode to the door, platform stilettos making me feel seven feet tall. I turned the bolt and was about to turn the handle when it moved on its own and the door swung violently inward, busting the chain lock and knocking me onto my arse on the carpet. I looked up, mouth open to protest, and saw Nick Austin standing there, holding a gun.

chapter twelve

For the second time that day adrenaline blasted me from dead drunk to stone-cold sober, and my intestines clenched like a giant fist had reached into my abdomen and squeezed.

I silently damned the stripper heels. Leaping up and running would have been easier for a newborn giraffe, so I shuffled backwards on my arse instead, feeling the carpet burn the backs of my thighs, and instinctively raised one arm to shield my face.

The shot never came. Nick pointed the gun at the floor and kicked the door closed behind him with the heel of a Blundstone boot. His hair was longer, a short beard covered his acne scars and he seemed wired: inky pupils, sweat on his upper lip, and neck muscles twitching like they were being jolted by an electrical current. Stained jeans hung off his newly thin frame, and with the red-checked flannel shirt he looked like a lumberjack on PCP.

'Baby Did a Bad, Bad Thing' was still playing, with lots of dirty bass, and I tried to say something but couldn't get my tongue to form the words. I wished I hadn't argued with Sean, and I wondered what Nick was doing in my lounge room, but never found out. Just as he opened his mouth to talk a loudspeaker boomed from somewhere outside.

'Police! Nick Austin, drop your weapon.'

The red dot of a laser sight wobbled around on his chest and I heard big boots, lots of them, running up the stairwell. Seconds later the front door burst open and Nick spun around, gun held up in front of him. I heard a loud pop, and a fine spray of red misted the air and then he was falling, right on top of me, crushing my chest and forcing the air from my lungs. I smelled sweat and blood and felt hot wetness soak the thin fabric of my top. He rolled over, elbow digging into my ribs, and pulled my face close to his, fingernails digging into my scalp. I tried to scream, but he'd winded me and nothing came out. He turned his head and his breath was hot in my ear.

'Warn Nerida,' he croaked. 'Warn J—'

Then the weight lifted off me, and a guy who looked like a soldier in a science fiction film shouted something unintelligible, kicked me onto my front and almost pulled my arms out of their sockets as he handcuffed my wrists.

•

'I put it to you that you remained in contact with Nick Austin while he was a fugitive.'

'No. I didn't.' I was sitting in a fluorescent-lit interview room somewhere in the rabbit warren of St Kilda Road Police Complex. Grey carpet, grey melamine table, chipped walls, and a video camera staring at me from a unit attached to the ceiling. It had to be midnight, and the hangover had long ago set in. I was dehydrated, it felt like a metal bolt was penetrating my skull just above my right eye, and my wrists and shoulders ached from the rough stuff and the handcuffs.

'Would you like to comment as to why Austin showed up at your residence?'

'I don't know. I told you, I told those other guys, he came in with a gun and the only words he said were after he was shot. Warn Nerida, warn J somebody.'

'Why did you let him in?'

'I thought he was my boyfriend.'

Dianne Talbot raised one skinny eyebrow. Duval's henchwoman was lean, hard and tanned as a stick of beef jerky. Her eyeliner was steel blue, her lipstick a translucent shade of plum, and she wore a navy pantsuit.

Sitting next to her was a man in a white shirt and blue-striped tie who I assumed to be her second in command. His name tag identified him as Detective Jefferson Archer, and he looked to be in his mid to late thirties. He had nice features and would have been cute as a twenty-something, but hadn't aged well. His dwindling brown hair had been shorn into a number one, a slight paunch jutted over his trousers, and the beginnings of jowls were melting away his jawline. He hadn't said much, mainly looked at me with hostile little eyes.

'And your boyfriend is Detective Senior Constable Sean Shields, is that correct?' Talbot continued, her voice a husky rasp.

'You know that, Dianne.'

'It's Detective Senior Sergeant Talbot.'

We sat there for a long while, maybe a minute. Talbot made notes. Archer stared at me and clicked his pen.

There was something I'd been meaning to ask.

'How did you know Nick was at my place? Were you following him?'

Talbot and Archer exchanged a look. Talbot dipped her sharp chin at him and he stopped clicking his pen and leaned forward, elbows on the table.

'You were under surveillance. Detective Sergeant Talbot thought Austin would try to contact you sooner or later, and she was right,' he said.

A creepy feeling filtered through me and I felt a little nauseous. Someone had been watching me for six weeks? Someone had been watching and I hadn't known? My only comfort was that I hadn't left the house all that much and I'd generally kept the bedroom blinds drawn. Suddenly paranoid, I wondered if I'd done a lot of unconscious nose picking and arse scratching. I hoped there hadn't been much to see.

Talbot slapped her folder shut. It was bulging with statements, witness reports and photographs and it had my name on the front.

'Right. You're free to go,' she said.

We all stood up. Archer said, 'You want me to escort her to the lobby?'

'No, I'll do it.'

Archer raised his eyebrows. As I got up I felt indentations in the back of my thighs where the vinyl chair had pinched the flesh. I was still wearing my denim skirt, but the Tactical Response Group had been nice enough to give me a clean t-shirt, and allowed me to remove my stripper heels and slip a pair of sneakers onto my feet.

Talbot led me down a corridor and into a lift. She inserted a card and we began to descend.

'How's Nick?' I asked.

'In hospital.'

I was getting a little sick of her surly attitude and decided to plead my case one more time.

'Look, Detective Talbot, I've been telling you the truth. I'll take a lie detector test if you want. Austin approached me and asked to follow me around for a book he was writing. I went to his house that day to pick him up for a ride-along and found the body. I didn't hear anything more from him until tonight. I'm guessing you had my phones bugged so you'd know, right? I was as shocked as anyone when he showed up. That's it. I've got nothing to do with any of this. I'm just innocently caught in the middle.'

I'd hoped the mild-mannered appeal to her better nature might work but when the lift reached the ground floor she hit the door-close button and got in my face. Her eyes were narrowed and up close she smelled of slightly astringent White Linen perfume, as well as the coffee and cigarettes I'd noticed on our first meeting.

'You think I'm unaware of all the shit you've been involved with over the past two years? You think I buy that you're just an innocent girl caught in the middle? That line might work with Christakos and Shields, but it doesn't run with me. Ever since the service knocked you back you've been insinuating yourself into all the police business you can. I don't know if you're one of those crazy law enforcement fans or a cop-fucker. Probably both. So I'm only going to tell you once. Stay the hell away from my investigation.' She stared at me, hard.

I couldn't believe the naked hatred on her face. I felt pressure behind my eyeballs, like blood had welled up in the sockets, and the muscles in my forearms twitched as I instinctively prepared to reach up and push her back into the elevator doors. But before I gave in to the impulse I noticed the corner of her mouth twitch and a triumphant glimmer in her eye.

She wanted me to go her. There'd be a camera in the elevator, they'd bust me for assaulting a police officer and I'd never get my licence back. I balled my fists and dug my fingernails into the skin of my palms instead, forcing a smile.

'Stay away? Gladly, ma'am.' I actually saluted her and she pursed her mouth, clearly disappointed I hadn't done anything. She didn't say a word as she let me out into the police centre lobby. Sean was waiting. She waved and nodded at him and he smiled back. Whatever. I ran over and hugged him.

'I'm sorry about tonight.'

'Don't worry about it.'

Over his shoulder I saw Talbot give me one last, dirty look.

chapter thirteen

My flat was still a crime scene so the police had booked Sean and me into a four star hotel on St Kilda Road. On the second day after the shooting, Chloe came to visit and we lay out by the blue-tiled rooftop pool under a sky bleached pale by the intense noonday sun. I was slathered in SPF 15, while Chloe glistened with Hawaiian Tropic tanning oil. She smelled like a piña colada and I wondered where the hell she'd got hold of the stuff. Surely the Cancer Council had outlawed it years ago.

When she'd first arrived I'd told her all about Christmas night and was a little miffed when she wasn't overly excited about the SWAT team taking down a homicidal crime writer in my living room. Had we gone through so much violence together that it now seemed routine? Or were the TV networks keeping the story on such high rotation that everyone was sick of it? Chloe seemed much more interested when I told her about the argument I'd had with Sean.

'You kiss and make up?' she asked, casually untying the back of her bikini top and flinging the microscopic scrap of elastane over the back of the moulded plastic sun lounge. She squirted more coconut oil directly onto her chest and began rubbing it in, seemingly oblivious to the glares the other guests were giving us from behind their sunglasses.

'You'd better put that back on,' I said.

'Why?'

'I think it's illegal.'

'That's stupid. Men can go topless.'

'They don't have tits.'

'I dunno, check out that fat bloke. He's got a better rack than you.'

We squinted over our sunnies, and the middle-aged man who had been ogling Chloe's breasts quickly turned away. She was right, he was at least a B cup.

'You'd better get used to it, babe,' I said. 'Women's boobs are so sexualised in our culture you'll have people telling you off for breastfeeding in public.'

'No they won't.'

'Why not?'

'Not gonna breastfeed.'

'You serious?'

'Makes your tits sag.'

'Bullshit.'

'It's true. Besides, I don't want some creature suckling at me like a piglet. It's gross.'

'Being grossed out is the least of your worries after shitting a watermelon.'

'Not doing that either.'

'You can hardly avoid it.'

'I'm already booked in for a C section,' she said, triumphantly lifting her can of Coke and taking a sip.

'Chloe, that's a major operation.'

'Have you talked to the girls at my agency who've had kids? Well, I have and childbirth is seriously fucked up. There's stretching, ripping, tearing'—with each word she stabbed a finger in the direction of her crotch—'cutting, hacking, stitches . . .'

I winced and instinctively crossed my legs.

'Chanel said they sliced her from arsehole to breakfast when she popped out the twins, and Juanita told me that after she had Jayden her moot looked and felt like a lump of raw meat the dog had chewed. No way, mate, I'm not putting my poor puss through that. She's for fun and profit only. Aren't you, babe?' She addressed the last remark towards her vagina, like an heiress cooing to a rat-sized mutt.

It was bad timing for the nervous-looking pool boy, who had chosen that moment to come over and tell her to put her top back on. He stammered his way through his request, his eyes fixed on the lifesaving ring on the far wall. She didn't argue with him, but she did get up and take about three minutes to comply, turning this way and that so everyone got a good look. One mother actually put her hand over her young son's eyes.

'Stop avoiding the issue,' she said when she finally sat back down. 'Did you make up or not?'

'I guess so. I apologised and after that we didn't really talk about it.'

'He doesn't want you to strip.'

'That was about the gist of it.' I swigged my bottle of water. I could have gone a proper drink, but lately I'd been trying to be good and hold out till five each day. Christmas Day excluded.

'The guy's serious then.'

'You reckon?'

'Shit yeah.' She nodded sagely and lay back on her lounge. Kids were screaming and splashing in the pool, apparently recovered from Chloe's display.

'When you first start seeing a guy, they think the stripping thing's pretty hot. But when they fall in love with you, they get jealous and want you all to themselves. Fair enough, when you think about it.'

'Chloe!'

'What?'

'It is not fair enough, someone telling me what I can and can't do with my own body. And that's not all. By telling me I shouldn't strip he's implying that there's something wrong with it and I'm, I dunno, *immoral*.'

I repeated his sarky remark about the ballet and Chloe cracked up. Annoying, since she was supposed to be on my side.

'Don't you wanna quit anyway? Isn't that why you did your detective course in the first place?'

'Well, yeah. I can't do it forever. But that's not the point. He shouldn't be telling me what to do. I didn't think he was that sort of person.'

'Honey, they all are. Curtis was just the same. Hated me stripping. That's why I try not to have any serious boyfriends. I mean, if he didn't want me to do it he should have kept me in the style to which I'm accustomed—then I wouldn't have had to work.'

I gave her a look over my sunglasses.

'What?' she said.

'That's very nineteen fifties of you.'

She shrugged. 'So? I'd swap places with you any day, babe. Sean's paying your rent, buying the food and the booze. Not only that, but he's a fucking spunk, everyone likes him and that accent makes me cream my jeans every time I hear it. Sure, he's a copper, but he doesn't act like one and he doesn't mind a smoke, which makes him okay in my books. Can't trust a person who won't have a choof every now and again.'

'I don't choof.'

'Yeah, well, I put that down to you growing up on a marijuana plantation. Too much early exposure put you off for life. Point is, you don't know how lucky you are. Plenty of chicks would kill to have a guy like Sean. Why don't you just relax and enjoy lying around on your arse, for once?'

'I can't.'

'Why not?'

'Feels weird, as though I owe him or something. I like having my own money.'

'I like having someone else's better!' She laughed and drained her Coke, then looked around for the pool boy so she could order another. 'Why the hell did I have to get knocked up by a broke journo? Why couldn't it have been some rich dude?'

'Maybe because you never fucked any.'

'Oh yeah, that'd be it.' She twisted in her chair. 'Who've we gotta blow to get some pool service around here?'

I couldn't see the pool guy either so I hoisted myself up and wandered over to the covered bar area, careful not to slip on the wet tiles. I had to suck in my stomach with a lot more force than usual and cursed all those indolent hours on the couch with Sean, drinking wine and eating cheese and crackers. One good thing about stripping was that it simultaneously provided cardiovascular exercise and a damn good reason to stick to a diet. I wondered if all the slothful evenings and indulgent snacks had actually been a ploy of his to fatten me up and keep me off the stage.

There was still no sign of the pool guy but I did see a menu mounted on a clear plastic stand, so I picked it up and looked it over. The usual hotel snacks: nachos, club sandwiches, potato wedges, chicken Caesar salad. I rang a small brass bell and leaned against the counter watching the television set that was bolted to the wall. Dr Phil was on, talking in his Fozzie Bear voice, telling a teary American woman that she couldn't change what she didn't acknowledge. I hadn't seen any crap shows for ages, since Sean hated daytime television almost as much as he hated cheese singles. I knew that both were bad for you, but couldn't resist their synthetic charms.

The good doctor threw to an ad break, but instead of a commercial for margarine or washing powder there was a news desk and a banner headline announcing a 'breaking story'. When I heard what it was I dropped the menu.

chapterfourteen

'Nick's escaped!' I told Chloe.

'Wasn't he half dead?'

'Just a pretty bad flesh wound. He knocked out a police officer, apparently.'

'Rock and roll.' She yawned.

'Fuck,' I said.

'It's not your problem, mate. Cops'll catch him eventually. More importantly, what about Sean, did you tell him you'd quit stripping?'

Luckily Chloe's mobile started singing: Madonna, 'Justify My Love'.

'Chloe's Elite Strippers, this is Chloe.' She was silent for a moment, then: 'I dunno, who's calling? Oh hey. Yeah, I'll put her on.'

I shook my head but she handed me the phone anyway.

'Hello?' I said.

'Hi, Simone, it's Elisabeth Austin. Liz. We met at the Summer Sessions?'

Nick's sister. Christ, what was it now? Probably wanted to talk about her brother.

'I remember. Hey, did you see the news about Nick escaping from hospital?'

'Um, yes.' She muttered something about it being an unfortunate situation and I got the feeling she really didn't want to talk about it. Pretty cold, considering it was her twin on the run. 'I'm actually calling about Curtis Malone's book. There are a couple of things I need to go over with you from a legal standpoint.'

'When?'

'As soon as possible. Are you busy at the moment?'

I groaned inwardly. The last thing I wanted to do was read what he'd written about the Emery Wade case, but if I didn't want Jimmy Olsen to slander me I was going to have to. I figured I may as well get it over with so I could race back and spend all afternoon by the pool.

'No. I'm free. Where do you want to meet?'

'Is St Kilda convenient for you? Our offices are based in Albert Park so it's handy for me. It's almost twelve, how about I buy you lunch?'

The thought cheered me somewhat. She probably had an expense account.

'Sure. Where?'

'Is upstairs at the Stokehouse alright?'

An expensive, two-hat restaurant on the beach. Was it ever. I livened up some more.

I left Chloe by the pool, changed into denim pedal pushers and a singlet top, and caught the number 16 tram down the wide, tree-lined boulevard that was St Kilda Road. After the junction the tram shunted right into Fitzroy Street, sliding past innumerable cafés, bars and restaurants. Just after it veered left on the Esplanade I jumped off and took the footbridge to the beachfront.

The temperature had to be somewhere in the high twenties, but it wasn't as stifling as it had been by the pool due to the light breeze floating in off Port Phillip Bay. The air smelled like summer holidays: sunscreen, salt water, hot chips and battered fish bubbling in hot oil. Out past the yacht club sailboats rose and dipped on the swell, and in the park near the foreshore families picnicked on the grass, shaded by chunky date palms.

The restaurant was in a nineteen-twenties weatherboard building painted dark olive with white trim; it had the feel of an expensive, minimalist beach house on Cape Cod. A waitress with a black shirt and apron and a long blonde braid led me through a room full of whitewashed wood, widely spaced tables and giant picture windows. As we made our way out to the large deck overlooking the sea I half expected to see toothy Kennedys lounging about drinking gin and tonics, contemplating a turn around the bay on the yacht.

Liz sat in the far corner wearing large round sunglasses and clutching a glass of white wine. Her silver-streaked blonde hair was carefully flicked, as before, and she wore a pair of expensive-looking beige slacks and a gauzy white sleeveless top with unobtrusive ruffles down the front. Her bronze bracelets were inlaid with mother-of-pearl and had probably cost quite a lot in a South Yarra boutique.

'Hey.' I nodded as I sat down opposite her. Close up she looked thin, her upper arms stringy. She'd been almost plump at the writers' festival. Not anymore.

The waitress poured me a glass of crisp pinot grigio from a nearby ice bucket, placed a menu in front of me, then quietly disappeared.

'I'm really sorry about . . . everything that's happened,' I said. 'How you holding up?'

'I'm alright. And you?'

'Not bad considering your brother showed up at my place with a gun.' I smiled, but the joke fell flat. Liz must have thought I was an insensitive cow because her mouth set into that schoolmarm line and she looked away. I guessed being the sister of a fugitive murder suspect wasn't exactly a barrel of laughs, but hell, being the supposed accomplice of one wasn't either. It was an awkward situation and I decided I'd quickly stuff my face, check the facts and leave.

'That the manuscript?' I pointed to the package and she nodded, still looking over my shoulder as though scanning the restaurant behind me. 'Shall we look over the pages now? Or you wanna eat first?'

Liz leaned forward, pushing her sunglasses onto the top of her head. I noticed for the first time that she looked a lot like Nick. Strong jawline, straight, prominent nose. Her grey eyes were puffy and red-rimmed.

'Simone, can I trust you?' she said softly.

I shrugged. 'I dunno. Trust me to do what?'

She grabbed her wine glass and took a big mouthful.

'Do you think he did it?'

'What?' It dawned on me that she'd lied about Curtis' manuscript. I was so pissed off I considered walking—until I saw fresh tears shimmer in her swollen eyes.

'Nick,' she mouthed, then sat back and looked around again.

'I don't know.'

'But you were there.'

'Unfortunately that's true. But it was after the fact.'

'The police think he's guilty.'

'Maybe. Maybe not. The official line is he's wanted for questioning. He ran. Shit. He's still running. They've got to bring him in.'

'Please keep your voice down,' Liz whispered. I looked over my shoulder. The nearest patrons were two tables away and deep in conversation. 'But do *you* think he's a killer?' She leaned forward, the table wobbled and I had to grab my wine glass before it tipped over.

'Didn't strike me as one when we first met, and I'm sure you don't think so, but believe me, you never know. Still, I don't think he was there to kill me last night.'

'He wanted your help.'

'Maybe.' I shrugged again. 'Look, Liz, I really can't say either way. All I know is I saw Isabella's body. I saw Nick with blood on his shirt.'

'How much blood?'

''Bout this—' I indicated a fist-sized area.

'His blood. From the festival. He was wearing the same clothes, right?'

'Yeah.'

'And there was a lot of Isabella's blood in his office?'

'More than I ever want to see again.' I felt sick having to recall it.

'If he'd killed her he would have been covered with it.'

She had a point.

'Yeah, I've thought about that. Unless, I dunno, he wore some sort of plastic raincoat he got rid of? Or maybe some other clothes, and then he changed back into the old ones.'

'But he was dead drunk, right?' she continued, leaning further forward, gripping the edges of the table.

'I thought so. He smelled like it. If he wasn't he's a great actor.'

'If he was that drunk, then how could he manage to change or get rid of his clothes? And if he wasn't that drunk, why did he pass out and leave the body there for anyone to find it?' She almost sounded angry at me.

I held up my hands. 'Hey, I agree. It doesn't make sense. I don't know what forensic evidence the cops have, but from what I've seen it doesn't really add up.'

She finished off the rest of her wine, grabbed the dripping bottle and refilled her glass. Rare for someone to finish a drink before I did.

'He's not a killer,' she stated.

'Statistically, women are most likely to be murdered by their exes. Especially when they leave. Apparently the divorce papers were on the desk.'

She shook her head and drank more wine. So did I, having to slug the stuff to keep up with her. The bottle was almost gone.

'What does your gut feeling tell you?' she asked.

'Seems unlikely, but then, why did he run? What's this all about?'

'I can't tell you unless I trust you.'

'Okay.' I was so exasperated I told her what she wanted to hear: 'You can trust me with your life and I believe your brother is innocent, cross my heart and hope to die.'

She narrowed her eyes. I had sounded kind of sarcastic.

'Honest.'

The waitress returned, and I ordered crab and cauliflower ravioli, followed by seared tuna with a white bean puree. Liz finished her drink and ordered just an entree: goat curd, roasted beetroot and rocket. No wonder she was so thin. I was already anticipating the cheese plate for dessert.

'Sure you don't want a main? I'll feel like a pig if you only eat salad.'

'Forget eating. I want to hire you.'

'To do what?'

'Shh,' she hissed. 'Someone could be listening.'

'Who?'

'The police. Nick called me three days ago . . .'

'You serious?' It came out a little loud and she gave me a worried look so I lowered my tone. 'I'm guessing you didn't call the cops.'

She shook her head.

'What did he say?' I asked.

'That he didn't kill Isabella, and he needed money or someone else was going to die.'

'He tell you who *did* kill her?'

'No.' She bit her lip.

'Who'd he say was going to die?'

Liz emptied the bottle into her glass, then finished it in one go.

'Me.'

chapter fifteen

'What? Who would want to kill you?'

'I don't know. No one. It's not personal, just someone using me for . . . leverage. Nick said if he didn't come up with the money it'd be me, then our younger brother, then Mum. Dad's passed away.'

'You think someone's blackmailing him? How much money does he want?'

'As much as he can get. At least a million, maybe more. I cashed in my shares and raised almost fifty thousand. I've put my flat on the market but it's going to take months to sell and even then it'll only be four hundred. He said he'd try and pay it back as soon as he sorted out the mess he was in. But I got the feeling he needed a lot more.'

'Mess?'

'That was as specific as he got.'

'Why do people usually need large amounts of money in a hurry?'

'Bad debts?' she suggested.

'Or blackmail. We already know he liked a drink. Did he gamble? Coke? Was he a kiddy fiddler?'

'No!'

'And all this is assuming he wasn't just scamming the money off you?'

'Why would he do that?'

'He'd need cash to leave the country. They would have frozen his bank accounts.'

'I know Nick better than anyone. He wasn't scamming me,' she insisted. 'And why would he show up at your place if he was about to leave?'

'No idea.' I shrugged. 'Couldn't have been to scab cash because I don't have any. Maybe he's just . . . unhinged?'

She bridled. 'He's not.'

'Did you see him? Do you know where he was hiding out for six weeks?'

She shook her head. 'No. I talked to him on my assistant's phone. I had to drop the money off in a park, so I didn't see him face to face. He said it wasn't safe.'

'Christ, sounds just like one of his books.'

The waitress came back with more wine and the entrees, so we kept our mouths shut until she was gone.

'Will you help him?' Liz implored. 'I think that's why he turned up at your flat. He needed help, and then the police . . .' Her eyes shimmered with tears.

'After Nick was shot he asked me to warn Nerida and somebody whose name started with J. Ring any bells?'

Her bronze earrings rattled when she shook her head. 'I don't know any Neridas, and a lot of people have names starting with J. Nick's ex-wife's name is Jenny, but she turned into a religious freak and he hasn't had anything to do with her for ages.'

Liz refilled our glasses while I nibbled on my ravioli. It was divine, but I had other things on my mind.

'What do you mean, help Nick?' I asked.

'Find him before the police or Rod Thurlow. There's a rumour Rod will hand over the money to anyone who catches Nick, dead or alive.'

I had to try very hard not to roll my eyes.

'How come you're so sure I can do that? The cops haven't had any luck.'

'That's because Nick's friends and family know he's not guilty and haven't been telling them everything. We don't want him in jail or shot dead, and we're not going to sell him out for the million-dollar reward. Even if you don't find him maybe you can at least discover why he had to run. That's the main thing. Then we can help him, and clear his name.'

That was debatable. If Nick was being blackmailed over something really sick, things could turn out worse. I didn't tell her that, though. She was Nick's sister, and as far as she was concerned he could do no wrong.

'I'm sorry, Liz, but I can't help. Why don't you try another investigator?'

'I wouldn't trust another investigator.'

'Have you been reading the papers? Because of your brother, I am not presently licensed, therefore I can't legally work for you.'

'Oh, fuck that.' She waved her hand dismissively and I was a little shocked. It was the first time I'd heard her swear. 'I'm talking off the books. Cash in hand. I've read Curtis' manuscript. I know you don't always stick to the letter of the law.'

I narrowed my eyes. 'He wrote that?'

'Yeah, but don't worry, we've taken out all the libellous stuff. Anything we thought you could sue Wet Ink over. Listen, Simone, I'm willing to pay you, and well. In with the manuscript is an envelope containing seven thousand dollars.

That's for a week. Five hundred a day plus the same again for expenses.'

Seven thousand bucks? My heart started to palpate.

'How'd you come up with that figure?'

'Nick's books. It's Zack Houston's daily rate. He doesn't usually charge so much for expenses but I figured you might need it. Should cover plane tickets if necessary, motels, bribes . . .'

It was ridiculous. I couldn't take the case. It was illegal, possibly dangerous, I'd been warned off by Talbot, and Sean would hit the roof. Plus there was the fact that everybody in the country was already after the guy. If the entire federal police force and any number of self-styled soldiers of fortune couldn't catch up with him, what hope did I have? Even if by some amazing fluke I did find him, wouldn't it be illegal not to hand him over to the authorities?

On the other hand, I really, really needed the money, and if I was careful Dianne Talbot would never have to know.

'I can't promise I'll find him.'

Jesus, I was as good as agreeing. My palms tingled and the electric feeling shot straight up my arms, making my neck veins throb.

'Of course.'

'And I can only give it a week.'

Sean was on double shifts for the next seven days. No awkward questions.

'I'll take what I can get,' Liz said.

Unfortunately, Liz couldn't give me much to go on. For all her talk, Nick didn't have a hell of a lot of family or friends. Their parents had emigrated from Poland before they were born; the dad was now dead and the mum in a nursing home. Their only other relative was a younger brother, Tom, who worked in IT in Sydney. Liz asked me not to contact him directly as she was sure he was under surveillance. The friends that Liz knew of were more like acquaintances from the publishing industry: Curtis, Desiree, Victoria Hitchens.

'I know that name.' I said. 'The tall blonde writer filming a doco at the Summer Sessions. Isabella's friend.'

'Ex-friend. Don't believe all the kissy-kissy stuff, it was just for the cameras. But yes, Nick met her through Isabella.'

'Think the ex-wife, Jenny, would be worth talking to?'

'The Christian? He hasn't spoken to her for at least two years.'

The conversation pretty much deteriorated from there on in. While I rather virtuously sipped a double espresso Liz finished the wine and reiterated the varied and innumerable ways in which Nick was the most wonderful brother on earth, slagged off Isabella and told me that it was actually good she was dead, despite the fact that Nick was now a fugitive murder suspect, because he could finally get closure on the relationship.

I got the feeling she'd been wound up tight for at least six weeks so I let her go for a while before finally signalling for the bill, propping her up as she staggered down the stairs, and then stuffing her into a cab. The coffee had cut through the wine and the food and my usual afternoon somnolence. I was raring to go.

Back at the hotel I headed straight for the business centre so I could get on the internet. Chloe had gotten sick of waiting for me and gone to the movies. Good, because I could get straight to it and didn't have to tell her about the case. Chloe was my unofficial sidekick, but she also had a big mouth: if she spilled to someone like Curtis, news of my clandestine job would be all over town. As to whether I'd tell Sean, I figured I'd decide later.

While I waited for the computer to start up I scribbled notes on scrap paper, realising I only had one piece of information that the cops didn't: Nick picking up forty grand in cash at Yarra Bend Park a few days ago. So what? I hadn't a clue what he'd done with the money, and no way of knowing if Liz and the rest of his family had actually been threatened and, if so, by who.

Maybe Liz had been right and Nick had come to me for help, although I didn't know why he would do that.

Of course, Liz was so obsessed with finding her brother that she hadn't even thought of Isabella. It was possible Nick was mixed up with some sort of major shit, but in any murder case it was important to find out everything you could about the victim. Perhaps Isabella had been involved in the same trouble, or maybe someone else had a motive to kill her.

I thought of Rod Thurlow. The victim's partner was always the main suspect, and I remembered the look on Rod's face when Nick and Isabella had commenced their vicious flirting at the writers' festival. Sure, Rod had appeared on TV looking heartbroken, and he'd put up a million-dollar reward for information leading to Nick's capture, but it could all be an elaborate smokescreen. What if he'd somehow found out about the kiss I'd witnessed? What if Isabella was having an affair with her ex-husband? And why did they break up anyhow?

I had so many questions and so few answers that my head was spinning. The only thing for it was to begin researching and asking questions. It seemed like an enormous task that was unlikely to produce much of a result, but I had to start somewhere. I motivated myself like I did sometimes when I was stripping: by thinking about the money.

I spent the rest of the afternoon and early evening doing internet searches on Nick and Isabella and printed out reviews, profile pieces, and a couple of articles that Nick had written. The two of them also turned up on past writers' festival programs, and radio interviews podcast onto the net. I even downloaded a picture of Nick at some sort of leftist meeting from an archived issue of the Melbourne University newspaper, *Farrago*.

Most of the hits I got on Isabella, though, were generated after her death. A crime writer brutally slaying his ex-wife then going on the run—it was the kind of ironic story the public pored over, and had shown up everywhere from the *New York Times* to the *Warsaw Voice*. I managed to get a fair bit of background on Isabella, but nothing that told me why anyone, apart from Nick, might have wanted to kill her.

She'd grown up on the Mornington Peninsula, attended a private girls school and then gone on to study writing at RMIT. Her father ran a boat-building business, and there was mention of her parents divorcing when she was a teenager. I'd always thought it more noteworthy if a person's parents weren't divorced, but maybe that was just me. She'd had her first novella, *The Liquidity of Desire*, published at twenty-seven. I checked out a few of the reviews, and although they were mostly positive, the book didn't sound like my cup of tea. It was variously described as 'lyrical', 'nuanced,' 'ephemeral', and 'utterly without plot'.

Although I hadn't found out anything particularly useful, the web search was a start. It was scary how much information about a person drifted around in cyberspace, available to all. I resisted the urge to google myself. I really didn't want to know. I did, however, search my dad. He had an unusual name, Mark Koputh, and I only got one hit: LinkedIn, a professional networking site. It even had a photo.

Mark had been a bohemian surfie in his twenties, but his fifth decade had seen him morph into a typical suit-wearing, middle-aged middle manager. The perma-tan was long faded, his blond hair had receded and greyed, and his big brown eyes seemed to have shrunk into pockets of fat. My mum had fared a lot better in the ageing stakes and I was glad I took after her. Still, he was the only father I had, and the only parent who didn't hate my guts, so I sent him a quick hello through the website.

Back up in the room a message on the hotel phone told me my flat would be ready to reoccupy the next morning. I packed most of my stuff, careful to shove the printouts and the cash down the very bottom of my bag, hidden underneath some dirty clothes. I didn't want Sean to discover them when he came back late from work. After eating a room-service chicken and avocado salad and drinking a half bottle of Jacob's Creek red, I washed my face and brushed my teeth and lay between the smooth, cool hotel sheets watching an incredibly silly documentary about koalas during which the narrator described two fighting males as 'furry gladiators'. Jesus. The program, combined with the sun, skulduggery and mind-numbing hours spent staring at the computer screen, meant I was out for the count long before Sean got back.

chapter sixteen

'All this rooting is melting my brain.' I wiped my forehead with the back of my hand. Despite the air-con I'd worked up a major sweat.

'I thought you liked sex.' Sean crawled up from between my thighs, kissing my belly and chest along the way.

'Yeah, but I've never had so many goddamn orgasms over a six-week period. It can't be healthy. You spoil me.'

'Well, Moneypenny,' he put on the Connery voice, 'you deserve spoiling.'

'Huh,' I snorted. 'Flagellating more like.'

'That'll cost you extra.'

I laughed, smacked his arm, then kissed him and tasted the both of us on his lips. Peach crumble and sea salt. Strange but true.

'You're the perfect man.'

'I am.' He lit a cigarette and I took it off him for a quick drag, handed it back and laid my head on the pillow, exhaling and watching the smoke wind its way to the ceiling. I was wondering if I should tell him about my new job.

'What time do you have to be at work?' I asked instead.

'Seven. What are you up to today?'

'Apart from going home and trying to avoid the media?'

'Uh-huh.'

'Might go for a run, stock up on protein, start my diet again.'

'You don't need to diet.' He stroked my belly. 'Curves are hot.'

'Yeah, but I'm not curvy, I'm straight up and down. When I put on weight I turn into a barrel.' I propped myself up on my elbow and had another turn of his ciggie. *Tell him*, urged my brain. *You're in a relationship here. Honesty is the best policy.*

I sucked in smoke, blew it out, handed the durry back.

'Sean, what would you say if I told you I'd been hired to look into Nick Austin's . . . disappearance?'

'What? What the fuck are you talking about?'

'I—'

'Are you completely out of your mind?' He sat straight up. 'It's illegal for a start, not to mention dangerous, and if you piss off Talbot one more time you'll—who's hired you?'

Best policy my arse.

'Whoa,' I said. 'Relax. It was a hypothetical. I'm not really doing it. I just wanted to see what you'd say.'

'So someone must have asked. Who?'

That was a point. Why else would I be asking what he thought?

'Rod Thurlow,' I lied.

'That tool? I hope you said no.'

'I said I'd think about it. It was quite a lot of money . . .' Once I started making stuff up I really couldn't stop.

'For god's sake, don't worry about money.'

'Not so easy when you haven't got any.'

Sean looked off into the middle distance like he was mulling something over. 'I'm serious, you don't need to worry. I've got a plan.'

'Oh.' I raised my eyebrows. 'What?'

He put the cigarette out and smiled at me, slate-blue eyes gleaming behind the veil of smoke. 'I'll tell you tonight. Wanna meet somewhere around Acland Street for dinner? Cicciolinas? Claypots?'

'Aren't you working a double?'

'I'll swap with someone.' He jumped off the bed and I studied his body while he searched for his towel: slim hips; medium-sized, nice-looking cock; good legs; red-gold hair in a small V on his chest; freckled forearms. Cute. Chloe was right, I was a lucky bitch. Watching him made me want to go again, but he'd found the towel and slung it over his shoulder. I watched his firm buttocks shimmer as he walked to the bathroom.

'Want me to order you up some breakfast?' he called over his shoulder. 'They actually do a great eggs florentine—spinach, hollandaise, sourdough toast.'

'No!'

•

My unit was in a wide street full of oak trees. Nobody appeared to be skulking about in the shadows, so I grabbed my mail from the bank of metal letterboxes out front, strolled up the shrub-lined path, unlocked the not-very-secure security door, and climbed the stairs.

I wandered around the flat first, like a cat whose territory has been invaded, bristling and sniffing around. Cleaning fluid and other people's sweat and deodorant scented the lounge room, and I noticed that the carpet was especially spotless in the section where Nick's blood had soaked in. The furniture and a couple of the framed posters were slightly askew, but

I was sure Sean would sort that out—it'd drive him mental otherwise.

My plan was to drink a formidable coffee, brainstorm while I was jazzed on caffeine, then plunge headlong into the case any way I could. Hopefully I'd be able to get a lot done over the next six days, with Sean rostered on twelve-hour shifts. I felt briefly guilty about not telling him what I was up to, but he'd left me no choice. The way he freaked out, he'd probably threaten to tell that bitch Talbot, just to stop me. The thought made me feel so indignant I sucked in my cheeks and pursed my lips. I knew relationships were supposed to be about compromise, but why did it all have to come from my side? He didn't want me stripping, didn't want me investigating, so what the hell was I supposed to do? I guessed I'd find out when he told me his mysterious 'plan'. I wondered what it was, before pushing the thought out of my mind. Like any investigation, the Nick Austin case was a sprawling, unholy mess and I had to start focusing on it right away.

I switched on the kettle, filled the plunger with coffee grounds from a tin in the freezer and looked over my mail while I waited for the water to boil. The first envelope was from my real estate agent. I opened the letter inside and it took a few seconds for the contents to sink into my brain. Notice to vacate premises. Sixty days. Refer to clause 32c in the lease.

They were evicting me. And they'd given me enough time that they didn't need a reason, so I couldn't go to the Residential Tenancies Association and kick up a stink. Tears spouted in my eyes. Bloody hell. I'd been in the place for four years, which was pretty much longer than I'd ever lived anywhere. I'd been a good tenant, always paid my rent on time, except for when I was really skint. Sure, the police had been around on more than one occasion but that wasn't *totally* my fault. I started thinking about all those newspaper articles I'd read in *The Age* about a rental housing crisis: skyrocketing rents, hundreds jostling to view properties, prospective tenants offering an extra twenty or fifty a week to secure a lease. Even upright citizens with respectable jobs were struggling to find a place to live. What hope did I have?

I realised how much I loved the apartment. It wasn't slick or fancy but it had a sweet little balcony that caught the sea breeze and it was close to the Elwood shops and walking distance to St Kilda. Not to mention my picturesque running track to the bay.

I dug my mobile out of my back pocket and immediately rang Sean to whinge, but he wasn't picking up. Damn. The kettle steamed, gurgled and clicked off so I filled the plunger and checked out the second envelope. Blank and unsealed, flap tucked into the back. Probably a flyer from a local resident advertising ironing or secretarial services or personal training. I shuddered. I probably could have done with a trainer to get me back to my fighting weight, but I'd had an aversion to them ever since one had tried to kill me. Waiting for the coffee to brew, I idly opened the envelope and pulled out a sheet of paper. It was blank except for three words printed in the middle.

You're dead, cunt.

chapterseventeen

I let go of the paper instinctively, like it was a snake or a spider, and it fluttered to the floor. My heart felt like it was fibrillating, and I sucked in a short breath that caught in my throat.

Standing very still, I listened for sounds, expecting assassins to burst into the kitchen with a knife. When none were forthcoming I began to calm down. I'd been through the house. No one else was there. Damn, I'd become a basket-case since my mum was shot.

Finally breathing out, I pulled one of Sean's clear plastic sandwich bags from a drawer and crouched down to place the paper inside, careful to touch only the edges. I stood up, got another bag and did the same with the envelope. I could ask Sean to get them checked for prints, but maybe I was overreacting. Probably just a poison pen letter, an arsehole neighbour wanting to make sure I left the block. Or maybe some stalker type who had seen me on TV.

All I knew was it couldn't have anything to do with my new case, because I hadn't even started yet and nobody except Liz knew I was investigating. I asked myself the same question the cops would have: Did I have any enemies? Heaps, if I was honest, although most of them were in prison or dead. They could have family, associates . . . but why now? Why not try to get back at me earlier?

I decided not to let it worry me. If someone really wanted to take me out they would have, rather than sending a gutless anonymous letter. I took my coffee and notebook to the lounge room, spread all my printouts across the table and got to work.

After an hour and lord knows how many milligrams of caffeine, I had a preliminary list of questions I wanted to ask and people I needed to talk to. Rod Thurlow, Nick's ex-wife Jenny, Victoria Hitchens, and possibly Desiree the sexpert, although I'd have to be careful with her because I didn't want Curtis finding out what I was up to.

First off I phoned the hotline Thurlow had set up for information pertaining to Nick. A woman's voice answered.

'Reward hotline. Can I have your name, please?'

'Simone Kirsch.'

'Do you have information on the whereabouts of Nick Austin?'

'Not exactly, but I know something that might be helpful.'

'Go ahead.'

'Thing is, I need to talk to Rod Thurlow face to face.'

'I'm afraid that's not possible. We just log the information and then—'

'He knows who I am. If I give you my number, will you tell him to ring?'

'I can't promise anything.'

'Just let him know I called.'

I hung up and checked the internet white pages for Victoria Hitchens, but like most beautiful, famous people she was unlisted. A general search told me she wrote historical romances and uncovered her website, a slick affair full of posed shots of Victoria wandering around cities like New York, Paris and Rome, leaning on the railings of bridges and staring prettily into the distance, like one of her heroines. In one photo she was actually writing, and I wondered if authors really did sit at their computers in Gucci suits, immaculately made up, blonde hair coiffed.

According to her brief bio, Victoria had been an actress before becoming a writer, and had gone to the same fancy girls school as Isabella.

Clicking the contact tab on her website, I sent an email asking her to ring me. I didn't know if she would read it, or even get back to me if she did, but it was a start.

As for Desiree, I figured I could always stake out Curtis' place if I wanted to find her. Failing that, I'd accost her outside the radio studio later in the week. She hosted a live sex-advice show every Thursday night, where listeners could call in and get tips on everything from auto-asphyxiation to anal beads.

Then there was Nick's ex-wife Jenny. They'd been together for over fifteen years, pre-Isabella, and I thought she'd probably know him better than anyone, and might be up for a good bitch session. But how to find her? I didn't even know her maiden name. In a profile about Nick that was published when his first novel came out they'd only mentioned her by her first name, along with the fact that she worked as a schoolteacher.

I googled the names 'Jenny' and 'Nick Austin' and spent an hour clicking on useless, unrelated links until I finally hit pay dirt: a picture of them both at a Miles Franklin Literary Award dinner years before: he'd been nominated but hadn't won.

Nick wore a dinner jacket and looked bright-eyed and positively baby-faced, while Jenny was dolled up in a black velvet dress, a maroon pashmina draped around her shoulders. She was a little thickset and had a hawk-like nose, broad lips and dense eyebrows. Her long brown hair had been tied back in a loose bun, and wavy strands curled around her shoulders. Dark, matt lipstick and chunky heels were a testament to the mid nineties. Jenny was alright-looking, but no match for Isabella's delicate, ethereal beauty.

Of course there was no maiden name attached, but as I stared at the photo I began to realise I'd seen her somewhere before. I shuffled through my printouts and found the picture of Nick at university. It had been taken at a Socialist Alliance meeting back in nineteen eighty-eight and showed Nick sitting slouched on a desk looking impossibly skinny and impossibly young, wearing a Billy Bragg t-shirt and attempting to hide his inflamed skin behind shoulder-length, dyed-black hair. In the middle of the shot, standing up with his fist raised, was a guy who looked like the leader of the group. Despite the scraggly beard and crazy-old-man hair he looked to be in his late twenties, and wore a flannelette shirt and an outraged expression. The name under the photo identified him as David Geddes.

Next to him was a chick with crossed arms and a spiky, bleached-white crew cut called Rachel Devries, and on her right, checking out Nick from across the room, was Jenny, wavy hair roped into two long plaits. She sat in a chair, one ankle on the opposite knee, wearing jeans, cherry-red Doc Martens boots and a t-shirt objecting to the Higher Education Contribution Scheme. Pity her protest hadn't succeeded. I owed almost ten grand from my uncompleted arts degree, but with my declared income so wretched, the government wasn't getting it back in a hurry.

Below the picture was her name: Jenny Clunes. Yes! I punched the air and uttered a triumphant whoop. Such small victories were incommensurately satisfying in the PI biz, and I began to feel like I had half a brain and was a useful member of society, rather than the fat, lazy sex addict I knew myself to be.

I jumped back on the computer and typed her name into the internet white pages. Okay. No J Clunes in Victoria. Maybe she'd got married again, or shared a house and didn't have a landline in her name. That was alright, I could live with that, as long as one of the Clunes in the directory was related to her. I picked up my phone and proceeded to call every one of them in Victoria.

Nobody answered. Goddamn Christmas holidays. All I could do was leave messages:

'Hi, I'm looking for an old friend called Jenny Clunes? I have no idea if you're related to her but I'm trying everyone in the book. We went to Melbourne Uni together back in the eighties. If you know her could you pass on my number? My name's Rachel Devries.'

Underhanded, but I doubted she'd be in a hurry to call back if she knew who I really was. I had no idea if the ruse would work. Maybe Rachel and Jenny hadn't been friends at all. Even worse, they could've been great mates to that very day, living next door and popping over to each other's houses for tea and Marxist theory every afternoon.

There was also the possibility that Jenny had no relatives in Victoria and I was gonna have to either call every Clunes in Australia or go begging my old boss to get her number and address. Tony Torcasio was an ex-cop, had contacts on the inside, and subscribed to extensive information databases that I couldn't afford. He was a nice guy but the last few times

I'd implored him for help, he'd given me a flat no, he didn't want to get involved. Guess I couldn't blame him.

I sighed, typed in 'Clunes' and changed the state to New South Wales. Over a hundred of the buggers. Just as I sighed and moved to pick up the phone, it rang.

'Hello?'

'Is this Rachel?' The voice sounded whispery and old. I didn't think it was Jenny.

'Yes, who's this?'

'Margaret Clunes. Jenny's mother.'

'Oh hi, thanks *so much* for calling back.'

'You knew Jenny from university?'

'Yes.'

'How?'

How?

'Uh, we were student activists together? Got involved in a lot of protests. HECS and . . .' I searched my brain. Equal pay for women? More of a seventies thing. 'Nuclear disarmament. Aboriginal land rights. Gosh, you name it, we protested about it!'

'Oh yes, I remember when Jenny got arrested. I was horrified!'

'Yep, pretty frightening,' I bullshitted.

'Sorry about the questions.' Margaret's voice was friendlier. 'I don't know if you've heard about the trouble with Jenny's ex-husband?'

'Mmm,' I said noncommittally.

'The media kept pestering her to talk about Nick, but she refused. Very sneaky they were too.'

'Oh dear.'

'Anyway, I'll hang up and call her, and pass on your number—that way she can call you if she wants.'

I briefly considered trying to wheedle Jenny's number out of her mum, but she seemed like a pretty switched-on old cookie, so I decided not to push it. Ten minutes later my phone rang.

'Hello?'

'Rachel?'

'Jenny?' I asked.

'Ye-es.' She already sounded suspicious. I guessed I didn't sound much like her old comrade. I knew I didn't have a hell of a lot of time before she slammed down the phone.

'Look, sorry about the subterfuge but I'm not Rachel, my name's Simone Kirsch and I—'

She hung up.

I wasn't beaten yet. I checked the display on my phone and was overjoyed to find she'd called from a landline. As I grabbed my bag and hurried to my car I prayed it wasn't a new number.

chapter eighteen

I parked the '67 Ford Futura out the back of my office, next to the Laser which I hadn't used for the past six weeks. Chloe's shitbox Crown Victoria was parked in the lot too, and I hoped she was having some sort of mid-afternoon, pregnancy-induced nap. I didn't want to have to explain what I was up to.

No such luck. Just as I was opening the back door, Chloe stuck her head and her bare tits over the railing surrounding her deck.

'Hey, mate, I was just about to call you. I'm bored out of my mind. Come up and have some bubbly.'

'Can't right now.'

'Why not?'

'Gotta check something in my office.'

'What?'

'Just some stuff.' I let myself in before she could ask any more questions, walked through the kitchenette, slid behind the desk and booted up the computer. The room was stuffy and smelled stale from being shut up for weeks, but I wasn't going to be there long.

While the computer got started I rooted around in one of the cluttered desk drawers for a CD-Rom. It contained a reverse white pages, where you could type in a phone number and bring up the name and address attached to it. Unfortunately they didn't make the CDs anymore—I'd bought that one from the post office when I was just starting my PI course—and with people moving house, changing numbers and buying mobile phones, it was becoming more redundant with each passing day.

I typed in the number Jenny had called from and held my breath. It got a hit. Barrett, P, 28 Bougainvillea Drive, Berwick. It could be her, remarried. Just to be sure I got on the internet and searched Jenny Barrett together with Berwick and turned up a hit on a Christian school in the area. Jenny was the head of the English department. There was even a photo. She'd obviously been home half an hour ago. If I left straight away maybe she'd still be there.

'Stuff, huh?' Chloe said behind me, and I jumped and fumbled to shut down the page, like a husband caught surfing sex sites.

'Yep.'

How could she be so big, yet so quiet?

'Who's Jenny Barrett?' She'd wrapped herself in a hot-pink sarong with a hibiscus print that stretched tight across her belly and matched the cowboy hat tilted back on her head. Her eyes shone in the low light. She didn't miss a trick.

I considered lying for a second or two, but knew I'd never get away with it.

'Nick Austin's ex-wife.'

'You're on a job, aren't you?' She flopped down on the blue armchair in front of the desk and grinned.

'Sort of,' I admitted.

'Sweet!'

'You can't tell anyone. Not even Sean knows. Someone's hired me to find out why Nick keeps running: they said he needs money and they think it might be blackmail or bad debts. They reckon he didn't kill Isabella.'

'Who hired you?'

'Sorry, babe, can't say.'

'Doesn't matter. It's just good to be back on a case. I've been so bored. Business is dead over the holidays, apart from New Year, which I've already organised. So, what do you need me to do?'

'Nothing, except maybe ease off on the sun.' She was tanned as a cow hide.

'No way. For once Melbourne gets a real summer. It's like the solarium for free.'

'You're browner than George Hamilton.'

'Who?'

'Listen, I don't want you running around doing anything crazy, you're about to pop.'

'Don't be sexist.'

'Excuse me?'

'I'm sick of people treating me differently. I'm preggers, not dying—I can still help. In fact, you need me. I look at things different to how you do, and I find shit out you wouldn't even think of.'

Damn her, it was actually true.

'Okay, you can help.'

'Good.' She smiled triumphantly. 'What angle you taking?'

'Gonna talk to people who knew Nick, find out what anyone would have against him.'

'Right.' She thought for a minute. 'Nick and Isabella were writers, so . . . there might be clues in their books, yeah?'

If you were watching some crappy show like *Murder She Wrote* there would be.

'Sure,' I said. 'That's a great idea. Why don't you get reading?'

It would keep her out of trouble and since she didn't usually read anything more literary than *Picture* magazine, I figured she'd lose interest soon enough.

'I'm off to the bookshop.' She hauled herself out of the chair. 'About time something exciting happened.'

I stared at her belly but didn't mention the obvious.

'Didn't you think Nick Austin was boring?' I asked. 'You seemed more interested in me and Sean.'

'That's before I was on the case. What is happening with you and Sean, by the way?'

I got up to leave. 'Let you know tomorrow. He's taking me to dinner tonight, got something important to tell me, apparently.'

Chloe started humming the wedding march. 'Dum-dum-de-dum.'

'Oh, fuck off,' I said.

•

Berwick was to the southeast of the city, about fifty k's away, one of those suburbs that had once been farmland and were now filled with housing estates. I took the Laser because she was less conspicuous than the Futura, and because I figured that if she wasn't driven now and again she'd seize up.

Forty minutes later I found the entrance to 'Boronia Estates' where Bougainvillea Drive was located. I drove through an unmanned gate, then around clean asphalt streets with names like Acacia Avenue and Waratah Way, maze-like roads taking me around in circles. The whole estate was scrupulously neat, and I was sure they had some sort of bylaw in place whereby you'd be publicly flogged for leaving your wheelie bin out or neglecting to maintain the nature strip. The place had the sterile, disinfected look of Disneyland or a display village and I couldn't see any sign of life. Perhaps everyone was on holidays or inside in the air-conditioning, glued to the plasma screen.

I wondered how much these plaster-pillared McMansions cost. Probably less than the inner city, but more than I could afford. With my erratic income I doubted I'd ever own a house, but it wasn't all bad. I could hold an entire conversation without once mentioning property prices. Not everyone could say that.

I finally found Bougainvillea, indicated left and crawled down the wide, empty street, counting out numbers until I got to twenty-eight. There was a big silver SUV parked in the driveway, its hatch open, a man loading in suitcases, a giant umbrella and beach toys: boogie boards, coloured balls, deflated rings with dinosaur heads.

The man had a trimmed beard and a full head of brown hair, styled like a schoolboy. He wore long beige shorts with a tucked-in, matching polo shirt, a tan belt and sandals, and he turned and waved as I cruised slowly by. I lifted a couple of fingers in return before pulling into the kerb a little past the house. Apart from the absence of long socks, he looked like a geography teacher I'd once had, and I had a feeling he'd sport the knee-highs whenever the weather cooled.

As soon as I stopped the nerves hit, then the heat, and I started sweating into the cloth upholstery. The bloke by the four-wheel drive presented a new problem. My plan, such as it was, had been to show up at the front door and beg Jenny to talk to me. From the looks of him, he'd probably try to accost me in a jocular fashion before I even got there. I craned my neck and looked around the car for a ruse. Clipboard? Too many questions. Collecting for charity? He hadn't seen me knock on any other doors.

Then I noticed a tube of wrapping paper in the rear footwell, left over from before Christmas. I grabbed the street directory from the seat beside me, parcelled it with the last of the paper and got out of the car, holding the package together with my thumb.

I hustled towards the house like I was frazzled and in a major hurry, not much of a stretch since the sweat had already plastered strands of hair to my forehead. As I approached he straightened up and turned to me, wiping perspiration off his brow with his forearm. He'd made neat work of the packing and the back of the vehicle looked like a finished jigsaw puzzle.

'Hi there.' He started offering his hand but I pretended not to see it.

'Hi.' I put on a harried expression and didn't stop. 'Thank god I didn't miss you, Jenny inside?' I held up the present as I passed.

He nodded, looking slightly confused.

'Thanks,' I called over my shoulder as I walked between the entrance columns and through the open front door.

Liz had described Jenny as a religious freak, and I'd half expected the McMansion's interior to resemble the house from the seventies horror flick *Carrie*. However, there were no obvious religious icons in the entrance hall, no crucifix with an anorexic Jesus attached. Straight ahead was a flight of beige carpeted stairs with the sort of wooden gate people install to corral toddlers.

I stuffed the fake present into my shoulder bag and took a deep breath before announcing myself.

'Jenny,' I called. 'Yoo-hoo.'

There was no immediate answer so I poked my head around an archway into the lounge room. Another archway connected the living room to a dining room and I guessed that the kitchen was around the corner next to it, just out of sight. I heard clattering and a streaming tap.

'Hello, Jenny?' I said it a little louder the second time, then retreated to the hallway so I wouldn't look too bold. My heart was thumping and blood rushed to my head. Cold calling was almost scarier than getting shot at.

'In the kitchen!' she sang out.

I followed her voice to a large room furnished with granite-look benches and a silver stove and fridge. The windows looked out onto a grassy backyard where a young boy played tennis-on-a-stick. He must have been about five but wore an outfit that made him seem like a miniature adult. Long shorts, button-up, short-sleeved print shirt and teeny trainers. A baby crawled in a playpen nearby. Jenny stood at the double sink, wiping down the drip tray with a Chux.

'Hey there,' I said.

The expectant smile froze as soon as she saw me. She'd have seen my face on the news, and after the phone call would know exactly who was trespassing in her kitchen. Her mouth dropped open.

She looked like she had in the pictures, just a little older and broader. She'd tamed the hair to a wavy, shoulder-length bob, wore similar shorts to her husband and kids, and a plaid, sleeveless blouse that buttoned up the front. As well as the anguished saviour, I'd anticipated an Assembly of God type outfit with a headscarf and Amish-style apron, so I was pleased to find her so normal looking. She even wore a touch of brown eyeliner and some coral lipstick. I wasn't sure where Liz had got the idea she was a religious nut.

'What—'

'I'm Simone Kirsch.' The words all came out in a rush. 'We spoke on the phone earlier? I'm sorry to barge in like this but I really need to talk to you.'

'How did you find—?'

'I'm a private detective.' I shrugged modestly even though I felt quite pleased with myself. 'It's kind of what we do.'

'Get out of my house. Now.'

chapternineteen

I'd anticipated as much. Time for the sob story I'd been concocting on my drive down the freeway. I stuck my palms out, all non-threatening-like.

'Please, Jenny, just hear me out. I know you've probably read about me in the papers, but I'm not here to hassle you or cause any trouble. I just really need your help.' I paused for a quick breath. She didn't interrupt, which meant she was listening. Good.

'Your ex-husband came into my office one day and from then on in my life's been a mess. I've been implicated in a murder and lost my investigator's licence, and then Nick breaks in the other day, so the police think we're in cahoots. I'm just trying to understand what's going on and why he'd do that, so I can hopefully clear my name and get my licence and my livelihood back.' I'd run out of air by the end so I sucked in another deep breath. I opened my eyes wide, imploringly, and tried to look as though I was about to cry.

'I don't know . . .'

'I have no one else to turn to.'

I was banking on the fact that, contrary to popular belief,

most people liked to help. And if she really was a major god-botherer, then how could she refuse? I also tried to imagine I was a puppy. A really sad one who'd been separated from his mum too young and trucked off to the pound. I very nearly whimpered and peed on the lino.

She sighed. 'I don't see how I can possibly help you.'

'You were married to him for years and I don't know the guy from a bar of soap. I just need to ask a few questions, get to the bottom of this.' Sounded lame, even to me, but I kept it up, operation puppy-eyes making my retinas smart.

'We're about to go on holiday.'

'It'll only take five minutes. Please. I'm desperate.'

She glanced at her small gold watch, which wasn't so good. I had one card left to play. I didn't want to do it, but I hadn't come all that way for nothing.

'If you've seen the news then you probably know I used to work as a stripper. I became a PI because I wanted to get out of that life and, as well as wanting to help people, it was the only other thing I was good at. If I don't get my investigating licence back I'll be forced to . . .' I looked down as my words trailed off, feeling like a total turncoat. I really hated that victim stereotype of strippers and generally did what I could to dispel—not reinforce—it, but in the heat of battle you used what you could.

Jenny sighed again, dropped the dishcloth on the sink and crossed her arms. The hard look had left her eyes.

'I really don't want to talk about my ex-husband,' she said. 'That part of my life is over. I've been doing what I can to avoid journalists and—'

'I know what you mean, they've been hassling me no end.'

A squeal from outside. I turned to look. 'Are those your kids? They're gorgeous.' I tried to appear clucky, but probably just looked squinty and cross-eyed.

'Joseph, the youngest, is. The older one is Isaac, from Gordon's first marriage.'

'They're sooo cute.'

'They're a blessing . . . but a handful just the same.' Jenny paused and looked me over. She wore glasses with thin gold frames that matched her watch, and behind them her eyes looked enormous. I felt like a bacteria under an electron microscope.

'Okay. Five minutes. I'll get Gordon in to watch the kids.'

'Thanks sooo much,' I gushed, more out of relief than gratitude.

She called him in then took me down a beige-carpeted hall. The churchy theme was subtle, but it was there. In between the family photos lining the walls hung framed prints with bible verses, and photographs of waterfalls taken with a really long exposure, so the water looked all fuzzy. Devotional sayings were etched onto the posters in fancy calligraphy.

I caught glimpses into bedrooms on the way down the hall. All were neat with well-made beds. The older kid had a Superman duvet, the younger one a crib shaped like a car.

At the end of the hall Jenny opened a door onto a small bedroom that had been converted into an office. It contained a desk with a Compaq computer, pine bookshelves, a Swiss ball and an office chair. Her arts degree and teaching diploma had been framed and hung on the wall, and a netball trophy sat atop the bookshelf.

Jenny took the Swiss ball, bounced on it slightly, and offered me the chair.

'Sorry, it's a bit crowded.'

'Not at all. Nice place.'

'I never thought I'd move back to the suburbs. But after years of unrenovated terraces, rising damp, leaking taps and rusting bathtubs it's nice to have something new. And the neighbourhood has a real sense of community, not like the inner city where no one even knows their neighbours. It's a great place to bring up kids . . . Now, what did you want to know about Nick?'

She had me there.

'Gee. I know we only have five minutes, but, everything. You met Nick at Melbourne Uni?'

She nodded. 'I was two years ahead of him, but we both took the same creative writing seminar. He was very shy back in those days, sort of hid behind his hair, embarrassed about his skin. I only noticed him because of his writing: the most beautiful descriptive passages, truly moving. Really amazing stuff.'

I smiled encouragingly. People loved to talk about themselves, and once you got them going . . .

'Everybody else was ripping off Charles Bukowski and Raymond Carver, writing grungy pieces about living in Carlton and taking drugs and vomiting and passing out. Mind you, these were usually the trendy kids with wealthy parents, who'd gone to private schools. Nick grew up in the country and was boarding with a family out in Eltham. He had a night job stacking supermarket shelves so he could pay his way.'

'And you got together after that?' I was trying to hurry her along. If I only had five minutes I didn't want misty-eyed reminiscences, I wanted dirt.

'Yes, I actually made the first move, believe it or not.' She shook her head thinking about it. 'You have to understand, I was very . . . bolshie back then. Involved in student politics. Quite shameless. I invited him to the pub, and we argued about literature over too many beers, and then I invited him—'

'He always drink a lot?'

'Oh, no. Not like the rest of us. He was quiet and mainly used to sit back and observe everyone. I drank more than him, back in those days.' She pushed her glasses up and smiled at me as if to say: can you believe it?

'So, was there anything that—?'

She ignored me, on a roll. 'From then on we were pretty much inseparable. He moved into my room in a share house in Carlton, but after a year the house disintegrated, when my flatmates got into heroin. We got a place of our own, a fleabag studio in an ugly block near the housing commission flats. The next year I did a dip ed,' she nodded towards the framed degree, 'and started working in a girls school. Nick finished uni after his honours year and briefly considered doing a master's degree, but he said he wanted to be in the real world rather than academia. Thought it helped him to write. He took a lot of different jobs, casual work, manual labour, stuff that was physical more than mental, and wrote when he wasn't working. Back in those days there weren't that many jobs about, so he got quite a lot of writing done.'

Was it just me or was there a sour little twist to her lips?

'When did you get married?' I tried to speed things up.

'In ninety-five. We'd been together for six years. We were still pretty broke, living in our one-bedroom flat, so the wedding took place at a registry office and the reception at a Turkish BYO restaurant on Sydney Road.'

'No kids?'

'Nick thought he was too young. He thought it would cost too much and he said he'd rather spend the money on travelling overseas. Not that we ever did. The baby thing was a point of contention, plus the fact that I was basically supporting us. He did work hard when he actually got work, and spent a lot of time on his book . . . Finally, he had a completed manuscript and he sent it off to the Vogel awards. He was shortlisted, didn't win, but got published. I was so proud. I really was. I didn't know what it would lead to . . .'

She went on to tell me what I already knew from Nick, about the book not selling, the difficult second novel. I let her go because I didn't want to interrupt her flow.

'. . . In the end I encouraged him to teach. It was a steady income, and he could always work on his next book at night or in the holidays. He got a good job, and we moved, finally bought a house. Prices weren't as bad as they are now. Things were quite comfortable, but I don't think Nick ever really took to teaching and he was having a lot of trouble with his next book. Writer's block or something. When I look back I suppose he was depressed, in a low grade way.'

'He start drinking then?'

'No. You're a bit obsessed with that, aren't you? He was never a drinker. That came later.

'Anyway, I didn't even know he was writing a crime novel until he told me he'd sold it. Can you believe that? He must have known I'd think it was a waste of his talent. Have you read his first book?'

I shook my head.

'It was beautiful. Nuanced. I really thought he was the next Tim Winton, you know? But, inexplicably, the crime novel sold ten times what his literary novel did. I don't know, appealing to the lowest common denominator, I suppose. I mean, look at what rates on television these days. Don't get me started on the dumbing down of society. But Nick was happy. He took a little time off, worked on the second in the series and did the rounds of writers' festivals again. We weren't raking it in, nowhere close, but he could afford to take a six-month sabbatical.'

I sneaked a peek at Jenny's gold watch. We'd gone way past five minutes, and I hadn't learned anything useful.

'I think essentially Nick was introverted. He didn't like teaching because it was draining for him to get up in front of people, be the centre of attention. He always had to have a glass of wine before a writers' festival panel. But that's all it was in those days. Just a glass of wine. He was much happier home alone, writing, or even stacking supermarket shelves where he didn't have to talk to anyone and could be alone with his thoughts.'

'How come you guys broke up?' I was getting antsy.

'I'm getting to that. After the first three crime novels came out he was invited to go on a . . . what did they call it? A "writers' roadshow". Basically a minibus with about six authors crammed in, driving around to regional centres in Victoria, South Australia and New South Wales, doing workshops and talks and visiting schools and what have you. It was a four-week trip and Nick jumped at the chance. He'd get paid—not much, but enough to allow him to have another month off school and be a writer instead of a teacher. Even though I knew I'd miss him, I was glad for him to go because I knew it would make him happy. Of course, I didn't know what would transpire.'

'What did?'

'Isabella Bishop.' Her mouth twisted again. 'She was on the tour too. When he came home Nick was happier than I'd seen him in ages—full of energy. He even started exercising at the gym and working on the screenplay of his first Zack book. He kept putting off going back to school, which concerned me—we had house payments—but I was delighted he wasn't moping about being the archetypal depressed novelist anymore.'

'Until?'

'He dropped the bombshell. A few weeks later he upped and said he wanted a trial separation. Looking back I suppose I should have known something was up, but at the time I was hit for six. I suggested counselling. He refused. I asked if there was someone else, he denied it. He packed his stuff and wouldn't tell me where he was going and I didn't hear a word from him for two months. One day I was married and the next it was like our entire relationship had never existed. And that was that. Do you know how I found out he was seeing Isabella?'

I shook my head.

'The Sunday magazine in *The Age*. A glossy article on how creative types find it living together. They had an artist couple, two musicians, and Nick and Isabella representing the writers. There were a lot of smoochy pictures of them living in some rundown warehouse in Fitzroy and quotes that said they were poor but happy, and that when they could actually keep their hands off each other they loved working side by side, finally being around someone who understood what they went through.' Jenny rolled her eyes, snorted air out of her nose. A bitter laugh stuck in her gullet.

'I wanted to be a writer too, you understand, only I didn't have the time. I had to work, keep body and soul together for the both of us. What made it worse is that somebody told me about the lead-in time those magazines have. The interview would have been done at least six weeks before. He'd moved in with her straight away. It was obvious they'd been together since the roadshow. It had probably started the first day. Anyway, a month or so after our divorce was finalised he married her, in New York I think. I heard they took a big trip. America, Europe. He had always wanted to go.'

'Gee,' I said. It was an old story, and a familiar one. 'How awful for you.'

'It was. I really hit rock bottom after that. I wasn't a Christian in those days, I didn't have the Lord to turn to, so instead I got involved in drinking, drugs, promiscuous sex . . . anything to dull the pain.'

'No way.' I tried to imagine Jenny as a school-teaching crack whore but couldn't quite manage it.

'It's true. Of course, I know now that it was all a cry for help. I'm just lucky that my cry was heard and I was saved. I would have died otherwise, I'm sure of it. One morning I was staggering out of an all-night pokies place, trying to figure out how I was supposed to get the money together for a bottle of vodka to get me through work, when I was approached by Gordon.' She nodded to the yard where he was playing with the kids. 'He was ministering on the streets with a few other parishioners. Normally I'd have told them where to go, but something about what they were saying just hit a nerve. They took me in, gave me guidance and love and it was like I'd finally come home, been reborn. I was baptised not long after, and a year and a half ago ago I married Gordon. He'd lost his first wife to cancer. Nine months later we had our little miracle, Joseph. Doctors had told me I was too old to conceive naturally, but with prayer . . . well, the results speak for themselves.' She looked out the window and beamed.

'Wow. I'm glad everything worked out in the end,' I said, while thinking, my god, what a massive waste of time. I hadn't learned anything about Nick, except he'd been a bit of a cad—or was it a bounder? I'd always gotten the two confused.

One last-ditch effort: 'While you knew him, did Nick have any strange kinks or vices? Any episodes where he lost his temper, any murderous rages?'

'Not while he was with me. Of course, he changed when he met her.'

'Really?'

'Oh yes. I saw him a year after they'd got together, when we were finalising the divorce. It was a terrible time, and if I hadn't had the support of the congregation I would have fallen apart. He tried to take the house, you see, when I was the one who'd saved the deposit and paid for most of the damn thing. I know it was her doing, she had him wrapped around her little finger, but still . . .'

'How had he changed?'

'He was like a different person, drinking heavily, smoking—which he'd never done. He had a sneering, contemptuous air about him that I'd never seen before and worst of all there was a darkness shrouding him. A terrible darkness.' She fingered the tiny gold crucifix around her neck.

'Darkness? What do you mean by that, exactly?' I asked, majorly confused.

A cloud passed over the sun and the children's shrieks outside seemed muffled, far away. She leaned forward, her voice a whisper.

'I never would have recognised it if I hadn't become a believer, but I knew what it was straight away.'

'What?' I was leaning forward and whispering too.

'Satan.'

•

Back in the Laser I had a quick slug of whiskey from the hip flask in the glove box, chucked my notebook back into my bag and started up the car, pulling out onto the deserted blacktop, but something was wrong. I couldn't control the steering, and a weird thumping came from the wheel well.

I rolled to a stop by the kerb, got out and inspected the driver's side front tyre. It was totally deflated, the wheel rim scraping the road.

I supposed I could change it myself, but screw that: I was paid up and calling roadside assistance. I dialled the number on my mobile and wandered around the car as I waited for an operator. Damn. The rear tyre was flat too. Rounding the hatchback I looked at the other side. Same story.

I shivered despite the heat. You didn't get four flats at the same time unless . . . I squatted and looked closer. The rubber had been slashed through by something very big and very sharp. Straightening up I glanced around, aware of my heart thundering in my chest. The street was deserted. No kids. No noise. No cars. I couldn't see a soul, but I had a disturbing feeling that someone could see me.

I remembered the letter—*You're dead, cunt*—and checked the back seat and under the car. No one was there and all I did was scare myself more. I jumped in the front and locked the door.

chapter**twenty**

Claypots was in St Kilda, just south of Acland. The restaurant was famous for its super-fresh seafood and strict no-bookings policy, and as I hurried across Barkly Street, I saw the place was already packed, and it was only six thirty.

Inside, diners hunched over crammed wooden tables which harried waiters angled their hips to squeeze between. Pans clattered in the open kitchen, and I smelled sizzling garlic, pungent coriander and the smoky scent of octopus and squid, no doubt covered in chilli and curling on a grill.

There was no sign of Sean, but I was sure he'd be out back. We'd come to Claypots a few times since he'd returned and the courtyard was our usual spot. Surprisingly, considering his appetite for vodka and Marlboro Lights, he followed a pretty healthy, semi-vegetarian diet.

The courtyard was laid with gravel, the tables nothing much to look at, and the seating a mix of wooden benches and bottle-green plastic chairs filched from a cheap outdoor setting. Coloured light bulbs dangled from a paling fence and in the far corner a tree straggled up from the rocky ground. With the humid summer evening and the aroma of pounded spices and bubbling oil, I could almost imagine I'd wandered into some roadside food stall in South East Asia, and guessed that was another reason Sean was so fond of the place.

I spotted him at a tiny table for two in the corner, wearing his striped work shirt with rolled-up sleeves. He waved and I hurried over.

'Sorry I'm late,' I said. 'Got a flat.'

It was sort of the truth.

'No problem. You want my seat?' He stood.

'Thanks.'

I liked to be flush up against a wall in public places—it made me feel vulnerable sitting with my back exposed—and Sean, sweetheart that he was, always obliged. The creepy sensation was particularly bad that evening, after the note and the tyres. I guessed I should tell Sean, but figured maybe later. I didn't want to ruin dinner and I knew he'd demand every last detail of the tyre slashing. With my licence cancelled, what possible excuse could I have for tooling around the 'burbs?

Sean had already collected cutlery and paper napkins for us, and glasses that had more in common with jam jars than Reidel flutes. A tapas plate was at the ready plus a bottle of champagne, wedged into a plastic ice bucket.

'You beauty,' I said, spying the booze.

'Not only that, I scored us the last whole snapper with chermoula,' he boasted.

Daily specials were crossed off the blackboard as soon as they ran out. The snapper was always the first to go.

I reached for the bottle and noticed the orange label as I dug it out of the crushed ice.

'Shit, is this Veuve Clicquot?'

He nodded.

'Fancy,' I said, remembering Chloe hum the wedding march. A ridge of panic spiked my spine.

We thunked, rather than clinked, our glasses. I took a big gulp of French champagne that filled my mouth with an ocean of tiny, delicate bubbles and tasted smooth, creamy and immeasurably better than the shite I usually drank. Smiling broadly to hide my unease, I popped a marinated octopus leg in my mouth and gnawed vigorously. Cuban salsa filled the air and beams of low orange sunlight seeped through gaps in the fence.

'So, what did you want to tell me?' I asked as casually as I could.

Sean smiled, his lips turning up at the corners, the light's peachy gleam offsetting hair that would have been described as titian had he been the tempestuous heroine in a Mills and Boon romance.

'Do you think the snapper's enough?' he stalled, squinting at the blackboard menu on the exposed brick wall. 'Maybe we should get the Andalusian claypot as well . . .'

I drew my fist back and whacked him on the arm, a little harder than I'd intended.

'Shit!'

'You deserved it.' I narrowed my eyes. 'Tell me what the goddamn Veuve's about.'

He sipped his champagne, really drawing it out, until finally he said: 'How do you feel about moving to Vietnam?'

In my mind I saw a giant billboard with the words *What the Fuck?* spelled out in thousands of glowing bulbs. In real life I just sat there with my mouth hanging open like a grouper trawling for bait fish.

Sean sat forward in his seat, talking fast, body bouncing involuntarily, like a kid at Christmas.

'I've been offered a job with the Federal Police, an intelligence position, gathering information for local and international law enforcement agencies on all sorts of stuff.

Drugs, human trafficking, smuggling, you name it. It's a two-year contract, based in Ho Chi Minh City—Saigon—but there'll be lots of travel. The money's great, they pay for housing and medical insurance, airfares, an overseas bonus, and there's annual leave. I know I keep telling you, but Vietnam's amazing: insane cities, dense jungle, white sand beaches, incredible food, and on top of that you're a stone's throw from Thailand, Cambodia, Laos . . .'

'You sound like you want to accept,' I said.

'Look, the Asian Squad's been great, but this position seems like the perfect way to utilise my language skills. I can be of much more use over there.'

'Let me get this straight.' I spoke slowly. 'You want me to move overseas with you?'

'Uh-huh.' He nodded.

'What'll I do there?'

'Well, running a house is a full-time affair. Cleaning, cooking, ironing. I'll expect you to go to market every day . . .'

I raised my eyebrows.

Sean laughed. 'You should see the look on your face. I'm joking. I've got you a job, if you want it.'

'What?'

'Investigative assistant to the senior liaison officer. Yours truly.' His grin was a mile wide.

'State coppers wouldn't take me, no way the feds would.'

'They will if I insist. Besides, you'll be working in a civilian capacity, you won't be sworn in. You'll need a police check though. You don't have a record—' squinting—'do you?'

'Arrested a few times, charged once, never convicted,' I muttered. My mind reeled. Vietnam? Just up and leave? What about my business?

'I've just started the agency.'

'And there's too much heat on you to run it. Why not stick it on the backburner for a couple of years, get more experience working with the police, then come back when everything's blown over? Hell, if things go well you could even apply for a job as an officer and forget the PI shit. Isn't that what you always wanted, to be a cop?'

'I used to.'

'And why was that?'

I shrugged. 'I dunno, sounds wanky, but to help people, I suppose. Exploitative scumbags have always pissed me off and I thought there'd be a fair bit of job satisfaction bringing down bad guys.'

'Fair enough.' Sean crossed his arms on the table and looked at me steadily. 'In your opinion, what are the most common cases an inquiry agent is hired to investigate?'

I sighed. There was no point trying to lie.

'Insurance claims, WorkCover fraud, cheating spouses. Tracking down defaulters so credit companies can repossess their cars.'

We were silent for a bit, sipping champagne. Damn him. It was as bad as arguing with my mother. I tried another tack.

'What about Chloe?'

He was ready for me. 'You'll miss her, of course, but we'll be coming back to Australia at least once a year, and she can visit anytime.'

An image popped into my head: Chloe tottering around some crazy South East Asian city on spike-heeled platforms, using a combination of mime and pidgin English to hit the befuddled locals up for ganga. I shuddered. Far as I knew she'd never been further north than Surfers Paradise.

'What about the baby?'

'You arranged to babysit?'

'Hell, no.'

'Look. The contract doesn't start till the middle of the year and she's just about to pop, right, so you'll be around for the birth. Having a kid takes up a lot of time and she'll probably be out of action for the next two years anyway. Chances are you won't be missing much. You really into newborns?'

'Not exactly.'

'Right, so by the time we get back it'll be two or three. They're cute at that age, don't puke on you so much and you can actually talk to them. No mess, no fuss.'

'Chloe won't be happy.'

'She'll have her hands so full she probably won't even know you've gone.'

Maybe I had tickets on myself, but I doubted that.

Sean continued: 'Opportunities like this come up, you've gotta take a risk and grab them. You want to apprehend real bad guys, or poor bastards who can't keep up payments on their cars?'

He had me there. He had me on pretty much everything, although there was one point we hadn't yet covered.

'You realise you're suggesting we move in together for two years. What if it doesn't work out? That's the biggest risk of all.'

'Don't be afraid to go out on a limb, that's where all the fruit is.'

I groaned. 'Spare me the motivational quotes. You really serious? You really want to do this?'

'Yes.' He reached across the table and squeezed my hand.

'What if I said I couldn't move to Vietnam.'

'Then I wouldn't take the job.'

'You'd give it up for me? Why?' I asked.

''Cause I'm in love with you, you idiot.'

chapter twenty-one

I woke up at nine, naked and sweating, the electronic chime of a mobile phone piercing my brain. Sean's side of the bed was empty, and I dragged myself across a tangled expanse of sheets in search of the noise. My handbag lay slumped on the floor and as I hung my head over to dig around inside, blood rushed painfully to the back of my eyeballs.

Lying down again I stared at the unfamiliar number lighting up the display, and as I waited for whoever was ringing to leave a message, I attempted to measure the extent of my hangover and ascertain how, exactly, I'd gotten to bed.

Turned out Sean had brought two bottles of Veuve to Claypots, the fish hadn't soaked up either of them, and I'd had the bright idea of going for after-dinner cocktails at the Vineyard. If I was wasted I wouldn't have to contemplate the daunting prospect of moving halfway around the world with someone who'd just told me he loved me.

I had vague memories of groping Sean under the table at the bar, no recollection of the cab ride home, and hazy, strobing visions of animalistic sex on the lounge room floor. I kicked free of the twisted sheet and raised both legs, pointing my toes at the ceiling. Red and brown scabs crusted both knees. There was no clever excuse for carpet burn. Everyone knew exactly what you'd been up to, roughly where, and in precisely what position.

I checked voicemail, discovered Rod Thurlow had been ringing, popped three Nurofen Plus and called him back. He was at his home in the Yarra Valley, and suggested we meet later that afternoon in town. Maybe I was still drunk, but I was determined to go to see him. Neutral ground was no good to me. I wanted to see where Isabella had lived.

By ten fifteen I was manoeuvring the Laser along winding blacktop, through small towns full of craft 'shoppes', and densely wooded corridors of national park. Sunlight flashed through ghost gums and lit up groves of bracken. Bellbirds pealed, and the warm air gusting in the windows smelled of eucalyptus and tasted of dust and dried-up twigs. Cicadas murmured, sharp and shimmering.

The well-judged combination of codeine and ibuprofen had suppressed any headache, and my hangover was of the dozy, brain-dead variety. Bad for interviewing skills, but good for stifling nervousness, especially since I had to talk to a man whose fiancée had been brutally murdered. Not for the first time I wondered why the hell I wanted to do a job that involved so much unpleasant shit. I flicked open the glove box and found liquid courage in the form of my hip flask, now half full of warm whiskey. I'd have a slug right before I went in—real breakfast of champions when mixed with the five cheese singles I'd eaten while driving.

Despite living in Melbourne for four years I'd never actually been to the Yarra Valley. I'd always imagined it as a narrow gorge filled with the same scrubby brush I'd just driven through, so I got a shock when I rounded a bend and the landscape opened right up. The place was huge, an honest-to-goodness valley about five flat k's across that wouldn't have looked out of place in France or Italy. Rows of grapevines covered gentle slopes that curved towards meadows of lush grass. Rustic farmhouses dotted the landscape, jersey cows milled in paddocks, and yellow flowers bobbed their heads at the side of the road. The air smelled of grapes and hay, and even the quality of the light had changed. The harsh beams that had sliced through the eucalypts had been replaced by a soft glow, as golden and syrupy as an aged sauterne. Two huge butterflies gambolled past the car, as though inserted by some Hollywood CGI whiz.

It was so pretty I almost burst into tears. I revised my hangover status to 'brain-dead yet emotional'. I could have lost it watching a Kleenex ad with toddlers and fuzzy ducklings, and knew I'd better be careful. If Rod's bottom lip so much as trembled while he talked about Isabella, I was a goner.

I checked my map, realised I'd missed the turnoff, doubled back and found a red dirt road cut into one of the ubiquitous vine-covered hills. I drove slowly, gravel popping as I negotiated the bends, and suddenly Rod's place came into view.

'Holy shit,' I whispered and let out a low whistle.

At the end of a poplar-lined drive sat my dream house. Except 'house' was too modest a word for this two-storey stone Tuscan villa on top of the hillside.

I rolled the Laser up to the spiked iron gate, leaned out my window and hit the intercom attached to the wall. No one replied, but the wooden double doors at the front of the main building swung out and a pumped-up Aryan blond in a black quasi-military outfit emerged. He stalked down the driveway past silver-leaved olive trees and flowering shrubs in large terracotta pots. Slipping through the gate, he circled my car, examining it as though it might have been a giant mobile bomb. Finally he crossed his arms and stood by my window.

'Hi,' I said, chirpy as an Amway saleswoman. 'I'm Simone Kirsch, here to see Rod.'

'You have an appointment with Mr Thurlow?' Hitler Youth asked, accent disappointingly Australian monotone.

'He's expecting me.'

'See some ID?'

I dug out my wallet and flashed my driver's licence. He hit the button on a plastic tag hanging off his belt and the gate slowly opened.

'Turn left, park in the garage. I'll escort you to the house.'

I did as he said, drove about twenty metres and found a garage cunningly disguised as an eighteenth-century barn. I turned off the engine and glanced in the rearview. The boy in black was still a good ten metres away so I quickly whipped the hip flask out of the glove compartment, unscrewed the top and took a couple of hefty gulps. The tepid whiskey stung my throat and brought tears to my eyes. I took another slug for good measure, coughed and shoved the flask back in the glove box, popped a Fisherman's Friend mint in my mouth and crunched. Between the alcohol and the menthol my face was on fire.

He walked me to the main building in silence and demanded to check my bag before he let me in the front door.

'Why?'

No answer. I handed it over. Wasn't much in there except the mints, phone, makeup, and a couple of tampons bulging fluff out of their plastic wrappers.

Inside, we passed a cavernous living area filled with tasteful antique furniture, Turkish rugs and the sort of massive fireplace in which you could easily spit-roast an entire wild boar. We climbed a sweeping stone staircase to the next floor, and padding along the hallway I glimpsed bedrooms with four-poster beds and French doors overlooking vineyards and distant mountain ranges.

I'd met a fair few rich folks in my investigatory dealings, but had never run across a spread like that. Reminded me of a boutique hotel, or a poxy movie where some middle-class ponce restores a gorgeous manor in Tuscany or Provence and finds themselves *and* true love in the process.

When we reached the end of the corridor my escort knocked on the open door and walked in. I poked my head round the frame and saw a huge double room with a large wooden desk at one end and a lounge area at the other, filled with furniture that managed to be both overstuffed and understated. A flat screen TV the size of a small billboard adhered to the wall opposite the couch, built-in bookshelves flanking either side. Rod sat behind the desk, which was empty except for a wide, thin LCD computer monitor, wireless keyboard and mouse. His ginger hair was crew cut, like I remembered, but he'd swapped the military get-up for an open-necked white linen shirt. Mozart or Beethoven wafted through the air, one of those symphonies they always played in commercials for luxury cars.

Rod looked at me and nodded, then dismissed Nazi-boy.

'Thank you, Dean, that will be all.'

Dean? I'd been hoping for Gunther, Klaus or Helmut. Disappointing. He didn't even click his heels or perform a clipped salute.

'Sorry, Simone, I'm just finishing up an important chapter. It'll only take a few moments. Have a look around, make yourself at home.'

Just before he turned his attention back to the screen he gave me a quick up and down and, judging by his expression, approved of what he saw.

I'd figured he responded well to ultra-feminine women, recalling Isabella's floaty outfit, and Rod flirting with Chloe at the writers' festival, so I'd worn my girliest item of clothing: a moderately frilled white sundress just long enough to cover the fucked-up knees. Made me seem non-threatening, less like a hard-arsed PI, and wouldn't have looked out of place on a model prancing through fields of sunflowers in a feminine hygiene ad. In my line of work it could be advantageous to be underestimated, and that's exactly what most folks did when they discovered I'd flaunted my modest jugs in most of the titty bars in the greater Melbourne area.

I wandered over to the bookshelf to study the mix of gleaming hardcovers and pristine paperbacks, tilted my head to examine the spines and got a shock when I realised every single book was one of Rod's. Editions from all over the world lined the shelves, sporting different covers, titles translated into dozens of languages. A framed poster for the film version of his first book, *Lethal Entry*, hung on the wall, a pumped-up Jean-Claude Van Damme posing in the foreground in torn army fatigues with an AK47 slung over his shoulder. A dishevelled ingenue clung to his leg, lips parted, head level with his crotch, while behind them a helicopter detonated in spectacular fashion.

I glanced back at Rod. Despite possessing a typing style best described as 'hunt and peck', he performed like a concert pianist, raising his hands before swooping them down, stabbing his index fingers at the keys. While he worked his face contorted, lips twitching as though mouthing the words. He punched the keyboard one last time, sat back, blew out some air and rolled his broad shoulders, then slapped his palms on the desk, hoisted himself to a standing position and smiled.

'Sorry to keep you waiting, but when the muse strikes . . .'

So far he was playing charming, so I decided to go along with it.

'Don't apologise. It must be tough writing a book. You do many drafts?' I thought it was a safer question than 'Where do you get your ideas?'

He walked around the desk. 'Just the one.'

'Really? Wow.' I was sure Nick had told me he did three or four.

'Of course, I outline every last detail before I start. Failing to plan is planning to fail, in my opinion.'

As he approached I noticed brown slip-on shoes made of soft leather and beige pants constructed of the same fabric as the shirt—a finely woven linen that shimmered when he walked and skimmed his bulky muscles, giving him a leaner, taller frame. When he stood beside me I smelled aftershave that must have cost a bomb but was way too sweet and musky for my taste.

Suddenly remembering why I was there, I told him I was sorry about Isabella and was a little taken aback when he grabbed both my hands, squeezed and sort of jigged them up and down.

'Thank you, Simone. I won't lie to you, it's been incredibly hard, but I'm trying to be strong and take it one day at a time.' He let go of my hands and I was relieved when he didn't lunge in for a hug.

'Would you join me on the terrace?' He nodded towards the wide Italianate balcony outside the open French doors. 'I'll call up for some drinks. What would you like? Coffee? Tea? San Pellegrino? Wine?'

My eyes must have lit up and given me away.

A small smile. 'Let me guess. You're the sort of lady who savours a cold climate sauvignon blanc?'

'Got it in one.'

'Then may I be so bold as to suggest our own, Villa Bella, riesling? Before you protest, it's not sweet like the rieslings of old, but dry with a crisp, grassy finish and the subtlest hint of fruit. Marvellous.'

'Sounds lovely, but—'

'Be a shame for you to come all this way and not sample such nectar.'

'Okay, you've twisted my arm. But just a little. I'm driving.'

'Of course.'

From his pants pocket he plucked a shiny, rectangular black object that looked like one of those all-in-one computer/camera/mobile phones, spoke softly into the device, then placed his hand on my elbow to steer me out through the double doors.

chapter twenty-two

The balcony was made of sandy, rough-hewn stone and decorated with antique wrought-iron furnishings upholstered in worn brown leather. Delicate flowers spilled from clay urns, and attached to the wall was a terracotta mask in the shape of a lion's face, dribbling water into a small pond. The sound made my bladder twinge, but I decided not to break the seal just yet.

Sitting opposite Rod at a small round table, I checked out the view. The villa's three buildings formed a U shape and framed a courtyard with a rectangular swimming pool made of grey tiles and enclosed by a low stone fence. Neat lawns, hedges and the odd statue surrounded the pool, and the open end of the U provided a spectacular vista of vineyards and distant mountain ranges. Not for the first time I realised I was seriously in the wrong line of work.

A butler appeared, pushing a cart that rattled over the coarse flooring. Jesus. An actual butler. Or maybe he was a valet? He wasn't wearing tails but he did have on a nice black suit and tie. I felt like I was either in a movie or tripping on some exceptionally strong acid. He set the table with two large glasses and a plate of gourmet snacks: a washed rind cheese, fresh figs, olives, home-made crackers and thin slices of pear.

The wine tasted of melon, green apples and grass, and shat all over the casks of riesling I'd guzzled as a dedicated underage drinker.

'Beautiful,' I said.

'The wine?'

'And the house. Everything.'

'Thank you, but it's nothing without Bella. I bought it for her and named it after her. The estate is actually a reproduction of the Villa Rossa in Siena. We took our first holiday together there, and it's where I proposed.'

'Where did you and Isabella first meet, if you don't mind my asking?'

'Not at all. It was at the Perth writers' week, last February. We were both married to other people at the time, and I'm not proud of that fact, but when twin souls find each other, there's not much you or anyone else can do about it. We both knew it was bigger than both of us . . . Do you have anyone special in your life?'

'I'm kind of seeing someone . . .'

'Mmm . . .' He gave me a slightly pitying smile. 'Not everyone has what Bella and I shared. It's a once in a lifetime thing. Maybe rarer. Many people never get to experience that sort of . . . transcendent love.'

It was at that point I decided not to mention Isabella snogging Nick behind the tree.

'So,' Rod asked, 'why exactly did you need to see me?'

I trotted out my excuse about wanting to find out everything I could about Nick so I could clear my name and get my licence back. I wasn't quite sure if he bought it, but as long as he talked to me I didn't care.

'An exchange of information, then? Seems like we both want the same thing, for Nick Austin to pay for what he's done.'

'You're a hundred percent sure he's guilty?'

'A hundred and ten. Jilted lover, classic case—if he can't have her then nobody can. From the moment Bella and I met, Nick refused to let her go. He couldn't accept that she'd had enough of the drinking, the abuse.'

'Abuse?' This was news to me.

'Don't tell me you've been taken in by his Mr Nice Guy routine?' Rod cocked a carefully trimmed brow. 'She never admitted he actually struck her, although I wouldn't be surprised. I do know there was pushing and shoving, and on one occasion he punched a hole in the wall, right next to her head. It was the mental abuse, though. They say that's the worst, don't they?'

'What sort of mental abuse?'

He didn't reply, just shrugged and sort of waved his hand in the air.

'Did you see any of this?'

'First hand. When Bella told him she was leaving I went with her to collect her belongings. He'd been drinking, as per usual, and started to smash her things. I tried to intervene, foolishly thinking I could reason with him, man to man . . .' He shook his head. 'I'm afraid it descended into fisticuffs.'

'Who won?'

Rod raised a small smile and flexed his large, square hands.

'I see,' I said. 'Why do you think he drank so much?'

'Why does anyone succumb to vice? He was weak-willed, obviously. I don't buy into all this namby-pamby psychological claptrap about addiction being a disease, or a reaction to some childhood trauma—self-medicating to drown the pain.' He scoffed and took another sip of his wine. Setting down the glass he leaned forward and tapped the side of his head.

'It's all up here, Simone. Triumph, tragedy, success or defeat, every possibility is contained within the human brain. You have to decide exactly what you want in life, then put in the time and the effort to achieve it. If you fail, you've no one to blame but yourself. It's my belief that quitters never win and winners never quit. I apply that philosophy to every facet of my life and I don't think I'm being conceited when I say I'm a winner. I mean . . .' He gestured to the grand spread around him before continuing.

'I've never resented successful people, rather I let them inspire me and I make sure I learn from their achievements. Nick, on the other hand, is the envious type: a child coveting another's toy. If he can't play with it, or steal it, he'll destroy it in a fit of pique. It never occurred to him to attempt to emulate my success and better himself. His reaction was to try and tear it all down. And by god, I'm going to make him pay.'

'Is that why you put up the reward? Better chance of turning him over to the cops?'

'Nick Austin will be lucky if he's turned over to the cops.' Rod's expression froze. 'He never should have crossed me. Never. People think my books are bullshit, but I've been there. I've done things to people who didn't even deserve it as much as Nick fucking Austin. I'm going to make him suffer. I am going to mess him up like you won't believe. Death, torture, they're too good for that fucker. I'm going to think up something special. I want him to suffer like Isabella suffered.'

I'd come into the meeting thinking Rod was a pompous, arrogant but generally harmless git. The sudden darkness in his eyes made me unsure. I swallowed before I asked my next question, instinctively aware I shouldn't show any bias towards Nick.

'Any truth to the rumours you want him dead or alive?'

The shadow lifted and his mouth turned up at the corners. The affable, pompous git was back, but now I didn't believe it for a second.

'Alive, preferably, but he is a dangerous fugitive. If one of my men, or even a concerned citizen, was forced to defend themselves and something happened to Austin, well, I wouldn't hold back the reward. It's only fair.'

'What do the police think about that?'

Rod laughed, like his scary moment hadn't even happened, which disturbed me even more. 'Oh, they hate me,' he said, 'especially that bull-dyke Dianne Talbot, but I don't care. If they'd done their jobs properly I wouldn't have had to put up the reward. If it wasn't for me the case wouldn't still be in the media. You know they hauled me in for questioning and acted like I was guilty when Isabella's body was found? Kept me there for hours, even though I had a perfectly good alibi. A breakfast meeting with my agent in Melbourne. Hundreds of people saw us.'

'Did Isabella have any enemies?'

'Just Nick.'

'Who was Isabella's publisher?'

'Brandenburg, same as me.'

'Any good friends I could talk to?'

'Isabella was a lovely person, but we pretty much kept to ourselves. My fault, I suppose: I didn't want to share her. Oh, she had acquaintances in the publishing industry and at RMIT, where she acquired her master's. She attended festivals, ran creative writing workshops and mentored the occasional aspiring writer. I could give you some numbers, but no one stood out to me as a particularly close friend. Really, we spent most of our time here. Do you see the building adjacent to the pool? It was her own studio cum pied-à-terre where she could create to her heart's content. Sometimes, when inspiration struck, I wouldn't see her for days.'

'No best girlfriend?' I thought of Chloe, who knew more about my life than I did.

He shook his head.

'What about Victoria Hitchens?' I ventured, thinking about the blonde romance writer whose name kept coming up.

'That whore?' He sneered like a growling dog—another crack in his veneer.

'Excuse me?'

He fought for composure. Won. 'I'm sorry. It's just that they'd known each other since high school and Isabella thought Victoria was her friend—until Victoria turned on her and started saying terrible things behind her back. Jealousy, once again. Oh, she had the material success, but not an iota of Isabella's talent. A hack. She'd never have been published if it wasn't for her looks, which, I have it on good authority, have had a little help from the plastic surgeon.'

Meow.

'You don't suspect her, though?'

'Of course not. She may be a bitch, but she's no killer.'

'What did your ex-wife think of Isabella?'

'Not much, but don't worry about her, she's quite happy living with a more-than-generous settlement and a bronzed toy-boy on the Côte d'Azur.' He narrowed his eyes and the flat, shark-like look was back. 'You seem determined to absolve Nick.'

'Oh, god no. Just playing devil's advocate.' I grimaced and performed what I hoped was a non-threatening shrug. 'Why did Isabella go to his house that day?'

'She wanted him to sign divorce papers. I didn't know. I would have forbidden her. I wish to god she hadn't.'

'Isn't it usual to send them, or get someone else to serve them?'

'Yes, but she was at her wit's end. He kept trying to put it off, pretended he hadn't received them, disputed the separation date, that sort of thing. She'd talked once about forcing him to sign in front of her, then delivering the papers to the court so we could start proceedings and hurry along our wedding, but I told her it would be madness to see him. If only she'd listened.'

The butler had glided in and topped up my glass, so I sipped some more wine and nibbled at a fig, then a piece of nutty-tasting cheese.

'Why did you do the writers' festival talk? I mean, if Nick was so messed up and unstable.'

'I didn't want to at first, but Isabella convinced me. She really needed the publicity for her new novel. The market for literary fiction is very tight in Australia, but she always sells very well on the festival circuit. She's such a beautiful speaker the audience can't help but rush out and sample her work. Also, it was a chance for us to finally be on a panel together. Why should we let a petty jerk like Nick stop us?'

I didn't mention that it also looked like an opportunity for Isabella to have the two of them fight over her and sit in the middle like the cat who'd got the cream. I tried one last tack.

'Was Isabella in any trouble that you know of?'

Rod frowned. I reframed the question.

'Maybe something Nick had gotten her into. Something to do with money? Blackmail?'

'What on earth are you talking about? Nick, I can imagine, but Isabella? That's absurd.'

'Sorry, I—'

'The police raised similar questions. They even intimated she was having an affair. I was outraged.'

I had the feeling I'd pushed it as far as I could and decided to finish up. I wanted to keep him onside in case I thought of anything important to ask later on.

'Thanks, Rod.' I smiled ingratiatingly. 'I guess that's it. Must be my turn to talk. What did you want to know?'

'Everything you told the police and every single detail about your dealings with Austin. Even if it doesn't seem significant to you, it might provide a clue as to his whereabouts. You don't mind if I record?' He pulled a tiny digital recorder out of his pocket and set it on the table. Made me uncomfortable, but I could hardly say no. I took a deep breath and another gulp of wine, and had just opened my mouth to speak when his fancy phone thing buzzed. He held out a palm as a signal for me to stop, and answered.

'Mmm-hmm. Yes, I see. No, it's not, but I can make it.' He rang off and looked up. 'I'm afraid I have to meet my agent for lunch. It's rather urgent.'

'Did you want to do this later?' I suggested.

'Not so fast, young lady. You've got your information, I want mine.'

'But if you have to go . . .'

He squinted into the distance for a little while, tapping his manicured fingernails on the table top, before simultaneously clicking them together and pointing at me.

'I have a plan.'

'Yeah?'

'I'm taking the chopper to Melbourne.'

'Harley?'

'No, helicopter. You ever flown in one?'

'Can't say I have.'

'Well then, you'll definitely have to come. You can share your information on the flight, then have a spot of lunch with us at Rockpool.'

I was a little taken aback. The day was progressively morphing into an episode of *Lifestyles of the Rich and Famous.*

'What about my car?'

'I'll get Dean to drive it down. By the time we've finished lunch and put you in a limo, it'll be waiting outside your house.'

I didn't like the idea of the blond security guy inside my car, and conducted a swift mental tally of what it contained. Bag full of clothes and wigs, half a hip flask of whiskey, nothing overly incriminating. The rego stuff in the glove box wasn't a worry as I was sure they already knew where I lived. A sweep for bugs and tracking devices and a quick paranoid check for severed brake lines would be a small price to pay to avoid driving home, and I had to admit I was just the teensiest bit keyed up about getting a helicopter ride into the bargain.

'Okay.'

'Splendid.'

When I uncrossed my legs and stood up I realised I really, really needed to pee.

'Can I use your bathroom before we go?'

'Certainly.' Rod walked me into his office and pointed to a door behind the desk.

The large bathroom contained a big old claw-foot bath, more terracotta tiles, and showcased another killer view over the vineyards. When I sat down on the polished wood toilet seat to pee I realised I must have been more dehydrated than I thought. Despite a major urge, all I could come up with was a minor trickle. After I'd washed my hands I cupped them for a few gulps of tap water, patted them dry on a fluffy chocolate-coloured towel, then nosed around the medicine cabinet. Aveda products, aftershave and a packet of Cialis. I received all the usual spam emails. Wasn't it the same shit as Viagra? An unbidden image of Rod pumping enthusiastically away on top of Isabella flashed into my mind and I felt vaguely ill and awfully glad he hadn't made a move.

Leaving the bathroom I heard Rod talking to someone in the hallway about getting the chopper ready for the flight. I was right behind the desk and the computer was still on, its screensaver comprising thousands of tiny, drifting stars. Unable to help myself I nudged the mouse with the back of my hand so that his Word file sparked back to life. I leaned forward to read it and was taken aback by what I saw: *The quick brown fox jumped over the lazy dog. The quick brown fox jumped over the lazy dog. The quick brown fox jumped over the lazy dog . . .*

The sentence was repeated down the whole length of the page and I realised he must have been writing it when I first came in. He'd lied about finishing an important chapter—either that or his muse wasn't much chop. What was his game? Did he think it would impress me, seeing the genius at work? I wondered what else he'd lied about.

I didn't think he'd killed Isabella—his grief and anger had seemed pretty genuine—yet I doubted he was being completely straight with me. Or himself, for that matter. He gave the impression of being the sort of person who put a spin on things, creating his own version of events to suit his view of both the world and himself. Everyone did, to a certain extent, but Rod had a pretty severe case of it. He couldn't have been completely blind to Nick and Isabella's flirting at the festival, could he?

I suddenly realised Rod had stopped talking, so high-tailed it to the doorway and almost smacked into him coming through.

'Ready to go?' He smiled, teeth so white and perfectly formed I wondered if they were real.

chapter twenty-three

Rod's chopper roosted on a purpose-built landing pad in a field behind the villa, gleaming in the sun. It was sleek and black with a pointy nose, long tail and a hint of the military about it, rather than the bubble-shaped craft I'd been expecting.

Despite the fact it could accommodate five passengers in leather seats in the back, I sat next to Rod in the cockpit, dazzled by an instrument panel so full of clock faces and controls it looked like we were about to nip into space and attempt a quick moon landing before lunch.

He flicked some buttons and switches in front of him, fiddled with something overhead, and the engine started a high-pitched whirr before the rotors began to thwack. He handed me a headset with a microphone attached and raised a lever between the seats. The machine wobbled and began to rise. Rod saw me watching him and assumed I was interested.

'This one's the collective control stick.' He tapped the lever. 'Raises and lowers the bird. The throttle between my legs is the cyclic control which I use to steer. It inches the axis of the main rotor in the direction I want to go. I push the foot pedals to work the rudder connected to the tail rotor. Left for left and right for right.'

'Easy-peasy,' I said.

'Not exactly.' His tone was stern. 'Flying a helicopter is a very complex business. You want to know the number one cause of helicopter crashes?'

'Not really.'

'Pilot error.'

I must have looked ashen. 'Don't worry,' he said. 'Been flying these babies since the eighties.'

I did feel sorry for him, despite my suspicions, his self-important boasting and his ostentatious spread. It had to be hell losing someone you loved, just like my mother and her boyfriend, Steve. Although 'boyfriend' didn't sound quite right when you thought of their ten-year relationship and how they had planned to grow old together. I remembered how I'd felt when I thought Alex was dead, sort of scraped out and empty and sick. Just thinking about it made me teary, so I ruthlessly derailed that particular train of thought.

The chopper dipped and rose, following vine-rowed slopes and swooping over lush fields and houses so quaint and charming they had to have been two-hundred-dollar-a-night B&Bs. Rod circled the valley, followed the blacktop out of town, turned down the music and asked me to tell him everything I knew about Nick. So I did.

Well, most of it. I didn't tell him about Isabella and Nick's kiss because I thought it would piss him off, and for all I knew, rage could easily be a contributing factor in 'pilot error'. I also didn't mention Liz, or the money Nick had needed to borrow off her. Client confidentiality, plus I'd given my word. I did, however, disclose that Nick had implored me to warn Nerida and someone whose name started with J. Rod told me that he didn't know any Neridas and that J was not really enough to go on. True.

By the time I'd finished we were coming into the city, banking over the Collingwood housing commission flats, then red-roofed, tram-line-bisected Fitzroy and finally floating above the wide, tree-lined streets, bluestone buildings and park-dotted blocks of the CBD. I picked out landmarks: the Rialto tower, Fitzroy Gardens, the MCG. In the distance, perched on the broad blue curve of Port Phillip Bay, St Kilda glittered in the summer sun. A few seconds later we were crossing the brown swathe of the Yarra River and heading for the helipad on the riverbank opposite the Casino.

'I'll admit I enjoy the fruits of my success. I won't lie about that.' He lowered the collective control, manipulated the throttle and we began to descend. 'But I work damn hard for it and I think I deserve it. Plus, I make sure I put something back. I'm passionate about the environment, I've visited with the troops in Iraq, who just love the Chase books. I occasionally do writing workshops with people less fortunate, street kids, prisoners. I think it's good for the public to see the many different facets of Rod Thurlow. People know me as the best-selling scribe, or the Hollywood power broker, but are unaware of my charitable works.'

'Which prison?' I asked.

'Sorry?'

'Which prison did you do the workshop in?' I was acquainted with a few folks in the big house.

'Port Phillip.'

I shuddered. 'You meet a guy called Emery Wade?'

He shook his head. 'I don't recall any of the names, although I do remember being amazed and a little disturbed to have so many felons as fans. Chase Macallister is a very upstanding character and the books have a real moral message.

I can't imagine how those offenders identify with Chase, but they do.'

'Everyone's the hero of their own story,' I said, and felt quite clever, especially since I had started to come down from the mid-morning wine and was getting that dirty feeling at the back of my eyeballs.

He scoffed and shook his head. 'Not those fellows.' And then he floated the chopper down right in the middle of the landing pad, soft as a feather.

chapter twenty-four

Rockpool Bar and Grill was part of the Crown Casino and entertainment complex, right on the Yarra. We entered the building from the river promenade and found ourselves in a cool, high-ceilinged space with lots of mahogany wood, the chairs and banquettes covered in dark blue upholstery.

The waitress-slash-model greeted Rod by name and showed us to a table out on the terrace where a man was sitting in my favourite position, back to the wall.

'Ah, there he is. Brendan!' Rod waved on the way over.

I really didn't know what an agent was supposed to look like, but realised I'd been anticipating a grey-haired man in a suit, or a fifty-something blonde with shoulder pads and a lot of gold jewellery. Brendan was neither.

He appeared to be in his early thirties, tall and thin with a pointy face and light brown hair that curled at his collar and had been plastered to the rest of his head with a touch too much gel. He'd buttoned his shirt up to the collar but hadn't worn a tie, and that, combined with the mirrored sunglasses wrapped around his face, made him look like a young bogan slicked up for a court hearing.

'Who's this?' Brendan snapped, looking me up and down.

'Simone Kirsch,' said Rod.

Brendan's head moved back on his stalk of a neck and I wished I could see what his eyes were doing behind the opaque shades.

'Simone, meet my agent, Brendan Reed.'

Brendan didn't offer a hand so I just smiled and said, 'Hey.'

The waitress asked if we wanted something to drink.

'Another bourbon and Coke.' Brendan rattled his glass.

'Bottle of Krug,' Rod said. 'The ninety-two.'

'What's she doing here?' Brendan addressed Rod after the waitress left. 'I thought we were going to talk.'

'And talk we shall. I've booked us a private room at the Cigar Bar for two o'clock.' He sat down and motioned for me to do the same. I hesitated.

'If you guys want to be alone, I can scoot off home.'

'Nonsense.' Rod turned to Brendan. 'Simone has been assisting in the search for Austin. Which reminds me, I have to make a call.' He pulled out his phone and stood. 'You know, I've half a mind to see if I can't convince her to join the team permanently. Maybe that's what this investigation needs. A woman's touch.' He walked off.

'His pecker needs a woman's touch, more like,' Brendan muttered under his breath.

I raised my eyebrows. 'I take it Rod's not one of your favourite clients?'

'He's my only client.'

I raised them some more.

'Oh, I make money,' he laughed sourly, 'don't you worry about that. I just don't have the cachet of being a best-selling author.'

'Write a book then.' I hoped the champagne would come soon.

He stared at me, shook his head and drained the dregs of his drink. Ice clattered in his glass.

'So, what's your story?' he said. 'Angling to be the next Mrs Thurlow?'

'What the hell are you talking about?' I said.

He smirked. My phone started ringing so I checked the caller ID. Sean. I put it on silent, not in the mood to lie to a detective about my whereabouts.

'Rod attracts his fair share of gold-diggers,' Brendan said.

'Gimme a break,' I said, before thinking of something. 'Is that what you reckoned Isabella was?'

'Aren't you all?'

My mouth actually dropped open at that one. I was just about to insult Brendan back with a creative combination of the nouns *rat* and *face* and a crude slang word for the female genitalia, when Rod returned.

'I've got some bad news,' he told me.

'Nick?' A little fillip in my stomach.

'No, it's about your car.'

'What happened?'

'There was an accident.'

'Shit.'

'Don't worry. It's not too bad and Dean got away with cuts and bruises. He's taken your car to my personal mechanic. Has a bit of axle damage and needs some panel beating and a new windscreen, but it'll be fixed in a couple of days and I've already paid for it, so you don't have to worry about that.'

'What happened?'

Rod frowned harder. 'Someone tried to run him off the road. According to Dean a white car deliberately sideswiped him and he rolled, landed upside down in a ditch.'

'Did Dean see who it was?'

'Here's the worrying part. The driver was wearing a mask—one of those plastic things for kids you buy in the supermarket or a joke shop? He pulled up and started to get out of the car, but when he saw Dean he jumped back in and took off. You know anyone who doesn't like you?'

chapter twenty-five

I woke up early the next day, and already the morning was hot and bright, streaks of sunlight beaming through cracks in the blinds. Sean wasn't in bed but I could hear him clattering around in the kitchen. I got up, eyes crusted, hair at the back of my neck matted with sweat.

Stupidly, I opened the curtains and nearly hissed and burst into flames, before turning and seeing myself in the mirrored wardrobe opposite the bed.

The huge mirror was great for sex, not so good for avoiding a glimpse of yourself first thing in the morning. I grabbed the roll of flesh that bulged between my singlet and undies and thought about lunch the day before. *Steamed chicken breasts*, I said to myself. And a run. But first, caffeine.

I tottered into the kitchen. Sean was ready for work, crisp shirt, damp hair, smelling of Tommy Hilfiger aftershave.

'Hey, babe.' I gave him a hug, or more accurately, lurched into him. 'Coffee.'

He hugged back and patted me on the arse. 'Kettle's just boiled. I was full of plans to ravish you last night, but you were out for the count when I got back.'

'Big day.' I got the tin out of the freezer, the plunger from the cupboard.

'It was like a sweatbox in here. The whole place was locked up tight and you smelled like you'd been on the piss.'

I'd staggered into the limo at two, drunk, but not so drunk that I didn't think to have the driver walk me to my flat and help me check the place for intruders. He hadn't even raised an eyebrow. After that I'd made sure all the windows were locked and the blinds drawn and I'd spent ages trying to figure out what was going on. Had someone really tried to run me off the road, or had Rod orchestrated the whole thing because he wanted access to my car? Later in the afternoon I'd watched TV for a few hours before falling into bed. No wonder I felt so drowsy—I'd had over twelve hours' sleep.

'Big day drinking.' I decided it was a five scoop morning, dumped in the grounds and filled the pot with hot water. The freshly brewed coffee smelled chocolatey.

'Drinking with who?' Sean asked as he stirred organic honey into his porridge.

I almost told him Chloe, but something about his forced casualness made me think he'd probably rung her the day before, after he'd tried calling me.

'Myself.' I attempted to push the plunger down, not easy with so many grounds and the fact that before coffee I had all the strength of a newborn kitten.

The kitchen blinds were slatted open and I could see the treetops. The leaves were technicolour green and tiny sparrows quavered on the branches.

'I love these oaks,' I said, suddenly sentimental, knowing that wherever I ended up, I'd be out of the flat in two months.

'Plane trees.'

'Aren't plane trees those flat-topped things in Africa?'

'Different sort of plane tree,' Sean said, taking over the plunging for me.

'They look like oaks.'

'Seen any acorns around?' The veins on his arms bulged as he forced the mechanism down. 'How come you were drinking alone?'

'Had a hangover. Best thing for it.'

'That's not good.' He frowned. 'Neither is this ridiculously strong coffee. You have to look after yourself.'

He took his porridge and cup of tea out onto the balcony and I followed with the plunger and a cup, but only as far as the dining table in the living room. I could still talk to Sean through the sliding glass door, no sense making myself a sitting duck.

The first sip of the evil brew hit my stomach and shot into my arteries and veins. The world started to come into focus.

'Have you thought any more about Vietnam?' He turned his chair around to look at me, and seemed puzzled as to why I was sitting inside.

'I was a little too drunk to really think of anything yesterday . . .'

'Well, stay off the booze today, yeah? Take it easy.'

'Sure.'

'Sorry I haven't been around lately.'

'It's not your fault.' I blew on my coffee, sipped, felt the hairs on my arms stand on end.

'After New Year's I'll have four days off. We should go somewhere. Down to my mum's in Torquay?'

'Mmm, be good,' I said.

Sean must have mistaken my pensive mood for deliberating whether to move overseas with him, and he launched into an excited ten-minute monologue outlining all the great things about the country and the job while I nodded, occasionally interjected with a 'sounds great', and weighed up the costs and benefits of telling him that someone wanted to kill me.

The drawbacks were many: I'd have to explain where I'd been when someone screwed with my car, which would make it obvious what I was up to, and he'd disapprove and probably jump to the conclusion that I was getting threats because I was looking for Nick. We'd have an argument and he'd insist I give it up, perhaps even threatening to tell Detective Talbot, who, out of spite, would cancel my PI licence for the rest of my natural life. I'd not only have to drop the case and give Liz her money back, but Sean would insist I hide out somewhere boring and safe—say, the Australian Federal Police College in Canberra—and there was the next two years mapped out for me and I'd feel even more trapped than I already was.

Of course, there was one rather large advantage to be gained from telling Sean: not dying. But if someone really wanted to knock me off they could have done it any time, and it would have been especially easy if they hadn't sent a note to warn me of their intentions. So what the hell was going on? Did someone just want me scared and out of the way? Why? There wasn't enough coffee in all the world to get my head around it.

I realised Sean was asking me a question.

'Sorry?'

'I said, what are you up to today?'

'Thought I'd go into the office, pay some bills, say hi to Chloe, maybe the gym . . .'

. . . call Liz, hunt down Victoria and Desiree.

'You need money?'

'No.'

'Sure?' He reached for his wallet but I waved him away. He checked his watch. 'Shit, I should get going,' he said.

'Drive me to the office?' I didn't think it would be wise to leave the house alone.

'Where's your car?'

'Mechanic.'

He frowned. 'Again? I thought the RACV checked it out before you bought it, gave it a good rating.'

I shrugged.

'Sure you don't wanna take the bus?' he said. 'I gotta leave in five.'

'Be ready in thirty seconds.'

I drained the rest of the coffee, threw on lightweight stretch jeans, a clean singlet and thongs, grabbed my small backpack and stuffed the death threat inside, just in case I decided to show it to him. I'd shower at work.

I stuck so close to Sean as we walked to his neat but battered white Saab that I bumped into his back when he stopped to unlock the door.

'Whoa, you alright?'

'Yeah, sorry, still half asleep.'

It wasn't a long drive but I checked for tails all the way, pretending to admire the architecture on Glenhuntly Road, which mostly comprised blocks of sixties brick flats.

I kissed Sean goodbye, let myself into my office, logged onto the internet and actually did pay some bills, then had another coffee and tried to work out what to do about the threats. It was ridiculous, I couldn't live like this, locked up tight and jumping at my own shadow. If I didn't tell Sean, then who else could help me?

My old boss, private investigator Tony Torcasio? He'd tell me to go to the police.

Sam Doyle, the ex-gangster I'd met on my last case? He was a nice bloke, had sent me whiskey and was always asking after my mother, however he didn't exactly have police connections and anyway, he was based in Sydney.

Alex?

Why hadn't I thought of him before? He had connections in the service yet wasn't actually working, which meant he might be more inclined to doing things a little off the books. We already shared one rather large secret, what was one more?

chapter twenty-six

I ate a small tin of tuna in spring water I found stashed in the office kitchenette and felt instantly thinner, showered in the closet-sized bathroom, blow-dried my hair, and spent about twenty minutes putting on makeup of the 'I'm not wearing any' variety.

I decided against calling and forewarning Alex; it would only give him a chance to tell me to piss off. I just hoped he was home, and that Suzy wasn't. If Alex's new bride caught me sniffing around her man there was a high probability of an out and out catfight. She'd certainly taken a swing at me in the past.

My Ford Futura was out the back, but I wasn't going to take it and make life easy for my stalker. Instead I scoped out the street through the venetian blinds at the front of my office, and when I didn't see any immediate threat, locked the door behind me and hailed the first cab that came along. I told the driver to take me to Mentone via the coast road. It would take a little longer but was more scenic and had fewer lanes than Nepean Highway, making it easier to spot anyone on our tail.

I spent a fair bit of time twisted around in the back seat, staring out the window, and when I was satisfied we weren't being tracked, sat back, checking out the big glass-walled beachside houses on my left, and the sparkling, sailboat-studded bay on my right.

Less than half an hour after I'd hailed the taxi, we were pulling up in front of Alex's place in Mentone, a modern-looking block of four apartments constructed of blue rendered concrete, glass and panelled steel. It was the kind of thing proudly advertised as 'architect designed' in the real estate lift-outs, which always made me snigger. Who the hell else was going to design a goddamn building?

Alex's flat was on the upper floor, overlooking Beach Road and the thin patch of parkland that bordered the bay. I stood in the park under a straggly pine and gazed up at his huge balcony, looking for signs of life. Nothing. Crossing the road I strolled around to the rear of the building where the six-foot-high corrugated-metal gate blocked the entrance. As I lifted my finger to ring the buzzer, my heart was thumping and I realised my pulse rate had steadily increased from the moment I'd decided to come. It wasn't fear of Suzy, because I knew she worked pretty regular hours at the Flinders Street Police Centre, and if she answered the intercom I could run like hell. I wasn't even worried about my would-be assassin at that moment because I was confident I hadn't been followed.

That left Alex.

It was because of him my heart was in my throat and I felt nauseous and dizzy. Get over it, I told myself, to no effect. Recognising the cause of my jitters only made them worse. I had to remember I was there because I needed his help, not for a romantic rendezvous. He was married and I was living with Sean, and besides, I didn't do that sort of shit anymore. Neither did Alex, I guessed, until I recalled the Christmas party and how he'd told me I could make it up to him: *I was thinking something along the lines of what happened at the pub . . .*

Remembering the intense way he'd stared at me when he said it made me swallow involuntarily and I felt a familiar tingle run up and down my inner thighs. Maybe it was just as well no one was answering the buzzer. I felt like a bit of a dick, though, not having asked the cab driver to wait.

'Hey,' someone shouted from the street adjacent to Alex's.

I turned. An old man in a wide-brimmed hat and long-sleeved shirt stood in the front yard of a brick bungalow. He wore gardening gloves and held a pair of pruning shears.

'Who you looking for?' he said.

'Alex Christakos.' I crossed the road so we wouldn't have to shout. 'Friend of mine.'

'The copper with the dicky arm?'

'Yeah.'

'Just missed him.'

'Damn.'

'Went down the tavern.'

'Tavern?' I checked my watch. It wasn't quite ten.

The guy saw me looking and grinned.

'It's twelve o'clock somewhere, love. Mentone Arms. Down Beach Road just before the surf club.' He swiped sweat off his forehead with his shirtsleeve. 'Might head down myself after I finish this.'

'Thanks. Maybe see you there. His wife's not with him is she?'

'No, why?' A sly grin.

I found the tavern fifty metres down the road, in between the surf club and a fish 'n' chip shop. It was a squat brick building with a board out front advertising pensioner lunch specials: pork roasts, chicken schnitzels and discounted pots of beer. The inside was dark and cool, with a low ceiling and bar on the right-hand wall. Televisions screened racing and football, and an arch to the left led to a TAB area for betting. I heard faint, chirruping chimes and guessed the poker machines were hidden somewhere further back.

The only patrons were a couple of old codgers sitting at the bar, who turned and looked when I walked in, and Alex, sitting at a high round table, who didn't. He was busy sipping a pot of beer and studying a form guide. My heart picked up again, drilling so fast I thought it might give out. I took a second to study him from behind.

He wore much the same outfit he'd had on at Christmas, faded black t-shirt and an old pair of jeans. He still hadn't cut his hair and it curled almost to the collar of his t-shirt, the fabric of which was so thin it outlined the bones of his broad shoulders and the curve of his back. I was overcome with a sudden urge to press my breasts against him, smell his neck and run my fingers down his spine.

I took a deep breath. Christ, I was worse than a bitch on heat. Could have done with a bucket of cold water, or maybe a quick spray with the hose. I tried to think of Sean, but his face had gone all blurry and he seemed far away, as though he'd never come back from 'Nam. I had to approach before Alex turned and saw me ogling like a playground pervert.

'Hi,' I said.

He glanced up and it took him half a second to realise who I was.

'Simone.' He smiled, then frowned. 'What are you doing here?'

'Just passing, thought I'd drop in. Your neighbour told me you'd be here.' I climbed onto the bar stool opposite.

'Want a drink?'

'Nah, I'm trying to cut—'

'Give me a break. I'm already living with one reformed alcoholic.' He got up, went to the bar and soon returned with a whiskey to supplement his beer, and a glass of champagne for me. He carried both the glasses in one hand, not a good sign. Meant his right arm wasn't back to normal.

'Whiskey in winter, champagne in summer, yeah?'

'That's right.' I couldn't believe he'd remembered. I'd said that to him, what, a year before? 'So, Suze back off the booze?'

'And coffee, sugar, preservatives, non-organic vegetables, deep-water fish.' He counted them off on his fingers. 'We're trying for a baby.'

'Oh.' My guts clenched, but I shouldn't have been surprised. Alex had already told me having kids was one of the reasons he wanted to get hitched. 'Good luck.'

We clinked glasses.

'Seems like everybody's popping out sprogs these days,' I said, thinking of Chloe.

'Even you?'

'Huh?'

'Put on a bit of condition.' He poked me just above the waistband of my hipster jeans. 'Thought you might be in the family way.'

'*Bitch.*' I involuntarily sucked in my stomach. 'That's low.'

Alex laughed.

'Settle down, Simone, looks good. Men don't mind a bit of extra padding, gives us something to hang on to.'

That gave me an image I really didn't need. There was a short, not entirely comfortable silence in which we sipped our drinks and I feigned interest in a replay of a Manchester United game on one of the TV screens.

'How's Graham?' I asked. Alex's Burmese.

'Most people inquire after my wife.'

'Your cat's friendlier.'

He grinned and swung his leg under the table so that our knees were touching.

'Tell me,' he said, 'why are you really here?'

'Somebody wants to kill me.'

'What's new?'

'Shit, Alex, I'm serious. I really need your help.' I pulled out the note in the plastic sandwich bag and slid it across the table.

He gave it a cursory glance and shrugged. I moved my leg away because my knee was tingling and it was getting hard to concentrate. Alex frowned, just for a moment.

'That's not all,' I said. 'I think the same guy slashed my tyres and ran my car off the road. I wasn't driving, but I could have been.'

'What do you want me to do about it? Call the cops like a normal person. Christ's sake, you're shacked up with a serving member of the state police. How hard can it be?'

'Sean doesn't know.'

Alex shook his head.

'Can you promise to keep a secret?' I asked.

Alex gave me a disparaging look. 'Simone, I'm really not in the mood for any girly *let's keep a secret* bullshit, especially when it comes to my best mate.' He downed the rest of his whiskey, chased it with a sip of beer and turned his attention back to the form guide.

The dismissive act made my face prickle. Who did he think he was? I didn't so much want to sniff his neck as slap his face. I was sick of his superior attitude and the fact he was a total hypocrite.

'No bullshit girly secrets? You told Sean and Suzy about what happened at your buck's party, then?'

'Of course not.'

'Well?' I asked.

'Well nothing. You think you've got something over me?'

'Not any more than you've got over me.'

We stared at each other across the table. His expression was flat and I knew there was no reasoning with him. So I told him what was going on, and why I didn't want to inform my boyfriend, and after I'd done that I asked very nicely for him to not mention to Sean that I was looking for Nick Austin.

'Just tell him.'

'I can't.'

'You don't really have much choice.'

'But if you could make some inquiries . . . You have lots of good mates in the service and it wouldn't be corrupt, just helping out a friend.'

'I'm not working for the Ethical Standards Department anymore and I don't really give a shit about corruption so much as what happened last time I *helped out a friend . . .*' He held up his arm and concentrated on making a fist, but his fingers wouldn't fold. 'And the time before that.' He jerked down the front of his t-shirt to show me the puckered bullet scar on his shoulder.

I didn't know how to respond. Everything he said was true. Helping me out had left him near death and out of work. He had every right to be pissed off. And if I was honest with myself, was it really his help I needed, or did I just want to be near to him, getting off on the amphetamine rush of infatuation? If so, then I was a selfish, immoral bitch. Sorry for myself, too, I noted as my eyes filled with tears. Somewhere in my conniving little head I must have hoped the crying would placate Alex, but it just made him colder.

'You know, I was glad when I heard you were moving to Vietnam,' he said.

'What?'

'Yeah, Sean told me and I thought, thank Christ, I'll finally have her out of my life. More fucking trouble than she's worth.'

I sat there with my mouth open, trying to work out exactly what Sean had said.

'But I haven't—'

'Canberra first, then Ho Chi Minh? I can't imagine even hitmen want to spend time in our nation's capital so you'll be quite safe there. Maybe you should leave now.'

I searched his eyes. They were triumphant, venomous. I should never have come. Alex was right. We weren't friends. We had nothing in common except Sean and a grubby sort of attraction to each other. He had his form guide and his procreation and his expensive flat that he was probably trying to trade in for a family home further out in the suburbs, and unless I was up for some quick, dirty encounter that was too meaningless to even make a blip on his moral radar then he didn't have much use for me. Screw him.

'Fine. I will leave.'

'Good.'

'Bye then.' I stood up and felt a mix of shame, anger and unrequited bullshit slop around my veins. 'Have a nice life, Alex.'

'Oh, I will.' He finished his beer and turned his attention to the form guide as I walked out the door.

chapter twenty-seven

I called Liz from a public phone in the park opposite Alex's place, pretended to be someone else in case her phone was tapped, and arranged to meet her at one pm in a café in Albert Park.

It was a five-minute walk to the station, where I boarded a city-bound train and stared out the window and seethed all the way from Mentone to South Yarra.

As the train left Richmond I pulled myself together, strengthening my resolve, and by the time it shunted past the MCG I'd made up my mind. I'd forget about Alex once and for all and chalk down his buck's party to a bout of bad behaviour never to be repeated or thought of again. It had been a crush, stupid and childish, and it was time to act like a grown-up instead of a boy-crazy teenage girl.

Sean was great, we got on really well, and as for his opinion on my stripping, well, I was kidding myself to think that any guy would be pleased I was doing it. Hadn't Alex said as much? Sure, domestic life lacked the excitement of the early days of our relationship: a crazy fortnight of love triangles and flying bullets, hyped up on a cocaine-like combination of infatuation and adrenaline, but tough shit. That was life and life wasn't a naff, straight-to-video action movie based on one of Rod Thurlow's books. Well, not most of the time.

Moving overseas would be exciting enough and the job was a fantastic opportunity only a certified dickhead would pass up. I knew I'd be stuck desk jockeying at first, but if I kept my head down and worked diligently they'd eventually have to throw me some fieldwork, surely. Canberra was a bit iffy, but that was only for a few months.

As the train pulled into Spencer Street Station I realised I'd made my decision. I was going to Vietnam. I felt like calling Sean and telling him straight away, but thought it'd be better to do it in person, after a glass of champagne. He'd be stoked. I got off the train and looked up at the high, wavy ceiling and had an expansive feeling, like life was opening up rather than closing down and trapping me.

I breathed out, strode up the concrete ramp to Spencer Street to find a tram, and felt light on my feet. I'd made my decision, organised my life, put all my ducks in a row. *And all your eggs in one basket*, whispered a voice in my head. I ignored it.

There was, of course, the small matter of the death threats, but I had a solution to that, too. I phoned my ex-boss while I waited for the tram.

'Tony, can you talk?'

'Sure, what's up?' He sounded wary. He usually did when I called. It was another good reason to leave. Everybody in this town had obviously had enough of me and I had no favours left to call in. Still, I wasn't asking for favours this time.

'I want to hire you.'

'To do what?' he asked.

'Follow me.'

'Huh?'

'I think someone's stalking me, and I want you to follow, catch him in the act and then hopefully I can identify him. Don't worry, I'm flush, I can pay.'

'When?'

'Tomorrow, say nine till five?' I suggested.

'I was doing some surveillance . . .'

'If you can't, then one of your subcontractors?'

'Nah, I'll do it, get someone else to take over the factory job. What's the brief?'

'Start outside my flat. I'm gonna leave about eleven am and just sort of drive around and run some errands. There'll be some in-vehicle surveillance, some on foot. Sound alright?'

'Too easy.'

'I don't need to tell you to make sure you're not spotted.'

'No, you don't. How many years I been doing this?'

•

Victoria Road, Albert Park, was a wide street full of lattice-trimmed terraces that had been converted into restaurants, bookshops, clothing boutiques and the sort of stores that specialised in expensive scatter cushions and fancy lamps.

The café doubled as a deli, and built-in shelves held gourmet produce for sale: arborio rice, quince and plum pastes, imported spices in ornately decorated tins. A rack by the door contained flour-dusted spelt and sourdough bread. Ladies who lunch, latte-sipping mums and real estate agent types in suits and ties sat chatting, sounds bouncing off the polished wood floor.

Liz was squished into a table by a glass case heaped with cheese, olives and cured meat. I walked over.

'Hi.'

'Hey. I've just ordered a sandwich. You want something?'

'I'll go.'

At the counter I passed over the cheese plate and pinot for a chicken and avocado salad, black coffee and water, feeling slimmer, purer and more righteous by the second.

'What's going on?' Liz leaned forward as I slid into the chair opposite. She looked even thinner than she had at the Stokehouse, if that was possible, her flicked-out hair more grey than blonde.

I told her most of what I'd found out and she seemed impressed that I'd tracked down Jenny and got an audience with Rod, even though I hadn't actually learned much. Our lunch arrived and Liz took a bite of her turkey salad sandwich while I blew on my coffee.

'Has Nick contacted you again?' I asked.

She shook her head as she chewed.

'You don't have any contact details for Desiree, do you?' I asked. 'An address or phone number?' I really didn't want to get Curtis involved.

'She's pretty private. Hardly anyone knows her real name, although I think Nick might have. All I have is an email and a post office box.'

'No worries. She does her radio show tonight so I'll see if I can "bump" into her at the station. Speaking of agents, you know anything about Rod's, Brendan Whatsit?'

'There's been a lot of speculation about that guy. Rod doesn't even need an agent. I mean, you've met him, he's pretty assertive and brokers most of the deals himself. Brendan doesn't do much except handle the contracts and apparently Rod pays him a *lot* more than ten percent.'

'Why?'

'Your guess is as good as mine. Is he Rod's bum boy? His illegitimate son? An old friend he owed and wanted to give a ride to? Believe me, this has been discussed ad nauseum at cocktail parties and writers' festivals for years. No one knows. I've never actually met him. What's he like?'

'Bit of a weasel.' I told her about our lunch.

'He doesn't seem to have liked Isabella. Do you think . . . ?'

'Don't get your hopes up. I'll have a bit of a dig, though. Can't discount anything at this stage.' I ate a couple of forkfuls of chicken salad. 'Another person I can't reach is Victoria Hitchens. I've tried everything. Any contacts?'

Liz thought about it while she brushed crumbs from her mouth. She bundled up the paper napkin and laid it on top of the sandwich. She'd only taken two bites.

'You doing anything New Year's Eve?' she said.

'Why?'

'Victoria's having a combined New Year's Eve party and book launch on a boat on the Yarra. Great view of the fireworks, tickets are the hottest property in town.'

'How would I get one?'

Liz reached down the side of her chair and pulled her big, caramel-coloured leather handbag onto her lap. She retrieved a long wallet with lots of compartments, slid out a slender envelope and waved it in front of my face. I opened it to find a gold embossed invitation.

Victoria Hitchens and Caravelle Press
cordially invite you to a masked ball to celebrate the launch
of Victoria's new bestseller

Masquerade

New Year's Eve
7 pm to late
MV Neptuna
Crown Promenade
Mandatory Fancy Dress

'Her publicist used to work with me at Wet Ink,' Liz explained.

'Won't she be disappointed you're not there?'

'There'll be so many people she won't even notice. And the last thing I feel like is a party, everyone staring, asking me questions about Nick.'

'You don't happen to have an outfit, do you?'

'Yeah, I got one made, but . . .'

'What?'

'No way it'll fit you.'

I stopped chasing around the last piece of chicken with my fork.

'I'm not saying you're fat,' she said, seeing the look on my face, 'just more muscular, sort of . . . broad around the back.'

Nice save, sorta.

'No worries. I'll go to a costume hire shop.'

She frowned.

'What?'

'I was talking to a friend the other day who's going. Every costume place in town seems to be out of masquerade ball-gowns. My friend actually flew to Sydney to hire something, maybe—'

'By masquerade ball we're talking those corseted, Frenchy, *Dangerous Liaisons* style outfits, right?'

'Uh-huh.'

'I've got it covered.'

Liz raised her eyebrows.

I did. I'd remembered that one of Chloe's girls'd had something made for a Marie Antoinette-turns-porno-slut themed show. I was sure she'd let me borrow it if the price was right.

chapter twenty-eight

After lunch I strolled around Albert Park for a while, wandering into shops, touching jewelled candle holders and embroidered pillow cases that I couldn't afford and didn't really want anyway. The sales assistants seemed to sense it and after a few snooty looks I was back out on the footpath, at a loose end. I was too wired for another coffee, couldn't have a real drink because that'd wipe out the rest of the day, and I still had five hours until Desiree's sex-advice show. Going home or to the office was out of the question as I didn't want my mad stalker to pick up my trail, at least not until I had Tony there to watch my back. I passed a sportswear shop, which reminded me I really ought to put in a couple of hours at the gym, but I didn't have my gear. Unless . . .

Half an hour later and five hundred bucks broker I walked out of the shop with a whole new workout outfit, including shoes and socks. The bill had taken my breath away, but shit, I needed new runners and had hardly spent any of the money Liz had paid me for the job.

The gym was opposite the Elsternwick railway station and sat above a chicken shop on Glenhuntly Road. If the wind was right you could smell chips and gravy in the aerobics room. It was a big barn of a place and not the slightest bit stylish or trendy, which suited me fine. The women dressed in bike shorts and big floppy t-shirts, and most of the men had abundant back hair and wore nylon running shorts that ballooned at the thigh so you could see their jocks, if they were wearing any.

I felt out of place in my new, matching cotton-lycra tights and sleeveless tank, but soldiered on nonetheless, doing an hour on the treadmill then another of free weights for every muscle I knew of, and some I didn't. By the time I'd finished my legs were so wobbly I barely made it down the stairs to the change room.

After the gym I called Sean and told him I had something important to tell him. He was finishing at nine and we arranged to meet at a bar in the Royce Hotel, right across the street from the St Kilda Road Police Complex and walking distance from the radio station in Southbank where Desiree was doing her show.

I parked my butt on a low cinderblock wall opposite ROCK FM at seven o'clock, an hour before Desiree's broadcast was due to start. The area was semi-industrial and the building two storeys of brick, with mirrored windows and double doors out front. I'd peeked through when I first arrived and saw a security guard behind a perspex screen. Looked like everyone had to sign in before gaining entry and I hoped that applied to Desiree too. I remembered her and Chloe's mini-catfight at the writers' festival, Chloe saying, *like, that's your real name?*, and I wondered what it actually was. Kylie? Bertha? Liz had told me Nick knew, but I couldn't ask him.

It was still light and I flipped through my file on Nick while I waited. I was just coming to the depressing realisation that my internet printouts and scribbled notes led to absolutely nothing when a sleek black Mercedes with tinted windows pulled up, a driver in front and two figures in the rear. The man in the back, a chunky guy in a dark suit, jumped out, ran around to the other side of the car and opened the door. A tall woman with a sleek red bob stepped out.

I ran across the road towards her, stuffing the file back into my bag.

'Desiree!'

I was totally unprepared for what happened next. The chunky guy came at me and shouldered me in the chest, and I dropped like a G-string at a buck's party. The driver, thinner and dressed in the same kind of suit, ran over. Both of them pulled guns.

'Get on your front! Hands where we can see 'em!'

I was too winded to move and lay on my back wheezing, attempting to suck in air.

'Whoa, guys, hold up, I know her.' Desiree laid manicured fingernails on the first guy's enormous besuited bicep, and he reluctantly lowered his arm. 'Simone Kirsch, right? I met you at the Summer Sessions. Curtis' friend?'

I couldn't actually talk so I nodded yes to the name question and shook my head for the Curtis one. The men re-holstered their weapons, and the driver held out a hand to help me up. I stood up, doubled over until I got my breath back.

Desiree wore a knee-length pencil skirt and a tight, vaguely S&M-looking halterneck top. 'Sorry about that,' she said, 'they thought you were someone else.'

'Who?' I panted.

She ignored my question. 'What are you doing here?'

'I need to talk to you about Nick Austin.'

'I don't think so.'

As she walked away I grabbed her wrist and the suits advanced. When I let go they backed off, just.

'Do you know where he is?'

'Of course not.'

'Do you think he killed Isabella?'

'No.' She crossed her arms.

'Who did?'

'I have no idea. What's it to you, anyway?'

'I'm trying to help Nick, and you're not doing him any favours by lying.'

Desiree sucked in her cheeks and lifted her Roman nose. The big guys were looking over, ready to shoulder me again, so I inched forward, speaking quick and quiet.

'I think whoever killed Isabella is after Nick and they're also after you. Why else would you have armed bodyguards?'

'The books I write ensure I get more than my fair share of strange fans.'

'You didn't have security at the festival.'

She turned to leave. I didn't dare approach with the goons ready to go me, but I did raise my voice.

'Why does somebody want to off you? What does it have to do with the money Nick's paying?'

Nothing.

'For fuck's sake, Desiree, I'm on your side.'

She was ignoring me, climbing the steps to the radio station, when in an instant it became clear. How could I have been so stupid? Bodyguards. *Like, that's your real name?* Nick in my flat telling me to warn—

'Nerida!'

She stopped, slowly turned.

'After Nick was shot he said to warn Nerida and J somebody. You're Nerida, aren't you?' I was talking softly so the bodyguards couldn't hear.

She paused like she was wrestling with something.

'I was Nerida Saunders. I'm not anymore.'

'How did Nick contact you?'

She didn't answer, just shook her head, but something in her face seemed to soften and I pushed on, sure I was in with a chance.

'Then who's J?' I kept my voice low. 'Is it short for Jason or Jayden or what? Has Nick warned him, too?'

She chose her words carefully, clearly not prepared to admit to any contact with Nick. 'Nobody can find JJ.'

'JJ?'

'He's a poet . . .' Her eyes misted over for a second and she wobbled slightly on her heels. I wouldn't have been surprised if she'd sunk to the concrete step, rested her head on her knees and started to cry, but she didn't. She blinked rapidly, straightened her back, sniffed and checked her watch. 'I have to go.'

'Do you want me to try and find JJ?'

'Stay out of it, Simone, unless you want to end up like Isabella.' She put her hand on the door handle, started to push.

'Desiree, what's this all about?' I pleaded. 'Give me a hint, at least.'

'You want advice?' Her face was composed now, all hard planes, sharp cheekbones, Cleopatra eyes glittering like a cat's.

'Anything.'

'How's this? False fingernails and anal stimulation just don't mix. It's from chapter three.' She opened her handbag and handed over two books wrapped in black fishnet and held together by hot pink ribbon. A fuchsia sticker announced 'Sizzling Summer Reads, Two for One Special'. The first was her autobiography, the second the sex tips.

'Christmas promotion,' Desiree muttered, then looked over my head and addressed the guards in a clipped tone.

'Make sure she's gone by the time I've finished my show.' She slipped inside the station.

Damnit. She knew exactly why Nick had run and she wasn't going to tell me. I wondered if Curtis had an inkling as to what was going on. It would mean I'd have to talk to him and he'd find out I was up to something, but maybe that was a sacrifice I had to make.

What was the connection between Desiree, Nick, Isabella and this JJ dude? Who wanted to off a bunch of writers, why, and how the hell was I gonna find out?

I followed the short concrete path back down to the roadway. One of the guards had the boot up and was removing a bucket full of rags and car polish. Inside were two Louis Vuitton suitcases, stacked on top of each other.

'Desiree going somewhere?' I asked.

The guy straightened up and slammed the trunk.

'Piss off.' He pointed.

'Sure.' I stuck my hands in my pockets and started down the street. The sun had just set and bright orange clouds streaked the darkening indigo sky. It was almost time to meet Sean. I walked to the end of the road and turned left, pretty sure the street I was on was parallel to St Kilda Road. If I kept going for a couple of blocks I'd be able to hang a left and hopefully pop out not far from the police complex and the bar.

As I walked, my mind raced. I didn't know shit, really, but discovering that Desiree was Nerida made me feel like I was finally getting somewhere.

I was curious about the Desiree/Nick connection. He was the only one aware of her real name, as far as I knew. Had they had a fling? At least I had another avenue to investigate. I also wondered what JJ the poet's story was, and itched to get on the internet and do a search. If I couldn't find out anything on publicly available sites then maybe I could get

Tony Torcasio to check everyone out on one of the many databases he subscribed to.

Where the hell was the street that connected to St Kilda Road? I kept trying to turn left, but ran into lanes blocked by brick buildings that made up the arse end of the Victorian College of the Arts. Irritating, because I ached from the gym, my hip and shoulder smarted from where I'd connected with the tarmac, and I was sweating in the heat. I badly wanted to flop into a comfy chair at the Amberoom and could practically taste the glass of crisp, cold sparkling I was determined to order.

The sky was darkening and the air glimmered with that mysterious twilight afterglow. Urban crickets, hiding in the walls of converted factories and scrappy patches of weeds, started their summer-evening chorus. In the distance trams dinged their bells, and I heard cars swishing across the Kingsway overpass en route to the airport or the western suburbs.

I also heard footsteps.

I glanced over my shoulder. A figure strolled a block behind, runners squeaking on the sidewalk.

My heart revved and I tried to calm myself down. Just a dude walking along a footpath, not a crime, no big deal, and besides, I'd been careful all day. No car, just an unpredictable mix of taxis and public transport. I'd kept looking over my shoulder the whole time. I was sure I hadn't been followed.

I relaxed a little. God, I really had to stop being so nervous and rabbity. Not everybody was a crazed stalker, out to slit my throat. Just to reassure myself, I looked back one last time.

My heart didn't so much rev as stop completely. The guy was only half a block away and something was very wrong with his face. As he picked up speed and closed the distance between us I finally figured out what it was. He was wearing a mask.

chapter twenty-nine

My legs, already weary and sporting a deep ache from the gym, nearly went out from under me. Then the guy started sprinting and I literally felt adrenaline spurt from the gland and didn't have to tell myself to move, I was running, thongs slapping the pavement, arms pumping. My backpack slapped my shoulders and buildings blurred as I flew by.

I knew I couldn't keep up the pace for too long; already my chest was tight and I could hear him gaining ground behind me. I glimpsed a crossroads ahead. Desperate to get off the deserted street I darted left, praying it led to St Kilda Road.

It finished in a dead end at the back of something called Arts Building B.

I stopped, planning to swivel and take a frantic swing at my pursuer, maybe catch him off guard, but he was too quick. Before I could turn he slammed into the back of me, we fell to the concrete, and for the second time in an hour my skin was scoured and I was gasping for breath.

I didn't have enough oxygen in my lungs to scream, so I bucked and wriggled, frenzied as a vet-bound feline. He grabbed the hair at the base of my skull like I really was a spacked-out cat, lifted my head off the footpath and pressed something sharp into the side of my neck.

I stopped thrashing and stayed perfectly still except for a slight shudder as I breathed in footpath-flavoured air. The guy was astride me, basically sitting on my butt. His fist was tight and my scalp burned where he was ripping out hairs. His scratchy breathing was amplified by the mask and he smelled of sweat, cigarettes and something sweet and boozy. Bourbon? Funny what you notice when you're sure you're going to die. I also observed an abandoned hair elastic on the pavement in front of me and was just debating whether it would be gross and unhygienic to wear something I'd found in the street when a vein throbbed, right near the point of what I assumed to be the knife. Or maybe it was pressing on an artery? Words like carotid and jugular sprang to mind and I finally focused on what was happening to me.

'Fancy meetin' you here,' my assailant said. He had a whiny ocker accent and a raspy voice. I couldn't remember hearing it before.

'Who are you?' I choked out.

'Your worst nightmare.'

Corny, but it turned my spinal cord to ice.

'No, really,' I gasped and tried to swallow. Impossible with my head reefed back. 'Who are you, what do you want?'

'Who am I?' His laugh was a wheezy staccato intake, like Mutley the cartoon dog. 'Who do you reckon? I'm the king, baby, the fucken king.'

I thought he was truly unhinged, until he jerked my head to the side and bent down. The cheap plastic mask had a black painted quiff, pink sneering mouth, and dark brows above cut-out eyeholes. Elvis.

'Be-bop-a-lula,' he said, pushing my face back into the concrete and sitting up again. My lower back throbbed, my arse went numb and I decided not to mention that Gene Vincent had actually recorded the song first. He took his hand off my hair but kept the knife in place.

'I like Elvis,' I mumbled, partly because it was true, mainly because I'd read somewhere that if you could establish a personal connection with an attacker they were less inclined to gut you like a trout.

'I fucken don't.' He was tugging at my backpack strap now, pulling it off my shoulder and sliding the bag down my arm. 'Tunes for pooftas and old cunts. Acca Dacca's the go, but the costume shop didn't have Bon Scott.'

I willed someone to walk past the lane, but the College of Arts was shut up for the holidays. A car drove down the adjacent street, headlights pointing the wrong direction to illuminate the dead-end lane. Even if I screamed I doubted a driver would hear me over the engine, and it was likely to get me stabbed in the neck.

I heard Elvis Mask dump the contents of my bag onto the footpath, my notes sliding out of a cardboard folder, keys and change jangling. What did he want with my stuff?

'You're the guy who sent me the letter, right? Slashed my tyres, ran my car off the road?' Although I was acting casual and conversational, I felt stupid as self-pitying tears glazed my eyes.

'Clever girl. You work that out all by yourself?'

'How'd you find me?' I asked, still attempting the personal connection thing with a bit of ego-appeal thrown in. 'I was looking over my shoulder all day. You must be good.'

'I am,' he said matter-of-factly. 'Plus I got a knack for being in the right place at the right time.'

'Huh?'

'Thought the evenin' was a write-off when the slut showed up with them Claytons cops. Couldn't believe it when you run up and the fat one knocks you arse over tit. Fucken bonus.'

It took me a second to pick up on the ramifications of what he'd said and I wondered if I'd heard him right. He'd been threatening me two seconds after I'd started investigating for Liz *and* he was the guy Nick had warned Desiree about? I didn't get it. What was the connection? Despite the danger I couldn't help but ask.

'Why are you after Desiree? What did Nick and Isabella do? And JJ?'

He didn't reply, just shuffled through my files.

'Okay then, what have you got against *me*?' I asked.

Still nothing, just the sound of papers being stuffed into a bag.

I searched my memory, desperately trying to find a link, and remembered Desiree telling me to stay out of it unless I wanted to end up like Isabella. Shit, I'd found her body, it had been in the news . . .

'Did you . . . ?' I had a hard time getting it out. 'Are you the one who . . . ?'

Another zipping sound, then he shifted his weight, grabbed the scruff of my neck, and once more I caught a whiff of the fags and chemical-smelling sweat as he leaned forward. Out of the corner of my eye I glimpsed his gloved hand holding a huge hunting knife with a black rubber grip and a blade of shiny stainless steel. Every cell in my body seemed to dissolve.

'Did I what?' he cooed softly into my ear, an Aussie thug's version of coy.

'Is—Isabella.' Her name stuck in my throat. 'Is it because I found her body? I swear, I didn't see who did it. I didn't find any clues. I just, I just spewed my guts out and ran.'

'I know. Saw you piss-bolt down the street,' he said.

He had to be Isabella's killer. I was dead. I let out an involuntary whimper.

'Awww.' He released my hair, clumsily patted my head and put on a goo-goo voice, as though talking to a toddler. 'You scared? Don't worry, I'm not gonna kill ya—well, not today. I don't have the, whatchamacallit? Facilities. I don't have the right facilities.'

Facilities? What the hell was he talking about? He was crazy, had to be. The mask, the different voices.

'Why do you want to kill me at all?' I croaked, hoarse with fear.

'That's for me to know and you to find out. Tell you what though, it's going to be a hell of a show.'

Show?

His palm thumped my head again, an evil child tormenting a pet.

'You know what I like about you, Simone? You don't run whingeing to the snouts, even though you're rooting one of the filthy fucks. Now, I reckon you're probably so scared you're about to piss your little panties, but I'd stick with that policy, yeah? Make things hard for me and there'll be penalties, yeah? Know all about your friend Chloe, the banged-up slapper. And your mum in Sydney with that faggot brother of yours. Oh, hang on, they're not in Sydney, they're up north with the ferals for New Year's. Then there's your boyfriend. Don't think we can't get to him just 'cause he's a dog cop. I could waste him easy. One bullet.' He made a shooting noise in the back of his throat and coughed his abrasive laugh.

Anger at him threatening my friends and family caused a familiar red mist to cloud my vision, but it was tempered by paralysing fear and all I could do was lie there inhaling concrete dust and shaking, thinking about how he'd said 'we'. Was it a slip of the tongue? If not, who was 'we'? And were my mum and Jasper really up north? I'd thought they were in Sydney.

He finally got off me. My lower back tingled as the blood flowed back in.

'Be seeing ya,' he said.

chapterthirty

The freak in the mask walked off and I lay on the roadway shivering, astonished to find myself alive. After a few minutes I sat up and checked my bag. My wallet had been opened and appeared as though it had been riffled through, and the Nick Austin file was gone.

I tried to remember what I'd had in there. Printouts of articles I'd found on the web. Notes I'd scrawled about my conversations with Jenny and Rod, diagrams connecting people, question marks, circled names. Near impossible for anyone else to decipher.

Had he taken my file in the hope it would lead him to Nick? No wonder Nick was running. Of course, that raised another question: if Elvis Mask really was the murderer, why hadn't he killed Nick when he'd slaughtered Isabella? Nick had been out cold, would have been easy. Dead men couldn't make pay-offs, but pay-offs to who, for what reason, and what the hell did it have to do with me?

I knew there were quite a few people who wouldn't have minded catapulting me into the next life—relatives of bad guys who'd met worse ends, and the odd scumbag I'd had a hand in sending to jail—but I just couldn't figure out the Nick Austin connection. Nothing about the whole damn mess made sense.

I grabbed my mobile from my bag and sent my brother a quick text asking if he and Mum were still in Sydney, then hauled myself to a standing position, a full-body ache leaching from my muscles right into my bones. Shuffling derro-like out of the lane, I winched my shoulders to my ears in anticipation of mask-guy leaping out, gibbering old song lyrics and hackneyed threats. They didn't relax until I finally shambled onto St Kilda Road and saw the police complex ahead.

For once, the office block full of uniforms and guns seemed a warm and kindly place and I instinctively made for it, ready to tell Sean and Detective Talbot everything. I pulled out my mobile to call Sean, see if he was still at work or waiting at the pub, but it beeped before I could dial. A message from Jasper: *Nah, sis, drinkin mango daiquiris @ Beach Hotel Byron. Wish u were here. When u gonna make up with ma?*

My body pulsed like I'd just licked a live wire. Someone really was watching them, someone who knew more about their whereabouts than me. My phone chirped again—another text, from a private number: *Penalties.*

I was at the steps that led to the lobby of the police complex and stopped short, whirled around and scanned St Kilda Road. Cars and trams hurtled past and the warm evening air was filled with beeping horns and ringing bells. Men and women in suits bumped into me as they brayed into cell phones, shiny shoes thwacking the pavement.

The guy could have been anywhere and I wouldn't have recognised him; I didn't have a clue what he looked like without the mask. All around me headlamps blazed and tail-lights flared, traffic signals flashed red, amber and green—so much light and movement it was dizzying. Much as I wanted to race to the cops and throw myself upon their mercy I just couldn't, not until I came up with some sort of plan to guarantee nobody else got hurt.

I was walking away from the building slowly and carefully, hoping the guy could see I wasn't trying to make things 'hard' for him, when I felt hands dig into my ribs from behind and I jumped, letting out a mouse-like squeak.

'Whoa, babe, it's just me.' Sean was laughing until he saw my face. 'Shit, sorry, hon. Is something wrong?'

I shook my head, no, before I felt warm tears stream down my cheeks.

'What's wrong?' He held me at arm's length, looking me up and down, and I followed his gaze, taking in my dirty singlet and ripped jeans, rust-stained around the knees from reanimated carpet-burn scabs.

I had no idea what I was going to say until the words were already out of my mouth: 'I fell over!' I laughed a little too hysterically through the tears.

'What?'

'Yeah, just now. I was getting off a tram and I fell down the steps onto the footpath.'

'You're not usually that unco. Are you pissed?'

'No! I was just at the gym—' I pulled one of my new trainers out of my backpack to prove it—'and I went so hard on the squats and lunges that, like, my legs went all wobbly. Seriously, I can hardly walk.' I thumped my quads with my fist for emphasis.

'Are you really hurt?' he asked.

I shook my head and forced another carefree laugh, just in case Elvis Mask was watching. 'Nah, I think I started crying from the shock and embarrassment more than anything. Tell you what though, I could use a drink and a cigarette.'

He studied my face a few seconds longer, like he was deciding whether to believe me or not, then laughed and wiped the tears from my cheek with his thumb.

'Yeah, me too.' He hooked his arm through mine and we crossed St Kilda Road to the Amberoom, on the ground floor of the Royce Hotel. Outside tables catered for smokers and I hoped my attacker would be able to see me from the footpath, laughing and joking, and realise I wasn't about to dob him in. I couldn't live with myself if I got anyone else killed.

The bar had been renovated with lots of brown suede, amber lighting and a shimmering gold-beaded curtain that made me think of that seventies nightclub Studio 54. It was a little bit fancy and I figured that with my torn jeans and dirty singlet I'd better stay outside while Sean went in to buy drinks.

He returned with champagne for me and a vodka and cranberry for himself and threw a packet of Marlboro Lights and a book of matches on the table. As I sipped my drink I watched him take off his jacket and loosen his tie.

The pushed-up sleeves, open shirt and tousled hair gave him a kind of dissolute look and I had a sudden urge to pounce, push him to the footpath and straddle him. It was weird, but almost getting wasted made me frisky as a rabbit on Spanish fly. Must have been some evolutionary, biological thing, a last gasp at passing on the genes.

I realised Sean was asking me something.

'What was this news you had to tell me?'

'Oh, it wasn't all that special . . .' I sipped my champagne.

'Don't make me interrogate you. I can do incredibly painful things with phone books and bags of oranges.'

'Well . . .' I drew it out until he leaned over like he was about to pinch me. 'Hitch up the tuk-tuk, baby, we're going to 'Nam.'

His face split into a huge grin and he grabbed me and pulled me onto his lap, spilling my champagne and making me squeal. People looked over, but Sean didn't care, just bent me backwards and kissed me, old Hollywood style. A couple of suits at the next table stuck their cigarettes between their teeth and applauded. If Elvis Mask *was* watching he'd be damn sure I hadn't dobbed him in.

'That's awesome,' Sean finally said, pulling me back into a sitting position. 'Just one thing. Tuk-tuks are from Thailand. It's cyclos in Vietnam.'

'Whatever.' I drained what was left in my glass and noticed my hand was still shaking. 'Get me another champagne.'

chapter thirty-one

The next day was New Year's Eve, and Tony followed me, as arranged. I went to the gym, had a late breakfast at the Turtle Café, did a little grocery shopping, tried on clothes I couldn't afford and finally went home, waiting anxiously for Tony's call. If I could just find out who the guy stalking me was . . .

'There was no one there,' Tony said.

'You sure?'

'Sure I'm sure. I was watching for six hours. You sound disappointed.'

'Nah.'

Just a day late, and a buck short, as per usual.

'It's frustrating,' I said. 'I'm sure he'll be back as soon as you leave.'

'Want me to stay on you? I could do another hour or so, but the wife and I are going to a party.'

'No, it's fine. Thanks, Tone.' I hung up the phone.

At five o'clock I drove to Balaclava, keeping a lookout for guys in Elvis masks, seeing none. I had to meet the girl with the masquerade costume upstairs at Chloe's at six and thought

I'd put in a little time at the computer first: do another internet search, reprint the stuff that had been taken along with my file, see if I could learn anything about JJ.

As I booted up the hard drive I heard a thudding bass line and a stretchy, groaning sound coming from the ceiling that indicated people were moving around above me. Just because the girls were working on New Year's Eve didn't mean they weren't celebrating as well. Chloe's flat was gonna be party central while they got ready and when they stopped over between shows.

I was glad she wouldn't be alone. Just thinking about Elvis Mask gave me a shiver that rippled up from the base of my spine and shook my shoulders. Was it more terrifying because I hadn't seen his face? I desperately wanted to call the police, but realised it would be stupid to take that risk unless I knew who was after me and why.

If only I could find Nick. He knew the answer, and when I was done throttling him for ruining my life, I'd ask what it was.

I googled Nick Austin, Isabella Bishop, Desiree and JJ all in the same search line without expecting to get a hit on such a broad query, but I did. Just one. I clicked on the result and a PDF file opened up. A program for a writers' roadshow. Writers' roadshow . . . I realised I'd heard of it before—Nick's ex-wife Jenny had told me it was where he and Isabella first met. And Desiree and the mysterious poet JJ, it seemed. I printed out the document and leaned back in my chair, skimming through it.

The event was described as a 'regional literature initiative' sponsored by the government through the Australia Council for the Arts, and had taken place three years earlier. Basically, they'd packed a bunch of writers into a minivan and driven them around country Victoria, South Australia and New

South Wales where the authors had held talks at schools and libraries and conducted writing workshops. The trip had taken six weeks and covered several thousand kilometres. Desiree hadn't been there for the whole thing, I noticed. She'd just put in a couple of days in Broken Hill, running a workshop entitled 'Writing Real Life'.

I flipped to the back of the document and found the participants' biographies. JJ's full name was Jerome Jones and his photo showed a good-looking black guy in his late twenties, wearing a black suit, skinny tie and pork pie hat. I read on: *Jerome Jones, aka JJ, is a Nukunu person from the Southern Flinders Ranges. An award-winning poet and playwright, he is currently completing a PhD in Creative Writing at the University of Adelaide.*

The good old 'I'm getting somewhere' buzz started humming through my brain. Theories and scenarios flitted in front of my eyes, and one in particular seemed to make sense.

Far as I knew, the roadshow was the only place they'd all been together at the same time. Elvis Mask was after all four of them, so what if something had happened on that trip? But what? It wasn't like a randy football team or drug-fucked rock band had come rolling into town. Didn't writers spend all their time hunched behind desks, or lounging around bars in cravats and elbow patches, pontificating on the death of the novel? They weren't troublemakers. What could they possibly have done to make that psycho so hell-bent on eviscerating them?

I needed to speak to JJ, and the other writers who'd been there. Looking through the rest of the bios I discovered there were three more; judging by their pics, they were all aged in their fifties or sixties. Cecelia Levy wrote children's books, Thomas Finch's forte was historical fiction, and Albert Da Silva was a literary author.

I could bugger around for hours searching the hard way, like I had with Jenny Clunes, but I didn't have time. After New Year's, Sean had four days off and most if not all of my operations would have to be suspended. I needed to find out as much as I possibly could, and fast.

I called Tony and asked for one final favour. He said he'd get on it, find the authors' details and text them to me.

Glancing at the time in the bottom right-hand corner of the computer screen I discovered it was after six. If I didn't motor I'd miss the boat. Literally.

chapter thirty-two

The metal steps clanged as I shot up the back stairs. All the strippers' drivers had congregated on Chloe's deck and were sitting at the green plastic outdoor setting or leaning on the railing between the potted palms, chatting, smoking and drinking Coca-Cola out of sweaty red cans. I waved to them on my way through.

Inside it was chaos. Fifteen or so dancers milled around in various stages of undress, applying body glitter and false eyelashes, laughing, screeching, drinking champagne. French perfume and cheap body-spray mingled, hovering like a mist in the air, making my nose twitch and my eyes water. Loose sequins crunched underfoot and the carpet was covered with so many boa feathers it looked like someone had just butchered a flock of multicoloured chickens. A couple of girls were showing each other moves on the practice pole as 'Sexyback' boomed out of the stereo.

The scene made me nostalgic for New Years past as I remembered Chloe and me getting ready, high on nerves and the odd line of low-grade speed. Part of me wished I was performing, feeling sexy in fishnets and feathers, getting a rush from the applause and the sheer fun and abandonment of dancing around naked. It was hard to let go of, but I had to. I guessed we both did, now that she was a single mum to be and I was, well, pretty much an unemployed housewife.

My best friend reclined on her red lip-shaped couch, drinking champagne and shouting into her mobile phone. A stretchy baby-pink tube top rode up over her belly and a black skirt in the same fabric slid below.

I picked up the bottle of sparkling from her desk, found a plastic cup, filled it, and had to remove a rather brutal looking black dildo from the couch before sitting down.

Chloe hung up the phone, put her arm around my shoulder and kissed me on the cheek.

'Happy New Year, mate. It's been fucking crazy here, everybody wanting last-minute shows. Don't wanna do one?'

'Can't.'

We pressed our plastic cups together and took a sip.

'Don't give me any crap about drinking,' Chloe said.

'Wasn't gonna.'

'There's that much other shit around I haven't touched. Fucking Curtis. Soon as this parasite's out I'm going on a binge. Right in the hospital room. What do you reckon? Coke, E's, bit of Louie. Maybe a trip. I haven't had acid for years.'

I felt exhausted just thinking about it.

'You might have to wait until you finish breastfeeding.'

'Fuck that. The thing's having a bottle.'

I couldn't be bothered arguing with her.

'How's the case going?' she whispered.

I told her a few things, leaving out the death threats. I didn't think I should stress her unnecessarily, given her condition.

'How are you going with the books? Any clues?'

'I couldn't get through *Thrill City*,' she admitted. 'The first bit was okay, this chick brains a speed dealer with a replica Harley, but then she just sort of wanders around thinking about shit and I got bored. I like Nick's books, but then I get so into them I forget I'm supposed to be looking for clues. Rod's are okay, but they're a bit unrealistic. Every time his hero gets in trouble he has this mini jet pack that gets him out of it. Dunno about the sex scenes either. What's a pudendum?'

'A pussy?' I wasn't exactly sure myself.

'Oh. Thought it was a sexually transmitted disease.'

'Well, keep going. You might find a clue yet. Here—brought you some more books.' I handed her Desiree's Christmas two-pack. As long as Chloe was reading, she wasn't out following me around. 'Is the chick here with the dress? I really have to get going.'

'Porsche!' She waved at one of the pole girls then pointed to me.

A dark-haired Italian-looking girl disentangled her long limbs from the pole. She was all of twenty-one, my height and had a classic gymnast's body except for the fake tits. She disappeared into Chloe's bedroom and came back carrying a plastic-sheathed gown with the reverence of a Renaissance Madonna holding the infant Jesus.

'Portia, is it? Nice to finally meet you. I'm Simone.'

'Not Portia, *Porsche*.'

A lame joke popped out before I could stop it: 'You look more like a Ferrari.'

'I know.' She sighed. 'But that name was taken.'

'How about Datsun 180Y?'

Porsche appeared unamused and looked me up and down with an expression that said she'd heard all about me and wasn't sure she approved. I couldn't win a trick. The straight world thought I was too bent and the bent world assumed I was too big for my thigh-high boots. Chloe's phone trilled Abba's 'Happy New Year' and she picked it up and waddled to the desk to answer.

'I don't think I should lend you the costume,' Porsche said.

'Why not?'

She huffed and rolled her eyes as if it were so obvious I shouldn't have bothered asking.

'Firstly, I was going to wear it tonight. Secondly, I don't want it wrecked. Or *stretched*.' She stared pointedly at my midsection. 'This gown is custom made. The skirt is attached to the bodice with Velcro for easy removal and the corset, fully lace-able at the back, can be released with a zip that's hidden at the front. The fabric's from Italy and the outfit was vital in me taking home the runner-up sash at the Miss Erotica state finals. It cost me over a thousand bucks, it's original and I'm sooo sick of people copying me. Like, I was doing pearls and then everyone started doing pearls?'

I didn't tell her it had all been done before. Schoolgirls, secretaries, police women, harem girls, nurses, brides. Girls working hot had shoved in and pulled out anything that would fit up their twats. Vibrators, fruit and veg, you name it. I'd heard of live frogs, but I didn't know if that was an urban stripping legend. I wouldn't have been surprised to find out it was true.

'I'll take very good care of it.'

All I got was a sour look, so I continued: 'And, you know, if you've lost income from not wearing it I'll hire it off you. How's a hundred? No? Two.'

Nothing.

'Two fifty and I'll get it dry-cleaned. I'm not even stripping out of it, just wearing it to a party.'

After a long pause she said, 'Okay.'

'Show me how to put it on?'

We went into Chloe's bedroom. Tiara, the skinny blonde, and another girl were smoking out of a glass pipe. I thought it was some kind of newfangled bong until I remembered Chloe telling me about Tiara's fondness for ice. Tiara started, thinking I was Chloe, then gave me a challenging look when she saw me check out the pipe.

I ignored her. I didn't give a shit what she did. It was none of my business and I'd never been an angel. They left soon after. The room smelled of burning chemicals, like when you accidentally throw plastic into a fire.

I undressed to my knickers and bra and Porsche helped me slide into the corset and step into the full, hooped skirt. She had to loosen the laces.

'Lucky you have such small boobs or there's no way you'd fit,' she said.

I sighed and looked skyward.

chapter thirty-three

The cab dropped me off at the eastern end of the casino, just before Queens Bridge, and I power-walked along the promenade to the dock where the party boat was moored. The riverbank and restaurants were packed with people, all there to see the fireworks, and my get-up prompted a few people to nudge each other and wolf-whistle.

The MV *Neptuna* was hard to miss, a two-storey paddle steamer all done up with lights, orchestral music emanating from the top deck. A red carpet, its entry barred by two burly security guards, stretched from the promenade all the way up the gangplank and was surrounded by press photographers. Women in glittering ballgowns strolled down the carpet, arm in arm with men wearing flamboyant suits. Their feathered and sequined masks were attached to sticks so they could easily expose their faces as they posed and simpered for the paparazzi. I recognised a few people from the social pages at the back of the Sunday papers: weathergirls, pay-TV hosts, socialites.

I slipped my mask on. It was made of black felt, shaped like cat's-eyes and secured to my head with a thin band of elastic, which suited me just fine. I didn't want anyone seeing my face. The bouncers scanned the barcode on my invite and unlatched the velvet rope to let me in.

Photographers asked who I was, but I ignored them, hitched my skirts and rushed up the gangplank. Cinderella in reverse, racing *towards* the ball. Once I was onboard a liveried waiter handed me a glass of expensive-tasting champagne and I followed the rest of the crowd through a lower deck done up with red velvet curtains and gilt-edged mirrors. I couldn't tell if the place was supposed to resemble a fancy brothel or a salon in the Palace of Versailles.

The top deck was open to the sky, and decorated with more of the ornate furniture I'd seen below. Couches, poufs and Louis XIV chairs had been pushed to the edge of a dance floor packed with guests chattering and quaffing champers. Coloured lanterns dangled from the railings, and at the rear of the deck I saw a small stage and a table stacked high with copies of Victoria's new book, *Masquerade.*

On either side of the table huge cardboard stands held blow-up images of the front cover. Under the title a beautiful blonde in a ballgown had lowered her mask and arranged her features into an expression of orgasmic rapture. In the background a mysterious caped figure stood beside a horse and carriage in front of a country manor.

To the left of the stage, in the corner, a string quartet played a waltz. With everyone in costume it was easy to imagine you were at a masked ball a couple of hundred years ago—if you ignored the neon lights of the Melbourne skyline on the north side of the Yarra, and the glowing casino tower on the south. Could have been a fun party if me and Chloe had been able to run amuck, but I was there to work. Not that I had a clue how I was gonna play it. I hadn't even glimpsed

Victoria Hitchens, and didn't know how the hell I'd approach her, or what I'd say when I did.

I wandered around for a while, eating canapés, trying not to drink too much, and smiling at people in a vague sort of way. Everyone had their own interpretation of the theme, and even the century, with some men in wigs and waistcoats and one guy going around like a harlequin, although he could have been part of the staff. Most of the women had gone the corset route and I was confronted by an awful lot of up-thrust breasts, some soft and pillowy, others poking out of bodices like baseballs.

Engines rumbled and water churned as the boat began pulling away from the dock, the smell of brine and diesel mixing with the perfume and hairspray of the guests. Other boats passed, strung up with coloured lights and blasting out cheesy disco or thudding electronica. We sailed past Federation Square, the tennis centre, Olympic Park and the botanical gardens, before heading back to the city. At this point the band stopped playing and a woman who looked a little like a fairy godmother took the stage and tapped the mike.

She introduced herself as Victoria's publisher and spoke for a while about how wonderful Victoria was, how many copies her books sold, and told the crowd a little about *Masquerade*, calling it 'a sweeping, turn-of-the-century saga of one woman's journey from the slums of Bucharest to the French royal court and eventually stardom on the great stages of Europe. A story of ambition, love, loss, betrayal and the wild triumphs and bitter tragedies that result when someone refuses to give up on a dream.'

She finished: 'It gives me great pleasure to welcome the woman of the hour, our lovely author, Victoria Hitchens.'

The band struck up a triumphal march, the crowd parted like the Red Sea, and Victoria made her appearance. She was done up like a Disney princess in a jewel-encrusted ivory gown, her tiny waist corseted tight and her massive jugs squeezed halfway up to her chin. Her long blonde hair was immaculately coiffed, the front strands piled on her head and secured with a diamante tiara, the rest hanging loose in waves of bouncing ringlets. I couldn't believe I'd compared myself to Cinderella. Next to her I was an ugly sister, for sure.

'Thank you so much for coming,' Victoria said, her voice low and newsreader-smooth. 'And for helping to celebrate the launch of my third novel, *Masquerade.* The idea for the book first came to me on a trip to France. I was visiting the Palais Garnier—the Opéra National de Paris—and saw an old gelatin photograph of a beautiful woman onstage in eighteen twenty-two. On my return to Australia the image continued to haunt me and eventually became my heroine, Gisele. I feel so privileged to have been the one to tell her story, and I hope you'll enjoy taking this journey with her too. As my wonderful publisher said, *Masquerade* is about believing in your dreams, having the courage to overcome adversity, and the transformative power of true love.'

As everyone applauded I heard a snort behind me and turned to see who it was. A man in a heavily brocaded evening jacket was leaning over the railing, smoking, and gulping from a wine glass covered in greasy fingerprints. He looked forty-something, with a ruddy, bloated face and thinning hair mussed by the breeze. I figured he'd been on the booze for the better part of the day. And maybe something else. The rims of his nostrils were red and matched his bloodshot eyes.

'Don't you believe in the transformative power of true love?' I asked, mock-serious.

He rolled his eyes and flicked his cigarette butt overboard, straightened up and moved closer to me. A little too close.

'Spare me. If I have to hear about one more plucky heroine getting her bodice ripped by evil Count Van-der-fuck I'm going to shoot myself in the head. Of course, it is a nice little earner. The ducks love it, moistens the gussets of their support hose. Do I know you?' He had a slightly camp, vaguely English-sounding accent which I was sure was put on.

'I don't think so. My name's Vivien, I work for Wet Ink Press.'

Vivien had been my stripping name so I always used it as an alias: easy to remember and just rolled right off the tongue.

'Hamish Kingston, otherwise known as *Mr* Victoria Hitchens.' He swayed slightly, and not just from the movement of the boat.

'Her husband?'

'Nicely deduced. Ten points for you.'

'How long have you been married?' I asked.

'Too fucking long. Ha ha. Ten years.'

'Children?'

'You have to have sex to have children.'

I pretended to laugh at his joke while he stared drunkenly at my boobs, the tops of which were wobbling above my corset like a couple of crèmes caramels. There was something deeply creepy about him, but if he'd been married to Victoria for ten years he'd have known Isabella too, so I stuck around. Wouldn't hurt to find out what he knew.

'I haven't actually met your wife, but I did know a friend of hers. Isabella Bishop? Terrible what happened.'

'Mmm,' he grunted and lit another cigarette. 'Well, people are capable of all sorts of things.'

'You think Nick killed her, then?'

'Only met him a couple of times. Seemed nice enough, but I wouldn't have been surprised if she'd provoked him. She *was* the type. I knew her quite well, she used to go out with a friend of mine, back in the days when it was all happy families and everyone was still alive.'

A waiter walked past, and Hamish clicked his fingers and grabbed another red wine from the tray.

'And bring some snacks,' he told the waiter. 'Not that horrible vegetarian tart, either. I want the Peking duck, and that thing with the salmon on it.'

'What type?' I asked him.

'Huh?'

'You said Isabella was *that type*. What did you mean?'

'A ball-breaker, drama queen. If she wasn't actually playing around on James she'd make him think she was. Great screaming rows, but she loved the attention. Even more than the money.'

'What money?'

'James was—is—an investment banker, like me. Market was going through the roof in those days: seriously, we could do no wrong, bloody rolling in it. Always said I wanted to earn my first million by thirty-five, but I'd made a fair bit more than that by thirty. Course the market's gone to shit now, but jeez we had some fun. Pity James was stuck with her. Not that she wasn't gorgeous, but what a nightmare. Now, I'd never advocate violence against women, but what she needed was a good smack. James never touched her though, supported her so she could swan around uni pretending to be a writer, then she paid him back by running off with one of her married lecturers.' The waiter arrived with a tray of canapés and Hamish took a handful, actually releasing his glass so he could eat. He licked his fingers suggestively. 'Say, why don't you take off the mask?'

'Not till midnight.'

'You're quite the mysterious minx, Miss Vivien. You know, I'm hoping that by twelve everyone will be sufficiently lubricated that the party might start to resemble the only good scene in *Eyes Wide Shut.*' He wiggled his eyebrows so that I'd get the point.

'What would your wife think about that?'

'Unfortunately, she doesn't believe in the transformative power of a good screw.'

He laughed at his own joke, then moved in close and put one clammy hand on my bare shoulder and kneaded it a little. His fingers felt greasy.

'Actually,' he said, looking from left to right and lowering his voice, 'I'm thinking it might be time for another bump, if you're so inclined.' He sniffed and rubbed his nose. Nice of him to give me so many visual clues.

'I would, but I've just seen one of our authors.' I pointed into the crowd. 'Maybe later?'

'I'll look forward to it.' He gave my shoulder another squeeze.

chapter thirty-four

Hamish headed downstairs to the bathrooms and I did my best to melt into the crowd, wondering why every sleazebag in the country seemed drawn to me. Maybe the residue of stripping clung to me like cheap perfume. Talking to Hamish had made my skin crawl and I doubted he'd told me anything useful. Only one thing stuck in my mind. What had he meant by *back in the days when everyone was still alive*? Was he just talking about Isabella, or other people who'd died?

I kept an eye on Victoria, but couldn't get near her; she was surrounded by people, constantly getting her photo taken and still being trailed by the two-man documentary team. Still, she'd been sipping champagne for over an hour and no woman's bladder was an island. She'd have to go sometime. I ate more canapés, avoided her husband, and bided my time.

Just before nine everyone gathered on the deck to watch the start of the fireworks, and I noticed Victoria slip away. I followed her downstairs to the lower deck where the toilets were located, close to the rear of the boat, and waited outside, pretending to inspect a black and white photograph of an olden-days showgirl. When she came out I almost missed her.

Instead of walking past me to ascend the stairs, she slipped off to the stern.

I followed and found her leaning on a railing, looking over the water as she lit a cigarette. She jumped slightly when she saw me.

'Sorry,' I said. 'Didn't mean to scare you.'

'Oh, it's not that. For a second I thought you were a photographer.'

'You hiding?'

'As long as it takes to have a ciggie. Can't have pictures of me smoking up a storm.'

'Why not?'

'I'm patron of the bloody Cancer Council. You try and leak this I'll deny it.'

'Secret's safe as long as I can bludge one off you.'

'Sure.' She handed me a pack of Winfield, which surprised me. I would have thought she'd have some fancy brand, Cocktail Sobranies, Cartiers or at least Dunhill. I noticed something else incongruous about her as well. Her voice wasn't nearly as well modulated as it had been up on stage. She wasn't exactly a bogan, but her vowels had lengthened and a slight ocker accent was peeping through.

'Damn this is good.' She sucked back deeply and put one foot up on the railing, not so much a poised princess as a plumber on smoko. 'Can I've a sip of your champagne?'

'Go for your life.' I handed it over.

'I hate these things,' she said.

'Cigarettes?'

'No, book launches! Does that sound awful? Most people would kill to have a book published and here I am, complaining . . .' She looked at my face. 'I'm sorry, but have we met? It's a little hard to tell with your mask. You can take it off, you know. Isn't it digging into your skin?'

'A bit.' I slid my mask to the top of my head.

'I do know you. You're from Brandenburg, right? Publicity? Editorial? I remember your face. God, this is embarrassing, but I meet so many pe—'

'We've never actually met, but I would like to speak with you. I'm Simone Kirsch.'

'I've heard that name.'

'I'm a private—'

'The stripper who found Isabella's body! Jesus. What are you doing here?' Her eyes were wide and her mouth was hanging open. She didn't look angry, just amazed. 'I know I didn't invite you and I doubt my publicist did.'

'I'm trying to help Nick.'

'Why? Didn't he burst into your place with a gun?'

'Yeah, but he wasn't trying to hurt me. I think he wanted my help. I'm working on the theory that he didn't actually kill Isabella and someone's setting him up and blackmailing him in the process. I just need to find out why.'

So much for a clever ruse. I hoped to hell she liked Nick and didn't yell for the cops.

'Did someone hire you?'

'I'm not at liberty to—'

'It was Liz Austin, wasn't it?'

Much as I tried to keep a poker face, my eyes must have widened, giving me away. Victoria smirked and took a last drag of her cigarette before stamping it out underneath her dainty slipper.

'She's older than Nick by four minutes, yet she's constantly acting like his mother. She never liked Isabella from the get-go, was always a bitch to her, apparently, a surrogate mother-in-law. I thought it was weird, like maybe there was some *Flowers in the Attic* brother–sister action going on, but maybe that's just my dirty mind.' Her laugh turned into a hacking cough.

'I can't confirm or—'

'Listen.' Victoria lit another cigarette and offered me one. I shook my head. 'I like Nick, even though I don't know him all that well, and I'd bet any money he didn't do it. But I don't have a clue who'd want to blackmail him or set him up. I don't see how I can help.'

'You've known Isabella for a long time,' I prompted.

'We're not exactly friends.'

'But you used to be. You went to school together, didn't you?'

'A long time ago in a galaxy far, far away. I should get back upstairs to the party.'

I'd gone to so much trouble, I couldn't let her go just yet. There was a sudden crack and I jumped, but it was just the fireworks starting. Oohs and aahs drifted from the top deck as a shower of multicoloured sparks fell from the sky.

'Everyone'll be watching the light show. Sit down, relax.' I pointed to the metal bench that followed the contours of the hull.

'I'll need some more champagne . . .' She pouted prettily and a touch of the old princess was back.

'Sure, wait here.' I ducked out into the corridor, down to the middle of the boat where I'd noticed the galley as I'd first come in. I poked my head in. The catering staff were all looking out the portholes, trying to see the fireworks. I grabbed a half-full bottle of Pol Roger and a clean glass from a tray left on a stainless steel bench, and motored back to Victoria before she could up and leave.

'Tell me about Isabella.' I sat next to her.

Victoria sighed and drank some champagne. 'I met her when I started at St Katherine's in year eleven. I was just a public school bogan on a scholarship and she'd been there all her life so she intimidated the hell out of me at first. She was exquisitely beautiful, fiercely intelligent, well spoken, poised. Next to her I was a bit of a geek.'

I gave her a look. 'Piss off,' I said.

'No, really. I had braces and mousy hair and was taller than everyone and flat as a tack. They nicknamed me "Plank" and made fun of the way I'd put "but" at the end of each sentence. "But what?" they'd ask. I got out of that habit pretty quick. I don't think we ever would have been friends if we weren't both smokers. We first bonded over sly ciggies in the toilets, and then later in class. We were both top in the humanities, bottom in maths. That's how I'd got the scholarship. I was good at English, but Isabella was better. I beat her in drama though. We wanted to be actresses or writers or both, and were always making up stupid plays and performing them at assemblies.

'Then Isabella had to leave at the beginning of year twelve. Her dad left her mum, ran off with some tart and hid all the money in some offshore account and that was it. There was no more money for school fees and she had to go to the local state school. The one I'd just left, ironically.'

'Couldn't she get a scholarship, if she was so good at English?' I refilled her glass.

'It was too late in the term and anyway, I had the last one. I didn't see much of her for the rest of the year but we caught up when we'd finished school. We both applied to do acting at the Victorian College of Arts but didn't get in. I took a year off to work, got a job in a clothes shop on Chapel Street, and Isabella was accepted into RMIT. Professional writing. I actually got into the acting course the next year—they like you to have a bit of life experience—and although Isabella was happy for me, I could tell she thought it was a bit shallow. She was deadset she was going to write the Great Australian Novel, but I think she did more swanning around in coffee shops smoking Gitanes and drinking black coffee than actually writing anything.

'I'd met Hamish by then—I actually sold him an Armani suit—and then Isabella started going out with his friend James. We all had a lot of fun. I had the student life, still worked in the shop a couple of days a week, but didn't have to worry about money. The boys were loaded. There were a lot of parties and holidays and fast cars. Maybe Isabella was right, maybe I was shallow, but she couldn't talk, she was getting into it too, despite her superior air, like she was a deep and meaningful artiste and the rest of us weren't.'

'So when did you have your falling out?' I asked, trying to hurry her along. The fireworks would be over soon and people would come looking for her.

'When I had my first book published. I'd tried the acting thing for a couple of years after uni, but it wasn't really going anywhere. I had the looks by that stage, I suppose, but maybe I wasn't as good as I thought I was. I got a few bit parts in soapies, a couple of ads. I tried my hand at writing a script so I could cast myself in the main part, but it was pretty dreadful. I didn't really know what I wanted to write about. Then one day I was reading this book about writing which suggested you write what you enjoy reading. I'd always had a secret addiction to historical romances that I'd never admitted to Isabella—she would have taken the piss—so I started to write my first book in that style, just to see if I could do it. I had plenty of time in between auditions and my part-time job. I used to take around a little notebook and scribble in it all the time, not daring to tell anyone what I was up to. What if I failed? The story was about this girl who grows up in the suburbs of Melbourne in the twenties and wants to be an actress and ends up in Hollywood. Bit of wish fulfilment, I suppose. One of my customers at the boutique actually worked for an agent, and I gave it to her to give to him and the rest is history, I guess. Hamish was shocked. He had no idea what I was up to or that I'd be capable of such a thing.'

'And what about Isabella?'

'She was furious!'

'So that's when you and Isabella fell out?' I asked Victoria.

'Yep. I was shocked, but I should have seen it coming. We always did have a bit of a rivalry and here she was, very publicly slaving over a novel for five years, and I come up from behind and pip her at the post. Me, the shallow actress!'

'How old were you then?'

'Twenty-six. I got a lot of publicity because I was so young, and had been on TV, however briefly, but I was shocked when it became a bestseller. I never even thought I could write a book, let alone get it published. Isabella eventually finished *The Liquidity of Desire*, but I don't think it sold very well.'

I thought of what Rod Thurlow had told me at the Villa. 'I heard the relationship ended because you started bitching her out. You were jealous of her talent.'

Victoria laughed incredulously. 'Who told you that? What a crock. She was slagging me off to anyone who'd listen, telling them I was a hack and I'd only got published because I was young and good-looking and I'd slept with the right people. She started hinting that I was too dumb to have even written the book—hello, scholarship to St Katherine's?—and she told everyone I'd had every surgery under the sun.'

'Have you?'

'Only my nose and my tits. Pretty standard for an actress. She was saying I'd had ribs removed and full-body lipo. Bullshit. I was always skinny!'

'How about when she met Nick?'

'By that time me and Isabella weren't friends, although we did see each other at festivals and functions. I thought Nick was a nice guy. We actually had lunch after they broke up. He called me, wanted to talk. He was desperate to get back together with her and asked me what he should do. Shit, I didn't know. I think she really did love him, but she couldn't handle being poor, she was freaked out by it, ever since her dad took off. Plus Nick was too nice for her. She was the type who'd walk all over the good guys, always go for the man's man, the real cock of the walk.'

'Like Rod Thurlow?'

'That dick? The trouble with those alpha types is they're like that all the time. In business, in their personal life. They go for everything in the same way they go for money.'

'Like Hamish?' It slipped out.

Victoria looked confused until I told her I'd talked to him earlier.

'He doesn't seem too happy about your success,' I said.

'He's not. He used to be okay, believe it or not. But he's turned forty and the markets have taken a dive and he's losing his hair . . .'

'Mid-life crisis?'

'Putting it mildly.'

I poured her another glass of champagne.

'So you don't know of any trouble Nick and Isabella might have been in?'

'Uh-uh.'

'Did you hear about anything happening on the writers' roadshow where they first met? Something that might have involved Desiree—the sex writer—or a poet called JJ?'

'Sorry, but I have no idea what you're talking about.'

'That's okay.'

Victoria lit another cigarette. She had a relaxed, glittering look in her eyes and seemed like she was in no hurry to get back to the party.

'It's funny talking about Isabella. Despite all the shit she said about me, I always missed her after our falling out. She was smart and witty and I'm sorry she's dead. People always ask if the heroines in my books are me and I usually say partly, but you know what? I think I've based them more on Isabella than myself.'

'How come?'

'For all her faults, Isabella was as headstrong as they come. She wanted something, she'd go for it, and she didn't care who she pissed off or offended. Me, I'm too polite, too worried about what other people think. I want to please people. I write what they want me to write. Show up at things like this and act all la-di-da like a successful female author should. I wear the suits and boof up my hair for the website pics. It's not really me. Most days I get around in ugg boots and trackie-daks with food stains all down the front. Maybe it's easy for me to play a part because of the acting, I don't know. But I do know I couldn't base my protagonists on myself because I'm hardly ever in conflict with anyone.'

'What about Hamish?'

'Only in a passive-aggressive way. It would make for a bloody boring story. Isabella could be a narcissistic bitch and a tart and she manipulated people to get what she wanted, but she was never dull. I've always sort of admired her for that.'

'Maybe you need to rebel a little.'

'Maybe I've already started.' Victoria grinned.

She stood up to get back to her guests and I thanked her for her time, told her it had been nice to meet her. It had. She was a cool chick, nothing at all like I'd expected.

Before she took a step her mobile rang. She extracted it from a small jewelled purse and smiled when she saw the display.

I thought of something I hadn't asked.

'One more thing,' I said. 'When I was talking to Hamish he said something about a few people being dead, I think. I don't know if he was just drunk or if he was talking about someone other than Isabella.'

Victoria held up one finger to me as she talked into the phone.

'Hey, babe. No, it's fine. I'm glad you called. I miss you too. Can you hold on for one sec?' She covered the mouthpiece while she spoke to me.

'Probably referring to a guy we knew whose body turned up a couple of months ago. He went to Briarly College with Hamish and James, studied economics with them, and they all worked together at McMahon's bank. He was always a bit of a sleaze so I wasn't terribly sorry to hear he was dead. You probably read about him in the papers. Shallow grave in Daylesford. Lachlan Elliot?'

Lachlan Elliot. The dead investment banker that Curtis and Andi had been writing about. The one that ice-fiend Tiara claimed to have known. Was there a connection between his and Isabella's murders?

As I left, Victoria was getting all giggly and throaty as she talked into the phone and I realised she probably did believe in the transformative power of a good screw, just not with Hamish.

Back on the top deck of the boat I ordered a glass of New Zealand sauvignon blanc as the fireworks continued to crack and burst overhead. I was happy Victoria had been so forthcoming and felt a certain satisfaction at having done everything I could with what little information I'd had. Now I could finally relax. There was nothing else I could do until the boat docked after midnight, and hell, it was New Year's Eve.

I leaned back on the bar, sipping the wine and watching the end of the light show, thinking that with Sean off work for the next few days I'd be having an enforced break from the case. It would be good to have the time to figure out what to do about the psycho who was threatening me and practically everyone I knew. I was beginning to realise I'd have to tell Sean what was going on, but I had to think about how to word it first, and we'd both have to come up with a plan to ensure no one got hurt.

If I told Sean, that would be it for me and the Nick Austin case. I hated not being able to finish what I started, but at least I'd have done all I could. I'd give Liz back the remainder of the money, less expenses, and she could decide if we'd take the information I'd gathered to the police. I wondered if the cops would make anything of the Isabella/Lachlan Elliot connection.

I hoped that my being cooperative would inspire Detective Talbot and her mates to ease up on the whole 'cancelling the licence' thing, but even if they went ahead, I guessed I didn't actually need it anymore. I was off to start a whole new life overseas. Jesus. It hadn't quite sunk in yet. I wasn't looking forward to telling Chloe. And I wasn't too keen on moving to Canberra for six months, but that was a small price to pay. I'd fucked it up royally and there was nothing left for me in Melbourne. Time to blow the popsicle stand.

I downed the wine quick smart, getting a nice buzz and feeling pretty positive, all things considered. I turned to order another, but a guy in an oversized velvet suit wearing a mask like mine pushed in first and ordered a bourbon and Coke. He had a raspy Australian accent, maybe one of Victoria's mates from the old days. The barman handed him the drink and he asked how much.

'Open bar, dude,' the barman said. 'It's free.'

'Fucken bonus.' The guy disappeared back into the crowd.

I froze. When the barman turned to me and asked what I wanted I couldn't speak. Elvis Mask had smelled of bourbon, he'd said 'fucken bonus', and when the guy in the velvet suit pushed past me I'd smelled that same chemical sweat. It still lingered in the air.

chapter thirty-five

I snapped out of my inertia. Where the hell had he gone? Standing on the bar railing I hoisted myself up, craning to look over the crowd. Holy shit. He was trotting down the stairs. Victoria was down there. No. It couldn't be. Nick hadn't told me to warn her. She hadn't been on the writers' roadshow. It didn't make any sense.

The barman, who couldn't have been a day over nineteen, was looking at me funny, like he wasn't sure he should serve me another drink.

'Get security,' I yelled over the sound of the crackers and the crowd.

'What?'

'Security!'

'We don't have any security. It's a book launch.'

'What about those big guys checking invites?'

'They're not on the boat.'

'Jesus. Down on the bottom deck, there's a guy who's probably got a knife!'

He just stood there looking at me like I was mad. A few

seconds before I'd been leaning on the bar, calmly watching the fireworks.

'Call the water police, do something!' I screamed, taking off after the guy. I didn't want to go anywhere near him, but I couldn't let him hurt Victoria. He must have seen the invite when he'd gone through my bag. I'd led him there. It was all my fault.

I pushed through the revellers, spilling drinks, calling for them to help me, shouting that there was a man on board about to kill Victoria Hitchens. Everyone looked at me like I was crazy or on PCP, but there was no time to explain.

Once through the crush I took the steps three at a time, looked around wildly for something to use as a weapon and spotted an extinguisher next to the fire alarm. I smashed the glass and a deafening bell rang out as I wasted precious seconds wrangling the device from the wall. People began to come down the stairs, looking for the fire, pointing at me.

I ran out to where I'd last seen Victoria.

I was too late. She was lying on her back and the guy was hunched over her like an evil gargoyle, hunting knife held high.

'Hey, fucker!' I screamed. I'd had an idea about spraying him with the foam but in my panic I didn't have a clue how to work the nozzle so I rushed at him and smashed the extinguisher into the side of his head. The momentum carried me forward and I rolled on top of him. The knife clattered onto the deck. I hoped I'd knocked him out.

I hadn't. Before I could get up he'd grabbed me and rolled me over so he was on top, then raised his right fist and smashed me in the face. Bony knuckles slammed into my cheekbone and my head was forced to the side. I must have blacked out for half a second, and when my vision cleared I realised I was lying next to Victoria and she was groaning and shuddering as a red stain spread across the front of her gown.

No.

The guy was still on top of me. I looked up. He'd retrieved the knife, and blood smeared the blade.

The fireworks reached their crescendo. Classical music boomed as giant flowers of light burst open behind my attacker. Below the mask his nose was long and narrow, deep furrows ploughed either side of his mouth, and he'd twisted his thin lips and broken yellow teeth into a cheap facsimile of a smile. He began to wave the knife back and forth in front of my face and his mouth was moving as though he was humming a tune, but I couldn't hear it over the din. I was so scared my legs spasmed and my feet shook. I'd met some bad bastards but this guy was fucking crazy. You couldn't reason with psychotic freaks. I started to wish he'd just get it over with, stab me instead of torturing me with the anticipation.

And then something hit him on the side of his head.

He shifted on me, looked back, and I saw the barman and a few of the waiting staff armed with brooms and mops. They were trying to whack him with the handles so they didn't have to get close. He got up off me then, let out a roar and lunged at them and they freaked and ran back inside. I did the only thing I could think of: staggered to my feet, scrambled over the railing and threw myself into the Yarra.

Despite the summer heat the river was freezing. I gasped involuntarily as I went under and got a lungful of oily water, came up hacking and spitting and surrounded by voluminous skirts which had puffed up with trapped air. I tried to bat them down with my arms as I frantically trod water.

The fireworks had finished and the air was full of a burned-out, gunpowder smell. I caught sight of the *Neptuna*, moving away from me towards the docks. The barman was yelling something from the deck and pointing. He threw a life ring but it was too far away. My heart was up in my throat, and I swivelled my head. The Yarra was full of boats, mostly big passenger vessels. They wouldn't see me. If I got hit or dragged into propellers . . . The shore was about ten metres away and I started swimming but the dress was dragging me down and then something else was too.

Someone had grabbed my foot.

I tried to swivel but it was impossible in the dress and then Elvis Mask was on me, scrambling up my back like a rat, pushing me under. River water flooded my mouth and nose, scalding my sinuses, gushing down my throat. His hands were all over my back and neck and his fingernails were scratching me, and the more I struggled the further down I went.

I went limp. There was no air in my lungs and my dress was saturated so I sank rapidly, taking the bastard down with me. He quickly let go, floating up, and I opened my eyes to coloured lights shafting through dirty water. Boat engines emitted muted clanks and I felt strangely calm—until my chest started burning and every cell screamed for oxygen. I kicked up, surfaced, gasped and he grabbed me again, this time around my hips, fingers clenching the skirt. I kicked again, slowed by the water, but when my foot hit his body I thrust forward. As he yanked me back, the Velcro connecting the skirts to the bodice ripped free and I was released from the sodden material, heading for the riverbank, swimming for my life.

chapter thirty-six

I sat in the same grey interview room at the police complex, dried off, hair still damp and stringy. The police had taken away what was left of Porsche's dress and given me a dark blue tracksuit with a Victoria Police logo to wear. Sipping a cup of soapy instant coffee I couldn't stop shivering, even though it was warm in the room. Probably still suffering from shock. My cheek throbbed where I'd been hit, and although the ambos didn't think it was broken, they wanted to take me to hospital for an X-ray to make sure. I'd refused and insisted on St Kilda Road and Detective Talbot. I had to stop the madness once and for all.

Dianne Talbot looked like she'd just come from a New Year's Eve party. She wore smoky eye makeup, gloss over the usual plum lipstick, and her bob was kicked out at the ends. A sleeveless little black shift dress showed off her sinewy arms, and silver heels made her calf muscles stand out like tennis balls.

'The attack on Victoria Hitchens is connected with Nick Austin,' I said.

That got her attention.

'But I'm not saying anything until you do something for me. I need my mother and brother, and my friend Chloe, in protective custody and I need to know that Sean is safe. The same with Liz Austin and her mother and brother.'

'What's this about?'

'I'm not saying anything until I know they're alright.'

An hour later Talbot was back, telling me that Jasper and Peta were with the Byron Bay coppers and Chloe was at the St Kilda Police Station on Chapel Street. Sean was on his way. Liz had refused to leave her flat, so was under police guard. No one was happy about it, apparently, but I didn't care.

Talbot and her offsider, the paunchy Jefferson Archer, sat in front of me. Talbot had a file with my name on it that appeared to be even fatter than the last time I'd seen it. The video camera was in the corner, red on-light an unblinking eye.

'How's Victoria?' I asked.

'In surgery. Looks like she's going to make it. The bones in her corset stopped the knife from penetrating her heart.'

Relief flooded my chest. Thank god.

'Have they caught the guy who attacked us?'

'No.'

'Found his body?' I asked hopefully.

A headshake.

'How'd he get on the boat?'

'Mugged a guest and stole his clothes and his invitation. The man's at the Alfred with head injuries.'

'You ready to talk?' Archer growled. 'You said the attack had something to do with Austin. Was he there?'

'No, I don't know where he is. But the guy who stabbed Victoria is the same one who killed Isabella. He and his cronies set Nick up for the murder and are demanding he pay out a large amount of cash. I don't know what they've got over

Nick, but they're also threatening to kill Nerida Saunders—aka Desiree—and a performance poet slash uni lecturer called Jerome Jones, from Adelaide. Desiree and Jerome were on a writers' travelling roadshow thing with Nick and Isabella a few years back. That's the only way I can connect them. Victoria wasn't, so why she was targeted I don't know. I also don't know why they want to kill me.'

''Cause you're a pain in the ass,' Archer suggested. Talbot shot him a censorious glance and he looked down and clicked his pen.

'I started getting death threats just after Nick got shot in my flat,' I said.

'Why didn't you report them?' Talbot asked.

I shrugged. 'I didn't take them seriously at first. Thought someone was just trying to wind me up. But then I was attacked by the same guy who stabbed Victoria. He was wearing an Elvis Presley mask and he held a knife to my throat.'

'And you didn't report that, either?'

I hated Archer's smug, jowly face. 'No. He said he'd kill my family, Chloe and Sean if I talked to the police. Which is why I just asked you to protect them. He knew exactly where my mum and brother were, even though I didn't, and he said, *Don't think we can't get to them. We.* That's why I reckon he's not working alone, plus he's too fucking deranged to be organising the whole thing himself. Someone else has to be pulling the strings.'

'How come you know all this about Nick Austin? Detective Talbot told you to stay out of it.'

Time for the ruse I'd made up in the hour they'd left me alone.

'I was, but the timing of the threats made me think it was connected to Nick so I did a little digging around, trying to find enough information to protect myself. I wasn't breaking any laws.'

'Why'd you want Liz Austin in protective custody?'

'I have reason to believe she's in danger if Nick doesn't cough up enough money.'

'How did you find out this mystery . . . cabal are squeezing Austin for cash?' Talbot asked.

'Because the same person who told me Nick's family were in danger also lent him forty grand to pay them off. Wasn't enough, though. I think that's why he won't go to the police. He gives himself up, they don't get paid, and his family and friends get killed in retribution.'

'So who lent him the cash?' Talbot asked.

'Look, I promised I wouldn't say.'

Talbot rolled her eyes, flipped through her file and scanned a printout.

'We already know Elisabeth Austin withdrew forty thousand dollars from her bank account a week ago. Liz. That who it was?'

I shrugged. You didn't break client confidentiality, especially when you were working illegally.

Talbot sighed. 'We've had her under surveillance.'

Shit.

Archer piped up. 'She wouldn't have hired you to look for him, would she?'

'My licence is suspended.' I tried to look sincere. 'That would be against the law.'

I was there for hours, being honest when it counted, telling half-truths when I had to, and refusing to answer the occasional question if I thought it might incriminate me. They kept trying to trip me up but I stuck to my story, refused to implicate Liz over the forty grand, and said I'd managed to slip past the party security without an invite.

I let Talbot know that Isabella had been acquainted with Lachlan Elliot, but if this news got her juices flowing, she didn't give any sign.

By the time someone had formally typed up my statement, it was three in the morning on New Year's Day.

A uniformed officer escorted me back to the same hotel on St Kilda Road that Sean and I had stayed in after Nick was shot in my flat. Sean was waiting for me, Chloe had the adjoining room and there were a couple of cops in the suite across the hall. You needed a swipe card to access specific floors so it was pretty secure, and would suffice while they figured out what to do with us. I wasn't sure what was going on with my mum. It was too late to call so I resolved to ring in the morning.

I thanked the copper and used a card to get into the room, opening the door carefully in case Sean was asleep. I hoped he was so we wouldn't have to have the 'big talk'.

No such luck. All the lights were on and he was sitting out on the balcony. Gauzy curtains trembled and unfurled in the warm predawn breeze. I said hello, but he didn't reply, or even look at me.

It could have been the same room we'd had before: identical beige stylings, fake mahogany desk, TV opposite the bed. My overnight bag sat on a chair. Sean must have gone home and packed it. He knew the drill.

I glimpsed myself in the mirror and saw that my hair had dried stiff and frizzy and my cheek was turning from red to purple, marking the spot where pain radiated out along the bone. The tracksuit wasn't a real good look either.

I should have showered, but was too bone tired. I took a singlet from my bag and a pair of Sean's boxer shorts from his, changed and pulled my hair into a ponytail. Stooping to open the fridge I plucked out a half-bottle of chardonnay and found a wine glass on a tray next to the kettle and the too-small coffee cups. Then I joined him on the balcony, the bad girlfriend, ready for my ear-bashing.

'Hey, babe.' I bent down and kissed his cheek.

He didn't react.

I flopped into the chair opposite and poured a glass of wine. Yellow as vitamin B piss and oaky as hell, but it'd have to do. Sean had a few little bottles of vodka in front of him, and the tin that contained his pipe and stash of grass. Except for the tie he was still in his work outfit: black pants and a striped shirt, rolled up to the elbows. He dragged on his Marlboro Light and looked towards the botanic gardens where the elms were huge hulking shadows. Beyond the gardens the lights of the eastern suburbs twinkled. Sound drifted up to us from St Kilda Road: speeding cars, sirens, hooting drunks.

'I'm sorry,' I said, for about the trillionth time in my life.

He still didn't say anything, or look at me, so to fill the silence I launched into an abbreviated version of what I'd told the cops.

'Bullshit.' He finally turned, his blue eyes arctic.

'What?'

'I'm not an idiot so don't treat me like one.' His Scottish accent got stronger when he was mad, and he started rolling all his r's. 'Strange that you never mentioned the death threats.'

'I didn't think they were ser—'

'You see, I don't really buy that. I think you couldn't tell me because you were hiding something—the fact you'd been hired to find Nick Austin.'

'No.'

'For fuck's sake, Simone, we were in this same room when you asked me what I'd think if you took the case. You were fishing. You did take it. It's the only explanation that makes sense. I noticed you acting weird and distant, but I put it down to the fact you've had a lot of shit to deal with, not to mention the whole moving overseas thing. I didn't say anything because I didn't want to pressure you.' He paused and shook his head. 'You really went and threw it all back in my face, didn't you? Do you have any idea what being in a relationship means? Any idea at all?'

'I—'

'It's a partnership, it's two people who care about each other supporting one another, working together, being honest, not lying and sneaking around. Do I really mean that little to you?'

'Sean.' I reached out my hand, laid it on his forearm.

He shrugged it off and stood up.

'I'm going to bed,' he said.

chapter thirty-seven

I slept fitfully, pain jabbing my cheekbone whenever I rolled over and accidentally rested my injured side on the pillow. Sean was curled into himself, his back to me, and each time I tried to put my arm around him he inched further away until he reached the far side of the mattress, teetering on the edge. I checked the red display on the digital clock every five minutes, it seemed, and by eight in the morning decided I'd had enough, and got up.

I showered and tried not to wake Sean as I dressed in jeans and a singlet, slipping thongs onto my feet. I grabbed my handbag, left the room and knocked on the door opposite. The copper, a young guy with a crumpled suit and dishevelled hair, yawned and escorted me down to the breakfast buffet in the restaurant adjacent to the lobby. The room was only half full, and he sat at a different table, drinking coffee and reading the paper.

I loaded up my plate with soggy scrambled eggs, collapsing tomatoes and small, pale sausages. A waitress poured me a cup of burnt coffee and I washed it down with some unnaturally pink juice that had been labelled 'guava' but tasted mainly of sugar.

Once it was all in my mouth there was no need for chewing. The food disintegrated into savoury water and I pushed the plate away. I couldn't help going over what Sean had said the night before and mentally attempting a moving speech in response. I saw myself starting with the teeniest bit of justification, laying on a big slab of contrition, and concluding with a double whammy: pleas for forgiveness *plus* hopes for our future life together. All going well, he'd take me in his arms while a crowd cheered, music swelled and the American flag waved in the background. I wondered if I'd get away with Victoria's quote about the transformative power of love. Probably not.

Oh god. I was so tired I was delirious. My eyelids felt raw and scratchy and my face still throbbed and twinged. I knew I should get it checked out but doubted there was anything the doctors could do for a cheekbone, short of a full head cast with two little nose-holes to breathe through. It crossed my mind to call Chloe to come join me so we could start drinking mimosas, but she usually slept till midday and was known to become violent if roused any earlier. I didn't want to deal with Sean until I had to, and preferably with a couple of cocktails under my belt to shield me against the sickening reality of my own bad behaviour. I tried to imagine how I'd feel if he'd done the same thing to me and realised he was right. I'd been a shit.

I waved over the middle-aged waitress.

'Can I get a glass of champagne?'

'We don't serve alcohol with *breakfast*.' She gave me a look.

I sat back. Could it get any worse? Well, yeah. I could be lying in the ICU at Prince Alfred like Victoria, stab wounds to the chest.

At a loss and not wanting to go back to the room I dug my mobile out of my bag and checked the messages. Twenty.

Twenty was bad. A few were from my mum so I took a deep breath and called her back. I owed her an explanation as to what was going on, and I figured that once I'd talked to her, dealing with Sean would be a piece of piss.

Soon as she answered, I did my spiel: the grovelling apology followed by approximately five minutes of half-truths that didn't seem to be convincing anyone. Silence after I'd finished. Ten seconds that felt like ten years. Finally she spoke.

'I see you haven't taken any of my advice. If anything, you've attracted more violence and negative energy into your life. I'm only going to say this one more time: it's up to you to control your spiritual destiny. I know people who can help you out with that, but not until you're ready to admit you have a problem.'

'I don't need help.' I was tearing up a paper napkin and rolling the sections into balls. 'I'm not going to be a PI for much longer, or a stripper. Me and Sean are moving to Vietnam. I'm getting a government job.'

That was supposed to be my trump card and I expected her to be surprised and happy. She was neither.

'You sure about that?' she said coolly.

'Sure about what?'

'Sean called me last night to let me know what was going on, and we had a nice long chat. He seems like a really good guy.'

Too good for you, I translated when she paused.

'The sense I got,' she continued, 'was that he's unsure the relationship is strong enough to withstand the pressures of working together and moving overseas. He's not convinced you're ready for that sort of commitment. And I'd have to agree. If you haven't worked on yourself and your problems, then moving to another country is just running away. And running away never solved anything. It's a coward's way out.'

The napkin was completely decimated and there was an intense pressure behind my eyes that I felt could only be relieved by flinging the remaining guava juice at the window overlooking St Kilda Road. I didn't, just breathed hard through my nose thinking up bitchy comebacks. *From which top fifty self-help books did you cobble together that shit?* was number one.

'So where are you staying?' I asked mildly. 'Are you still with the police?'

'No. I'm home.'

'But they're outside, right?'

'I told them their presence wasn't necessary. Jasper's going up to Brisbane to see some friends and I'm off to a two-week yoga retreat.'

'You can't,' I said.

'Really?' By the tone of her voice I could tell she was arching an eyebrow. 'Not only did I organise and pay for it months ago, but I refuse to be held hostage to this . . . darkness you surround yourself with. It's horrifying, quite frankly, and I won't be caught up in it. Not anymore.'

She hung up.

I rang back.

A recorded message told me her phone would be switched off until the fifteenth of January.

I sat there, stunned. She was blowing off the police protection and blithely skipping along to a yoga workshop, feeling secure in the knowledge that because she had good vibes, the universe would look after her. Fucking *hippies*. Unless she had a death wish since Steve had passed on. Couldn't discount that either. I wondered if it were possible to force people into police protection. I doubted it. Christ.

chapter thirty-eight

Still at the breakfast table, I fiddled with my phone. Most messages I had no intention of dealing with. I opened a text from Tony: *Emailed those details. T.*

So I had the phone numbers of the other writers who'd been on the roadshow. I looked around. No sign of Sean. Wouldn't hurt to give them a call, just to see what they had to say. I could always pass on any info to the cops, assist their investigation, win myself a few brownie points . . .

I pushed back the chair, threw my napkin on the table and walked through the lobby to the small glassed-in business centre where all my research on the case had started. I found the numbers in my inbox and called them one by one.

JJ's phone rang out, neither Thomas Finch nor Albert Da Silva picked up, and I cursed the summer holidays. I didn't anticipate having much luck with Cecelia Levy, either, but she answered on the third ring.

'Hello.'

'Cecelia?'

'Speaking. Who's this?'

'You don't know me but it's possible you've heard of me. I'm a private detective, Simone Kirsch.'

'I read about you in the papers. That business with Nick Austin.'

'That's me. Were you and Nick friends?'

'Acquaintances, I suppose. We met on a writers' thing where we went around in a minibus to rural areas for six weeks. He was a nice fellow, we got along very well, but I haven't seen him in three years. What's this all about?'

'I'm trying to help Nick,' I said. 'I believe he's been set up for Isabella Bishop's murder and I'm trying find him before some really bad guys do. He's in a lot of danger and I think it all goes back to the roadshow.'

'The roadshow? You must be joking.'

'I'm not. Can you tell me about it? Anything unusual happen? Any trouble?'

'Nothing apart from a few flat tyres. Oh, and no one turned up to a book signing in Wilcannia but that was because the local footy club was playing in the grand final. We packed in the signing and went along to watch! I suppose the only thing to happen of note was that Nick and Isabella started a romance. Oh, and JJ broke a few hearts. Poets . . .'

'Did JJ really annoy any of the locals? Stir up any green-eyed boyfriends or husbands?'

'Goodness, no. Most everybody loved him. He did workshops with the kids and organised poetry slams in the evenings. People came from miles away to read their work. It was wonderful.'

'Nerida Saunders get into any strife?'

'Who?'

'Desiree.'

'Not at all. She was a lovely, polite young lady despite her unsalubrious past. It was all a lot of fun, and to tell you the truth it reminded me of being on school camp, many years ago. Why do you assume there was trouble?'

'Isabella's dead, and someone wants to kill Nick, JJ and Desiree. The only connection I've got between them is that roadshow. I dunno. Maybe I'm clutching at straws.'

'My god, I wish I could help, but there really was nothing . . . unless something happened that I didn't know about. I suppose that's possible. The younger members of our troupe were thick as thieves, used to stay up late drinking in the local pubs while all us oldies were tucked up in bed. They never acted as though anything bad had happened, except for a few nasty hangovers. If there was any trouble they kept it very well hidden. Writers are observers, you know, so I'd like to think that either myself or one of the others would have noticed something.'

'Okay, well, thanks for your time.'

She must have picked up on the disappointment in my voice.

'Sorry I couldn't help. Actually, there are some pictures of the trip, if you'd like to have a look. They're on a photo-sharing website. Isn't this new technology just marvellous? I'll give you the address. Maybe you'll be able to find a clue.'

Yeah, right, I'll get out my magnifying glass. I didn't say it; no need to be a moll. She was a nice lady.

I typed in the URL and was redirected to a site called Flickr.com. I scrolled through the online album. In the first picture the group posed with their luggage around a white Tarago van, waving. Subsequent photos had them posing in front of town signs, and there were candid shots of all the authors conducting talks and workshops and signing books.

In the first photo Nick and Isabella were on opposite sides of the van, and it was interesting to note how they moved closer in successive photos, until in the last one Nick's arm was around her shoulder and her hand had twined around his waist. The group stood in front of a two-storey sandstone pub with a nineteenth-century gold-rush look about it. The large second-storey veranda was decorated with latticed ironwork and held up by ornate columns you'd have tied your horse to at the turn of the century. A sign on the front said Empyre Hotel.

Knowing what had happened to them made the photo kind of poignant, and I studied it for a moment. They looked so happy, and so damned young. Less than three years had passed since then, but Nick didn't have the dissipated, slightly bloated look he'd sported when I'd first met him, or the haunted, haggard appearance I'd seen when he'd burst into my flat. He looked fresh-faced and boyish; Isabella, with her longer hair and very little eye makeup, could have passed for twenty-one.

I checked out the rest of the photos. JJ wore a natty suit with a skinny black tie and trilby hat. Thomas Finch was so tweedy he should have been holding a pipe, Albert Da Silva looked like an eccentric swinger uncle with his long grey hair, open-necked shirt and velvet jacket, and Cecelia was clad in a print dress that made her look like someone's grandma, which she probably was. Desiree wasn't there as she'd only shown up in Broken Hill, but there was another guy hovering at the edge of the photograph who looked completely unaware that he was in the shot. At first I assumed he was a local because of his red-checked flannelette shirt, Ned Kelly beard and worn Blundstone boots, but I quickly realised he looked familiar. I'd met him, or at least seen him, somewhere before.

It wasn't the guy who'd attacked me. The nose and mouth were all wrong. So where the hell did I know him from? My worn-out brain wouldn't give it up so I called Cecelia back.

'Sorry to disturb you again, but the guy in the last photo with the flannie and the beard. Do you know who that is?'

It took a little while for Cecelia to boot up her computer and connect to the internet. I heard her tapping on the keyboard and humming softly. Finally she said: 'Oh, him. He was a bit of a weirdo. Knew Nick from university, lived in the area, and just showed up at one of the readings. Afterwards he ended up coming out to lunch with us. One of those anti-government, hermit types. Lives alone with no electricity or phone, no car. I don't remember what his name was, but I remember thinking he must be schizophrenic, the way he was going on about spy satellites and surveillance and the military sending out radio waves that get inside your head. He ended up having a huge argument with Thomas about politics. Thomas is quite conservative and this chap was actually an anarchist, I believe. Nick looked terribly embarrassed by the whole thing.'

An anarchist. I knew who the guy was. I minimised the internet window and clicked on the downloads icon, hoping the photo was still there. It was. Nick and Jenny at the Socialist Alliance meeting, and the wild-eyed guy with his fist raised. Even though it had been taken twenty years before I could tell it was the same person. David Geddes.

An anarchist who lived like a hermit in some bush shack. No friends, no phone, the perfect guy to hide out with. I recalled the worn red flannelette shirt and dirty Blundstones Nick had been wearing when I saw him last. There were a lot of flannies in the world, and it could have been a coincidence, but . . .

'Where was the photo taken?' I asked, blood pumping.

'Castlemaine. An hour and a half north of Melbourne. It's just past Daylesford.'

I considered calling Detective Talbot, but stopped at the thought of a bunch of cops turning up at what might be Nick's hideout. I probably hadn't convinced the police he was innocent, and even if I had, Nick didn't know. What if he and Geddes came out waving guns? Victoria Police had a reputation for being trigger happy at the best of times. I couldn't risk it.

Still, if I went up there on my own, or with Sean as backup . . . I didn't know if he'd be in it, but it might smooth things over between us if he was. I reckoned half the reason he was pissed off at me was because I hadn't included him. Sean hated injustice as much as I did, and if I laid out all the evidence he wouldn't want Nick punished or killed for something he didn't do.

Just before logging off the computer I checked my inbox. There was a new email and I felt a weird flutter when I saw the sender. Mark Koputh. My dad. Stupidly excited, I opened the email straight away. After a few lines, I wished I hadn't.

Hello Simone. It was a surprise to get your email after so many years. Since there was no contact after your last visit I'd assumed, given the unfortunate 'incident', that we'd mutually come to the conclusion that it was best not to stay in touch. After all, we hardly know each other, haven't lived together since you were an infant and have only seen each other once in, what is it, the last fifteen years? I apologise that I took so long to get back to you, but I'm afraid I wasn't all that sure how to respond. Suffice it to say, I've talked it over with Beverly, and we both feel that it's probably for the best if things remain the same. Tyler and Ashley are in their late teens and don't need any distraction from their studies, or any sort of harmful influence. I'm sorry if this sounds harsh, but we're well aware of the lifestyle you've chosen and, quite frankly, I don't think we have anything in common, or that I've got anything to offer you. Best to nip it in the bud. No hard feelings, and I wish you all the best in your future endeavours.
Mark

Some chicks might have cried. My first reaction was boiling rage. Who did that fat fuck think he was? *All the best in your future endeavours*? That was the corporate equivalent of 'piss off and die'. He was supposed to be my flesh and blood. Jesus, even my mother wasn't such a stone cold bitch. I couldn't believe Mark and his neat-freak wife were still angry about the 'incident'. I'd been a teenager, for god's sake. A teenager visiting LA who'd just been through a whole world of shit. Sure, I'd got high, brought some stranger home and broken house rules, but wasn't that par for the course? It was bad behaviour, but adolescents did that sort of stuff all the time; what about forgive and forget? I was sure it was all coming from Beverly, the puritanical slag. Still, my dad should have stood up for me.

I didn't dignify his email with an answer. Instead I went straight to the room I was sharing with Sean. The cop protecting me was so engrossed in his newspaper he hadn't even noticed I'd left.

I let myself in and found the bed empty. Sean wasn't in the bathroom or having a cigarette on the balcony either. He was gone. Really gone. He'd left a scrawled message on hotel stationery. *I can't do this anymore*, was all he wrote.

chapter thirty-nine

I picked up the Ford Futura from outside my place, drove through Elwood and St Kilda, spent about ten minutes weaving around deserted streets in South Melbourne, and when I was sure I wasn't being followed turned onto Kingsway, hit the Westgate Freeway and sailed over the curve of the bridge, heading for Castlemaine.

There was hardly any traffic, and below me the fuel refineries and container yards sparkled in the sun.

The weather didn't match my mood. I was exhilarated, near breathless with anger and listening to Rage Against the Machine's 'Killing in the Name of'. How many people had cast me off in the last couple of days? And all because I wouldn't behave like they wanted me to. Alex because I wasn't a compliant bit on the side, Mum because I didn't align my chakras and finish my uni degree, Sean because I couldn't be housetrained, and my dad had snubbed me because I wasn't some white-bread, corn-fed, bible-studying yank goody-two-shoes with a dumb-arse name like Kimber.

Screw them. I was a fairly average stripper and a damn good PI and I wasn't going to change for anyone. I was going to find Nick, figure out who was threatening me, and to hell with everyone who thought I couldn't. I turned the music up loud.

An hour and a half later I turned off the Calder and onto the Pyrenees Highway, passing hills dotted with farmhouses and thickets of gum trees. The area was elevated, and puffs of white cloud skimmed the hilltops.

As the speed limit dropped to sixty a sign welcomed me to Castlemaine, and I found myself driving down a wide boulevard lined with elm trees, their leaves deep green against the bright blue sky. It was hot and dry, and the air was spliced with crisp, medicinal eucalyptus.

I turned at a roundabout where a sign announced 'Town Centre' and drove along wide, almost deserted streets past a mixture of grand old buildings and smaller, newer shops. The town hall looked like a castle and sat next to an old sandstone telegraph station. Ornate pubs and bank buildings lined the streets, alongside antique shops for the tourists and discount stores for the locals. I eventually spotted the Empyre Hotel and parked in front, grabbing the photograph I'd printed off at the hotel's business centre. I'd zoomed in on David Geddes and cut out the others, and although it was black and white and a little blurry, he was still recognisable.

As I walked up to the building I realised that it wasn't actually a pub anymore. The downstairs area had been turned into a fancy restaurant, and a sign on the outside of the building advertised boutique accommodation upstairs. I peered through the open door where a young blonde waitress in a long black apron was setting tables. She saw me and walked over.

'I'm sorry, we don't open until midday.'

'That's okay.' I held out the piece of paper. 'I'm looking for this man. Name's David Geddes. You don't know him, do you?' It was a long shot.

She shook her head. 'Sorry. Doesn't look like the sort of guy who'd come here.'

'Do you know where he *would* go?'

One side of her mouth tugged up. 'By the looks of him you might want to try the Commercial. Turn left at the corner and one block down. On the highway by the roundabout.'

'Thanks.'

I left the car and walked past a couple of cafés, an art deco theatre, Castlemaine Cycles and a toy store with crazed-looking stuffed sheep in the window and then I was standing in front of the Commercial Bar and Grill. The building was two storeys of cream and grey brick with a corrugated-iron awning and small windows covered with so much overexcited signage it was impossible to see in. *Sizzle Steaks! Roasts! Seafood! 2 Pool Tables!!!*

The arse end of an air-conditioner poked out above the pub door, dripping water on the stoop, and a sign on the wall advised I was entering *The Smoking Gun Bar.* As I pushed the door in I hoped it wasn't prophetic.

There were five blokes inside wearing jeans and blue singlets. A couple of them were in flannelette shirts, which made me feel like I was getting closer to finding Geddes. Two were playing pool, three sat at the bar, and when I walked in they all turned and stared at the same time. It was like something out of a western and I wouldn't have been surprised if one of them had spat on the floor and said, 'Looky here, Jed, thar's a stranger in town.'

I felt like hitching up my jeans and tipping an imaginary cowboy hat, but just nodded and slid onto an empty stool. The barman, thin and tall with a shock of thick grey hair, stared at me with a faintly alarmed expression.

'Glass of champagne, mate,' I said, instantly wishing I'd said bourbon or beer. What if they didn't have any? But he walked through to the bistro, dug around in a fridge and pulled out a fresh bottle. While he was fiddling with the cork I looked around.

The public bar was the size of a large living room, with scuffed, unpolished wood floors, brown walls, and old lace curtains hanging from the windows. The furniture consisted of a few raw pine tables and chairs and a potted ficus lurking over by the toilets. On the wall above the bar there were some rather odd murals, including one of King Kong with a teeny Faye Wray in his simian palm. Directly above the top shelf liquor—ouzo, Jack Daniels, Southern Comfort—a sign read *Welcome to the House of the Mouse.*

The barman set the champagne glass in front of me. 'Four bucks.'

I paid and took a sip. Better than the house bubbly in a lot of city establishments and the price was certainly right. I decided I liked the pub. When he brought my change I slipped a two-dollar coin into a tin raising money for local Vietnam vets.

'Who's the mouse?' I asked.

'The publican. He's the mouse and, well, this is his house.'

'Fair enough.'

Everyone had stopped outright staring, and the click of balls meant the pool players had gone back to their game, but I could feel the surreptitious glances. The youngest guy at the bar cleared his throat.

'Passing through?'

He had a dark goatee, wore wraparound sunnies indoors, and tribal tattoos snaked from his shoulders to his wrists.

'Actually, I'm looking for someone.'

'Yeah?'

The pool sounds stopped. Everyone was eyeballing me again. I could feel the weight of stares on my skin.

I dug out my printed picture of David Geddes and handed it to Goatee, who passed it on to the bartender. The pool players came over, holding their cues.

'Why you wanna find him?' the bartender asked, handing the paper to a pool guy with squinty eyes and a shaven head.

'You a jack?' Shaven Head moved his mouth like a cow chewing its cud.

The atmosphere had turned hostile and a small bud of fear unfurled in my stomach. Not enough to stop me, though. I'd seen the recognition in the bartender's eyes. I drained my drink, asked for another.

'Do I look like a fucking jack? Jesus, I'm not a cop.' I leaned on the bar with an offended expression on my face, searching my brain for a ruse. Private detective would be on a par with copper. What to say? Sipping my second drink, it came to me.

'It's just . . . nah, don't worry about it. It's stupid . . .' I shook my head.

'What?' Goatee leaned forward. I got the feeling he fancied me.

I took the picture from squinty guy and I stared at it wistfully.

'I . . . I think the guy in this photo might be my real dad.'

chapterforty

'Why didn'tcha say?' The barman broke into a crooked smile and topped up my glass.

'Whaddaya mean you *think* he's your dad?' Squinty said, unconvinced.

I took a big gulp of champagne and launched into a long, convoluted impro about a family New Year's party that ended with me and my bush-pig older sister Sharon getting into a punch-up—my swollen cheek added veracity—after which she'd spat that her dad wasn't my dad and had let slip that I'd been conceived when my parents split briefly, many years ago. I made my fictitious mum out to be a bit of a slut, and said I'd talked to her and she'd narrowed it down to a couple of contenders for fatherhood and now I was on the hunt. By the time I'd finished the story and the third glass of champagne I nearly believed it myself.

The blokes all exchanged glances and finally the barman spoke. 'We know Davo. Lives around here.'

'Where?'

'Happy Valley.'

Christ, it sounded like a mental institution.

'Nearby?'

'Ten minutes, just out of town,' said Goatee. 'I've picked him up hitchin'.'

'Sure you wanna meet him?' The bartender bit his lip.

'Why wouldn't I?'

'Might not like what you find. He's a bit . . . different.'

'Don't bullshit her, Rick.' Goatee sucked on his bottle of premixed bundy and Coke. 'He's fucken mental.'

'I don't care. How do I get to Happy Valley?'

'I can show you where I drop him off, on Collers Road,' Goatee said. 'Need a ride?'

'Car's up the road. I'll follow if that's okay.'

He shrugged.

Before I left I slapped a fifty down on the bar.

'Thanks for your help, guys, next round's on me.'

The champagne, combined with success in locating David Geddes, had made me a little giddy so I slugged some water while I followed Goatee's dust cloud. The road was unpaved and wound around farmhouses, paddocks and grassed river flats. When we turned off on Collers the road narrowed and climbed, and the forest became dense. Goatee pulled to a halt in what looked like the middle of nowhere and got out of his car. I stayed in mine, dust settling on my sweating skin. Magpies warbled, the engine ticked and his boots crunched gravel.

'Nice car. A sixty-five?' He leaned a forearm on the roof of the Futura.

'Sixty-seven. Where's this house?'

'No one's seen it, but I've dropped him off right there. See the driveway? Bit grown over, 'cause he doesn't have a car.'

I turned to look out the passenger seat window and could just make out an overgrown track. No sign, no letterbox, nothing. My heart was beating hard. I tried not to get my hopes up, but it was just too perfect a hideout.

'I see it. Thanks.'

'You want me to come with you? He's a crazy old coot.'

'Nah, I'll be fine. Tell you what though, if I'm not back at the pub in two hours, you might wanna send out a search party.'

'No worries. Hey, you smoke?'

By the way he lifted his eyebrows I didn't think he meant tobacco.

'Very occasionally.'

He licked his lips.

'Do you root?'

'Never.'

He frowned, then laughed and punched me softly on the shoulder.

'You're just joshin' me. Cheeky. See you back at the pub, okay?'

'Will do,' I lied.

He got back in his ute, revved the engine like he was preparing for a drag race and performed a screeching U-turn, kicking up dust and pinging rocks off my car, before tearing off like a bat out of hell. Boys.

Soon as he was gone I drove slowly up the road, looking for somewhere to park. No way was I cruising down that driveway. If Nick was there he'd take off like a startled rabbit. About five hundred metres later I found a rutted fire trail, turned off, bounced along and stopped when the car was hidden from the road. I went to the boot and swapped my thongs for an old pair of Dunlop Volleys, left my handbag and packed a small backpack with my water bottle, camera and a pair of binoculars.

I returned to the overgrown drive and walked down it as quietly as possible, stepping around dry twigs and ducking to avoid prickly vines. The heat intensified the smell of eucalyptus until it was almost overpowering, and sweat stuck my singlet to my skin. I wished I'd changed into shorts, although the jeans protected my legs from clumps of spiky plants.

The driveway went on for more than a kilometre, angling down. Bright red and blue rosellas swooped through the trees and dun-coloured pigeons scrabbled in the undergrowth. Occasionally I heard the rhythmic thumping of a kangaroo or wallaby bounding through the scrub. A dog barked in the distance and I stopped and stiffened, but it didn't bark again and I continued on.

After about ten minutes I was beginning to think I'd missed another near-invisible turnoff when I finally glimpsed a small clearing at the bottom of the drive with a ramshackle wooden hut in the middle.

I backed up a bit, went off the driveway and picked my way through the bush, along a natural ridge that overlooked the shack. Twigs cracked, plants pierced my thighs through the denim, but eventually I found a big rock hidden behind a clump of blackberry, climbed up and sat on it. I took the binoculars out of my bag and found that when I adjusted them I could see the house through the gaps in the tangled vines.

The place looked like a one-room job, built on wooden poles. Steps led to a small veranda that leaned at a dangerous angle. The windows were too dusty to see through properly, and I didn't catch any movement inside. All I heard was birdsong and a distant creek, water burbling over rocks.

I trained the binoculars on the yard. It was full of junk: rusting forty-four-gallon drums, plastic milk crates full of yellowing newspapers and empty long-neck beer bottles, a battered Toyota LandCruiser propped on stumps.

I sat watching, waiting for something to happen and hoping that if it did, it would involve Nick Austin walking out of the front door of the house. A treeful of cicadas began a shimmering song. Sunlight filtered through the trees, sweat itched my neck, and when I scratched the skin stung. I scooped my hair up into a ponytail. I couldn't stop thinking about Sean leaving, and my dad blowing me off and everything else that'd gone wrong, but I didn't care. Anger was bloody energising, and probably the only thing that was keeping me awake. I hummed Rage Against the Machine. Fuck 'em all.

An hour later I'd seen no movement from the house and was pretty sure no one was home, but couldn't discount the fact that somebody could have been asleep in there, or quietly reading. Wanting to move things along I searched the ground around the boulder for smaller rocks, picked up a few the size of golf balls, and pegged them at the house.

The first one hit the dirt in front of the shack, but the second clanked onto the rusted corrugated iron, the sudden noise silencing the cicadas. I held my breath. Nothing happened. I chucked another onto the roof and waited. No one was home and I guessed Geddes was in town. It crossed my mind that he might have shown up at the Commercial and the guys were telling him his long-lost daughter was looking for him. Jesus. If he popped out of the bushes then I'd, well, pretend I was a bushwalker who'd gotten lost. He was harmless, wasn't he? Not like he'd shoot me or anything.

Bugger it. I was going down to check out the house.

I bashed through the brush back to the driveway, and picked my way down, involuntarily jogging down the last, steep section and staggering into the clearing. I felt exposed out in the open: my heart thumped and I had to remind myself to breathe. The sound of the creek was amplified and I smelled the cool mossy scent of fresh water and river rocks.

I circled the house. Assorted tools and building materials were scattered underneath it: a rusting chainsaw lay next to a woodpile, along with an axe poking out of a block. I had an urge to grab the axe, but it looked heavy and I thought carrying it would only freak me out more.

The Australian bush had always struck me as spooky. I kept thinking I heard something moving and whirled around, eyes straining to see past the thicket of twisted gums, but there was never anything there. I made a deal with myself. Check the rest of the grounds, check the house and you can hightail it back to Melbourne to figure out another plan.

Rounding the back of the shack, I found a metal garbage can and opened the lid. Fat flies buzzed out and a rotten stench nearly made me gag. I wished I'd thought to bring my latex gloves from the car. I gingerly picked out a big green garbage bag, set it on the ground and ripped it open, separating the detritus by kicking it apart. Old cans mainly. No-name dog chow and beans and Campbell's Chunky Beef Soup. A couple of Cadbury's wrappers, old sachets of instant mashed potato and just-add-water pasta meals. And some bloodied gauze bandages.

My skin prickled. Nick's bullet wound.

I squatted and rooted around some more with a stick, trying not to gag from the smell and the maggots, and found empty packets of antibiotics and painkillers. The prickle was turning into an electric shock. He'd been staying here, I was sure of it. Was he still here, or had he taken off? I had to get inside the house, find out what I could before anyone came back.

I stood up and smiled, wishing all my doubters could see me now. You had to admit, I was pretty shit-hot. Not even the cops had got this far. I swigged from my water bottle, walked to the front of the shack, and was about to take the first step to the veranda when my whole world turned upside down.

chapterforty-one

The leaf litter rattled, a whip cracked, and my feet went out from under me as I was hauled into the air by my ankles. It took me a few seconds to realise I was caught in a net, dangling like an orange in a bag. Nylon rope dug into my nose and cheeks and forced my arms to curl spastically into my sides. I strained to push against it but was stuck tight. Blood rushed to my head and I thought I was going to be sick. The rope creaked and the tree branch it was tied to dipped and groaned. I spun slightly and saw the cabin door open.

A man walked onto the veranda holding a blue heeler by its collar. He removed the muzzle from its snout, and the dog barked gleefully and pranced down the stairs. It jumped under the net, turning in excited circles, yapping and licking my trussed-up face.

Even upside down with one eye forced shut against the netting, I could tell the man was David Geddes. Wild grey hair tied in a ponytail, long bushranger beard. He wore an old checked shirt with the sleeves cut off, thick green socks and lace-up boots. Knobbly knees poked out of ripped khaki shorts.

If my face hadn't already been red and engorged with blood, I would have flushed with shame. God, I was an idiot. Everyone had told me he was paranoid. Probably had the whole place rigged up.

'Hi, David, think you can cut me down?'

He reared back on hearing his name, nostrils flaring, eyes wide.

'Who are you? How do you know my name?'

'I'm a friend of Nick Austin's. Simone. Nick's told me about you.' It was a struggle to move my lips against the rope and I sounded like I'd had a full dental block. 'I need his help. I'm in a lot of trouble.'

That was an understatement.

'Nick? I don't know anyone called Nick.'

Sure.

'You were at Melbourne Uni together.'

He shook his head and his eyes darted from side to side.

'Please, let me down. I think I'm going to spew.' It was true. My stomach felt like it had fallen into my lungs, and there was so much pressure in my head I thought my eyeballs were going to pop. My injured cheekbone throbbed in time with my heartbeat. I couldn't take much more.

Geddes walked back up the stairs into his hut and the dog bumped me with its snout, causing me to spin. By the time I'd completed a full revolution David was back, standing in front of me with a rifle and a bowie knife. Oh god. Just how crazy was he?

He grabbed the net and pulled it down so my face was resting against the dirt, then cut the rope, and I crumpled to the ground like a sack of spuds. The dog got really excited, slapped its paws onto my chest and barked in my face. Geddes pulled him back by the collar.

'You had no right to trespass. This is private property.' His voice was grizzled, like he was carrying a throatful of phlegm.

'Sorry.' I struggled, still unable to move. When he approached with the knife all I could do was tremble. I held my breath as the glinting steel swept past my face, but he was only cutting the net away. Soon as he was done he jumped back, sheathed the knife in his belt, grabbed the rifle and pointed it at me.

I untangled myself and sat up, rubbing my ankles where the rope had cut in.

'Your backpack. Throw it over here.'

I slipped it off my shoulders and chucked it to him. He dug in his shorts pocket and pulled out a roll of silver gaffer tape, threw it at me.

'Tie your ankles.'

I did one layer, kept it loose.

'Tighter, keep putting it around.'

When I finished he cut the tape with the knife and gaffed my wrists in front of me. He returned to the house and emerged with a packet of Port Royal tobacco and a long-neck of beer, sat on the middle step and rolled a cigarette.

The dog was sniffing around, barking in my ear.

'Kropotkin! C'mere!'

The mutt backed off when called, trotting to the base of the stairs, keeping a smug eye on me. Had to have been responsible for the bark I'd heard. Geddes must have muzzled it and they'd both hid in the house, probably watching me through a gap in the wood.

'Nick must have told you who I am,' I said, trying to keep my voice calm and even. 'The cops shot him at my flat, which wasn't my fault—I didn't know they had me under surveillance. I saw the dressings and the antibiotics. I know he's been here. Please, just tell me where he is. The guy who killed Isabella is after me too. I don't want Rod Thurlow's reward money and I'm not working with the police. I just need Nick's help. Please.' The wild energy that had got me up to Castlemaine suddenly dissipated. I was starting to crash and burn.

Geddes, infuriatingly, just sat there, smoking his rollie and swigging beer.

'I don't know any Nick.'

'Yes you do.' I was going to argue the point but suddenly didn't have the strength. I brought my thighs up to my chest, rested my head on my knees and closed my eyes. I wondered if goatee guy had taken my 'send out a search party in two hours' request seriously. I hoped so.

I wasn't sure how long I remained in that position, taped by my wrists and ankles. Five minutes, maybe ten. I heard Geddes smoke and drink and the dog chew at a patch of fur. A twig snapped and the bushes rustled on the other side of the clearing.

I lifted my head. The dog had its nose up, but Geddes seemed to be in his own little world. The shack blocked a large section of my view, and the dog ran behind it, barking.

'Aren't you going to see what it is?'

'Probably a roo.'

'I wasn't a roo.'

'You were coming down the driveway. Nothing back there but blackberries.'

But the mutt was really going crazy and Geddes frowned and stubbed out his rollie on the sole of his boot. He was just getting up when the dog yelped in pain. The undergrowth crackled, and it limped out, dragging itself under the house. Blood trailed in its wake.

'What the fuck?' muttered Geddes, standing up and grabbing his gun.

He turned, and stopped. I followed his line of sight.

Oh Jesus. A figure in cargo pants and a navy tracksuit jacket had entered the clearing and was marching around the house. His face was obscured by an Elvis mask.

'Stop!' Geddes hoisted the rifle to his shoulder and looked down the sight.

The figure halted and held up his hands in a gesture of surrender.

'Who are you?' Geddes called.

'It's the guy who killed Isabella,' I shouted. 'Shoot him!'

Geddes just stood there, looking through the gun sight. Elvis Mask inclined his head like a bird examining a worm and inched forward, dolly steps at first, becoming longer and faster each second Geddes failed to even cock the rifle. What the hell was wrong with him?

'What are you waiting for?' I screamed so loud my throat felt shredded. 'He'll kill us. Just fucking shoot him!'

As he closed in Geddes lifted the gun off his shoulder, held it like a baseball bat and took a swing. Elvis Mask had incredible reflexes: he ducked as the momentum swung Geddes around, then jumped up and rammed him in the shoulder so he lost the rifle and fell face first onto the ground. Elvis Mask leapt on his back, grabbed his hair by the ponytail and smashed his face repeatedly into the earth. Then he slipped the knife out of Geddes' belt and crouched behind him.

Geddes struggled to his knees, bleeding from the forehead and mouth. I tried to yell at him to look out but I didn't have time. Elvis Mask lunged and grabbed his throat from behind with one hand, forcing him to arch back. With the other hand he brought the knife around and plunged it into Geddes' belly one, two, three times. Blood spurted from the wounds and flicked off the blade. Geddes didn't scream, just made a sound like he'd been punched in the guts, and pitched forward.

chapterforty-two

Elvis Mask wiped the knife on the tail of Geddes' shirt and chucked it behind him. I shuffled back until I hit the tree trunk, but he walked past me, sat on the step and removed the mask.

I thought I'd reached the absolute limits of terror, but as soon as I saw the gaunt face and hollow eyes with teardrop tattoos underneath, I realised I hadn't been close. He'd let me see his face. I knew what that meant.

He picked up the long-neck of beer, guzzled it and frowned.

'Fuck, warm as piss.'

Then he grinned. His teeth were terrible. The ones that weren't missing were yellowed, chipped and broken, and his skin wasn't much better. Deep creases rutted his cheeks, and a couple of sores had scabbed over like he'd been picking at them. His hair was light brown, receding at the front, longer at the back. The dog whimpered beneath the house. Since the stabbing, Geddes hadn't moved or made a sound.

'G'day, Simone. Didn't get ta introduce myself last time. Name's Watto. Told ya I'm a lucky cunt.' He took off the tracksuit jacket and dug around in its pocket. Underneath he wore a blue singlet. Wasn't a gram of fat on him. Jail tattoos and track marks traced up his sinewy arms.

He pulled out a glass bowl—an ice pipe, just like Tiara had been smoking from—tapped crystals out of a tiny plastic bag, sparked a lighter and inhaled until there was no more smoke. Leaning back on his hands, he closed his eyes and turned his face to the sky. It was more than a minute before he finally spoke.

'Fuck yeah. That is the shit. That is the fucking shit.' His whole body shuddered briefly and he looked at me. 'You ever done crystal?'

I didn't answer.

'It's better than sex. Better than ten orgasms, all in a row. Want some?' He proffered the pipe. 'Last-time offer, act now. No? Well, fuck ya then.'

He rolled a cigarette using Geddes' tobacco, got up and started pacing around the house, rubbing his hands together. I could see between the old crates and rusting tools underneath and glimpsed him stop at the woodpile. When he jerked the axe out of the stump I had a momentary spurt of adrenaline so pure that everything in my line of sight wavered for a second, but he chucked the axe to one side, lifting the stump instead. He carried it over and set it in front of me. What the hell?

The cigarette dangled from his mouth as he squatted behind the stump. He produced a small digital video camera from his pants pocket and balanced it on the wood, pressed record. A little red light blinked at me.

'Say something,' he said.

'What?' I croaked.

'That'll do.'

As he examined the screen I heard a shrill version of our voices play back. He reset the video, lit another cigarette off the butt of the old one, and strolled back to the woodpile humming a tune that sounded a lot like Bon Jovi's 'You Give Love a Bad Name'.

He picked up the chainsaw and pulled the cord and when it didn't start I let out the breath I didn't realise I'd been holding. He rooted around under the shack, found a tin of petrol and poured some into the chainsaw. When he pulled the cord again the machine sputtered. I had a brief moment of hope before he tried again, and the chainsaw buzzed into life. He walked back, saw held high, and I realised I was as wet as if someone had just poured a bucket of water over me, sweating uncontrollably: forehead, underarms, every goddamn pore. I could hardly see and I didn't know if it was from tears or perspiration.

I tried to speak, but my mind was blank, my tongue sandpaper. I knew I should move, but I was inert with terror. He tested the saw out against the veranda railing and it chewed right through the wood, chips flying, giving off a burnt smell. I imagined the searing pain of it eating into my arm, visualised bone flecks, arterial blood spray, dabs of my own mangled flesh hitting me in the face.

Something clicked in the connection between my mouth and my brain.

'Help! Somebody help me!' Even as I yelled I realised it was useless. No one was around, and if they were they wouldn't hear anything over the rumble of the saw. Watto, aka Elvis Mask, turned and started coming towards me and I managed to get to my feet, but it was only for a second. I was hobbled; my ankles banged together, and I fell to my knees.

Watto was laughing like a madman, his small eyes black with pupil and the corners of his mouth clogged with dried-up spit. I squeezed my eyes shut, anticipating white-hot agony, but opened them when I heard a shout.

'Hey—fucktard!'

Watto was blocking my view, so I couldn't see who was yelling.

A gunshot fractured the air, the clang of a bullet striking metal, and I watched as the chainsaw arced out of Watto's hands and fell towards me. I threw myself to the side and rolled as hard as I could. The saw hit the ground near my face, still roaring, digging up dirt and flinging it in my eyes. I rolled again and heard another shot. Watto sprinted into the bush as a guy wearing shorts and nothing else chased him as far as the edge of the clearing. The topless guy turned and walked towards me. He was thin, with bleached blond hair and a swatch of gauze taped to his side.

It was Nick Austin.

chapterforty-three

Nick switched off the saw and ran over to Geddes, tried to roll him and jerked his hands back in horror. They were covered in blood.

'Oh Jesus. Oh fuck,' he said.

'I told him to shoot.' My voice hitched up in my throat. 'Why didn't he shoot?'

Nick got up and stepped backwards from the body.

'It's a replica. I've got the only real gun.' He turned and threw up into the dust.

I heard an engine; it sounded like a car coming down the drive. Nick heard it too. He looked like the dog had: tensed up, ready to bolt.

'Untie me!' I yelled.

He ran into the house instead.

I shimmied over to the knife Watto had used to kill Geddes, fumbled the blood-slicked handle with my bound hands and sawed through the tape around my ankles. I stood, nearly fell, and followed Nick into the shack.

'Get this tape off my wrists.'

He didn't respond. He'd chucked on a t-shirt and was stuffing things into a sports bag.

'Please,' I pleaded. 'The car could be that psycho coming back.'

He zipped the bag, slung it over his shoulder and took the knife. He'd just started to cut when he looked over my shoulder and stopped.

'Fuck.' He threw the blade to the floor and spun me around, arm circling my waist, gun to my head. I looked out the dusty windows and saw why. A police car had pulled into the clearing, and a fat uniformed cop got out of the driver's side, gun drawn, making a beeline for Geddes' body. The passenger door opened and a woman with a brown bob emerged. Detective Talbot, talking into her radio. The uniform kneeled by the body, shaking his head. Talbot and the uniform squinted at the windows and pointed their guns.

'Come out with your hands where we can see them!' she yelled.

Nick dragged me onto the veranda.

Talbot's eyes widened as she realised who we were.

'Put down the gun, Nick,' she said. 'It's all over.'

'Back off or I'll shoot her.'

'Nick didn't kill him.' I pointed at Geddes with my tied-up hands and jabbered, trying to get it all out before it was too late. 'The guy who murdered Isabella and stabbed Victoria Hitchens did. Crack addict. Five nine, receding brown hair, wiry build, hollowed-out face, teardrop tattoo under each eye.'

But all her attention was on Nick.

'Put the gun down, mate. We know you didn't do it. If you come in with us we can sort out the whole mess, yeah?'

Nick sagged for a second, and I thought he was going to surrender. Instead he moved his hand to the back of my head, grabbed my hair and cocked the gun. The click echoed in my ear. Were there any bullets left? He'd only fired off two shots so I didn't see why not. Just how desperate was he?

'Step the fuck away from the cop car and throw your guns over here.'

'We can't, Nick.'

'Just fucking do it!'

They stood there, pointing their guns at him, while he pressed his pistol into my temple.

'I said, throw down the guns or I'll blow her fucking brains out!'

Uniform looked at Talbot. Talbot waved her hand as if to say, stay where you are. Nick breathed heavy, pulling my hair out by the roots.

'Nick,' she said.

He let out a sigh, shifted behind me and jerked the gun. There was a blast of hot air and a bang so loud it altered the pressure in my left ear and I thought I'd been shot until I saw the uniformed cop crumple to the ground, a dark stain spreading on his navy trousers.

'Shit,' the cop said. 'Shit, shit, shit.'

Talbot threw her gun towards Nick, ran to the moaning copper and tossed his gun over too, before taking off her jacket and holding it to his leg. Nick marched me down the stairs, forced me to pick up the guns and pushed me towards the police car.

I turned to Talbot. 'There's an injured dog under the house!'

Nick shoved me into the passenger seat, grabbed the cop's revolvers out of my hands and slammed the door. He slid into the driver's seat, thrust the weapons in his bag and chucked it on the floor. After a jerky three-point turn, he tore up the driveway, bumping over rocks and ruts in the road. The radio babbled. Nick shut it off. Finally he spoke.

'How'd you get here?'

'Huh?'

'You drive? Got a car?'

'Yeah. Fire trail, five hundred metres up.'

I half expected to run into a phalanx of cop cars when we emerged on Collers Road, but it was deserted. Wouldn't be long. Nick found the fire trail and parked the police car next to my Ford. We got out. Nick was so jumped up he looked like he'd had a hit of the crack pipe himself. He stood at the driver's side.

'Gimme your keys.'

I dug in my pocket and used them to open the passenger door first.

'You're not coming,' he said.

'What?'

'There's some shit I've got to take care of. It's dangerous. Nothing to do with you.'

Everything hit me then. The chainsaw, Sean, my father's brush-off and Mum refusing police protection and telling me I was evil. A righteous anger seemed to spring from the earth and stream through the soles of my feet. I tingled with it, felt like I was going to spontaneously combust.

'Nothing to do with me?' I yelled. 'My whole life turned to shit since you walked into my office and I don't know why. I lost my job, my flat, my boyfriend and almost my life. That fucking psycho has been after me and my family—'

'Your family?' Nick frowned, confused.

'And you, you fucking cocksucker, say it's *nothing to do with me*? Either you tell me everything that's going on, right now, and take me with you, or I chuck these fucking keys as far as I can and leave you to shoot it out with the police!'

Even though he was holding three handguns, Nick had the freaked-out look guys got when a formerly compliant woman went ballistic. Nice guys, at least. Not-so-nice guys tended to smack you in the face.

'Okay, get in the car.'

'It's my car and I'm fucking driving.'

'Alright. But can we leave, now?'

We swapped places and I slid into the driver's seat, reversed down to the road, did a U-turn.

'I can't believe you brought this car.' He looked around, disgusted. 'What real-life PI drives such a conspicuous car? We're gonna have to ditch it. It's ridiculous.'

I shifted into drive.

'Shut the fuck up,' I said.

chapterforty-four

Nick directed me out of town and back down the Calder, which I didn't think was such a good idea—wouldn't be long before the highway was swarming with cops. He sat up straight, like he was looking for something, and when a service station appeared he told me to pull over before we reached it.

'What the hell are we doing?'

'Don't want them to see the car, but I do want us to go in there and smile for candid camera. Makes us look like we're on our way to Melbourne.'

'Aren't we?'

'No. Adelaide. You got a mobile phone?'

'Why?'

'You'll see. Put it on silent and give it here.'

I did as he said, handing him the phone.

Inside the store he clutched my upper arm while we walked around picking up energy drinks and plastic-wrapped sandwiches. I attempted to wriggle out of his grip, but he held on tight.

'I'm not going to run away,' I said.

His voice rasped in my ear: 'Makes you look kidnapped instead of an accessory. I shot a cop, they're gonna come down like a ton of bricks.'

Outside, Nick saw a truck driver climbing into his cab and hustled me over.

'Hey, mate,' Nick said, 'where you off to?'

'Sydney, mate.'

'Not Queensland?'

'Nah.'

'No worries.'

If I hadn't known what he was up to, I never would have seen Nick slip my phone under the driver's seat.

'Nice idea,' I told him on the way back to the car. 'They trace the phone as it goes past the signal towers.'

'It's in the next Zack book.'

We didn't say much the first hour, both tense, expecting sirens and flashing red and blue lights. Nick slumped low on the bench seat with a gun in his lap and I sat straight, hands gripping the wheel. I didn't want to draw any more attention to the car and concentrated on sticking exactly to the speed limit. Nick tuned the radio to a local station, but there was nothing about us in the news headlines. An hour later the newsreader mentioned a shooting in Castlemaine. No details. I relaxed a bit.

'You going to tell me what's going on?'

'I stole some money.' He sighed.

'Whose?'

'I don't know. I thought I knew, but it turned out I didn't.'

'And . . . ?'

'For your own safety, the less you know the better.'

'Safety? It's a little late for that. I almost got dismembered.'

He stared out the window, refusing to say more, so I

forced him to listen instead. I told him everything that had happened, hoping it might prompt a reaction. No such luck. If anything surprised him, he kept it inside, and he refused to confirm or deny any of my theories. Frustrating, but I was sure I'd get it out of him later.

We took back roads and obscure highways through the Grampians National Park, passing craggy sandstone mountains, eucalypt forests and grassed valleys. In Hamilton we stopped for petrol, once more parking away from the station. I took a blonde wig from my stash of disguises in the boot, stuck on a cap and sunglasses, filled up a couple of jerry cans and bought another couple of Red Bulls. I was running on caffeine and adrenaline and nothing else.

By the time we crossed the border near Mount Gambier, Nick had fallen asleep. The sun was setting and the landscape had flattened, dense bush replaced by sheep runs and vast fields of wheat lit up peach in the afternoon light.

By the time it was fully dark we were on the coast road, had passed Robe and were ten k's out from a place called Meningie. The Futura, which tended to shudder and stall in city traffic, was purring like a kitten. I was so tired I was hallucinating little creatures scurrying on the edge of my vision. The Red Bulls had well and truly worn off. I nudged Nick.

'Dude, wake up. I'm rooted. You're gonna have to drive.'

'What time is it?' He sat up and blinked.

'Just past eight.'

'Want to stop? Motel, few hours' sleep?'

I couldn't think of anything better, but I stalled.

'Only if you tell me everything.'

'I will, after a shower and something to eat.' He sighed. 'Reckon it'll be safe?'

'If we do it right.'

In Meningie I drove past a motel on the highway and parked down a deserted side street a few blocks away. I pocketed the keys, put the wig and cap back on, and left Nick in the car while I doubled back, cars and trucks rolling past, headlights forcing me to squint. The night was hot and crickets twittered in the nature strip. A park fronted a lake on the opposite side of the road and the water smelled brackish.

The place looked like every other motel in history: reception attached to a small restaurant and a long, single-storey L-shaped building enclosing a concrete car park out back. Eighty-five bucks, a false address and one fake American accent later I was inside an unpainted brick room with a double bed, a bar fridge and a television chained to the wall. I dumped the backpack I'd taken from the boot, walked back to the car and drove us into the centre of town where I bought McDonald's, a couple of bottles of wine and a pack of cigarettes. Parking the car on the same side street we walked back to the motel, making sure there was no one at reception to watch Nick sneak in.

Soon as we were inside I cracked open the screw cap on a bottle of Geisen sauvignon blanc, poured it into two thick tumblers, and handed one to Nick. I finished the first in three gulps, poured another.

Nick looked at his.

'I haven't had a drink in six weeks.'

'Yeah?'

'Needed to stay sharp, couldn't let down my guard. After what happened to Izzy . . . if I hadn't been passed out drunk I could have saved her.'

'You don't know that.'

He stared at the glass.

'One won't hurt,' I said. I wanted to get him a little tipsy, thought he might loosen up and start talking.

He took a tentative sip.

'Nice. Tastes expensive.'

'Yeah, well, I thought I deserved it. Besides, I've still got five grand of Liz's cash.'

'Huh?'

'She hired me to find you. I'd say we're gonna need it.'

We sipped our drinks and looked around the room, clocking the double bed at the same time. There was no additional single, no couch. Cosy. I looked at Nick and I swear he actually blushed.

'So what's the plan?' I asked to get our minds off the sleeping arrangements. 'Find JJ in Adelaide?'

'First off I'm going to change the hair.' He opened the sports bag and pulled out five packs of dye, all different colours.

'Can I shower first?' I asked. 'I feel disgusting. I stink.'

'Sure.'

I was out in ten minutes. Wet hair combed, wearing an old pair of shorts and a t-shirt I'd found in the backpack. I sat on the bed and Nick handed me another wine. It tasted a little different from the first—probably because I'd just brushed my teeth.

'Should I go black?' He held up one of the dye packs.

'Sure. Just don't forget to do your eyebrows or you'll look like an incompetent goth.'

He disappeared into the bathroom while I drank wine, watched some home improvement show on TV and lit a cigarette, ignoring the no-smoking sign. Hungry as I was, I didn't want to scarf down the Maccas right away, because a full stomach would make me crash and I wanted to get some more information out of Nick first.

He came out of the bathroom half an hour later with black hair and very dark eyebrows. He'd dyed his beard and shaved it into a goatee.

'You look like a stage hypnotist,' I said and giggled a little hysterically.

'Long as I don't look like me.'

'Tell me about this money that you stole.' I got straight to the point. 'Is that how you and Isabella could afford to go overseas, get married in New York?'

He raised his new eyebrows and looked like he was about to say something, but the late news came on so he turned it up and sat on the bed next to me to watch. We were the lead story.

'*Victorian Police have staged a massive manhunt for fugitive author Nick Austin after a shootout earlier today in the Victorian town of Castlemaine. One man is dead, a police officer was shot and injured, and a woman was taken hostage.*'

Our photos flashed up on the screen and I had to sit forward and squint to make them out properly. Exhaustion was really messing with my eyes. They showed an old publicity still of Nick, a mug shot, and an artist's impression of what he looked like with blond hair and a beard. I got the bikini picture, of course. No one mentioned my car. I guessed no one had seen me drive it except for tattooed goatee guy, and he didn't seem to be exactly law abiding himself. It was only a matter of time, though . . .

The report finished with a warning that Nick was armed, extremely dangerous, and not to be approached.

'Oh god,' I said. 'This is huge. Maybe I should dye my hair, too? It's too hot to be wearing that ratty wig.'

Nick didn't say anything, just studied me for a moment. Freak. I riffled through his stash of dye, picked out a pack of blond and lay back on the bed and opened the box, trying to read the instructions. All the little letters danced in front of my eyes. I sat up and rubbed my face.

'Jesus. I can't believe how tired I am. I'm fucked.'

'Go to sleep.'

I shook my head from side to side, movements exaggerated.

'Not until you tell me about the money. Where'd you steal it from?' I got up to refill my glass, bumped my hip on the chair on the way over, swore and picked up the bottle. I couldn't keep it steady, and wine slopped over the side of the glass. I took it back to the bed and sat down a little hard, spilling wine on my bare legs.

'Shit.'

Nick plucked the glass out of my hand.

'You're drunk.'

'Only had three glasses.' It was true. I'd started on an empty stomach, but still . . .

'Lie down.'

'So forceful! You know, if this was one of your Zack books we'd already be making mad, passionate love in the motel room and I would've come instantaneously and with no foreplay or oral sex. Sooo unrealistic.' I started giggling again. Somewhere in the recesses of my brain I wondered why I'd just said such a stupid thing.

Nick frowned. I started kicking his foot.

'Tell me about the money. Tell me, tell me, tell me, tell me, tell me,' I singsonged, kicking harder each time. I was behaving like a psychotic three-year-old. The thought made me snort like a pig, and the snort made me laugh uncontrollably. I doubled over, finally calmed down, swung my head back up and stared at the brick wall. It was breathing. Man, I'd been dog-tired and traumatised before, but it had never had this effect. The feeling reminded me of my crazy drug-taking days when once, for a laugh, I'd mixed champagne with a couple of strong Valiums. Holy shit. I turned to Nick.

'What did you?' I slurred. It was difficult to form words. 'In my wine. What?'

He didn't answer. The hypnotist facial hair combined with my blurred vision made him look especially sinister. I stood and made a break for the door, but he grabbed me around the waist and hauled me back, threw me on the bed. I struggled and he pinned me down. What the hell was going on? I tried to yell. He put his hand over my mouth. My limbs became heavy and I felt myself slipping. I was under the sea, sinking, and consciousness was floating on the glinting surface, too far away to reach.

chapterforty-five

I woke up with a dry mouth and stuck-together eyes, wondering where I was. The ceiling was made of rough concrete, the wall opposite naked brick. There was a TV on a bar fridge and a really bad picture of a sailing boat over by the door. Sailing boat . . . sinking . . . it came back in flashes: Nick drugging me, pushing me onto the bed like some mad date-rapist.

I looked down at my body, lying on top of the floral bedspread. Still clothed, didn't appear I'd been ravished, but I stuck my hand down my pants and had a quick feel, just to make sure. Nope. Everything appeared to be in order. I leapt up, almost fell over, and looked in the mirror for any other suspicious signs: strange stains, crusty white stuff adhering to my person. Nothing.

My gaze landed on a handwritten letter on the small laminex table, two fifty-buck notes next to it.

Simone, sorry about the sleeping tablets, but they shouldn't cause any lasting damage. I've taken your car and Liz's money and left you cash to get a bus back to Melbourne. I hope you'll tell the police that I dropped you there, and not let on where I'm really going or what

I look like now, although I know I don't have any right to expect you to comply. I started this and it's up to me to finish it. I don't want to put anyone else in danger. Thanks, Nick.

He hadn't wanted to rape me, he'd wanted to ditch me. I reread the note. Nice sentiment, Nick, but I was already in danger and he wasn't doing me any favours leaving me in bum-fuck South Australia with nothing but a bus fare. There was a strong possibility he'd get his head blown off by either the cops or the bad guys, and then I'd never know who was after me and my family and we'd all have to spend the rest of our lives in police protection or dead. I mentally kicked myself for not forcing him to spill straight away. I should have threatened to drive the Futura into a tree.

I turned on the television and made a coffee, putting three sachets of International Roast into one small cup. Vile, but it was the only way to get enough caffeine out of instant. Sipping the hideous brew I watched the morning news: Nick and I were still top story, but they now had a picture of my car, video footage of me and Nick at the service station and a recent photo, a close-up of my face. Sean had snapped the picture in Apollo Bay, after I'd found Isabella's body.

I felt hollow in the guts and couldn't tell if it was guilt, regret, or just nostalgia for how it had been when we'd first got together. I'd well and truly fucked things up despite my promises to myself.

I threw back the last of the coffee. There was no time for sentimentality, and there was no going back to Melbourne and the mess of police statements and recriminations that would ensue. Nick thought he had to finish things? Well, so did I. Finding out who was behind the threats and the killing was the only way to make sure what had happened to Mum three months ago didn't happen again.

Only problem was, I couldn't cruise around as myself. I picked up the ratty blonde wig and stuck it on my head. The wig was so obviously fake it *looked* like a bad disguise. Synthetic strands scratched my face and within seconds my scalp started to sweat. I glanced around the room. On the floor by the bed was the pack of blond dye I'd been examining the night before. I touched my hair. For once it was in pretty good condition, but that was about to change. Oh well. Desperate times and all that. I put on the gloves and headed for the bathroom.

At ten o'clock the cleaner was hanging around the doorway and I was trying to drag myself away from the mirror. I looked completely different, not to mention super tarty, ultra-dark eyebrows clashing with the new blonde hair. I doubted even Sean would recognise me if we passed in the street.

I checked out at reception and, still using the accent, asked the old guy behind the desk about an internet café and a bus to Adelaide. He told me a coach left from the Caltex servo around midday and let me use the computer in the office to get on the net, which was nice. I had a feeling I'd get away with a lot more as a perky Californian blonde than I had as a surly Australian brunette. I wrote down JJ's address and phone numbers from the email Tony Torcasio had sent, and ambled down the highway to the petrol station, the hair inciting more car horns and lewd suggestions than ever before. I didn't know how Chloe dealt with it. Actually, I did. It was *not* getting propositioned she couldn't stand.

At the Caltex I used a public phone to ring JJ's home and mobile numbers and, as per usual, got no answer on either. I wondered if Watto had got to him already. I discovered the bus arrived at midday but didn't leave until twelve thirty, after all the passengers had been forced to chow down on deep-fried food at the diner. It was only ten forty-five and Nick already had a substantial head start so I decided to hitch it, hoping I'd be able to tell if an outback serial killer type tried to give me a lift. As it was, an old couple picked me up and proceeded to harangue me for the next hour and a half about hitchhiking's dangers. They got so frothy about all the perverted things that could happen to a young lady on our nation's highways that I briefly wondered if they intended to take me back to their purpose-built dungeon and have their evil, senior-citizen way. They didn't, instead dropping me off at JJ's address so I wouldn't have to wander the mean streets of Adelaide alone. I left them with effusive thanks and a sincere-sounding promise to never get in a car with a stranger again.

JJ's place was in North Adelaide, on the fringes of the city, a rendered-brick thirties-style apartment block on a wide, flat road. The street was lined with paperbark trees and rustic-looking renovated cottages and was deserted. Actually the whole city had seemed deserted as we'd driven through it, past churches, parks and historic buildings. Maybe everyone had gone on holiday, down to the coast.

Heat radiated up from the pavement and the air smelled like hot tar, gum trees and dried-out grass. The temperature had to be in the mid thirties at least, but there was very little humidity and the dry air scoured my throat and nose.

I followed the signs to flat number two, which had its own stone stairwell and small balcony and was sheltered by a European-looking leafy green tree. Acting like a normal person, I knocked first on the old-fashioned wooden door. There was no answer and no sound or movement when I put my face to the opaque glass panel. I tried the handle. Locked tight.

I descended the stairs, walked around to the back of the apartment block and got a shock. My car was parked next to a Hills hoist. Nick had got rid of the zebra seat covers, dangling mirror ball, St Christopher medal and various other accoutrements that made my vehicle look like it belonged to a Mexican pimp. I put my hand on the bonnet and although it was warm from the sun, I could tell it hadn't been driven recently. I wondered if Nick had dumped it, or if he was still around.

I climbed a set of wooden stairs leading to a small porch at JJ's back door, and saw a broken window.

'Nick, it's Simone!' He was armed and jumpy so I identified myself real loud.

Carefully avoiding the jagged glass I stuck my arm through the hole, turned the interior lock, and found myself in a small, bright kitchen with renovated period features and diamond-patterned black and white linoleum. An antique cabinet took up one wall and held cups and crockery. A built-in table and chairs, the sort of thing estate agents called a 'breakfast nook', nestled next to the windows.

The floor was clear of glass, which had been swept up and dumped in the bin, along with an empty baked beans can. There was a bowl with a swipe of tomato sauce in it, and a dirty coffee cup in the sink. I checked out the calendar on the fridge. It was for December the previous year and there was a line running from the fifteenth until the end of the month. Above the line, written in red, were the words *Broken Hill Residency.*

Little wonder no one could find him. He was probably still in Broken Hill. I crept through the rest of the house, feeling like a burglar and hoping I wouldn't find anything dead. The lounge room was neat. Polished floor, woven rug, fireplace and lots of art on the walls, some of it Aboriginal, most abstract prints. The furniture was an eclectic mix of thirties sofa, fifties wing chair, and modern stainless steel shelves filled with books.

The first bedroom had been converted to an office filled with more books, boxes and a desktop computer. I switched it on and explored the second bedroom while it booted up. JJ owned a wooden-framed bed set high off the floor, made up with dark blue linen. It had been slept in. A clothes rack appeared to have been riffled through, and shirts and pants were piled up on the bed.

The bathroom was tiled, with a bath and sink in a pale green colour that had been popular in the thirties. A damp towel lay crumpled on the floor with the clothes Nick had been wearing when I'd last seen him in the motel. So he'd stayed the night. Where was he now?

Back in the office I sat down in front of the computer and was relieved to find it had broadband internet and hadn't been password protected. I brought up Google search and got ready to type in *JJ Broken Hill* but after the first J the computer suggested the phrase for me. I really was hot on Nick's trail. The link he'd selected was a different shade from the others, so I clicked on it and was directed to the Broken Hill library's online newsletter, which informed me that their current writer in residence was Jerome 'JJ' Jones and that he was going to be there until January six. He had already conducted a few poetry and spoken word workshops at the library, and was MC-ing a 'Summer Slam' poetry competition at a Broken Hill pub that night.

I wrote down the library's number and went into the lounge room to call from the phone. Before I punched it in I hit redial, just to find out the last place called.

A woman picked up. 'Kit Kat Club, Adelaide's home of adult entertainment. How can I help you?'

I hung up. Interesting. Next I phoned the library.

'Broken Hill Library, Karen speaking.'

'Hi, Karen, I'm a good friend of Jerome Jones, your writer in residence at the moment? Uh, he's not answering his mobile and I was wondering if you had a contact number for him. Either that or an address.'

She gave an exasperated sigh. 'Is this some kind of a joke?'

'Sorry?'

'You're the third person to call up asking for him today. We take the privacy of our artists and writers very seriously. They come up here for some quiet time in which to create, and if he's not answering his phone I'm sure it's for a reason. The third person! What on earth is going on?'

'What if I said please? It really is quite urgent.'

'That's what the others said. And when I told them to leave a number so I could get Jerome to call them back they hung up! Would you like to leave a number?'

I hung up.

Three people? Me, Nick and who else? Watto? How did he know so damn much? Had he been here too? Back on the computer I checked the search history. Nick had looked up the Indian Pacific train line, and the Kit Kat Club combined with the name Travis. I scribbled the address for the club and checked out the Indian Pacific timetable. The train had left Adelaide at ten am and would reach Broken Hill at six thirty that night. What do you know, Nick would get there just in time to meet up with JJ at the poetry slam. He must have thought the car was too conspicuous to drive, and he couldn't take a plane with those guns he was toting. I searched airlines to find out which companies flew to Broken Hill from Adelaide and came up with one. REX, Regional Express. A five-fifty pm flight got in at seven and there was a seat available. Looked like I'd be able to make the Summer Slam too, if I had any money. I couldn't risk using my own credit card so there was only one thing for it. I called Chloe.

'Oh my god!' she squealed as soon as she heard my voice.

'Shut up and listen,' I said, before she could blow it. 'Where are you?'

'Still at the hotel, by the pool.'

'Is there a cop in earshot?'

'Yeah, he's pretty cute. I got him to rub Hawaiian Tropic on my back before. I think he got a hard-on.'

'Hang up and tell him you're going down to the business centre to check your email. Go straight there. Take your handbag. I'll call in ten.'

Ten minutes later I rang back.

'You there?'

'Yep.'

'Where's the cop?'

'Out in the lobby, reading the paper. Don't worry, he can't hear. My god, Simone. Where are you? Are you okay? The cops have gone ballistic. Sean's freaking out. Alex was here a little while ago and they had a big argument. Sean found out you went to Alex for help and wants to know why you did it and why Alex didn't tell him. Major scene. Are you with Nick?'

'Not anymore. Long story. I'm in Adelaide and I need to get to Broken Hill on a REX flight this evening. Can you book it with your credit card, give me a false name?'

'Won't you need ID?'

'Not without luggage. I can print out a boarding pass myself, walk straight onto the plane. Just email the itinerary to me and don't tell anyone.'

'Okay, doing it now. Aren't you worried they'll recognise you at the airport? You've been all over the papers and the telly here.'

'Somehow I don't think that'll be a problem.'

'What are you doing in Broken Hill?'

'Finishing this thing once and for all.'

Chloe did as I told her and I checked in over the internet and printed my pass. I closed the web browser and was just about to shut off the computer when I had an idea. I minimised the internet window and ran a search on all the files and folders using the term 'Travis'. In a couple of seconds I had a JPEG file, a photograph titled 'JJ and Travis'. I opened it. JJ had his arm around a blond surfie-looking guy in a neon-lit bar.

I checked the time. Two thirty and I didn't have to be at the airport till five. Searching the flat I found a small backpack, emptied my large one onto the lounge room floor, and packed a couple of outfits and some toiletries into the smaller one, leaving behind crap like the wig and my ugly grey trackie-daks that had so disturbed Nick all those weeks ago. When I was finished I stood up, nearly fainted, and realised I hadn't eaten anything for what seemed like days. I found a small tin of tuna in the cupboard and scarfed it over the sink, washed it down with a glass of water, then called a cab.

'Where to?' asked the dispatcher.

'Hindley Street. The Kit Kat Club,' I said.

chapterforty-six

Hindley Street was full of pubs, pokies and restaurants, all quiet on a hot afternoon in the middle of the summer holidays. The Kit Kat Club was in a plain brick building, jazzed up with pictures of bikini-clad females set into frames that lit up at night. In a nod to glamour and sophistication a small wine-red canopy covered the doorway, and a carpet of the same colour led to the interior where a yawning bouncer, obviously mistaking me for one of the girls, waved me through without demanding the ten-dollar entry fee.

I pushed through a heavy metal door and walked down stairs with orange lights twinkling at their edges, into a dimly lit, cave-like bar. The stage hugged the left-hand side of the room and an abbreviated catwalk jutted out from the middle. A dancer with waist-length blonde hair held onto a pole and gyrated half-heartedly in front of a lone customer. The only other guy sat at the bar, chatting to a buxom barmaid. He was the surfie from the picture, tangled blond hair and tanned, desiccated skin. His lips were pale and thin, burned by the sun. I slid into the seat next to him, immediately comfortable in the familiar environment, and ordered champagne.

'Travis?'

'Yeah.' His voice was raspy and wrecked. Cigarettes, seawater, late nights, all of the above.

'I'm Vivien.' I stuck out my hand and he shook it.

'Oh hey, you starting today or—'

'I'm here because I'm pretty sure Nick came in last night and I wanted to know what he spoke to you about.'

Travis just stared at me.

'Nick Austin?' I lowered my voice so the barmaid wouldn't hear. 'Australia's most wanted? He's changed a bit. Black hair, goatee, looks like he should be up on stage in an RSL club making the audience cluck like chickens.'

The barmaid put the champagne down and looked at me with a curious, searching expression and I resolved to keep an eye on her, make sure she didn't use a phone. It had been a risk to come, but Travis didn't exactly look the type to call the coppers or make a citizen's arrest.

'I don't know what you're talking about,' Travis said. 'I've never heard of anyone called Nick Austin.'

'Everyone's heard of Nick Austin. What about JJ? You know him? Jerome Jones. Black guy, performance poet, likes to wear Blues Brothers suits and a trilby hat? Him and Nick got involved in something a couple of years ago and now someone's trying to kill them. You know anything about that?' I sipped my champagne. It was flat.

'I've never met anyone called—what was it? JB?'

Clumsy. Travis might've been able to carve some gnarly pipes, but he was a terrible liar.

'Yeah you do. I've seen the photos of you on his computer. Look, I'm not a cop. I'm a friend of Nick's. I'm trying to help him. Trying to help all of us. I know there was some money stolen. I just need to know who it was stolen from because I reckon that's who's trying to kill us. If you can just tell me what you and Nick talked about . . .'

Travis lost it. He jumped off his stool and loomed over me.

'I don't know what you're talking about. You're off your head. Get the fuck out of my bar!' Emery boards scraped his larynx when he yelled.

The dancer had stopped swaying and the customer was looking around. Despite all the noise Travis looked more scared than enraged. He wasn't going to tell me anything. I finished the champagne and slid off my chair.

'Sorry to have disturbed you. I'll tell JJ and Nick you said hi.'

Travis looked horrified, as though a venomous snake had just slithered across his path. The barmaid was staring at me open-mouthed.

I walked back up the stairs. The bouncer was on his walkie-talkie and he bristled and squared his shoulders when he saw me, like a cat fluffing up and coming in sideways. After the madman with a chainsaw it just seemed lame, and I almost laughed.

'See ya, mate,' I said.

I walked down the street to look for a cab. Bit of a useless trip, except I now knew Travis had something to do with it. Why hadn't someone tried to knock him, though?

I saw a cab rank up ahead and made for it, until I felt a tap on my shoulder and whirled around. It was the barmaid. She was on the chunky side of voluptuous, wearing tight black pants and a sleeveless black top with a very low V-neck. Her face was pretty, doll-like, and her wavy, shoulder-length hair looked like it had come out of the same bottle as mine.

'Are . . . are you Simone Kirsch?' she asked shyly.

'No.'

'You *are* her. I knew it.'

'I get mistaken for her sometimes, but Simone has dark hair.' I edged towards the taxi stand.

'This is so embarrassing. And you can say no, but can I have your autograph?'

'What?'

She held out a pen and a copy of the *Adelaide Advertiser*, turned to page three where there were photos and an article about Nick and me.

'I'm a huge fan.' She squeezed her knees together and bounced a little.

Fan?

'What the hell are you talking about?'

'I've been following your career ever since you saved your friend Chloe from that kidnapper. I actually met Chloe a couple of years ago, at the Miss Nude finals at the Crazyhorse? I used to strip, but I put on weight when I had a baby so I don't anymore, I just work behind the bar, but, like, it's nice to see a stripper really kicking some arse, you know? I've got all your news clippings and—god, I hope I don't sound like a stalker, I'm not, I just think you're really cool. Sorry. I should shut up, this is so embarrassing and I'm making such a dick of myself, but if you could just sign this it'd be so awesome.'

I was reeling. I had a fan? Who wasn't a horny, middle-aged man?

'Would you like to go for a drink?' I asked her. We were standing outside an old sandstone building that conveniently housed a pub.

'Maybe a quick one? I told Travis I was going up the road to get everyone Red Rooster.'

I broke my first fifty at the bar and bought champagne for me, and Malibu and Coke for the barmaid. We sat up the back near the poker machines and I slid the newspaper in front of me and took the pen.

'Who should I make this out to?'

'Bethany. Oh god, this is so exciting.' She drummed her shoes on the polished wooden floor. 'You're such an inspiration. I mean, to me you are. Some strippers don't like you.'

'No?'

'They see you in the paper and they reckon it's not fair that you get so much publicity and they say stuff like, well, she hasn't even won any competitions, she probably can't even *dance* and who does she think she is, but they're just jealous.'

'Right. Look, Bethany, before I give you this autograph, can I ask you something?'

'Sure, anything.'

'Does Travis know a guy called JJ?'

'Yeah. He was totally lying back at the club. God knows why. Him and JJ have been mates since they were kids. JJ comes into the club a lot, he's cool and such a hottie. I can't believe he's, like, a uni professor. Cracks me up. I always thought poetry was boring as, but his poems are about, like, strip clubs and passion and getting fucked up. They're sexy!'

'Do you know of any trouble JJ might have gotten into in the last few years?'

'No. I know him and Travis used to be into some shit when they were younger, but JJ's pretty respectable now. He organises poetry nights, goes to that Adelaide writers' week, writes reviews and stuff for the paper.'

'Were you working last night?'

'Yep.'

'Did this guy come in? Nick Austin?' I turned the paper around. She frowned.

I took the pen and coloured in his hair and his eyebrows and drew a goatee on him and showed her the picture again. Her eyes lit up in recognition.

'Yeah! Shit. Was that Nick Austin? God, I had no idea. He was talking to Travis at the bar before they went off into Travis' office. I noticed 'cause Travis looked real freaked out and they were talking about the Red Devils.'

'The bikie gang?'

'Yeah.'

'What did they say?'

'I don't know. I just heard the name in passing. Noticed because the Red Devils are pretty much at war with the Assassins, and the Assassins are part owners of the Kit Kat. Silent partners, not officially on the books. A few years back the Devils firebombed their clubhouse and the leader of the Devils, this bad bastard called Craig Murdoch, he bashed the president of the Assassins in Melbourne and almost killed him and now he's in jail.'

I vaguely remembered hearing about it in the news at the time.

'Does the name Lachlan Elliot mean anything to you?' I asked.

'Never heard of him.'

'Ever been to Broken Hill?'

'No. But I know the Devils have a clubhouse out that way somewhere, some girlfriends of mine have gone up there to do shows. It's where they get the name. You know, from the red dirt and that.' She drained her drink and looked at her watch. 'So, what's a writer got to do with a bikie gang?'

I signed her newspaper.

'That's what I'm trying to find out.'

•

Soon as I got to the airport I rang Chloe from a public phone. I'd been thinking about our Mexican Christmas party. Tiara, the speed-freak stripper, had said something about murdered investment banker Lachlan Elliot being connected to the Red

Devils, but I'd been so drunk by that stage I couldn't recall the details. I needed her number. Chloe didn't answer, and I rang at least ten times, getting increasingly frustrated each time a message told me the phone was switched off. She never switched her damn phone off! The only other person I could think to call was Andi. She'd talked to Tiara, and she knew about Lachlan Elliot and the bikie gang. I didn't really want to ring her—even though she was my friend, she was also a journalist—but I didn't have much choice.

At least her phone was on.

'Andi, it's Simone.'

'Hellooo . . .' she said. I heard a click.

'Are you recording?'

'Nooo . . .'

'Bullshit.'

'Where are you? What's happening? Where's Nick Austin?'

'I can't tell you. I'm safe, though, and I need some information about Lachlan Elliot's connection to the Red Devil's.'

'Why?'

'I don't know yet.'

'I'll grab my notes. Let's see. Red Devils outlaw biker gang, started in the nineties, a breakaway group from the Lucifer's Warriors. Chapters in Victoria, South Australia and New South Wales, pretty small, estimated membership about eighty-five. Involved in all the usual stuff, drugs, particularly manufacture and supply of amphetamines, prostitution, yada yada yada. Although they're a relatively new, small club they have a vicious reputation. Their leader, Craig Murdoch, is in prison for serious assault.'

'Which prison?'

'Hang on a sec. Uh, Port Phillip.'

Port Phillip kept coming up. It was where Rod Thurlow had done his writing workshop, where Emery Wade was locked up, and now Craig Murdoch. I wondered about Watto/Elvis Mask. He had jail tatts.

'And what was Lachlan Elliot's connection to them?'

'Known associate, suspected of dealing, low level stuff. The sort of guy who liked to slum it, take a walk on the wild side. Pampered private-school kid who wanted to feel like a tough guy? I don't know.'

'Why would the bikers deal with someone like him?'

'He had money and from what I hear Craig Murdoch is a bit of a social climber himself. Likes to think he can mix in all circles. Before he went to jail he was in negotiations with a major film company to produce a documentary about his life, if you can believe it. Maybe Elliot gave him an entrée into high society.'

'And there was a contract on Lachlan Elliot?'

'That's the word on the street. Rumour has it he disappeared with a lot of money and a lot more drugs. Worth around a million, all up. The police think the Red Devils found and whacked him, but they can't prove it. What I want to know is why you're asking. What's all this got to do with Nick Austin?'

'I don't know yet.' But I was getting an idea.

'When you do will you give me an exclusive?'

'Maybe.'

'Jeez, thanks, Simone.'

A voice over the intercom said it was final call for the plane to Broken Hill.

'I gotta go.'

'I'm sure you do. Hey—give Sean a call, okay?'

Why? He'd broken up with me. I hung up, hoping Andi hadn't heard the airport announcement.

All the other passengers were making their way across the tarmac to the small, twin-engine Regional Express plane. The sun was a golden splotch inching towards the horizon, and a heat haze shimmered just above the runway. I handed my boarding pass to an air steward in a fluorescent vest, but before I could make my way through the glass doors I heard a commotion. Somebody was screeching behind me.

'Hold the plane! I'm here! Hold the plane!'

The steward was looking over my shoulder with a shocked expression. I turned to follow his gaze, but I already had a sinking feeling and a good idea of what I was going to see.

Loping down the terminal in high-heeled mules and a pink denim mini, blonde hair flying, holding her belly in one hand, a couple of women's magazines, her handbag and a boarding pass in the other, was Chloe.

chapterforty-seven

Chloe had to look twice before she finally figured out it was me standing there with the blonde hair and the pissed-off expression.

'Vivien! Just flew in from Melbourne, sure I was going to miss the plane.' She draped her arms around my neck and got her head in close.

'Go home,' I hissed.

'Shut up or I'll tell 'em this is a bomb, not a baby,' she whispered. 'Airport cops'll be here so fast your head'll spin.'

'Should she be flying?' I asked the guy. He frowned.

Chloe waved a crumpled piece of paper. 'Doctor's certificate. I'm two days under thirty-six weeks. Read it and weep!'

She let me go and grinned broadly at the steward. 'This is my sister! We've been planning this girls' weekend for ages!'

'In Broken Hill?' he drawled disdainfully as he scanned Chloe's pass.

'Miners, hon. They're fit and frustrated. You should come, might get lucky yourself!'

From the moment we strapped ourselves in I tried to persuade her to take the next plane back, but she wouldn't listen.

'You never should have ditched me at the hotel.'

'You might have been killed by a chainsaw-wielding ice-fiend.'

'I could have helped. We could have overpowered him together. You seem to have forgotten I'm your sidekick.'

'You're not a sidekick, you're my best friend. There's no such thing as a sidekick. It's a concept, a cliché from one of Nick's books.'

'I don't care. I'm sick of being left out of everything! I'm pregnant, not dead!'

The air hostess came along with her trolley.

'Water,' I told her.

'Just a Coke, love, ta,' Chloe said.

'When are you due?' The hostie smiled.

'A month, give or take.'

'Your first?'

'Uh-huh.'

'How lovely. Girl or boy?'

'A boy, I hope. I work with heaps of chicks. I'm over them.'

Below us an endless expanse of sand burned ochre in the setting sun. Scrubby bush peppered the desert like stubble. I stared out the window and seethed.

An hour later we started our descent, and in the orange light of the setting sun I made out a grid of streets: a large town plonked neatly in the middle of the desert.

Soon as we disembarked the heat smacked me like a fist.

'Jesus,' Chloe said.

The airport was a small, carpeted shed with a tiny cafeteria and walls painted with desert scenes. Having no luggage to collect we walked straight out and into a taxi waiting outside. Music was playing on the radio. 'It's the End of the World as We Know It'. R.E.M.

'Where to?' asked the driver.

'There's a poetry slam at a pub.' I dug around in my bag, looking for the address.

'Ah, that'd be the Silver City hotel.'

'Can I drop you at a motel?' I asked Chloe.

She crossed her arms and shook her head like a little kid. 'Poetry slam!' She pouted.

'Do you even know what a poetry slam is?'

'No.'

'It's a competition,' the cab driver piped up. 'You get up on stage and you've got two minutes to recite before the whistle blows. Five judges from the audience hold up cards giving you a mark out of ten. The middle three are tallied and that's your score.'

He caught my eye in the mirror and shrugged. 'The wife's entering.'

'What the hell is that?' Chloe pointed out the window at a rocky mountain bisecting the town and nearly blocking out the sky. 'Looks like a giant slag pile!'

'We call it a mullock heap. It's what's left over from mining. Sits right above the line of lode.'

'And what's that building on top of it?'

'That's a restaurant.'

'A restaurant, built on top of a slag—mullock heap? This place is bent.'

She sat back, pleased with the fact.

The song on the radio finished and local ads started playing. The first was a plug for Outback Whips and Leather.

'They even have a sex shop.' She nudged me, impressed.

The cab driver pulled up on what I assumed was the main drag. It was a wide street with more of those grand old buildings from the late eighteen hundreds. Sandstone courthouse, pub on every corner with the big veranda, lacy ironwork and Greek-style pillars for tying up your horse. I was all for historical shit but in the past two days I'd seen enough heritage listed structures to last me a lifetime. All I wanted was a narrow inner city lane with a modernist hotel on it. Something like the Adelphi: stark, minimalist, stainless steel edges so sharp you could sever an artery.

I paid the driver and asked if he knew of a bikie clubhouse in the area. The Red Devils. He scratched his beard.

'You don't want to be hanging around there.'

'But if I did, do you know where it is?'

He nodded.

'Give me your number?'

He wrote it on a card and I tipped him ten bucks. We stepped out and slammed the doors. The heat felt like walking face first into a wall.

The Silver City hotel was one of those huge corner pubs and it was packed. We walked up to the door and paid the five-dollar entry fee to a big woman with dyed red hair, a voluminous skirt, a leather vest and cowboy boots.

'Are you registering for the slam?' she asked. 'We've already started.'

'Shit, no!' Chloe declared.

A big island bar sat in the centre of the pub and we pushed through the crowd to get to it. Interesting mix of people. Cockies in moleskin pants, striped shirts and hats mixed with arty types in berets. There were young men and women who probably worked in the mines, labourers in boots and blue singlets and even a couple of hippies, which surprised me. Their natural habitat was the temperate coastal region of the eastern seaboard and it was rare to find them west of the Great Dividing Range. None of the subcultures minded a drink, though. Everyone was knocking back beer, wine and premixed rum and coke with gusto and the noise level was high—conversation mixing with the jazz playing over the PA. The crowd made me relax a bit. Safety in numbers. Watto always waited until you were alone.

I borrowed a fifty off Chloe, bought us both champagne and leaned back on the bar, scanning the room, but there was no sign of Nick. A small stage in the corner was draped in black and lit with a crimson spot. Round tables jostled for space in front of it, full of people clutching notebooks, A4 printouts and crumpled, ink-scrawled sheets of paper. A couple of French doors were set into the wall behind the stage and beyond them I glimpsed a carpeted hallway leading to a sweeping staircase. A sign above it read *Accommodation*. Next to the stage the judges' table was set up with scorecards, pens and paper, and three bottles of red. JJ was there in his black suit and trilby hat, drinking wine and talking to a fat guy in a t-shirt, beret and cravat. Chloe stood on the bar railing to see what I was looking at.

'Who's that?' she squealed. I didn't think she was talking about beret guy.

'Jerome Jones, otherwise known as JJ. Poet and uni lecturer. He's running this gig.'

'Jerome Jones . . .' She swirled the name around her mouth like a wine-wanker savouring an expensive vintage. 'Very tall, very dark, very handsome and very smart . . . I'm gonna do a poem, make him notice me.' She started moving through the crowd to the registration desk.

'Has to be original,' I shouted after her.

'Too easy,' she yelled back. 'There was a young lady named Chloe, who was awesome at giving a . . .'

I stood there sipping my drink and feeling a nauseous clench in my stomach that was either apprehension or hunger. In two days I'd eaten a few bites of a hotel breakfast, a sandwich and a small tin of tuna. Forget Atkins, just go on the run from the cops.

There was still no sign of Nick and I thought for a second that he might have double bluffed me, set up a false trail while he went off and . . . what? He was worried about JJ, wouldn't leave him to get slaughtered.

Unless Nick hadn't even made it to Broken Hill . . . Bloody scenes flashed before my eyes and my stomach lurched. Bugger it, if I couldn't stand not knowing, why didn't I just ask?

I pressed through the crowd, heading for JJ, nearly suffocating with the combined scent of sweat, spray deodorant and patchouli oil. Just as I was attempting to poke my head around the fat guy I felt a tap on my shoulder, turned and immediately recognised the black eyebrows and goatee.

Nick said, 'Shit, it *is* you,' grabbed me by the wrist and pulled me through the French doors into the hallway, out of sight of the bar. He pushed me up against a wall.

'I told you to go back to Melbourne.' He wore black trousers that were a little too long and a suit jacket I suspected he'd lifted from JJ's flat. His eyes glittered and his body quivered with nerves.

'Try reverse psychology next time. I tend to do the opposite of what I'm told.'

'And you brought your fucking friend.' He gestured towards the bar.

'No I didn't. She came on her own and that's your fault. If you hadn't stolen my money I wouldn't have had to call her for the airfare and she wouldn't have known where I was and got it in her head to come. Don't worry. She gave the cops the slip, didn't tell anyone.'

Nick didn't appear convinced, but he did seem to relax just a tiny bit.

'You haven't talked to JJ yet?' I ventured.

He shook his head. 'I know him. The crazy fucker won't cancel the slam. I thought it'd be relatively safe with all these people around, but I'm keeping an eye out just in case.' He tapped his jacket and I suddenly realised why he was wearing it in the heat. He had a weapon concealed.

'Give me one of those.'

'What?'

'I know you've got three. Freak's after me, too. Give me a gun.'

'You don't know how to fire one.'

'Neither do you, judging by your shithouse shot yesterday. How hard can it be?'

Nick looked from side to side. I could see him weigh it up. If Watto did show up, it would be two against one.

'Follow me,' he said.

At the top of the staircase we walked down a floral-carpeted corridor until Nick unlocked a wooden door with an old-fashioned key. The hotel room was chintzy: brass bed, patchwork quilt, doilies and dried flowers decorating antique mahogany furnishings. Lace curtains adorned double doors leading to the wide balcony that ran around the pub. It was stuffy inside and Nick flicked a switch on the wall to turn on an old wooden ceiling fan.

He slid his sports tote from underneath the bed and we sat next to each other on the sagging mattress while he unzipped the bag, pulled out one of the police issue Smith and Wesson's and handed it to me. The wooden grip was textured and the gun felt heavy in my hand. I held it gingerly, as though it might bite.

'Ever used one of these?' he asked.

'Only to smack someone in the face.'

'Sure you want to carry it? Hard to say you're a hostage.'

'Has been since I followed you to Broken Hill. I'll tell 'em I got Stockholm Syndrome, started identifying with my captor, like Patty Hearst.'

He grinned, frowned, then rested his head in his hands for a couple of seconds, before rubbing his eyes and sitting up straight. I got the feeling he'd almost reached the end. He was half the size he'd been the day he strolled into my office, and had scooped-out cheeks and violet skin beneath feverish eyes. I wondered if Liz had lost so much weight because of some psychic sympathy with her twin.

'Right.' Nick sniffed, taking the gun off me and cracking the barrel to show me the bullets. 'It's fully loaded. A revolver's single action so you've got to cock the hammer before you pull the trigger. Just like in the movies, right?'

'Sure.'

When he handed it back I practised tilting the hammer a couple of times, then slipped it into my bag. Australian PIs weren't allowed to carry guns and I'd never really been armed before. I wondered if I'd actually be able to use the weapon if it came to that. Just thinking about firing it made my heart thud against my rib cage.

'So what's the plan? We let JJ finish his slam then get him to safety?'

'Pretty much.'

'And after that?'

He looked into the middle distance like he was wrestling with something.

'Nick,' I said, 'come clean, seriously. I know everything. Or almost everything. I know someone's threatened to kill Liz and your brother if you don't pay them a shitload of cash. Most likely the same someone who sicked Watto onto me.

He told me that Chloe and my mum and brother were dead if I went to the cops. Sound familiar? I know you talked to JJ's friend Travis at the Kit Kat Club in Adelaide last night—about the Red Devils. You told me you'd stolen money off someone, so it's not too much of a leap to think it might be them, although I'm not sure why you'd be so dumb as to rip off a bunch of bikies.'

Nick stared at me. I went on: 'I'm thinking it all goes back to that writers' roadshow. Otherwise, why would Isabella, JJ and Desiree have someone after them? You were all together here in Broken Hill. The Red Devils have a clubhouse in Broken Hill . . .' I was thinking out loud by then. 'Of course Victoria wasn't with you, so Watto targeting her makes no sense.'

'Watto targeting you makes no sense.'

'I know. He sent me a death threat the day after I took the case. How could anybody have known what I was up to? All I'd done were a couple of internet searches . . .'

'Maybe he was following me, saw you, and became fixated? You said he's off his head.'

'That's not a reason to have my family tailed. Watto knew Mum and Jasper were in Byron when I thought they were in Sydney. Lot of organisation for a drug-fucked stalker.'

'Doesn't make any sense . . .'

'That's why I need you to tell me everything you know. If I find out who's behind all this I can tell the cops and protect everyone. I'm not going to be responsible for any more deaths. Not after what happened to my mum and her partner Steve.'

'Telling you won't protect anyone. It'll put you in more danger.'

'Nick, please. I just want to end this.'

He was quiet for a while. It was hot in the room, despite the slow-moving fan, and I could feel the hair at the back of my neck become damp.

'Me too. I'm ending it tonight.'

chapterforty-eight

The bed in the chintzy hotel room squeaked as I shifted my weight.

'How are you ending it?'

'I'm paying back what I owe.'

'But Liz said it was more than four hundred thousand. Much more.' I couldn't keep the incredulity out of my voice.

'Uh-huh.'

'How'd you get hold of it? Travis? Where is it?' I looked around the room, wondering how much space that much money actually took up. Had to be pretty bulky.

Nick lifted one side of his mouth. 'It's not in cash.'

'What then? Gang takes Visa?'

'You don't have to know the details. It's enough that I've got it, okay?'

'So what's the plan?'

'Soon as the slam's finished I head to a pub where I meet with the Devils and complete the transaction.'

'What if they take the money and decide to kill you anyway?'

He thought about it for a while.

'I was going to ask JJ to come along for backup. Wait in the car. Make sure I get out okay.'

'What about after you pay them off? You're still Australia's most wanted.'

'I disappear.'

'What?'

'Vanish. It's part of the deal.'

'How?'

'False passport. New identity. People do it all the time.'

'But, shit, your writing career.'

'Christ, Simone, that's the least of my worries. I fucked things up and now I have to make it right. It's the only way.'

Sounded like something I'd say.

'And what about that freak in the mask, Watto? He's still after me. Am I gonna be watching my back the rest of my life?'

'No need to worry, that's another part of the arrangement. They get the money as long as they leave everyone else alone.'

'I don't believe it.'

He pulled a mobile phone out of his jacket pocket and dialled a number.

'It's Nick. I have to speak to Craig.' He hung up.

I stared at him.

'Take a couple of minutes,' he said.

Amplified voices drifted up through the old floorboards, muffled applause, whistles, catcalls. Sounded like a vibe show at a buck's party. Who knew pub punters would be so into poetry?

'That hair . . .' Nick looked at me, shook his head and almost smiled.

'It's hot, right? I mean, gentlemen prefer blondes and all that.'

'You look like a crazy tart from one of my books.'

'I really don't think you're in a position to criticise, Martin St James.'

The mobile rang. Nick's face got serious.

'Simone Kirsch wants to speak to you, about the deal.' He handed over the phone.

'Simone.' It was a male voice. Deep, slightly Aussie, confident sounding. 'I've heard so much about you. You're quite famous in here.'

'Who is this?'

'My name's Craig, and I'm truly sorry to hear about your trouble with my, uh, associate. He served a purpose, but his personal problems have made him a liability to my organisation.'

'By personal problems do you mean he's a murdering drug pig who threatened my family and attempted to dismember me with a chainsaw?'

'Don't worry, your family is safe. He's bad for business and won't be around much longer, I can promise you that.'

'Why was he after me in the first place?' I asked, but there was no reply. The connection went dead. I turned to Nick.

'Was I just talking to Craig Murdoch, head of the Devils?'

'Uh-huh.'

'But he's in jail.'

'Doesn't mean he can't get access to a mobile phone. Don't tell me you're that naïve.'

'Reckon I can trust him?'

'Can't trust anyone. But I do believe he'll off his psycho henchman. Guy's completely out of control.'

As Nick and I made our way carefully down the stairs it became apparent there was a break in the slam. 'Everybody Knows', the Leonard Cohen song, was playing, the crowd had washed up against the bar, a substantial group of punters was outside smoking cigarettes, and Chloe sat at the judges' table.

JJ was right next to her, arm over the back of her chair, and the two of them were so focused on each other they didn't notice us approach from behind.

'You're gorgeous.' He sipped his glass of red.

'I'm fucking fat, is what I am.'

'I love pregnant women . . . so lush, luminous.' He checked his watch. 'Damn. Better announce the final results and give out the prizes. You staying here in town?'

'If I can find a room . . .' Chloe played with her hair, winding a strand around her index finger.

JJ grinned, leapt up, walked right past Nick and me and jumped onto the small stage. He was a little unsteady on his feet, his hat was askew and I noticed that the wine bottles were empty. The music faded out and JJ grabbed the mike, got the crowd's attention, telling them what a great night it had been, and thanking the poets, the audience, the publican.

'Before I announce the winners of the Broken Hill Poetry Slam there's one more poem I have to read, a haiku I composed just a few moments ago, inspired by everyone's talent, the wonderful city of Broken Hill, and a beautiful woman with a nice line in saucy limericks.'

A few people whistled and catcalled and Chloe preened.

JJ pulled a stained beer mat from his pants pocket and read off the back: 'Desert moon rises, In the red earth she flowers, Incandescent bloom.'

Applause. A lot of the women in the audience looked particularly misty eyed. I looked at Nick and we both rolled our eyes.

'He's laying it on a bit thick,' I said.

'Yeah, but it's working. Your friend better watch out.'

'You don't know Chloe. *He's* the one in trouble.'

We'd only taken our eyes off our surroundings for a couple of seconds, but that was all it took for everything to turn to shit. I looked back to the stage where JJ was opening an envelope, Oscars style, and glanced through the windows behind him. A police car had pulled up in front of the pub and the two cops who emerged wore bulletproof vests. Another police car, a four-wheel drive, was visible through the pub's double glass doors.

'Shit.' Nick clocked them at the same time and froze like a hunted deer.

'Might not be after you,' I whispered. 'Could be, I dunno, a drug raid or something.'

'Then what's she doing here?'

Detective Talbot slid out of the passenger side of the four-wheel drive, her brown bob sleek and a flak jacket over her usual pantsuit, bulking out her sinewy frame. A tall, brawny Aboriginal copper with a salt and pepper beard and a khaki uniform slammed the door on the driver's side, and the two of them crossed the sidewalk and entered the pub. She squinted, scanning the crowd, while he made for the stage and hopped up.

'And the winner is . . .' JJ, glassy-eyed with red and blinded by the spotlight, hadn't noticed them.

'Police!' The cop took the microphone. 'We have a warrant to search these premises. Nobody move.'

chapter forty-nine

The crowd booed and hissed and despite the order not to, began shuffling around chaotically. A few people tried to leave but all the doorways were blocked by uniformed cops. JJ bounded off the stage back to Chloe, looked up and saw me and Nick. The expression on his face rapidly morphed from 'I know you from somewhere' to 'Holy shit.'

'I'll explain later,' Nick said. 'Right now we've got to get out of here.'

Chloe hoisted herself up from her chair.

'You.' Nick pointed. 'Stay.'

'Make me.' She tossed her long blonde hair and stuck her hands on her hips.

Rage momentarily darkened his face, but instead of throttling her he turned and walked slowly and calmly to the corridor that led to the hotel stairs. JJ, Chloe and I followed, our actions hidden by the crowd. Nick glanced to the right, down the passageway, and I followed his gaze. A couple of cops stood outside the glass door at the end of the hall, backs to us. Nick started to jog up the stairs and the rest of us followed. We'd just reached the first landing when I heard a shout.

'Oi, you lot. Stop right there.'

We bolted, JJ helping Chloe, practically lifting her off her high-heeled mules. I felt the old pub shake as the cops thundered up the creaky hallway, simultaneously radioing for backup.

When we reached the top Nick was holding the door to his room open. We sprinted in and he closed it quietly just before the coppers reached the top of the stairs. He held his finger to his lips, crossed the room and carefully opened the balcony door.

Outside our pursuers were rattling handles and bashing on doors.

'Police, open up!'

'I'll check the fire exit,' one of them shouted.

A radio crackled and I heard a voice I was sure was Talbot's. 'Got the keys. I'm coming up.'

Nick slipped out the door and beckoned the rest of us to follow. JJ went first, holding Chloe's hand and pulling her along. I closed the door and brought up the rear. We walked lightly, sticking close to the wall so no one could see us from the street, Chloe on tippy-toes to stop her heels from clattering. At the end of the balcony stood another old two-storey building with a veranda of its own, a two-foot gap in between. Nick jumped across and kept going, not looking back. I guessed he'd scoped out the escape route as soon as he'd checked into the room.

JJ and I helped Chloe struggle from the first balcony to the second and by the time we'd got there Nick had disappeared. I leaned over the railing and looked down. The next building along was single storey with a flat concrete roof, and he was already halfway across it.

JJ climbed over, hung for a second and dropped. It was five foot, not much, unless you were about that tall, eight months up the duff and wearing four-inch heels.

JJ waited with his arms open, looking up at Chloe.

'Stay here,' I whispered to her, just before I jumped. 'Cops aren't after you.'

'Fuck that.'

I stumbled a bit as I landed and righted myself just as Chloe flung herself into space, falling towards JJ, a front-heavy human missile.

He caught her, but she landed hard and he staggered back, huffing out air and losing his balance. He swung a hand behind him to break their fall and when they hit the concrete I heard a sharp crack, like a twig snapped for kindling. I hurried over. JJ groaned.

'You guys alright?'

'Fine.' Chloe was dusting herself off.

'My wrist,' JJ said.

I heard voices coming from the pub veranda.

'Come on,' I said. 'We don't have much time.'

I helped JJ up and we ran to the edge of the roof where I'd last seen Nick. A set of metal rungs had been fixed into the wall as a ladder and he was waiting down the bottom, in an alleyway filled with rubbish skips. As I climbed down he whispered: 'End of the lane, turn left. Venue called the Demo Club. Tell the others. Meet you there.' He wedged his hands in his pockets and strolled off, still doing his 'act casual' thing.

Chloe got to the bottom of the ladder no problem: all those years of stripping in platforms had made her amazingly agile in heels. As JJ struggled down one-handed, I told her what the story was, said I'd meet them there and hurried off. I didn't want to get caught, and figured an expectant platinum-haired stripper and an injured poet dressed like a Blues Brother might stand out a tad in Broken Hill.

I turned left on the wide main drag, forcing myself to walk slowly, not looking back at the Silver City hotel. People passed me, heading to the pub. Word had obviously gotten around that something big was going down, and everyone wanted a look-see.

A block later I arrived at a long, low building with signs advertising a *Family Bistro*, *Keno* and *Live Entertainment*. *Barrier Social Democratic Club* was painted on an awning overhanging the footpath, so I guessed it was the place Nick had told me about.

I smiled at the bouncer, signed in at the front desk for temporary membership, giving a false name and address, and followed a carpeted corridor towards the bistro, where music was pumping. I doubted Nick would be in the gaming room—too many cameras.

The room was large and cavernous and the restaurant was closed, its bains-marie empty. Tables and chairs had been pushed back against the walls, exposing red carpet patterned with yellow swirls, making room for a dance floor in front of a small stage. Coloured spots lit up a four-piece band. They were performing a cover of a Pogues song—'Fairytale of New York'—and the lead singer was thrashing around drunkenly, doing a very convincing Shane MacGowan impression. The same song had been playing at Nick's the day I'd stumbled onto Isabella's body. Seemed like a lifetime ago.

I spotted Nick on the far side of the bar, hidden in shadow, watching the band with a funny expression on his face and drinking something that looked like straight spirits. I guessed if you were going to fall off the wagon then the conclusion of a police pursuit was the time to do it. I walked over.

'Hey,' I said. 'That was fucking close.'

He nodded but kept looking at the band.

'These guys were playing when me and Isabella were here as part of the roadshow. Pogues cover band. Guess what they're called?'

I shrugged.

'The Rogues.' He shook his head and grimaced as he sipped his drink.

The room was crowded with young people, well-dressed men and women in their early to mid twenties, all drinking, some swaying and singing along with the song. It surprised me. Guessed I'd expected a bunch of grizzled, smudge-faced miners wearing hard hats with lights attached to the front, hacking their lungs out into their beers. Place reminded me of a blue light disco I'd been to as a teenager, held at the local RSL.

'I know you don't want to tell me, but is Victoria's connection to Lachlan Elliot the reason Watto tried to kill her? Both her and Isabella knew him, he knew the bikies . . .'

Nick just shook his head.

JJ and Chloe entered the room and were mostly ignored, thanks to the band launching into 'If I Should Fall from Grace with God', which inspired the crowd to pogo, link arms and swing each other around as though performing a psychotic barn dance.

I ordered a water—fleeing from the fuzz had made me kinda thirsty—and when Chloe came over she ordered a red wine and a champagne.

'How's the wrist?' I asked JJ.

'Pretty banged up. Lucky I'm already anaesthetised.' He looked at Nick. 'What the fuck's going on, mate?'

Chloe handed JJ the red and took a slug of the champagne. Nick had just opened his mouth to speak when some drunken patrons staggered by and a female voice said, 'Disgusting.'

'You say something?' Chloe yelled after them.

The group stopped, turned. A large girl with frizzy red hair stepped forward, holding a Bacardi Breezer. She looked Chloe up and down.

'Yeah, I did actually. I said disgusting. Drinking in your condition. You should be ashamed of yourself.'

Chloe bristled and stood up tall on her stupid heels.

'Ashamed? I don't think so, love. Pretty soon I won't be pregnant but you'll still be an ugly bush-pig.'

'What did you call me?'

'Bush-pig. You heard.'

'Slapper.'

The band had finished their song and launched into a cover of 'Fiesta', a fast-paced ditty equal parts Irish-folk-punk and crazed mariachi band. The dancers thrashed violently around the floor.

Chloe and the red-haired chick launched at each other at the same time, all bared teeth and sharp fingernails. I pulled Chloe back, JJ assisting with his one workable hand. The girl's boyfriend grabbed her, but she broke free and slapped Chloe across the face. I was holding Chloe by the shoulders with all my might while JJ spoke to the boyfriend.

'Hey, keep a hold of her, will you. This is a pregnant woman here.'

'Control your own bitch,' spat the chick.

'Yeah,' said her boyfriend. 'What's it to you, you fucken boong.'

Chloe and JJ looked at each other and threw themselves at the offending couple as one. I couldn't hold her. I didn't try.

JJ shot off a couple of short, sharp punches—not bad considering he only had one hand. The guy staggered back and hit the floor. Chloe leapt at the chick and the two of them fell, Chloe on top, clawing at the girl's hair and attempting to lift then smash her head against the carpet. The couple's friends advanced and JJ sent a few wild swings their way but made no contact. One of them picked up a plastic chair and brandished it like he was a lion tamer. I looked to Nick to help and he reluctantly stood up and moved out of the shadows, towards us.

The band played on with lots of brass, whistles and yelping from the singer, but the dancers were peeling off, either to gawk at us or join in. Two big bouncers pushed their way through the crowd, but before they or Nick could reach us the redhead let out a high-pitched screech and Chloe actually got off her and stood still with a strange expression on her face.

'She's pissing on me!' the girl screamed, lying on the floor. 'The fucking slapper's pissing on me!'

Everyone stood back and watched. Fluid was gushing down Chloe's legs, soaking the redhead's dress, turning it from pale blue to navy. The bouncers finally arrived at the scene.

'Fuck's going on?' one of them said, face screwed up in confusion and disgust.

'Get an ambulance, mate.' JJ had his arm around Chloe's shoulders. 'Her waters just broke. She's about to have a baby.'

chapterfifty

The ambulance didn't take long and I wondered if it had been just up the road, staking out the Silver City hotel. Five minutes later two paramedics were crouched next to Chloe who was reclining on the pub carpet, swearing and clutching JJ's arm. The redhaired chick and her mates had scurried off quick-smart, threatening legal action and looking vaguely ill.

Nick nudged me in the ribs. 'Been nice knowing you,' he said.

'Huh?'

'It's almost time.' He glanced at his watch. 'JJ and I have to go.'

'What about me?'

'You'll be at the hospital with Chloe, surely.'

'For secret women's business? Give me a break, Nick, I'm coming to the pub. JJ can't help. He's half cut, doesn't know the plan or what Watto looks like, and—if you hadn't noticed—he's got a broken wrist and a better idea of what's happening to Chloe than I do. He's going with her, not me.'

'Fine.' Nick slammed down the rest of his drink and squatted next to JJ. I followed suit.

'Mate, I need to borrow your car. Where's it parked?'

'Sulphide Street. Couple of blocks. What's going on?'

'You're going to hospital with her and I'm paying the Devils what I owe them. I don't have time to explain.'

JJ pulled a set of keys from his pocket. Chloe seized my forearm, fake fingernails digging in.

'I want a contract out on that cocksucker,' she gasped.

'Who?'

'Curtis, the goddamn mother—' She stopped to let out a primal shriek. The Shane MacGowan lookalike stopped writhing on the stage and peered in our direction.

'Okay,' the female ambo said. 'It's off to maternity for you.'

'I'm not due for a month!'

The two paramedics hoisted her onto a stretcher.

'I'm booked in for a fucking caesarean!' she yelled. 'In Melbourne!'

They looked at each other and chuckled.

'Little bit late for that . . .' the guy said.

'My moot!' Chloe cried.

'Will I see you later?' JJ asked Nick.

'Probably not. I've got to disappear for a while. I just wanted to say . . .' He paused. 'Fuck it. I'm no good at impromptu speeches. Don't even know what I *think* until I see what I write. Cops ask you questions, you don't know a thing.'

'I know the drill.'

'Take care, mate.'

'Yeah, you too.'

They hugged. It seemed like Nick didn't want to let go. JJ looked puzzled, patted Nick's back, pulled away and followed Chloe out to the ambulance. I yelled that I'd catch up with her soon, but wasn't sure she'd heard.

Fifteen minutes later Nick and I sat in JJ's old Mitsubishi Magna, across the road from the pub. The hotel was on the outskirts of town, not a grand two-storey job but a squat concrete bunker with a corrugated-iron awning and blacked-out windows. A chalkboard on the side of the entrance advertised topless barmaids and five-dollar steak specials. A couple of Harley Davidsons and a few utes were parked outside. My mouth was dry. Nick gripped the steering wheel so hard his knuckles were white.

'Think they've got someone watching us?' I asked.

'Definitely. Got your gun?'

'Uh-huh.' I withdrew it from my bag and rested it on my lap. 'Reckon there'll be trouble?'

'I don't think they'll try anything. Want the money too bad, but I'll check on you from the pub. I reccied the place earlier, and you can see out the windows even though you can't see in.'

I nodded. He'd thought of everything.

'Then what do I do?' I asked.

'Whatever you want. Go see Chloe. Give yourself up to the cops.'

'What do I tell them?'

'Anything. That you escaped my evil clutches. That I killed Geddes. That I'm really Watto or Elvis Mask or whatever his name is, out of my mind on drugs. Just don't tell them the truth and don't implicate the Devils. That's part of the deal, yeah? No one grasses, no one testifies, they're happy and our families and friends are safe.'

'So they just get away with it?'

'There's no other option. They've got too much clout, Simone. It's why I couldn't go to jail. They'd have got me in there easier than on the outside.' He checked his watch. 'I'm going in. Thanks for this. And once again, I'm sorry for walking into your office that day, for losing you your licence, screwing up your life.'

'I probably would have screwed it up myself anyway, sooner or later.'

'You know, I kind of wish I was writing the next Zack book now,' he said. 'I've got the best idea for a female PI. A smart-mouthed, crazy ex-stripper who never, ever drinks green tea.'

'Bit far-fetched,' I said.

Nick smiled and got out of the car, then paused with the door open. 'Oh, before I go—take this.' He pulled an envelope out of his jacket pocket. It was the last of Liz's money.

'Won't you need it?'

'I'll be right.' He smiled. 'Bye.'

'Wait,' I said. Something had been brewing in my head ever since we'd spoken in his room at the Silver City hotel. 'You said you thought you knew who the money belonged to, but you were wrong. Was it Lachlan Elliot you ripped off? Victoria and Isabella knew him. He was in with the Devils. What if he was holding on to the bikies' money and they killed him because they thought he'd stolen it? Kind of makes sense . . .'

Nick just gave me an enigmatic smile, slammed the door and was gone.

I scooted over to the driver's seat and sat waiting, the gun on my lap hidden by a tourist map of Broken Hill. I was so tense my shoulders were bunched around my ears and my neck felt like a pillar of stone. Nick couldn't have been in the pub for more than a few minutes but time seemed to have slowed and stretched out, become elastic.

I wished I had a drink. I wished I had a cigarette. I found an old bottle of water rolling around in the passenger side foot-well and had a swig but it tasted stale and chemical, like the plastic had degraded in the heat.

A late model black van with tinted windows cruised past the pub a couple of times, but I couldn't see who was driving.

The vehicle stopped in front of the entrance and a man got out and walked into the building. He was chunky, with long hair and a leather bikie waistcoat.

After an excruciatingly long five minutes a cab pulled up and I nearly had a heart attack, thinking it was a police car. I squinted through the window. The driver got out to have a cigarette and I realised it was the same dude who'd picked up me and Chloe from the airport.

Finally Nick walked out of the pub, got in the taxi and drove away. A minute later the black van came back, the bikie got in and they did the same.

I guessed that was it. Nick had paid them off, was taking his false passport and getting the hell out of dodge. Craig Murdoch, hopefully, was going to dispose of his crazed 'enforcer'. I didn't see why he wouldn't. Surely he didn't need any more heat and just wanted to be left alone to carry on his business dealings, or work on his documentary or whatever it was he did behind bars. Nick had been right. They'd gotten away with everything, but it was the only way to ensure no one else would get hurt. I should have been happy—it was all over—but an uneasy, dejected feeling settled around me like low-lying cloud.

I wondered what was going to happen to me now that everything was finished. I'd go through a lot of shit with the coppers and they'd know I was lying and never reinstate my licence. My only hope had been the job in Vietnam, but that was up shit creek. There was always stripping to fall back on, but I was nearly thirty and the older you got the worse stuff you had to do to keep up with the younger, hotter girls. Not just nips and tucks but sick shit like sitting on witches hats and popping live animals out of your pussy. Forget erotica, the whole thing turned into a freak show.

What was left? I'd done hospitality and retail and they both made me feel like shooting myself in the head. I could always finish my arts degree, but who ever heard of a BA actually getting you a job?

I started up the Magna and thought about what to do. I could give myself up to Talbot or go see my best friend give birth. Both options were unappealing, but at least the latter would include a celebratory bottle of champagne. I checked the tourist directory for the location of a drive-through and the hospital, and picked up a bottle of Domain Chandon and a sparkly pink bottle-bag on the way.

I dragged my feet into the reception area.

'I'm looking for my friend, Chloe Wozniak? She went into labour at a pub in town.'

'The one screaming bloody murder about her caesarean and her fanny?' the nurse said, smiling. I smiled back.

'That'd be her.'

'She's in the delivery room. No time for the caesar. We told her not to worry, everything would snap back, good as new.'

'Does it?'

She literally hooted with laughter and slapped her palm against the desk. I resolved never to have sex again.

I heard the screams on the way down the green linoleum corridor. I'd had the misfortune of hearing Chloe 'make love' and had always thought it sounded like a person being murdered. That night was worse, more like she was being skinned alive.

The nurse poked her head inside the delivery room and spoke to someone. JJ emerged, wrist in a plaster cast, wearing a gown and gloves, both streaked with blood. He looked beatific.

'Simone! You made it.'

'How's the baby?'

'Fine. Coming quick though. You might want to gown up.'

I clutched the champagne to my chest as another howl emanated from behind the swinging doors.

'That sound. Can't they give her something for the pain?'

'Too late for an epidural and they don't want to risk peth. There's gas but I think it's doing more for me than her. Doctor's cool. How's Nick?'

'Paid off the Devils and disappeared.'

I quickly told JJ about Nick's plan.

'How'd he get hold of a million bucks?' he asked, incredulous.

'Not sure. I thought maybe Travis gave it to him. Nick visited the Kit Kat before he came to Broken Hill.'

JJ shook his head. 'No way. Travis is dead broke. His only asset is his beloved surfboard.'

'What about the club?'

'He just manages. Deals a little on the side, but it's small-time stuff.'

'Maybe the Assassins lent it? He's in with them, right?'

'You've got to be joking,' JJ laughed. 'Maybe Nick sold his house?'

'All his assets are frozen. House. Bank account. Rights to his books.'

'Well, shit, I don't know. How does someone get hold of a million dollars?'

And suddenly I knew. I couldn't believe I'd been so stupid, but it had all happened so fast, there hadn't been time to think it over.

Nick didn't have the million. Nick *was* the million. The bikies were handing him over to Rod Thurlow. Wanted, dead or alive. It made sense. The long hugs, faraway looks, him feeling he should say something profound. The story about disappearing was bullshit so I'd go along with it and help him.

And I had. I'd helped him kill himself.

'Well,' said JJ, 'however he managed it, I'm glad it all worked out in the end. You'd better get into the delivery room or you're gonna miss the birth. It's the most amazing experience, watching a new life come into the world.'

'Send Chloe my apologies and give her this.' I handed him the champers. 'There's something I have to do.'

In the hospital lobby I used the payphone to call the taxi driver who'd driven us in from the airport and picked up Nick. He pulled up in front of admissions and I got in.

'Remember me?' I took a fifty from Liz's envelope and handed it over.

'The good tipper.'

'You picked up a fare from the Bauxite Hotel about half an hour ago. Guy with black hair and a goatee. Where did you take him?'

The driver hesitated. I gave him another fifty.

'Red Devils' clubhouse,' he said. 'Outskirts of town.'

'Take me there.'

'I'm not sure it's such a good idea for a young lady to go out there on her own.'

'And I'm not sure I'm what you'd call a lady. There's another hundred in it for you, on top of the metered fare.'

He put the car in drive.

chapter fifty-one

We were in an industrial area on the south side of the giant mullock heap and everything was quiet, factories and warehouses dark behind chain link fences and steel roller-doors. The occasional street light emitted pale pools of radiance and signs warned of twenty-four-hour security patrols. Not that I could see any. The streets were empty of traffic.

I had no idea if Nick was alive or dead, although I had a feeling Rod Thurlow would want him alive, if only for a little while. What had he said? *I want him to suffer like Isabella suffered.*

We pulled up on a corner. I couldn't see anything resembling a clubhouse, not that I would have known. I'd heard some bad stories about biker do's and had generally avoided them, so my knowledge was pretty much confined to B-grade sixties films starring Jack Nicholson and Peter Fonda.

'Where is it?' I asked.

'A block up. They have surveillance video. Sure you want to do this?'

'Yep. Drop me off right in front of the place. I want them to see me on the cameras.'

He sighed, but did as I said.

'Why you want to go there anyway?'

'Trying to find a friend.'

We stopped in front of a building that looked like it had once been a small factory or workshop, although it was hard to tell—the perimeter was encircled by a heavy steel fence. He was right about the CCTV cameras. They were on the posts in anodised metal housings, the kind that swivel around and follow your every move.

'Here.' I gave him a hundred and fifty. 'Wait for me where you stopped before, yeah? If I'm not out in an hour call the Broken Hill police. Ask for Detective Talbot.'

'What's going on? Never heard of a local copper named Talbot. This something to do with that raid on the pub?'

'I'll tell you everything in an hour. Best gossip you ever heard. And I'll give you another hundred, swear to god. Just stay out of sight of the clubhouse.'

I got out of the cab and walked up to the gate. Solid steel, no handle or gap to look through. There was an intercom, though, and it hit me that I was often behind tall gates talking into them. Probably because I always had to question dodgy pricks who needed to protect themselves from the world.

I knew the drill so I pressed the buzzer and popped some gum in my mouth while I waited, thankful as hell for my new blonde hair.

'Who is it?' Gruff male voice.

'Candy.' I turned my voice a bit westie, stepped back so the camera got a good view, sucked in my stomach and pushed out my boobs. 'I'm the entertainment.'

'We've already got entertainment.' The voice sounded puzzled.

'Now you've got some more. Open the gate, mate.'

It didn't open. I was sweating, and not just from the heat.

'What did you say your name was?'

'Candy.' I rolled my eyes, chomped the gum. 'Craig sent me.'

'Craig who?'

'Murdoch. Who do ya reckon?'

'I didn't hear anything about it.'

''Cause I'm supposed to be a surprise. For the celebration.'

'What celebration?' Suspicious.

'Fuck should I know? I get a call from Craig at Port—we go way back—and he says how quick can I get on a plane to Broken Hill? Boys are having a special party so they need a special show and he knows me show's not the sort of thing you see every day, so, like, I said, Craig, I know we're mates 'n' all, but fuck off, I'm not going out the back of Bourke for one fucken strip. And he offers me a grand, plane ticket and a motel room, so I say, okay, whatever, fuck it, and here I am. Look, you don't want the show, that's fine. I've already been paid, I'll just go back to me motel and drink bourbon and watch telly before I fly back tomorrow. Easy money. Craig'll be pissed off, but it's not my problem he went to all this trouble to surprise yas and yas didn't let me in, aye?'

Something clanked and the metal gate rolled back. I waved the cab driver off and sauntered in, trying to sway my hips nonchalantly and give the impression I did 'special' shows at biker clubhouses every day. The building was squat and concrete, a bunker with no windows, heavily fortified with the same Colorbond steel as the fence. The car park that surrounded the building was empty, no van, not a single Harley. I remembered news reports about clubhouses being firebombed and shot up by rival gangs. One mob had actually crashed a van through a security gate and blown it up. Then there were the coppers to worry about. No wonder security was tight. Bikes were probably parked inside.

A door opened on the right side of the building and a fat bearded bloke who could have been a bikie from central casting poked his head out and waved me over. I ambled across, trying not to clutch my bag too tightly, hoping desperately they didn't search you before you went in, and that they wouldn't try calling Craig to check out my story. The gate clanked shut behind me.

I chewed my gum while he looked me up and down. He seemed plenty pissed, hyped on uppers, but he liked what he saw.

'Trev.' He stuck out a meaty palm.

'Candy.' I shook it. 'Grouse ta meet ya.'

'Fuck, you're a bit of a glamour compared to the chicks we normally get. City girls don't wanna come all the way up the Hill. You look familiar, but. I seen you somewhere before?'

I shrugged and tried to utilise my panic the way actors drew on stage fright. I'd once seen a doco on Marlon Brando and the Stanislavski method. I *was* a skanky yet up-myself bogan stripper-princess, slightly bored by the proceedings but fully aware of my sexual power.

'*Hustler, Penthouse, Picture, Oz-Bike.*' I ticked each one off on a finger. 'Plus I'm branching out into acting. You seen *I Cum in a Land Down Under*?'

He shook his head.

'It *was* mainly for the overseas market . . .' I talked through my gum.

'Where's all your stuff?' He nodded to my small bag. 'Youse girls usually come with suitcases full of costumes and props and shit.'

'Don't need any.'

'No?'

'Nah, I kinda use whatever or . . . whoever comes to hand.'

Trev grinned. 'Sounds hot.'

'Fucken oath.'

'Have to be to top the shows we got on tonight.'

I shrugged again. Like, whatever.

Trev stood aside to let me in. The entrance led to a small antechamber, obviously another security precaution, and he locked the outside door before opening the inner one. The interior of the building was a large, square open space with a corner bar in front of a large glass-fronted fridge filled with booze. The Harleys were parked inside next to a garage roller-door and the furniture consisted of bar stools, a few old couches and a couple of chrome tables. There were no windows, just a fierce air-conditioner and an extractor fan to ensure no one suffocated. A large painting took up one wall—a picture of a grinning devil head with the name 'Red Devils' above and the club motto below: 'Dead Man Riding'. Other walls were plastered with posters of naked chicks and bikes, individually and together, some relatively tame like the ones Chloe had done for *Picture* magazine, others looking like something out of a gynaecology textbook. The place smelled of oil and sweat and cigarette smoke. A plasma screen TV over the bar was playing a porno, but the sound was off and the fifteen or so bikies weren't paying attention to it anyway. They were huddled around in a rough circle as AC/DC blasted out of a huge silver sound system. 'Thunderstruck'.

'That's Channelle.' Trev nodded towards the crowd as he led me into the room. 'She's doing a beer show.'

'Cool,' I said, no idea what a beer show was.

'C'mere, darl.' He grabbed me around the waist and hoisted me up on the bar so I could get a good view. I had the feeling Trev was flirting, coming over all gallant and knights of the round table.

Channelle was dancing around the centre of the circle naked but for a shiny satin suspender belt, fishnet stockings and chunky heels. Her hair was shoulder length, bleached and permed and her makeup harsh: bright blue eye shadow teamed with hot pink lipstick made her look older than she was, which I guessed was late thirties. She was quite thin, but sort of flabby, like there was no muscle tone underneath. A faded rose had been inked onto one boob and when she turned I saw a washed-out shamrock branding one sagging flank. After she'd finished dancing around the circle she headed for one of the walls of the clubhouse and everybody let out a roar. She did a handstand and came to rest upside down, heels ripping the edge of a girlie magazine poster. Little by little she moved her legs until they made a wide V and all the blokes swarmed in close for a good look at her shaved pussy. You could always tell shaved from waxed: had a raw look, sort of a rash, like the stubble was trying to poke through the skin.

One of the guys, who was, strangely enough, shirtless and wearing a pair of Biggles-style aviator goggles on his forehead, ran to the fridge. The crowd roared as he returned holding aloft a stubby of VB. He twisted the top off and foam dribbled down the side. I suddenly got it. We weren't in Kansas anymore, Toto.

I tried not to look shocked as the shirtless guy went over to Channelle, tipped the stubby upside down and inserted it into her vagina up to the neck. It balanced. Channelle smiled bravely, her face red and puffy from the sudden rush of blood.

The guy slid the goggles over his eyes and removed the bottle, still holding it upside down, so the crowd could see that no liquid remained. I couldn't help thinking a fanny full of beer couldn't be good for you, the yeast alone likely to incite a terminal case of thrush.

Goggle-guy lay down on the floor, on a plastic drop-sheet. Channelle flipped expertly out of her handstand so that she was standing above his face. He opened his mouth and for a few seconds nothing happened, then the beer foamed out and he drank it, gargling and poking out his tongue. The gang went wild.

'Pretty good, aye?' Trev helped me down from the bar-top.

'Seen better.' I shrugged. 'There somewhere I can get ready?'

'Yeah, out back. Tulsa and Arizona are in there, but it should be okay.'

'So Channelle was just the warm-up bitch, huh?'

'Yeah. If that's for starters I can't wait to see what you come up with.'

A door behind the bar led to a hallway at the back, with doors leading off, all of them closed. Maybe they'd once been storerooms or offices. The clubhouse was claustrophobic and I started to feel that coming here had been a really dumb idea. Nick probably wasn't there anymore. At least I'd told the cabbie to call Talbot, but even if he did, could I stall them for an hour? And how would the cops get in without a warrant? Trev was hardly going to slide open the gate and roll out the welcome mat.

My mouth dried up and I started sweating again despite the powerful air-conditioning. Keep your shit together, I told myself. I had the gun. Six rounds, but there were fifteen of them, probably armed themselves, and I didn't even know whether I'd be capable of shooting, if it came to that.

Trev knocked briefly and opened one of the doors in the hallway.

The bedroom looked windowless, probably shuttered. A couple of thin, hard-faced strippers sat on a cheap floral bedspread under harsh fluorescent light. They wore long dresses in skin-tight, stretchy fabric, low cut, slashed up the thigh. The blonde's dress was hot-pink and Trev told me her name was Tulsa. Arizona wore electric blue, her hair was dyed rock 'n' roll black, and she looked up, startled, when we came in. They'd been deep in conversation and seemed totally wired, licking their lips and sucking at their teeth, pupils like black olives. Both were as skinny as Tiara and had the same twig arms, visible ribs and razor sharp clavicles. A glass pipe, identical to the one Tiara and Watto had used, sat on the bedside table, next to a lighter and a small square of folded foil.

'Fuck, Trev,' Arizona said. 'You scared the shit out of us. No guys in the girls' room, right?'

'Sorry. This is Candy. She's going on after youse. Craig sent her.'

Trev backed out of the room. The girls stared at me. Hard, crystalline eyes.

'You're the finale?' Arizona said.

'Uh-huh.'

'What do you do?' Tulsa, the blonde, asked.

'It's a surprise,' I said, and they both rolled their eyes. 'What do you guys do?'

Tulsa reached behind her and picked up a long, neon-pink object.

'We're the Texan Twins,' she said, and I didn't tell her that I was pretty sure Tulsa was in Oklahoma and Arizona happened to be a whole 'nother state.

At first I thought the item was one of those snake things you put at the base of doors to stop drafts, but a millisecond later I realised it was a double-ended dildo of similar length and girth made of some kind of pliable rubber. As she gripped it in the middle each bulbous end bounced up and down.

'Your show must be pretty extreme,' Arizona said, looking doubtful. 'They don't call us the backdoor beauties for nothing.'

If I ever get out of this damn clubhouse, I pledged silently, that's it, I'm quitting stripping for good.

'Cool,' I said. 'You guys know where the dunny is?'

'Down the hall.'

'Ta.'

I left the room and crept down the corridor, trying every door. All locked except for one at the opposite end, which turned out to be a small office. A desk sat in the middle and steel cabinets lined the walls. A table held a bank of TV screens displaying the CCTV footage. I saw the street I'd come in from, empty front and rear car parks and the beer show still going on in the main room. Another guy was lying on the tarp wearing the goggles this time. Who said vaudeville was dead? The final screen showed the strippers sitting on the mattress in their dresses, sucking from the pipe. The angle suggested the guys had installed a small camera in the light fitting. Pervy fuckers. Unfortunately for me there was no image of Nick bound to a chair in a storeroom, struggling like Penelope Pitstop tied to the railway tracks.

He wasn't there. Made sense. No black van, either. No Elvis Mask. They'd probably taken him directly to Rod.

I had to get out. I looked wildly around the office, heart beating fast. The desk was a mess: papers, computer, overflowing ashtray, biker magazines. I checked the top drawer and found a bunch of keys. Maybe they opened the locked doors. Maybe the locked doors led to a way out.

The first door revealed a small storeroom packed to the roof with cases of booze. The second led to a closet with nothing in it except a patch of carpet on the floor. I lifted it and found a padlocked hatch, tried each key with shaking hands, but none fitted. Was it a way out or did they have something stashed down there? Weapons? Drugs? I put my ear to the hatch, knocked softly, called Nick's name but heard nothing.

Right. I was seriously running out of time.

Another door opened onto a second bedroom, empty of people, and the last door onto a small workshop with bike parts and tools and a concrete floor. My heart sank, then rose. The back wall of the room was another roller-door. I hurried over. One key opened the padlock, the next the door itself. I winced in preparation for an ear-splitting alarm but it never came. Rolling the door up a little I slipped underneath and ran around the building looking for a way out. The fence was ten feet of slippery steel topped with razor wire. The ground was empty concrete and there was nowhere to hide. I raced to the front gate, praying the beer show was still in full swing and no one was in the office, scrutinising the television screens. I'd expected a mechanism beside the gate to open it, perhaps a handy red button, but there was nothing. Of course. Had to be in the antechamber Trev had led me through. I ran to the door I'd first entered but it was locked tight and none of the keys fit. My hands on the metal felt the thud of the music within. The thud suddenly stopped.

Damn. I ran to the back of the building, slid under the roller-door, closed but didn't lock it, and shut the door to the workshop. I tried to compose myself before re-entering the girls' room, but there wasn't really time. Arizona and Tulsa stared at me.

'Fuck happened to you?' said the blonde. 'Look like you just run the four-minute mile.'

I'd always worked well under pressure, necessity being the mother of invention and all that. I shook my head, held the bridge of my nose, tipped my head back and sniffed deeply.

'Faaaark.' I winced. 'I have just done the biggest line of the strongest fucken Louie I've had in my life. I'm peakin', mate.'

'You still *snort* speed?' the blonde asked, incredulous, just before she took another hit from the ice pipe.

I nodded, wiping my nose with the back of my hand as she handed the pipe to the brunette and leaned back on the mattress, eyes closed, enjoying the rush.

'Old school,' the brunette said, shaking her head. 'That shit'll kill you.'

The door opened and Channelle entered, naked and stinking of beer. Trev popped his head in.

'Youse are on now,' he told Arizona and Tulsa. 'Right now. I mean it.' He smiled at me before he closed the door and his small, even teeth made the grin look like that of an impish child—completely at odds with the beard and waistcoat.

'Great show,' I said to Channelle as she pulled a fluffy pink towel from her suitcase. 'Uh, can I borrow someone's mobile? Mine just ran out of juice.'

The others just stared, but Channelle said, 'Sure, love, use mine. Just make sure you give it back when I get out of the shower.'

'Thanks.'

'No worries.'

I fiddled with the pink flip-out phone until she went to the bathroom, waited till the other two gathered their lube and dildo and left, then slipped through the workshop again and underneath the roller-door. I stuck close to the wall, out of sight of the cameras, I hoped, and my hands were trembling as I fumbled in my bag. Past the cold metal of the gun I found my wallet and slipped out Talbot's card. No time to wait for the cabbie.

The line went straight to her messagebank. I rang three more times but she wasn't picking up. I left a message:

'Um, Detective Talbot? This is Simone Kirsch. You have to come save me. I'm being held captive at the Red Devils clubhouse in Broken Hill.' Not exactly true but I was sure it soon would be. 'I know where Nick Austin is,' I added. Another lie, but it was sure to get her attention. If she ever checked her goddamn messages.

Just as I was dialling triple 0 I heard a familiar mechanical scrape. The front gate was moving. My god. I couldn't believe my luck. Maybe some dude on a bike was coming in and I'd be able to slip past, run like hell to the taxi and escape.

I crept around the side of the clubhouse, staying in the shadows close to the wall, and peered around to the front. The gate slid open and the black van I'd seen at the pub began nosing in. I didn't know what to do. Wait for Talbot? Try to call triple 0 again? Channelle would be looking for her phone soon, Trev and the boys searching for me—expecting a thousand bucks' worth of depraved acts and getting awfully shirty if I didn't put out. The van's headlights were illuminating the empty car park, but I really needed to get out of there, and if I was fast enough . . .

I sprinted for the gate, heading straight for the metre gap between it and the van. Headlights blinded me, but just as I passed them I glanced up and saw the scooped-out rat face behind the wheel. Watto.

It was the last thing I saw before he swung open the driver's side door and I crashed into it, head first.

chapter fifty-two

I came to on a metal floor, unable to move, head throbbing. My hands were taped behind me and my feet were bound and I smelled diesel and road dust. Music pounded below the roar of the van's engine. Bon Jovi? No, something else. A song about being on a plane, snorting coke, getting all lit up. I'd stripped to it a few years back and remembered the pub with its tiny stage and red and yellow spotlights, but for the life of me I couldn't remember who sang the song.

The van turned a corner, I slid across the floor and my bare arm touched a motionless body. I felt fabric, but it was too dark to make out anything except indistinct shapes, or tell if the person was dead or alive. Nick? The road was dirt now, horribly rutted, and when we bounced across a pothole my head thumped on the floor and I was out again.

Next time I woke it was still dark and bumpy and my mouth was crunchy with grit and dust. The van stopped, and under the relentless pounding of cock rock I heard a door open and the whine of a rusty gate. The door slammed, the van jerked forward and we drove some more, stopped for another gate, and finally came to a halt, tyres munching gravel. The music cut off.

The side door rolled open and I kept my eyes closed, pretending to be unconscious. I'd done the same thing as a kid so my mum would have to carry me from the car. No one carried me that time, just grabbed me by the ankles and slid me out of the van so I whacked the stony ground with my shoulders, then with the back of my already aching head. I was being dragged by the ankles, top riding up, rocks ripping into my back and tearing into my hands and arms. I heard Watto's voice, a small way away. It wasn't him had my feet.

'Not the fucken house, you dickhead. The pen. And pick her up under the arms so you don't rip the gaff off her wrists.'

As the dragging continued I opened my eyes a little and saw a vast velvet sky studded with stars so numerous and swirling they seemed fake, like something from a film set.

Watto swore and muttered as he dragged the other person, then the sky was gone and I smelled tin and more dirt and dogs: old fur, stale urine, ancient, rolled-in cow dung. Watto dropped the other body beside me. After the scrape and clatter of a door being closed and padlocked, I heard the captors confer outside.

'Smoke, mate?' Elvis Mask.

'Not unless it's weed, need to kip for a few hours. Long drive.'

'You're fucken soft.'

'Who gives a shit? He won't be here till light, anyway.'

Their footsteps crunched as they walked away.

The body groaned.

'Nick?' I whispered. 'That you?'

'Simone?' He coughed.

'Yup.'

'You tied, too?'

'Uh-huh.'

'Where are we?' His voice was a rasp. 'Last thing I remember is that fucker king-hitting me then injecting me with something. What the hell are you—?'

'Long story. I finally figured you were giving yourself up to Rod Thurlow and got it in my head to save you.'

'Christ. That's why I did this, so no one else'd get hurt. You stupid . . .'

I'd thought he might at least be grateful so I manoeuvred myself around and kicked my legs in his general direction. Got him in the shins.

'Hey!'

'Enough with the self-sacrificing shit and the insults. We're here now and we have to find a way out.' My voice was a harsh whisper.

'My head's fucking killing me.'

'Mine too, and I'm cold, starving, thirsty and I really need to pee. They said he'd be here when the sun came up. Wonder what the time is now?'

'I have a watch with a light. It's pushed up my arm so I don't think the tape's covering it. I can reach the button with my other hand.'

I heard him rustle and then a blue light came on, faintly illuminating the tin shed we were held captive in. It was about eight by five feet and not high enough to stand up straight.

'Roll over.'

He did as I said and I wormed my way towards him, twisting and straining to check out the face on his expensive-looking watch. 'Four thirty. What time's sunrise around here?'

'Where's here?'

'Middle of fucking nowhere, couple of hours out of Broken Hill.'

'I don't know. Six, maybe?' he suggested.

'Then we've got an hour. Hour and a half, tops.' I shuffled to the door and tentatively pushed at it with my feet, trying not to make too much noise. It wouldn't give. 'They locked it.' The ground beneath my feet was hard-packed earth. The walls of the shed were tin. 'Maybe we can dig our way out?'

'I'm not going anywhere,' Nick said. Resigned.

'What?'

'I told you the deal. A million and they leave everyone else alone.'

'You can't be serious.'

'I am. You're welcome to escape yourself, but I'm not going anywhere. Besides, where is there to go? They've taken our guns, we're in the middle of the desert. You run into that scrub with no water you're as good as dead by the end of the day. Your best bet is to beg your way out of it. Swear secrecy. Maybe Rod'll help you. He's always had a soft spot for the ladies.' Nick uttered a bitter little laugh that made him sound like he was choking.

I backed up to one of the tin walls and tried to dig my fingers into the ground, but it was no use. The earth was too hard, and from what I could feel, the tin walls were embedded a long way down. Of course. If a dog couldn't dig its way out, what hope did I have? I quietly, involuntarily started to cry and when the tears ran onto my lips I tasted salt and dust. I felt along the wall behind me. A small nail was sticking out and I began to rub the gaffer tape that bound my hands against it, just like in the movies.

Unlike in the movies, Watto had wound around what felt like layers of tape and it was heavy duty shit. I might've had a chance if I'd had all night, but an hour? And then what? Overpower him with some judo moves I didn't possess? My shoulders cramped from lifting my wrists up to the nail but I kept going. Nick just lay there. Outside the sky was turning from black to grey. The half-light peeked through small holes in the tin. His acceptance made me want to kill him, but somebody else would do that soon enough. And not just to him, but to both of us.

'There's no begging, swearing myself to secrecy or throwing myself at Rod's mercy,' I told him. 'They're going to kill me too. Watto already had a go with a chainsaw and was going to video the whole thing.'

He sighed. 'I tried to make you go back to Melbourne. I told you to go to the cops in Broken Hill.'

'Why does he want to kill me, Nick?'

'That's the thing, I don't *know*. You don't have anything to do with what happened.'

'What did happen? Shit, you may as well tell me. There's not a hell of a lot left to lose.' I thought of the Red Devils' motto, 'Dead Man Riding'. We were Dead Men Sitting in a Dog Shed. I almost laughed.

'The bikies want the million because it's pretty much what we stole—well, when you add up all the drugs as well. Not that we got that much for them . . .'

'You stole a million in cash and drugs from a bikie gang. I'm sorry, but that has got to be the dumbest—'

'Hey,' he hissed. 'I already told you we didn't know it belonged to the bikies. And we didn't know about the drugs. I didn't want to take them, but . . .'

'Sorry, dude, you're losing me. Can you start at the beginning?' I kept worrying away at my bindings. 'Where did it start? On the writers' roadshow?'

'Yeah, in Broken Hill, funnily enough, same place me and Isabella fell in love. God, who am I kidding? I was in love with her the first time I saw her, trying to stuff that ridiculous old-fashioned steamer trunk into the back of the fucking Tarago van. We had our first kiss at the Demo Club and that same cover band, The Rogues, were playing "Fairytale of New York". Sorry, other people's romantic stories are just vomit-worthy.'

'Pretty much,' I admitted.

'We had a ball on that writers' trip. It was always me and Izzy and JJ sitting up late in pubs and hotel rooms, drinking red wine, laughing, talking shit. One time we even got stoned. It was like being a teenager again. No. It was like being the teenager I'd never been. I thought that she and JJ would get together for sure, and it's not like he didn't have a crack, but she chose me. I couldn't believe that someone like her would want me. JJ was cool about it. You've seen him in action. By the end of the trip he had a girl in every port anyway. It was a running joke between us. Sorry. I'm raving on.'

'It's okay.'

I'd never heard Nick talk so much. For all these weeks this was the story I'd wanted to hear and now it was too late: the information wouldn't make any difference.

'It was a joke at first. A stupid joke. We were all staying in the pub where the poetry slam was held, sitting out on that veranda, drinking wine. Nerida—I could never call her Desiree—had shown up for her life-writing workshop and we were grilling her for sick stories about her clients, trying to figure out who they were. She told us about this investment banker who was a real perverted arsehole, high on drugs most of the time, and who liked to do it in sight of this enormous stash of cash he always had hanging around the house. She said it had to be at least a hundred thousand, and he wouldn't even tip.

'I remember Izzy asked her why she didn't just steal some of it, and Nerida got a bit offended and said high-class callgirls *never* stole from clients and they *never* named names. It was sort of like a code, being a priest or a doctor or something.

So then of course we *really* wanted to know who he was and started this sort of twenty questions thing—we were pretty drunk by this stage—and Izzy got this strange look on her face and asked, "Is he from Melbourne?" And when Nerida said yes Izzy said, quite calmly, "It's Lachlan Elliot, isn't it?" Nerida got this surprised look on her face so we knew Izzy was right, not that me or JJ knew who the hell she was talking about. Turns out that Izzy used to go out with his friend.'

'James,' I said. The friend of Victoria Hitchens' sleaze-bag husband Hamish.

'Shit, you really have been investigating. Then, I don't know how it happened, but we started talking about how hard it is to make a living as a writer, especially compared to being a high-class callgirl. We'd all missed out on Australia Council grants that year and—'

'Sorry, what?'

'They're government literary grants, anything from five to thirty thousand dollars. I'd applied for twenty so I could take a year off just to write, didn't get it and knew I'd have to go back to full-time teaching, which I hated. And then we were railing about how it was so unfair that all sorts of mindless, unprincipled cocksuckers had *so* much money and we were so damned honourable, artistic and deserving, yet struggling to make a crust—JJ wasn't a lecturer then, he'd just started his PhD—and even though my books were doing well it still wasn't enough to live on. I don't know who suggested it first—JJ or Izzy, probably—that we should steal this Elliot guy's money and start up our own grant system. The Robin Hood foundation or something ridiculous like that. Nerida was just shaking her head, but Izzy was really getting into it, saying, "You're a crime writer, Nick, you could totally plan this thing," and we actually made up this—Jesus—heist plan then and there.'

'You weren't serious.'

'Hell no. Like I said, it was a joke. I'd forgotten all about it by the next morning. Never even crossed my mind until a long time later, when Izzy brought it up.'

'What was the plan?' I asked.

'It was that stupid and clichéd I'd never even try to get away with using it in one of my books. Izzy was gonna play the femme fatale, get invited back to his place for a tête-à-tête and slip the guy a Mickey, disable the alarm system or unlock the front door or whatever, and then me and JJ were gonna come in. Why we all had to be there, I don't know. Maybe to beat him up if the drugs didn't work? I can't remember. Then we were going to steal all the cash and go off on our merry way and just write and not have to work.'

'Wouldn't Elliot have known who'd stolen the money?'

'We were gonna give him some sort of drug that induced amnesia—not that any of us knew if one existed, or how to get it. Like I said, it was a drunken fantasy, not serious.'

'But Isabella brought it up again?'

'About a year after I left my wife and we'd moved in together. I regret that, by the way. Not leaving Jenny, because the relationship had well and truly run its course, but the way I did it. Sneaking around, having an affair. I should have just come out and said it. I've met someone, I don't love you anymore. Clean break. Instead, I took the easy way out. Or maybe it was more than that. Maybe I liked the excitement of the deception, gave me a thrill. And there I was saying Elliot was an immoral bastard. The whole thing with the article in the Sunday glossy, that was horrible.'

'Your ex-wife told me it appeared really soon after you broke up. You and Isabella playing happy families. I wouldn't have picked you to do something like that.'

'I didn't—well—the article was Isabella's idea. Her second book was being released and it's hard to get publicity and, shit, I didn't think it'd come out so soon. And you have to remember I was so fucking in love with Izzy, infatuated. It was like a drug and I'd have done anything—hell, if she'd asked me to run naked down Bourke Street singing "Yankee Doodle Dandy" I would have stripped off then and there. Only thing was, I could tell Izzy wasn't happy with our life together, which scared the shit out of me. I was terrified of her leaving, because I couldn't believe someone like me had ended up with someone like her in the first place and I knew I'd never get over her, even then.'

Sounded to me as though Isabella had done nothing to assuage his feelings.

'Were you paranoid she didn't love you?'

'Yes. No. I dunno. Looking back on it now I think she always loved me. Sounds pathetic? It was just the money situation. I was doing occasional relief teaching and we were both living on that and we thought I'd get half the money from the house Jenny and I bought but it didn't work out that way.'

'Didn't the article say you were broke 'n' happy 'n' living on love?'

'That was a load of shit. Izzy could never be happy being broke. She seemed to have a mortal terror of it. Probably why she always ended up with so many rich pricks. But then rich men and beautiful women always seem to go together, don't they?'

'So she *was* a gold digger?'

He turned his head. 'That's a pretty chauvinist generalisation. It's complicated. She grew up well-off but then her father deserted the family, left them destitute, and ever since then . . . having no money made her feel incredibly insecure.'

'If she didn't like being broke, why'd she become a writer?' I laughed.

'Some of us don't get to choose,' he barked.

He was still in love with her and I knew I'd have to stop slagging the bitch if I wanted to find out what had happened. My shoulders were cramping badly, but I didn't let up scraping the nail against the gaff. Felt like I'd gotten through one layer already.

'Sorry,' I said. 'So she brought up the heist plan? For real this time?'

'Yeah. She went on about it for months and months, telling me it really could work. I said she was being ridiculous. There was no guaranteed "amnesia" drug we could get our hands on, and anyway, I'm not a thief, a tough guy, the sort of person who'd ever do something like that. I couldn't live with myself, I told her.'

'How'd she convince you, then?'

'She didn't. She tried to do the heist on her own and she called me when it all went wrong.'

chapterfifty-three

Predawn light filtered into the dog shed. I kept rubbing my taped wrists against the nail in the tin while Nick spoke.

'Isabella said she was doing an appearance at a bookshop, and normally I would've gone but I had a deadline for my fourth Zack book and stayed home to write. It was late, but those things often run on, people go for drinks after. I hated not being there. I was always worried she'd meet someone else, someone better, with more money. I never said anything, that jealous shit only pushes people away.

'She called about midnight, whispering into the phone like she'd been crying, and told me she was in Lachlan Elliot's bathroom and the drugs weren't working. I asked what the hell she was talking about and she said she'd decided to go through with it, met up with him "accidentally" and went back to his place. Slipped him a couple of Rohypnol, but he was so wired from taking ice that they hadn't slowed him down. Said he was trying to rape her and I had to come to her rescue.

'I heard shouting in the background. Someone banging on the door. I told her I'd call the cops and come over, but she begged me not to get the police involved: they'd arrest her and I'd never see her again. I didn't think that was likely, but there was something in her voice. I knew if I called the police, she'd leave me. I just knew. She gave me the address and told me the security cameras were off and the gate and the front door were unlocked, so I raced over.

'It's funny. I was in this panic, yet I was weirdly calm, like it was a dream . . . I grabbed gloves and a wrench, which was the only thing resembling a weapon I had, parked the car well away from his house and strolled up to his place all casual-like, making sure no one saw me go in.

'It was a big place in South Yarra. New, flashy bachelor pad. Lots of black leather and chrome and shiny surfaces. They were on the couch when I got there and he was on top, shirt off, kissing her, and her dress was hiked up and ripped. She seemed to be struggling. Heavy metal was playing, Motorhead or something, so he didn't hear me coming up behind him.

'I took the wrench out of my pocket and hit him on the back of the head. Would have stunned a normal guy, but not him. He pushed off her, turned and lunged and we both hit the floor. I know what it is now. When someone goes crazy on that drug you need a SWAT team to restrain them and enough tranquillisers to kill an elephant.

'At the time I didn't know what was happening, except I was about to die. He'd pulled the wrench out of my hand easy as grabbing a lolly from a baby, and raised it, about to smash my face in, but it veered off, right at the last moment. Izzy had crash-tackled him, and it gave me half a second to roll away from the maniac. I grabbed the first thing I saw, this stupid sculpture of a Harley Davidson that had been sitting on the coffee table, made of chrome and about the size of a small cat.

'Elliot had one hand around Izzy's neck and the other pulled back about to belt her in the face and I swung the statue into the back of his head a lot harder than I had with the wrench, and heard the crack as his skull shattered. Most sickening sound in the world.'

'That stop him?'

'Yeah. That stopped him. He went down face first onto the polished boards. I looked at the motorbike and felt faint. There was hair on it, bits of scalp. I felt dizzy, like I was going to throw up, and I sank to my knees next to his body and rested the statue on his back. One part of my brain was still thinking like a crime writer, thinking, don't get any DNA on the floor. They can test for blood, even after you've cleaned it up.

'Izzy turned down the music and that helped me concentrate. I couldn't go near his head, so I felt his wrist for a pulse and there it was. Faint but even. I hadn't killed him.

'Meanwhile, she'd picked up Elliot's shirt from the couch—one of those banker-ish blue-striped things with the white collar—and wrapped the weapon in it. He's still alive, I said, we have to call an ambulance. She knelt on the other side of him and looked down, almost tenderly. "No, we don't," she replied, raised the statue and smashed it down onto the back of his head so hard that when she took her hands away the thing was still lodged in there. He convulsed, once, and was still.

'I stared, shocked, but I think she mistook my look for confusion because she smiled and said, "I wrapped it to stop the blood spatter. It would have flown off from when you hit him before. I did learn *something* reading your crime novels. Now quick, go to the kitchen and get some garbage bags."'

I was silent for a moment and took a break from rubbing my bonds against the nail. The cramp had spread from my shoulders, up my neck and melded with the pain in my head. Outside it was fast getting light and I saw Nick clearly, lying on the dirt floor, looking up at the ceiling. He seemed serene.

'You still could have called the police,' I said. 'Self-defence.'

'Not when you've just robbed somebody,' he said. 'Izzy had seen the money and she wasn't going to let it go. After we'd wrapped up Elliot's body and stuck it in the boot of his BMW—the garage was attached to the house so that part was easy—she showed me this secret room he had it stashed in. There was a lot more than a hundred thousand, almost five, all wrapped up neatly in plastic and already packed into suitcases. And the drugs, bricks of white powder, bags of crystals, vacuum-packed satchels of ecstasy tablets all stamped with little panda bears. There were even a couple of handguns. I told her we had to leave the drugs and the guns, but she said no: JJ had contacts in Adelaide, he could sell the stuff on. Besides, if we wanted to make it look like he did a runner, we couldn't leave anything behind.

'We packed a suitcase full of his clothes and toiletries and put everything except the money in the boot with the bagged-up body and the murder weapon. Oh, and a spade from the gardener's shed out the back. I drove his BMW to Daylesford and buried the body, then went on to Adelaide to see JJ, hugging the speed limit, nearly shitting myself all the way.

'Izzy stayed at the house and cleaned up some more, then turned everything off, reset the alarm, locked up and put the suitcases with the money into the back of our car and drove home. The next day she went to a signing at Readings in Carlton, which went very well, from what I heard. I dumped the shit with JJ and said he could do what he liked with it, keep the proceeds. I left the BMW to get stolen and god knows where it is now, probably rebirthed and in Western Australia or somewhere. I caught a Greyhound bus home under a false name and arrived back less than twenty-four hours after I'd left. No one even knew I'd been gone.

'Soon as I got home Izzy cracked open a bottle of French champagne and showed me the round-the-world air tickets she'd purchased while I'd been gone. She was dressed up to the nines, wearing her usual lipstick and a new vintage flapper dress, and she put "Fairytale of New York" on the stereo and began twittering on about all the places we'd see and how maybe we could get married overseas, maybe in New York, maybe on Christmas Eve, if they let you get married on Christmas Eve. I had half a glass of champagne, then went to the cupboard where we kept a bottle of cheap scotch that someone had left after a party. I didn't stop until I'd finished the whole thing.'

chapter fifty-four

'I wish you'd told me this before.' I'd worn away another layer of gaffer tape and was rubbing against the nail with renewed gusto, trying to ignore the pain, fear, thirst, and pressure on my bladder.

'Can't have a deathbed confession without a deathbed.'

'Stop talking like that.'

'Why? It's obvious you've got just as much of a death wish as I do.'

'What?'

'I'm assuming it's about what happened to your mother, because of that case last year? I kept trying to work out why you were so hell-bent on tracking me down, why you wouldn't let up and why you constantly put yourself in danger—even when I kept giving you an out.'

'I was working for Liz. Wanted to give her her money's worth.'

'It went a little above and beyond that—you wouldn't be here otherwise. I think you're punishing yourself for what happened. Like me. I put Zack through it in my last book, *Dead End*, so I know what I'm talking about. It was sort of cathartic to write after the whole thing with Lachlan Elliot. Not that I mentioned any details, nothing that could identify me.'

I couldn't believe it. Chloe had been right about clues in the books. If only I'd listened to her.

'But Isabella did, didn't she? That's why you ran out of the tent at the writers' festival. She mentioned specifics in *Thrill City*. The motorbike statue. His house. The haul of cash and drugs. It's what you were arguing about under the tree, before you kissed.'

He turned to squint at me.

'I was so damned paranoid about that statue—which ended up in the Yarra, if you're interested. But the police never mentioned anything about it being missing. They interviewed his friends, his cleaning lady. Even if they knew about it, the story never came out. But Craig Murdoch must have known.'

'How? Hard to imagine a biker reading one of her books.'

'No idea. But it got her killed and me and JJ identified. Nerida, aka Desiree, too.'

'But why were they after Victoria?' I asked.

'Dunno.'

'And me?'

He shook his head. Shrugged. 'Guilt by association? Who knows. It's all too late now.'

'There's got to be a way out of this.'

'Always have to solve the case and win the day, don't you? The plucky little stripper who could. Maybe, as well as the guilt thing, you're trying to impress Daddy. You said you hadn't seen your father in years. Perhaps that's why you're a PI.'

I glared.

'I'm not trying to insult you. Zack was going through the same issues in *Dead End*. It's a legitimate motivation.'

'I don't give a fuck about my dad, so why do you?'

'Since I'll never write again, it's nice to know I got my facts straight when I did.'

Was it just my imagination, or did Nick seem happier than he had since I'd met him? Writers, goddamn freaks. I was about to tell him so when the door to the shed was wrenched open. With all the talking we hadn't heard Watto and the other bikie approach. They stood silhouetted in the doorway. The sky was the palest blue and a bright pink glow emanated from just below the horizon.

'Rise 'n' shine,' said Watto, cigarette clamped between his teeth. He bent down and dragged me out of the shed by my feet, then took his hunting knife from its sheath. My heart seemed to drop into my stomach, or perhaps my bowels, but he just bent at the waist and cut through the gaffer tape on my ankles. He handed the knife to the other bikie, the fat one with the long hair I'd seen at the pub, and gestured for him to do the same. The guy frowned.

'Sure that's a good idea, mate?'

'I'm fucken sick of draggin' 'em around. Me back's fucked. And *he's* not going to try anything.' He pointed to Nick.

'What about her?'

'I fucken hope she does.' Watto grinned.

They hoisted us to our feet. Nick was led away to a large corrugated-tin shed a couple of hundred metres from the house, and Watto pushed me towards an old wooden farmhouse with a sweeping, bull-nosed veranda. I guessed they didn't want Rod Thurlow to know I was there.

'Nick!' I called. If I'd thought things were bad before, getting separated made them a thousand times worse.

'See ya, Simone,' he called back over his shoulder. A generator hummed somewhere out the back of the house and I had a feeling that this time, Watto had all the facilities he needed.

As he pushed me up the stairs to the veranda I took one last look around. Nothing for miles but desert and scrub, the red dirt lit up a heartbreaking crimson as the sun peeked over the horizon. I wondered if Chloe's baby was a boy or a girl. I was fucked.

The front door opened onto a long hallway. I glanced left and saw a lounge room with old, overstuffed furniture and two bikie-looking guys. A skinny one wearing leathers, asleep sitting up in a recliner, the other fat, wearing a t-shirt, smoking a bong and watching what had to be satellite TV. There was a handgun on the table and a shotgun leaning on the wall near the disused fireplace. Watto kept the knife to my back as he talked to the guys inside.

'Hey, Davo—wake up!'

The skinny guy in the recliner stirred.

'Thurlow's coming. Soon as he lands, get the money and bring it here. Any problems with those cunts, call me.' He looked at the fat one in the t-shirt. 'You finished cooking yet?'

Bong guy shook his head.

'Another couple of hours at least,' he said.

What was he making, a pot roast?

Watto pushed me into one of the bedrooms. Wasn't much there except a wooden chair in the centre of the room, and a laptop computer sitting open on an old school desk. The window was covered by a faded floral curtain, and a battered wardrobe stood at the back of the room next to a metal bed frame, no mattress. A bare hundred-watt bulb hung from the ceiling, attached to a frayed cord. What was really worrying was the blue tarpaulin spread out across the floor under the chair.

He pushed me onto the chair and gaffer-taped my ankles to the legs, but with only one layer this time. I flexed my wrists. The tape there was definitely looser. I tried to pull my wrists apart, but the tape hung on by a tough ligament of gluey thread. If I'd been stronger, if I'd exercised, lifted some weights in the last couple of months instead of sitting on my arse . . . I hadn't even eaten anything in the past few days. When had my last meal been? My stomach felt hollow and acidic. I was weak as a kitten.

Watto was over by the laptop, fiddling with a webcam attached to the top of the screen and a couple of small speakers to either side. I remembered him attempting to video his aborted chainsaw attack. Was he doing a snuff movie? Trying to make a few extra bucks on the side?

He looked at his watch, hunched over the computer to type something in, punched enter and then stood aside, lighting another cigarette.

A Media Player screen filled the monitor, and on it a blurry face. As the image sharpened I finally realised why he was going to kill me.

chapter fifty-five

The face on the computer screen had the same moustache and pale, grey-blue wolf eyes, but was thinner and paler. I'd always thought he looked like an actor playing a lawyer in a daytime soap; now he looked like an actor playing a lawyer who'd been in jail for almost a year. His hair was grey, the tennis tan had been replaced by a putty-coloured pallor, the pinstriped suit swapped for a loose cotton top. I could just make out the wrinkled bullet scar on his throat.

'Good morning, Simone,' said Emery Wade, the murdering bastard I'd helped put away.

It took me a few seconds to form words. 'I thought you couldn't speak. The bullet—'

'I had an operation.' The voice coming through the speakers was still deep, but with a hitch to it, like a scratch on a record.

'You're in jail.'

'I am.'

'You—you can't have a computer on the inside.'

'Indeed you can, if you've got a legitimate use for it, say, preparing your own or another's defence. I've become quite the jailhouse lawyer in the last ten months. What you can't have is internet access, but I've so many good friends in here it wasn't too hard to smuggle in Wi-Fi. Mobile phones are also banned, although quite a few of my associates seem to use them regularly for business.'

'Like Craig Murdoch?'

Wade smiled. 'He's my latest client. Imagine my surprise when I heard on the news that you'd gotten yourself involved in a little project of his.'

'Real coincidence, but that's Melbourne for you. Everyone knows everyone.' I didn't feel quite as brazen as I was trying to sound.

'Serendipity.'

'So, what, you guys teamed up and now you're going to kill me so I can't testify against you?'

'That's one reason. The other is that I'm going to derive a great deal of pleasure from your extended demise. I ordered Watto to draw it out from the beginning and I'm sure he scared you: the note, the slashed tyres, the mask. Knowing you were being watched, gradually realising that nowhere was safe. Did you really think you could fuck with me and get away with it? You stupid bitch.' He shook his head.

Watto was standing back, smoking and scratching a scab on his arm, watching like we were a mildly interesting movie.

'There'll be other people to testify,' I said. 'A whole roomful of cops saw you try to kill me and there's video of you basically admitting to murder.'

'I'll probably go down for attempted, but I can argue I was provoked by a rather unpopular and possibly mentally unstable inquiry agent, so I don't think I'll get more than a couple of years. As for the video, it was illegally obtained and is being struck from the evidence as we speak. And I have plans for the other witnesses—' he looked down, as though to consult a document—'most notably Alexander Nikolai Christakos and Sean Callan Shields.'

Jesus. Even I hadn't known Alex's and Sean's middle names. I'd never even thought to ask.

'Anyone can get got, as they say, inside of jail or out. You're in no position to argue with that.' He looked me up and down and smirked at his own joke.

I was all out of smartarse comebacks. The sun had risen and the room was hot and stuffy, but I would have sweated even if it had been forty below. Emery said something to Watto, and Watto unsheathed his knife and then time started doing strange things, speeding up and slowing down. Seconds flashed, then slowly dripped and all the while my senses became clear and the drab room filled with sharp detail. I saw every ripple in the light blue tarp, smelled Watto's chemical sweat and cigarette stench, and tasted metallic fear in my own dry mouth. I felt the hard edge of the chair bite the back of my bare legs and the sticky glue from the gaffer tape gum my wrists. The only sense that wasn't working was sound. Why was that? Everything was muffled, like noise underwater. Emery Wade said something to Watto, then disappeared from the screen. Watto put the knife back in its sheath.

What the hell was going on? With the knife away my hearing returned and also the power of speech.

'What's happening?'

Watto sighed. 'I fucked up the times. We're half an hour behind Victoria and he's gotta go to breakfast. Oh well. Gives me a chance for another hit.'

Half an hour behind? They must have taken Nick and me across the border into South Australia.

Watto left the room. In the distance I heard the low, love-the-smell-of-napalm-in-the-morning thwack of helicopter blades. Rod Thurlow, coming to collect his bounty. I struggled with my bonds, but Watto was back in no time with a six-pack of Wild Turkey and Coke stubbies and another wooden chair. He reached into his pants pocket and pulled out the pipe with the bulbous glass end and a little packet filled with clear crystals.

'Wade wants to watch it live, you know.'

'Oh,' I said, stupidly.

The helicopter got louder as it landed, and the machine whined as the rotor blades shut down. I tried to think of a plan. Rod Thurlow was my best bet. He had it in for Nick, but I didn't think he'd agree to the wholesale slaughter of yours truly. I'd really acted like I liked him at lunch. But how to get to him?

My mouth was dry as the landscape outside and I eyed Watto's drink. 'Can I have a sip?'

'Huh?'

'Your drink. I'm parched, mate.' I did my best at chummy. 'Even on death row they get a last meal.'

He looked amused and stalked over.

'Don't see why not.' When he held the bottle up to my lips I tried not to think about cold sores and other diseases, then wondered why in hell I was worrying. He kept tipping and I gulped at it like a lamb sucking on a bottle, and in seconds I'd demolished at least half.

'Fucken hell.' He pulled it away. 'Leave some for me.'

The Coke and booze fizzed down my arid throat and I could immediately feel myself getting a little sugar and bourbon buzz. I was still surreptitiously tugging at the gaffer tape, but didn't have enough strength to break through the final strand.

Strength. I remembered what Nick had told me about Lachlan Elliot, and ice fiends in general, how being off their tits cranked up the adrenaline so bad it took a team of coppers or paramedics to bring them down. Then I wondered how long Watto had gone without sleep. Surely the crazed energy and uncanny reflexes would have to subside the longer you stayed awake. Everyone had to crash sometime.

Not that I thought Watto would fall asleep, exactly. He was just then inhaling another hit. But I'd done my fair share of drugs and I knew that the more you took the less effective they became. The first taste was the strongest, and then the high gradually diminished. Unfortunately for me, it probably wouldn't come soon enough.

There was a knock on the door, and the skinny guy in leathers poked his head around.

'Looks like it's all here.'

'Bring it in.'

He hefted a grey Samsonite case into the room, and avoided looking at me in a way I kind of understood. I was all for chowing down steak and lamb, but didn't want to go to the slaughterhouse for a viewing.

The guy clicked open the suitcase and I glimpsed wads of bundled cash, more than I'd ever seen in one place.

'Fucken bonus.' Watto nodded his approval. 'Let Thurlow at him. What's he gonna do with the body?'

'Chuck it out the copter in the middle of arsefuck nowhere.'

'Tell 'em we'll have a little package of our own.'

The guy frowned. 'Dunno if Thurlow's gonna like that. He's here for Austin.'

'I don't give a fuck. By the time I've finished they won't even know what's in the bag.'

The other guy couldn't get out of there fast enough, and a shiver rolled its way from my ankles to my elbows as I looked at the knife sheathed in his belt and anticipated intense pain. What would it be like? I'd been cut bad in the past, but not ripped to pieces, shredded, like Isabella had been. I remembered the sharp searing and multiplied it to the power of ten, imagined the blade slicing through skin and muscle and tendon, scraping bone. I saw the hooked, serrated tip grabbing looped innards and could practically smell the blood, bile and shit.

And then what, after the horror? Nothing, at best, or hellfire and brimstone, if Jenny was correct. Somehow the nothingness seemed worse, harder for the ego to cope with. I couldn't let it happen. I didn't have a death wish. Not anymore. Nick was wrong.

Watto sucked down another hit and sat back, eyes practically rolling. I waited until he came around before I spoke. 'Watto, mate.'

'Yeah?'

'You know how up at Castlemaine you said I could have a hit on that pipe? Offer still stand?'

'Huh?'

'Can I have a go of that ice? You said it was like ten orgasms, all in a row, and I've never done it before. Shouldn't a girl get to experience that if she's only got half an hour to live?'

He twisted his mouth into a yellowed, gap-toothed grin. 'You like to party. I knew it. All strippers like to party. Can't believe you've never had this shit.'

'Just speed and E's,' I said.

'Speed's nothing compared to this.'

'So my friends tell me. Come on. Just one hit.'

Another thing I remembered from my misspent youth was that drug-fucked individuals, mostly, liked to share. It wasn't nearly as much fun being out of it on your own.

I didn't really think I had a chance of befriending him and talking him out of killing me, although the thought had crossed my mind. My main motivation was to buy a bit of time and energy. At that stage anything was worth a try.

He looked like he was debating it in his head for a bit as he squinted his eyes and silently moved his lips.

'Yeah, okay,' he said, finally. 'You're gonna love this.'

How about that? The guy who was about to rip my guts out was pleased for me, excited I was trying something new.

He scraped his chair over so he was sitting in front of me, shook a couple of clear crystal shards into the bowl of the pipe, then concentrated hard on keeping the lighter flame steady underneath so it didn't touch the glass. When the crystals melted and started to smoke he took away the lighter and placed the stem against my lips.

'Draw back. Slow and steady.'

I did as he said. The smoke tasted chemical and burned the back of my throat.

'Keep going! You don't want to miss any.'

I inhaled until I had no more breath. Elvis Mask took the pipe away, inhaled the last wisps himself then crouched in front of me, looking intently into my face.

'Hold it,' he said. 'Hold it in.'

I did as he said, felt like I was suffocating, and finally had to exhale. Nothing happened for a few seconds, and just as I was wondering what other brilliant plans I could come up with I felt a kind of tingling bubble up from my lungs and spread out everywhere: limbs, spine, head. My heart started thumping fast and heavy and I felt little fairies run their tiny fairy fingernails up and over my scalp. A deep, glorious shiver climbed my backbone and when it reached the base of my skull I had to tip my head back and close my eyes. Watto hadn't been kidding about the ten orgasm thing, except that it was even better, a climax encompassing the body, brain, neurons and every microscopic cell.

I wasn't sure how long my eyes had been closed for, but I was still rushing when I opened them, only it had changed from a blasting rocket to a smooth glide.

'Holy shit,' I said.

Watto's hideous face was in front of me but it didn't seem to matter so much. I was back, sharp, on top of the world, and felt like I could run the four minute mile if I had to. I'd get out of this, and if I didn't? Shit. No comedown to worry about. I actually giggled.

'Gimme some more of that fucking bourbon and a drag on your cig,' I said.

Watto looked delighted, clapped his hands and danced a little jig. He raced back to the computer and put a CD in the drive and while his back was turned I tried to force my wrists apart with all my might, which was considerably greater than it had been a few moments earlier. The tape didn't break but it did stretch some more and I thought maybe I could try wiggling and pulling a hand out of the sticky restraints, but then the speakers started blasting more of his beloved cock rock: Poison, 'Nothing But a Good Time'. I remembered it from pub strip shows and blue light discos years before. I started singing along and I couldn't believe I knew the words, but the way I was feeling, I pretty much knew everything.

'So, mate, how about you let me go and we really party?' I asked.

'Sorry, babe. Even if I was that fucking stupid my dick's useless, all the shit I've been doing. Not bad stuff, huh?'

'You're telling me.'

Normally a speed rush settled, but this bastard kept going.

'So, uh, tell me about yourself, Watto.' I fought the urge to grind my teeth.

'Whatcha wanna know?'

'You're working for Craig Murdoch and Emery Wade, yeah?'

'Uh-huh.'

'Where'd you meet?'

'Wade I met inside. He got me off an armed rob charge. Craig I knew before. I'm an associate member of the Red Devils.'

'And you're, like, their enforcer?'

'Yep. But I do other stuff too.'

'Oh yeah?' I acted interested, all the while wiggling my hands behind my back. But subtly, hoping he wouldn't notice. 'Like what?'

He leaned forward in his chair. 'I'm a writer,' he said proudly.

'Excuse me?'

'I'm a writer. I've written a fucking book.'

I tamped down the urge to laugh out loud. Jesus. Everyone was a fucking writer and I'd had enough of all of them.

'No shit.' I tried to look impressed. 'What do you write?'

'About my life. Like Chopper Read or that guy who wrote that book about breaking out of prison and going to India. Shanta-something.'

'*Shantaram*?'

'That's the one. You read it?'

'Yeah,' I lied. I'd seen it in friends' bookshelves, but the thing looked more like a doorstop than a book. 'It was awesome.'

'Fucken oath, and it sold a shit-load. Same with Chopper. That's why I reckon I've got a bestseller on my hands.'

'You've written a whole book?'

'Yeah.' He was getting defensive, like I didn't believe him.

'That's great. I just don't know where you'd find the time.'

'I don't sleep.'

'Oh.'

He jumped up and collected his backpack from where it was sitting in the corner, unzipped it and showed me a sheaf of paper and about a dozen small notebooks, covered in scrawl.

'You wrote about killing Isabella?'

'Yep.'

'You gonna write about me?'

'Probably.'

'Won't that sort of, I dunno, incriminate you?'

He rolled his eyes as if I were dense. 'I change the names.'

'Of course. Sorry. So you enjoy offing people?' I couldn't believe we were having this chat.

'If they've got it coming.'

'Think I do?'

'Shit yeah. Stupid bitches fuck with the wrong people. Dumb cunts. Like my mother. The cuntingest of all.'

Mother issues. Shit. I really didn't want to go there.

'Yeah. I know I was stupid, now.'

'Fucken oath you were.'

'Can you just tell me one thing before you kill me?' I asked.

'Depends.'

'Oh, okay, don't worry about it.'

'What was it?'

'Nah,' I said. 'You probably don't know anyway.'

'What? Fucken tell me.'

I sighed, like I was reluctant. 'Well, I just wondered how Craig figured out Isabella knocked Lachlan. I mean, your boss must be a pretty smart guy. Smarter than me. I can't work it out.'

Watto's eyes lit up like a little kid. 'It was me.' He sat up straight in his chair.

'Nooo, you're fucking with me.'

'It was!' he practically squealed.

'How?'

'I read her book.'

'*You* read *Thrill City*?' I couldn't keep the incredulity out of my voice and he took offence.

'I'm not a dumb cunt, I can fucken read. Fuck's sake, I've written a fucken book.' He pointed to his backpack.

'Yeah, I know. Sorry. I just didn't think it'd be your sort of thing.'

'Wasn't. I didn't read all of it. Picked it up mainly 'cause she looked hot on the cover and pics of hot chicks are hard to get hold of inside. Anyway, I was bored and flippin' through it in me cell and there's this bit, right, where this banker dude gets brained by a fucking miniature replica Harley. And when I was readin' it I was thinkin', I know that house, I know that replica and I know that banker cunt. Elliot. I was there when Craig gave him the fucken Harley for a present. So I went and showed Craig.'

'How'd you get hold of the novel?' I asked, although I think by that stage I already knew.

'When that rich cunt Rod Thurlow came to Port and did a writing class. He brought in a whole bunch of books for the prison library.'

chapter fifty-six

Poison segued into Joan Jett, 'I Hate Myself for Loving You'. Now I knew. Craig had put the hit on Isabella because of what she'd written. And Rod had an unintentional hand in it, by offloading her novel at the jail.

'Craig just wanted his money back, and to send a message that you don't fuck with us. He's in prison because of them.'

'I thought he was in prison for trying to blow up another clubhouse and nearly killing the head of the Assassins.'

'That's 'cause he caught them selling our shit. Our E's were the only ones in the country with that stamp. The cook checked and they were all the same chemicals and that.'

'And Craig thought Lachlan Elliot had split and sold the stuff off?'

'Until I read the book in jail and then his body was found.'

'Did you torture Isabella for information?'

'Not much. Just cut off her finger and she told me everything I wanted to know. Said the pro on the radio—Desiree or whatever—came up with the idea, the black bastard offloaded the shit, and Austin and that hot writer chick . . .'

'Victoria Hitchens?'

'Yeah. Said it was her and Austin knocked Elliot. Said that's how she got the idea for the book and knew about the Harley and that—through them.'

'She was lying. Victoria didn't have anything to do with it.'

'Thought she might be. Kept telling me she was innocent. Didn't know what to believe so I decided to knock them both.'

Christ. If only I could let Rod know what had really happened, that he had the wrong man. I had to do something. Only problem was, I was tied to the fucking chair.

My mind was racing.

Joan was singing.

Watto screwed up his nose. 'Ain't my CD,' he said. 'Bitches can't rock. I'm gonna fast forward.' He approached the computer.

His back was to me and the music was loud. I strained and flexed what little muscle I had left, felt my head almost pop, and my shoulder nearly dislocate, but it worked. I wrenched one sticky wrist free without him hearing. I leaned forward and ripped the gaff off my ankles while Watto was hunched over the laptop, fiddling with the mouse, looking through the song list. He seemed to settle on something, left clicked and straightened, and there was a brief moment of silence. Didn't matter. By that time I was behind him, holding the chair above my head. As he turned I brought it down full force.

The thing broke and he went down, but only for a second before he flipped and grabbed my ankle. I fell on my back, lifted my head and saw him reach for his knife. I was still holding a section of chair frame and reacted fast, smacking him hard in the temple and then once more on the back of his head. That did it. Finally the prick was still. I got up off the floor, still holding the splintered piece of wood, breathing hard and all lathered up like a racehorse. My heart was racing and my mouth was dry, so I grabbed another bourbon from the six-pack and nicked one of Watto's durries, flicking the lighter and drawing back hard.

I was so hyped up I was feeling kind of addled and like I ought to come up with a solid plan, but hundreds of thoughts crowded my mind and it was hard to settle on one. I realised that Joan Jett had just saved my life and went to the computer to put 'I Hate Myself for Loving You' back on, keeping an eye on Watto the whole time.

Perhaps I should have staved his head in then and there, but I wasn't real keen on murdering people, no matter how much better off the world would be without them. I'd already killed one person in my life, and even though it had been self-defence it still made me lie awake at night feeling like I would either go straight to hell or get reincarnated as something hideous, a tapeworm hanging out of the arse of a mangy mutt.

'Get your shit together,' I told myself. 'Tell Rod, rescue Nick, save Alex and Sean and yourself.

'Thanks, Joan,' I said as I downed the last of the bourbon and ground the cigarette out on the floor.

I heard a voice underneath the music and thought it was Joan replying, before realising it was a little early for the speed psychosis to set in. The computer had buzzed into life and Wade was back onscreen, wiping food off his moustache.

'Watto, turn that god-awful music off.' He squinted into his monitor, obviously wondering what the hell was going on. I stood in front of the laptop and waved.

'Where's Watto?' He frowned.

'Screw you,' I said, taking what was left of the chair and smashing the shit out of the web-cam.

I crept down the hallway, heading straight for the lounge room, hoping the bikies had departed, leaving their guns behind. They'd gone alright, but taken the weaponry with them. I couldn't imagine Rod turning up without an armed guard, so it had to be a regular mine's-bigger-than-yours circle-jerk out at the shed. With any luck they'd all shoot each other, Tarantino style.

I had Watto's knife in a sheath around my waist as I prowled about, but didn't know if it would do me any good. It'd been drummed into my head at some long-ago self-defence class that a knife could easily be snatched away and used against you by someone of superior force, which was pretty much every swinging dick around the godforsaken farmhouse. I wished I'd taken the splintered chair leg.

Outside the sun was getting higher in the sky and it had to be at least thirty-five degrees. The dirt had settled to a dull ochre colour and the saltbrush was straggly khaki. I couldn't see anyone but still felt exposed as I dashed from one hiding spot to the other: the dog shed, back of the van, a rusted water tank. A caravan was hooked up to a generator about twenty metres away from the tank, with an air-conditioner crudely installed and running, judging by the drips.

I knew the lot of them would never be able to fit in there, so planned on heading straight to the large tin shed that Watto's offsider had dragged Nick into. I peeped around the tank. Rod's helicopter was roosting on a concrete slab in front of the shed. I crouched, looked underneath the chopper and saw two pairs of legs, one in jeans, the other wearing a combat jumpsuit and lace-up boots, both guarding the door.

The helicopter shielded me from the men as I dashed to the caravan. From there I'd planned on ducking to the back of the shed, but a sudden sulphur and cat urine stench made me pause behind it.

I stood on tiptoe trying to look in one of the windows. The curtains had all been drawn, but there was a small gap and when I pressed my eye to the dusty glass I saw science lab beakers, lengths of rubber tubing, and bottles of every sort of chemical from rubbing alcohol to drain cleaner. A pile of matchboxes on a table had all had their striker panels removed and there was a whole heap of empty cold and flu tablet packets.

So that's what Watto had been talking about to the bikie in the lounge room, a methamphetamine cook. Perfect place for it, I supposed. No neighbours to clock the stink, no one to call the brigade and the cops if the thing caught fire. I scanned quickly for any weapons, realised I should have checked the black van or searched the house more thoroughly, and decided to backtrack just as soon as I'd seen if Nick was still alive.

I jogged to the rear of the shed and put my eye up to one of the many small holes in the rusting tin. Two Harleys were parked inside, and Nick was tied to a chair atop a concrete floor. Rod stood over him, stripped to the waist and covered in sweat, just like his action hero character, but much shorter. Rod's Aryan offsider, Dean, stood watching, as did the bikies I'd seen in the lounge room. Everyone was armed except for Rod, who was doing a fair job on Nick with his fists, stopping every now and then to deliver a verbose soliloquy on justice, righteousness and an eye for an eye. Nick's head hung forward and blood dripped from his nose and mouth, and I wasn't sure if he was conscious or even alive until Rod signalled his guard and the guy tipped a bucket of water over Nick's face and pulled his head back. Nick let out a groan and his eyes fluttered open.

'Wake him up,' Rod growled.

The guard slapped Nick's face.

'Now, you pathetic, murdering cocksucker,' said Rod, 'we're going to take a little joy-ride and you can see what it's like to skydive—without a parachute.' He turned to his men. 'Start up the bird.'

'Uh, Mr Thurlow,' the skinny bikie piped up. 'Craig has a package he wants you to dispose of at the same time.'

'Fine, whatever. Go get it, but be quick. We're leaving in five.'

The guy nodded and left.

Five minutes. Damn. I considered yelling out to Rod, but had a sudden flash of insight. He wouldn't want to know that Nick didn't kill Isabella. He hated Nick because he suspected she'd still loved him and if I told him he'd just spent a million catching the wrong guy, well, he'd probably refuse to believe it. I'd have given away my position for nothing and it wouldn't take long for Craig's guys to find me and shoot me. Speaking of whom, the biker who'd gone to collect my body was going to be raising the alarm any moment. Shit, shit, shit. I ran through the options in my mind, but there weren't many. Run into the shed to untie Nick, get sprung and we'd die together. Run into the desert and die lost and alone. What about the black van? If Watto had left the keys I might have had a chance, except the bikies would follow on their Harleys, and I'd die in a hail of bullets at the first gate.

I couldn't get to the van, anyway. I was hidden by the copter as long as I stayed between the shed and the caravan, but as soon as I made a break for the van the guards at the front of the shed would see me, not to mention the guy who was about to find Watto's unconscious body and come running out of the house. So many thoughts rushed through my mind I was paralysed, didn't know what to do.

Until I glanced back at the caravan and suddenly had an idea.

Probably wouldn't work, but I had to try something. It might at least create a diversion and buy me time to get to the van.

I ran back to the caravan, keeping a lookout for the bikie who was heading towards the house. His back was to me as his boots scuffed up ochre dust. I tried the door and was amazed to find it unlocked. Goddamn. Well, we were in the middle of nowhere . . .

I'd read stuff in the papers about meth labs. They were prone to exploding, and so full of toxic, flammable chemicals that law enforcement didn't go in without full Hazmat protective gear. I pulled my t-shirt over the lower half of my face and went inside. An extractor fan was going but the stink was acrid, and I felt noxious gases sting my eyes and coil into my lungs. Inside, propane bottles, coffee filters, betadine and bottles of kerosene shared space with jars full of match heads. What the hell did they do with all that crap?

I switched off the air-conditioner, left an extractor fan on and swept all the empty cold and flu packets from the laminex table to the floor. I grabbed a bottle of kerosene, squirted it around and picked up an intact box of matches. Soon as I'd jumped out of the caravan I struck a match. Blue flames leapt and I bolted, slamming into the dust behind the shed, sure the thing was going to blow any second.

It didn't.

Had the fire gone out? I peeked through another hole in the tin. Soldier-boy Dean had untied Nick from the chair and was dragging him across the concrete towards the open doors and the helicopter beyond.

And then—boom.

chapter fifty-seven

My shoulders jumped and I turned instinctively, poking my head around the corner of the shed and copping an invisible wave of pressure and heat. The windows exploded in a blur of jangling glass and orange flame, and black smoke unfurled, turning the caravan into a fireball. I ducked as burning shrapnel rained from the sky, scuffing the dirt and pinging off the shed. The air stank of melting plastic, smouldering tyres.

Glancing through a hole in the tin I saw everyone running outside and I knew I didn't have long if I wanted to make a move. I snuck around the other side of the shed and ended up by the helicopter, where Nick was lying alone on the concrete slab.

'Come on,' I hissed. 'Get up. Run to the van.'

Nick shook his bruised and bloody head so I started dragging him through the dirt. Not easy. Although he'd lost weight he was still a big guy.

Rod and Dean were standing at the rear of the chopper, backs to me, with two bikies and a guy I guessed was the chopper pilot. The skinny bikie with long straggly hair had come out of the house and was standing on the wraparound wooden veranda, weapon in hand, mouth open. Everyone swore and ducked each time another chunk of flaming debris rained down.

Then something big blew and a fiery propane tank burst straight out of the roof of the caravan like a surface to air missile. The lot of them hit the dirt, but it wasn't headed for the chopper, instead flying towards the house and crashing through the tin roof. Flames burst from the hole and a blast ripped the air as the tank detonated. The skinny bikie vaulted over the veranda railing as a new blaze roiled from the building. I'd almost got Nick out of sight behind the van when a figure came striding out of the inferno, untouched. He wore a backpack, carried the silver Samsonite case in one hand and a Wild Turkey stubby in the other and was bleeding from the side of the head. Watto.

He stared straight at me as he came down the stairs. 'What the fuck's going on?' he yelled.

Everybody turned, saw me dragging Nick and in seconds I was surrounded. Watto's guys pulled me back and held me. Rod's men grabbed Nick and hefted him into the helicopter. I struggled like a wildcat until Watto dropped the suitcase on the ground, reclaimed his knife from my belt and held the serrated tip under my chin. I froze.

'Who the hell is that?' Rod boomed over the sound of the helicopter rotors, squinting like he almost recognised me.

Rod's guard, Dean, had helped wrestle Nick's limp body into the chopper, and stood on the edge of the cabin, pointing into the distance.

'I can see a dust cloud,' he yelled.

'Get the binoculars,' ordered Rod.

Dean reached into the chopper and came out with a pair. 'Shit. It's a cop car. They're stopped at the first gate!'

'How many?' Watto barked.

'Looks like two.' Dean adjusted the focus. 'A black guy and a woman. I think it's that Talbot bitch.'

'Fuck,' said Rod. 'ETA?'

'Five, ten minutes? He's using a sledgehammer on the lock.'

'Let's get out of here—now.' Rod moved towards the helicopter.

'Me, the girl and Craig's money are coming too,' Watto said.

Rod frowned. 'There's not enough room.'

'Bullshit,' said the fat guy in the t-shirt. 'I looked inside. Seats five.'

'Too much weight and she won't fly, we'll run out of fuel,' said Rod.

'We'll be three soon enough.' Watto grinned at me, then scowled at Rod. 'You don't let me on that fucking chopper and me mates here'll shoot you out of the sky.' He downed the last of his bourbon and Coke and threw the bottle into the dust.

'Right, fine, let's just get out of here,' Rod said, heading for the aircraft.

'What about us?' the skinny bikie whined.

'How much ammo you got?' Watto asked.

'Stacks.'

'Bonus. One of you in the shed, one behind the water tank. They won't know what hit 'em. Burn the bodies and the cop car and piss off straight after. They probably called for backup after the explosion, but it'll take ages to get here.'

Watto pushed me into the chopper beside Nick, who was slumped against the far door, and threw the silver case on the floor. Rod perched in the seat opposite and Dean jumped in, slid the door closed and sat next to Rod, a mini bar between them. The pilot started the engine and it let out a high-pitched hum before the rotor blades started to thump.

Watto kept the knife pressed into my side and grabbed a pistol out of the back of his jeans using his free hand. It looked like the one Nick had given me. Rod's guard held the sort of large automatic weapon favoured by Colombian drug lords, and his trigger finger twitched when Watto pulled the gun. Watto noticed.

'Wouldn't, mate. One, I work for Craig Murdoch, and two, youse have a lot more to lose than what I do.'

Rod put his hand on Dean's arm, made him lower the rifle. He glanced at me and then suddenly realised who I was.

'Simone *Kirsch*?'

I attempted a smile and tried to appear calm and resigned to my fate, when in reality I was speeding off my dial and noting exits, weapon placement and the position of the automatic screen that separated the cabin from the cockpit. It was directly behind Rod and Dean's seats and it was open.

'What are you doing here?' Rod asked, genuinely puzzled.

'She's with me,' Watto said, like I was his girlfriend. 'It's grouse to meet you again, by the way.'

'What?'

'Did your writing workshop at Port Phillip. So inspired I went and writ a book of me own.' He slipped the backpack off and, juggling the knife and the gun, opened the top so Rod could see all the jumbled notebooks and paper inside.

'Know where I could find an agent?' Watto asked.

Rod looked horrified.

While they were occupied I put Nick's seatbelt on him, then clasped my own so it wouldn't look suss. Watto noticed and chuckled.

'Don't think youse'll be needin' those,' he said.

Rod looked at me and opened his mouth as though he was about to tell Watto to unhand me, then he shut it and looked away, like being an imminent murder victim was contagious. So much for his righteous real-life action hero shtick. Arsehole.

'Can you see the cop car?' I asked, and everyone strained to look out the window. I took the Wild Turkey ring pull from my pocket and surreptitiously wiggled it into the buckle of Nick's seatbelt until the top broke off and the bottom half lodged in the mechanism. I was hoping to jam it, buy us some time.

As we wobbled, then began to lift, I put my next plan in motion.

'Hey, Rod,' I said. 'How's it feel to be sitting opposite your fiancée's killer?'

'Nick had it coming.' He still wasn't looking at me.

'Nick didn't do it.' I smiled. 'It was this guy: Watto.'

I thought the short, sharp jab in my side was a punch, until I looked down and saw the red patch growing on my singlet. Watto had stabbed me just below the ribs.

'Shut your lying hole,' he growled.

'Dean, get a towel,' Rod ordered. 'Now.'

Dean reached under the bar compartment and came up with some paper towels, knelt in front of me and pressed them to my wound. Rod rolled his eyes.

'No, for the seat.'

I held a bunch of absorbent towels to my side while Dean carefully laid down the rest to protect the seat underneath, then scooted back to Rod's side.

'I don't believe you,' Rod told me.

'It's bullshit,' Watto said. 'She's just trying ta, you know, like, get us to—'

Rod sighed impatiently. 'Set us against each other.'

'Yeah.'

'Everyone knows Nick's guilty.' Rod sounded like he was trying to convince himself. 'He went on the run. The police have been after him for months . . .'

I talked fast. 'He ran because Craig Murdoch was threatening his family and blackmailing him. Isabella stole money and drugs off the Red Devils. It's all in her book.'

I winced and waited for the thump that was really a stab. Bam. There it was. One in the arm this time. Not too deep but I felt the burn and hot blood gushing.

'Motherfucker!' I gasped, in pain yet strangely exhilarated. 'They read *Thrill City* after you donated it to the jail library. They recognised Lachlan Elliot and the replica Harley!'

Bam, bam, two more hits to the arm and the blood was really spurting, but I could take it. I was so high I felt like laughing.

'Would you stop doing that?' Rod bellowed at Watto. 'Those seats are imported calfskin!'

His brow creased like he was thinking. Even if he hadn't read the book he must have remembered her reading out the excerpt. He looked at me again and exchanged a glance with his blond-haired paratrooper.

'Don't listen, she's full of shit,' Watto said, eyes darting.

'He wrote about murdering Isabella.' I pointed at Watto's backpack.

I winced, anticipating the next stabbing blow, but Rod and Dean acted as one and leapt on Watto. Dean grabbed the gun but Rod couldn't get hold of the knife and struggled with Watto's wrist. In seconds the three of them were wrestling on the narrow floor space between the seats. I unclipped my seatbelt, scooted across to where Watto had been sitting, by the window, and clipped myself back in. Snatching his backpack, I wedged it between my knees before reaching forward to push the handle on the sliding door. Blood leaked everywhere, running down my arm, staining Rod's imported leather upholstery, sticking to my fingers. As the handle released, the cabin filled with rushing air and the deafening thump of the rotors. The others stopped and looked at me. I slid the door open all the way and saw we were only fifty metres or so above the red desert sand, but it was enough to make me feel dizzy and weak in the shins. I started pulling scraps of paper out of the backpack. Some of them fluttered around the cabin, but most flew out the door.

'You fucken bitch!' Watto tried to crawl towards me with the knife but the others held him back. With one hand Rod grabbed a headset and mike, struggled into it and said something to the pilot I couldn't hear over all the noise. I pulled out a bigger sheaf of paper and chucked it, too.

'No!' Watto yelled.

I made eye contact with Rod as I held the backpack above the threshold, about to fling it into space. Watto was enraged now, inching forward, his lips curled back exposing pale gums and disintegrating teeth. Rod said something into his microphone and nodded at Dean. They released Watto at the same time and dived back to their seats, clutching at the belts. The chopper banked sharply left as Watto lunged for his backpack, and suddenly he was gone. No yelling, no sound. One second he was there and the next he wasn't. I looked out the doorway and in between the strands of hair whipping into my eyes I saw his body hit the ground and bounce, once, producing a small puff of dust. I felt like I was going to throw up. The chopper straightened and Rod shifted to the seat next to me.

'Help me close the door,' I yelled in his ear, but he ignored me and started trying to undo Nick's seatbelt. Jesus. He knew Nick wasn't the killer, but he was going to throw him out of the chopper anyway. And I bet I was next. He'd given more of a shit about his seat covers and couldn't let me live if I witnessed him murder Nick.

Rod tugged on the seatbelt and looked to Dean for help. Dean got on his knees between the seats, tried the belt, took a knife from his ankle strap and started sawing through the material. His weapon was still strapped over his shoulder but he'd left Watto's gun on the mini bar between the two rear-facing seats. Just behind the seats was the cockpit. Since the privacy screen was open I could see the back of the pilot's head and the instrument panel. I wasn't sure if I had a plan, exactly. Maybe I was acting on instinct, or maybe I was thinking that if I was going down then everyone else was, too.

I unclipped the belt, dived across and grabbed the revolver, climbed onto the seat and thrust the top half of my body into the cockpit.

Then I fired the gun.

chapter fifty-eight

The first bullet blew into the instrument panel, the second into a throttle next to the pilot. I felt a tug on my leg and metal pressing against my neck. The assault rifle, probably. I kicked back and screamed.

'Leave me alone or I'll blow his fucking head off and we'll all be fucked!'

I hadn't a clue what I'd hit but it seemed to be doing the trick. The rotors slowed. Whump. Whump. Whump.

Rod was yelling stuff to the pilot I couldn't understand.

'Lower the pitch! Autorotate!'

'I'm trying! Altitude's too low!'

The copter started swinging around, slowly at first, then faster and faster. We were descending and moving closer to the farmhouse: I saw smoke from the burning building each time we flipped that way. For a moment I regretted what I'd done, but the spin became so intense that after a few seconds all I could think about was hanging on. I tried to look back and see what Rod and Dean were up to but the force was too great so I hooked one elbow under the pilot's shoulder strap. He was too busy fighting with the busted controls to stop me.

The chopper was at a weird angle now and I wasn't seeing any smoke, just flashes of blue sky, glints of sunlight and terrifyingly close red earth and scrub. The pressure was intense, and as much as I tried to hang on, my arm began slipping out of the harness. I was just wondering how many seconds were left till impact when there was a god-almighty bang and everything went black.

The drug wrenched me out of unconsciousness and I came to with a start. I was on my back, underneath a scrubby bush about twenty metres from the twisted wreck of what used to be an Agusta Grand. I wondered if I still had all my limbs, and if so, whether they were working. First I wriggled my fingers and toes, then lifted myself up on my elbows to take a look. My jeans were torn and bloody and my arms were a mess of lacerations, blood and dust. My rib cage ached and my head throbbed. Everything hurt—but I was so wired the pain wasn't bothering me.

I heard a vehicle in the distance and sat up, suddenly remembering: Talbot and the other copper, heading straight for the ambush. I managed to stand and limped over to the wreck. The top and tail rotors were gone, the tail was askew and it looked like the chopper had landed nose first. Although basically upright, the cockpit was mashed and I didn't stop to look inside. Crumpled metal fragments littered the stony ground and I padded carefully on the hot earth, wondering when and where I'd lost my shoes. I felt sweat dripping down the back of my head, but when I touched the spot my fingers came back red and sticky and tangled with bleached blonde hair.

The doors on both sides of the cabin were gone. I poked my head inside, smelling fuel and smouldering electricals, and wondered if the thing was gonna blow. Rod and Nick were still strapped in, not moving, but Dean, and one of the seats, was missing. I couldn't see any guns or the suitcase with the million.

I jumped in and tugged on Nick's seatbelt but it was still jammed. I needed Dean's knife. Had it been thrown out along with everything else? I slid out of the opposite door and looked around, shading my eyes from the sun. Ten metres from the nose of the chopper the missing chair lay on its back, Dean's feet sticking out. I ran over, wondering if he was still alive.

He wasn't. His head was gone and all that remained was a jagged line of torn flesh, cracked bone and stringy, multicoloured tendon, already crawling with flies. The beige calfskin upholstery was stained red and the dust beneath the chair contained a pool of coppery-smelling, rapidly coagulating blood. I glimpsed one of the main rotor blades behind him and shuddered. I looked around for the severed head, then snapped myself out of it. Get Nick out. Warn the cops.

The knife was strapped onto Dean's ankle so I tugged it out, undid his shoulder harness and gingerly slipped the rifle over his torso, trying, and failing, to stop it from touching the meaty gore. I gagged bourbon, managed to hold it down. Small chunks of flesh adhered to the strap, but I put it on anyway, ran back to the chopper, and sawed through Nick's safety belt. He slumped sideways out of the door and hit the dirt before I could catch him. I dragged him as far away from the helicopter as I could and laid him in a grove of saltbush where there was a tiny bit of shade.

Flies crawled over his split lip and I thought he was dead, until his mouth twitched. I probably should have administered first aid but couldn't remember any and didn't have time—the bikies were about to shoot Detective Talbot and the other copper. I ran towards the burning farmhouse, vaguely aware that I was having trouble breathing. Hot, dry air seared my throat and jagged stones sliced my bare feet and I realised I still had the

Joan Jett song stuck in my head, the chorus repeating over and over again like a looped tape. I wasn't sure if anyone could see me so I zigzagged like I'd seen in movies and crouched behind a clump of spinifex when I was halfway there, lifting the gun to my shoulder and peering through the telescopic sight.

The bikies were hiding, but I could see the four-wheel-drive police car stopped at the second gate. The big bearded officer was smashing the lock with a sledgehammer and Talbot was inside, talking into a radio, hopefully calling for backup, but how long would that take?

'Hey,' I yelled, then ducked for a few seconds, before popping my head up again, meerkat-style. No one had reacted. Probably couldn't hear anything over the roar of the blaze. Looking through the sight again I saw the cop bust the lock and get back in the vehicle to drive the short distance to the house. I had to do something, considered firing at their car, but knew I was too inexperienced. I'd probably disable it or shoot one of them in the face.

They pulled up a safe distance from the burning building and opened the car doors. I saw something glint behind the water tank. One of the bikies. No way could I get him, but I knew what I could hit.

I trained the crosshairs on the tank itself and pulled the trigger. It was jammed. The fuck? Must have been damaged in the crash. I studied the gun. Out of bullets? Or was it a magazine? Shit. Everything I knew about guns I'd seen in action movies. Lock and load. What the hell did that even mean? Did you have to press a button? Slide some part that went chick-chick?

The sun was scorching, sweat ran down my face and flies buzzed, tickling the wound at the back of my head and clustering around my lips and eyes. I waved them away and then I saw it. A tiny switch the same gunmetal grey as the body, easy to miss. The safety catch. Dean must have engaged it as the chopper was going down. I flicked it over, got the middle of the water tank in the sights, and fired.

I hadn't been prepared for the recoil and the first shot went wild and thrust me backwards. I steadied, braced myself and fired again, pulling the trigger over and over and watching the tank piss water. Releasing my finger I swung the gun in the direction of the cop car. Talbot and the male cop had dived back in and were tearing off back the way they'd come, throwing up gravel. The other bikie emerged from behind the shed, and fired at the four-wheel drive. The back window blew out and the vehicle skidded across the road before steadying, bashing through the gate and speeding down the dirt road in a cloud of dust.

I stayed down, looking through the sight. The bikies briefly conferred outside the shed, then took off on their Harleys. There was nothing more I could do so I limped back to the helicopter, dry-mouthed, breathing raggedly and dizzy. I needed water and so did Nick. I climbed inside and opened the little bar fridge next to the remaining rear-facing seat. What do you know, four plastic water bottles and one bottle of Krug champagne. Intact. I made a basket out of my stretched t-shirt and piled the lot in. Jumped and whirled around when I felt a hand on my back.

'Fuck!'

'Simone,' Rod croaked. 'Get me out of here. I can't undo the belt.'

He waved his hand and I noticed it was at an odd angle. Broken wrist.

'I don't think so. A whole heap of cops'll be here soon. I want you just where you are.'

'The money.'

'It's around here somewhere.'

'If you get me into the van and drive me out of here, you can have it. All of it.'

'Dunno.' I pretended to consider it. 'I would, only Nick and I are going to need it for evidence. Speaking of which, can I borrow your phone?'

I dug around in his pocket and found his fancy phone, popped it in the pocket of my torn and filthy jeans and left him, taking my booty back to Nick. I swigged some water, then washed off Nick's face and held the bottle to his mouth. He was half conscious and gulped and coughed.

'What's happening?' he slurred. His mouth wasn't working properly, one eye was swollen shut and his lip was bulging and split.

'We're about to give ourselves up.'

'No.'

'It'll be okay. There's a way out of this. We've got evidence against them and no one has to know you were involved in Elliot's murder. Trust me.'

'I can't go to jail.'

'You won't. We're on the side of the angels, Nick. We're the good guys.'

Unconscious again, he didn't respond. I unwrapped the champers, dialled a number on Rod's phone, then popped the cork and drank from the neck as I listened to the ring tone. Sublime ice-cold liquid foamed into my mouth.

'Hello?' Andi picked up on the sixth ring.

'It's Simone.'

'Holy shit. Where *are* you?'

'Dunno, exactly. The South Australian desert, 'bout two hours out of Broken Hill.'

'You alright?'

'Not sure of that either. Listen, I don't have time to explain, but me and Nick need a good lawyer, the best. You do the court rounds. Know someone?'

'Yeah, I do.'

'Right. Tell him to charter a freaking plane and get to Broken Hill as soon as he can. Me and Nick'll be there in a few hours, probably.'

'What's happened?'

'What hasn't? Get your arse up here and I'll give you an exclusive. Bring Curtis, too. I think he's just become a dad.' I hung up and offered champagne to Nick. He shook his head.

'Water,' he croaked.

I dribbled some into his mouth, then sat back swigging from the bottle, humming Joan Jett and swatting flies. I really could have gone a cigarette, but hadn't seen Rod or any of his men smoke. I briefly considered wandering the desert looking for Watto's body and his ever-present packet of ciggies, but decided not to. It was too damn hot.

chapter fifty-nine

I ended up with a skull fracture, two broken ribs, stitches on my stab wounds, and more cuts and bruises than I could count, and after the Broken Hill hospital had patched me up they put me in a private room, handcuffed and under armed guard. I was thankful for the cruisy combination of prescription painkillers and crystal meth, without which I would have had the headache of my life. Nick and Rod had both been airlifted to Adelaide suffering from broken bones and internal injuries, and Dean and the chopper pilot were, I presumed, toe tagged and lying in the morgue. The docs had explained that being thrown clear of the helicopter meant I was less injured than if I'd been strapped in when we hit the dust. Something to do with the force of the accident. I wasn't really listening. I was just glad to be alive.

Detective Talbot and her partner, the piggy Jefferson Archer, had been questioning me for about an hour when my new lawyer walked in.

'Caroline Swift QC.' She introduced herself around, then nodded to Talbot. 'Hello, Dianne.'

Talbot crossed her arms and sucked in her cheeks. 'Caroline, fancy meeting you on such a high profile case . . .'

The comment jogged my memory and I realised I recognised Caroline Swift from newspapers and news bulletins, defending such diverse clients as murderers, drug dealers, alleged terrorists and student protesters. She looked late thirties, incredibly young to be a Queen's Counsel, and wore a designer navy skirt suit with black, spiked, patent-leather heels. Her blonde crop had been artfully styled. Talkback radio hosts hated her.

'Great shoes,' I said. They were.

'Thanks. I hope you haven't told them anything.'

I had.

'Nothing that would incriminate me.'

'Good.' She turned to the detectives. 'What's Simone been charged with?'

'What hasn't she?' Jefferson Archer held out the charge sheet in one plump pink hand. Caroline glanced at it and handed it to her assistant, a frazzled young brunette juggling a laptop bag and a small suitcase on wheels.

'May I please have some time alone with my client?'

'Sure,' Talbot said. 'Just remind her not to try anything. I've got most of the local area command guarding this floor.'

The cops left and it was just me, Caroline and her assistant.

'You feel well enough to talk?'

Talk? Could I ever. An hour later and Caroline still hadn't managed to shut me up.

After some to-ing and fro-ing between Caroline Swift and Detective Talbot, I was uncuffed. I'd told the lawyer everything except Nick's part in Lachlan Elliot's murder, and as she took off to fly to Adelaide she seemed pretty confident she could keep him out of jail, if not out of court.

The docs had told me to rest up, but as soon as I was left alone I put on my torn and bloodied singlet and jeans and wandered down to maternity. The nurse who'd admitted Chloe had just clocked on for the evening shift and looked me up and down.

'Jeez, love, you look like you've been dragged backwards through a mulga bush.'

'You're not far off. Is Chloe Wozniak still here?'

'Yep.' She told me the room number and pointed me in the right direction. When I reached the room I peeped in and saw Chloe asleep with a little bundle wrapped up on her chest. After flirting, sleeping was her next greatest talent. JJ and Curtis sat on opposite sides of the metal-framed bed, whispering to each other across it. I hung back for a second to listen in.

'When'd you say you met?' Curtis said.

'Last night. Poetry slam.'

'So you haven't . . . ?'

'Jesus, man. Ten minutes after we hooked up she was giving birth. I'm not that much of a player. What are you so jealous about, anyway? Chloe told me you were going out with the famous Desiree. Had a crack at her myself a few years back, she's one hot woman.'

Curtis lowered his voice so far I had to stick part of my ear in the door to hear.

'That was all bullshit,' he whispered. 'Wanted to get her jealous so she'd take me back before the baby was born. Me, Nick and Desiree cooked it up after I got a bit drunk and . . . emotional at lunch with our publisher a few months back. It was working too, until Desiree pissed off overseas without telling me. I swear, I never even fucked her.'

'Hey, you don't need to get angry, man. You should be thanking me. I got photos and video of the birth on my mobile. It was beautiful.'

I chose that moment to walk in. JJ had flipped open his phone to show Curtis the footage, and Curtis reared back so suddenly he almost fell off his plastic chair.

'That's disgusting,' Curtis choked. 'Put it away.'

'You want to get back with her you might have to change your attitude, my friend. She's one natural, earthy woman.'

Natural was not exactly the adjective I would have used to describe her, but, whatever.

'Hey everyone,' I said.

'Hey.' JJ smiled as though I'd just popped out for a second to the drink machine and wasn't covered in filth and blood. Curtis started laughing.

'Get the hair! You look like a total skank.'

I ignored him. 'Is the baby okay?' I asked JJ.

'Fine.'

'Girl or boy?'

'Girl.'

'Name?'

'I was thinking Phyllis,' Curtis said. 'After my gran.'

'Alkira,' JJ countered. 'It's Aboriginal for sky, and she was born in big sky country.'

Curtis snorted. 'Look at her, she's white as a loaf of Tip Top.'

'So?'

I tiptoed closer for a better look. The baby was all swaddled up in a pink bunny rug, asleep on Chloe's chest. Chloe started to stir. I sat next to her.

'We should leave the women alone for a while,' JJ said.

'Not too long. Andi's looking for you,' Curtis told me. 'We need an interview now if we wanna get the copy in for tomorrow's paper. Capiche?'

I couldn't hack him.

The guys left and I helped Chloe struggle into a sitting position. Her daughter woke up and started to wail and she shifted it against one of her swollen breasts so the baby could suck. I looked on in amazement.

'You're breastfeeding!'

'Yeah, well, my tits were sore and JJ and the nurse convinced me. Besides, my moot's wrecked and my gut's a lump of jello, so I was thinking I could book in with some surgeon in six months. Tighten up the lot in one go. What's been going on with you?'

I told her about my heroics, and showed off my injuries. She didn't seem particularly impressed after her unintentionally drug-free labour. Fair enough.

'What happened to Rod?' she asked.

'Intensive care, just like Nick. Coppers are waiting to interview him. He's up shit creek when they do.'

'And Emery Wade and that bikie boss, Murdoch?'

I told her I had no idea and that Caroline Swift had organised a safe house for us all to be whisked to until we knew what was going on. This time Chloe was impressed.

'Sweet. We can order in takeaway and watch DVDs and you and Curtis can help with the baby.'

My heart sank.

'Will there be cops there?' she continued. 'I really need a bong. Hey—you called Sean yet?'

'No point.'

Andi and Curtis arrived. Andi went up to the baby and coochie-cooed.

'Let's get this done.' Curtis looked at his watch.

'Sure, but we do it in the pub. I'm tonguing for a drink, a jukebox and a pack of smokes.' It had been hours.

'They won't let you in looking like that.' Curtis nodded at my torn, bloodstained clothing, scabby limbs and bare feet.

'We'll pop by our motel on the way. I've got shampoo and a couple of changes of clothes,' Andi said.

'You're at least two sizes smaller than me,' I told her. 'They'll never fit.'

'Have you looked at yourself in the mirror lately?' she replied. 'You're a skinny bitch. Must have lost ten kilos since Christmas Day.'

Waiting at the automatic doors while Curtis and Andi went to retrieve their hire car, I felt a claw-like hand on my arm and turned. It was Detective Talbot, hard faced and smelling of instant coffee, sweat and cigarettes. I pulled my arm away.

'You can't keep me here,' I told her. 'My lawyer—'

'I'm not trying to restrain you. I just wanted to say . . .'

'Yeah?' I crossed my arms.

'I wanted to say thanks. Amazingly, all the evidence at the crime scene supports the statement you gave, and Queensland police picked up the gang members just across the border, armed to the teeth. You saved our lives back there and risked your own by giving away your position. It was brave.'

I shrugged. More drug-fucked, really, but I wasn't about to mention that I'd been off my head on meth and still was, pretty much.

'I'll be recommending you for an award.'

'I'd rather you didn't.'

Dianne Talbot actually smiled at me.

'Tough shit. And we'll see about your operating licence. If you can keep quiet for a couple of months—I have a friend in licensing. No promises, but . . .'

I was stunned. A cop was being nice to me instead of bawling me out. Before I could thank her she'd disappeared back inside.

I did half the interview shouting through steam in the motel bathroom and the other half at one of the big historic pubs in town, ducking out once for a ciggie which I couldn't smoke because it hurt my broken ribs too much. The doctors had said I couldn't do anything for it except take painkillers and try not to sneeze, cough or laugh.

The interview was a quick one because they had to race back to the motel to email their copy and some photos to the night editors, but both made me promise to tell them all the gory details the next day. Curtis was particularly stoked that Emery Wade had been behind it all and bragged that it would mean a definite sequel to his current book, and a large advance.

I felt dirty talking to the press, but my new lawyer had sanctioned the interview, telling me it was important to get the real story out there before Rod Thurlow had a chance to launch his spin machine. I had a feeling she didn't mind the publicity, either.

By the time the two of them left, the sun had set in an orange fury and a fuzzy purple twilight had descended upon the town. Reporters with television cameras began converging in front of the police station, but no one recognised me sitting at the bar in Andi's black jeans and Ramones t-shirt, Debbie Harry hair in a ponytail, a cheap pair of service station thongs on my feet. My waist might have shrunk but my instep hadn't.

The champagne I'd drunk hadn't even touched the sides and I was still wide awake, wondering if I ought to go back to the hospital and beg for morphine.

A couple of local lads had approached me at the bar, but shied away when they clocked the cuts, bruises and seeping bandages. I kept my head down when the next bloke sidled up, until he ordered a beer. I knew the deep voice well.

'Alex?'

'Simone?' He did a double take. 'Jesus, I didn't recognise you. Me and Sean flew in on the five fifty-five from Adelaide. We've been looking for you.'

'Why?'

He scrutinised my face. 'You seem wired.'

'As a matter of fact I am. Good to see you.'

It was. My stomach clenched like he was a high school crush and I felt like I was going to fall off my barstool or jump him. Maybe both.

'What happened?'

'Have you got three days? The condensed version'll appear in *The Age* tomorrow morning.'

The endorphins triggered by seeing him were mixing with the last of the ice, getting together for the mother of all parties. My stomach leapt like a Jack Russell terrier.

'I can't stop thinking about you,' I said, like an idiot. 'About what happened at your buck's turn.'

'Forget about it.' Alex's eyes darted away, nervous.

All the drugs and the stress had combined into a kind of truth serum—nothing was stopping me.

'I can't.' I meant what I said. 'Do you think about it?'

'No.'

'Bullshit. You told me as much at the Christmas party.'

'Who cares? It's over and done with now.'

'Don't say that.'

'For god's sake.' He shook his head and ordered a whiskey from the barman. 'When I was available you didn't want me. Now I'm married, you do. Plus you're going out with my best friend.'

'Was going out with your best friend.'

'What?'

'He hasn't told you?'

I gulped more champagne and slapped my thongs against the rungs of the stool. I couldn't sit still and the bloody Joan Jett song was reverberating around my brain. I felt manic, weird, like if I didn't tell him the truth right then, I never would.

Alex pulled out his mobile phone.

'Shut up. I'm ringing Sean, telling him where you are.'

He fumbled with some buttons and I sang the song under my breath. *I hate myself for loving you.* He frowned as he held the phone to his ear.

'What did you just say?'

I slammed my drink down on the bar and it slopped over the sides. I couldn't hold it in any longer. I wanted to kiss him or hit him. I wasn't sure which.

'I said: I hate myself for loving you.'

He looked stunned for a second, until we heard a ring tone familiar to both of us. Sinatra, 'I've Got You Under My Skin'. We turned just as Sean emerged from behind a pillar.

chaptersixty

'They say you shouldn't eavesdrop if you're not gonna like what you hear,' Sean said. 'So, what actually happened at the party?' His jovial voice didn't match his eyes.

I didn't say a word. Alex closed his mouth, too.

'Come on.' His Scottish accent drew the words out. 'I'm talking to my girlfriend and my best friend. If anyone's supposed to tell me the truth it's you two.'

'I'm not your girlfriend anymore.'

'Huh?'

'You broke up with me.'

'No I didn't.'

I was confused.

'The note. *I can't do this anymore.*'

'I couldn't. I couldn't handle spending the day with you shut up in a hotel room, I was too pissed off. I went to the movies, a gallery, wandered around the botanic gardens. When I came back you were gone.'

'What?' He hadn't dumped me?

'Right now I'm more interested in what you two got up to while I was away.'

'We didn't have sex,' I said, immediately wishing I'd shut the hell up.

'What did you have, if you don't mind me asking?'

'You really want to know?'

'Sure,' Sean said.

'When I realised it was Alex's buck's party I ran to the bathroom and he followed me. We were both pretty drunk, and Alex still had his head injury and we just sort of kissed and fooled around, but nothing happened.'

'Simone.' Alex was pissed off.

'Kinda fooled around.' Sean rolled the words around his mouth. 'What does that mean, exactly?'

'Mate.' Alex shook his head and approached Sean. Sean stepped back. He laughed, but there was no humour in it.

'No, I'm really interested to explore the semantics. Did you touch her tits?'

Alex shook his head, but I was tired of all the pussy-footing around.

'Yeah, he did,' I said.

'Outside the clothes or inside?'

'Inside.'

'Good. Great. Specifics. Now we're getting somewhere. And did you touch him?'

'Yes, Sean, I did.'

'Shut the fuck up, Simone,' Alex said.

'Whereabouts?'

'Where do you think, Sean?'

He nodded thoughtfully.

'And did that part of his body touch any other part of your body? Apart from your hand, I mean.'

'Stop it, mate.' Alex turned back to the bar.

'We didn't have sex,' I said.

'So you keep insisting. Just answer the question.'

I'd never seen his deep blue eyes so unreflective. They were as flat and dead as a fish on ice.

'Yes, but only for a second. I pulled away.' I glanced at Alex, ready to throw a rope. 'We both did when we remembered—'

'Oh, you finally remembered me. How thoughtful. And how far in did it get before you so kindly recalled that I exist?'

'You weren't there for me, Sean.'

'Fuck's sake, save the bullshit for Oprah or your beloved Dr Phil. I wasn't there because I was in fucking Vietnam and I would have come back in a second except you didn't tell me what was going on. You know what Alex said before? He was right. You're always going to want what you can't have. Even if he did leave his new wife for you—doubtful now they've got a baby on the way—you wouldn't want him anyway. How ironic. I wonder why you couldn't just come out and say you didn't love me. Did you want me hanging around like a pathetic puppy dog? Did you like that? There I was thinking I'd give you a bit of space, time to think about things, and you actually go to such lengths to avoid me that you end up on the run with an accused murderer and nearly get yourself killed. I mean, Jesus.'

'I'm sorry.'

'No. You're not. I am.' He turned to leave.

'Sean,' Alex said.

Sean turned. 'And you—stay away from her if you know what's good for you.'

He walked out of the pub. Alex grabbed me by the shoulders, fingers digging in.

'Why'd you have to drag me into it?'

'I wasn't—' I started, but Alex was already out the door, running after Sean.

Later that evening I lay in bed in the motel room next

to Andi's, guarded by coppers, attempting to sleep. It wasn't working. The ice was still in my system and my thoughts kept flashing wildly: Sean, Alex, Mum, Watto, Dad, Emery Wade, Dean's headless corpse. I'd screwed everything up, again. When the bedside phone rang I was pleased for the interruption, and picked it up.

'Simone.'

It was Sam Doyle, the Sydney-based ex-gangster who'd been strangely concerned for me since my mum had been shot six months ago.

'How the hell did you get this number?' I asked.

'I may be out of the biz, but I'm still connected,' he said. 'Saw the news. How you doing?'

'Nice of you to keep taking an interest.' I hoisted myself up on one elbow and took a slug of the whiskey I'd purchased in the mistaken belief it would help me sleep. 'But I'm not exactly sure why.'

'I knew your mum, met you when you were a little girl.'

Met me? That was a joke. He'd kidnapped me before a sudden change of heart made him let me go, unharmed.

'I feel responsible for what happened to her and her partner,' he said. 'And to you.'

'That's nice.' I lay back on the bed. 'Is it your new Catholic guilt or do you still fancy her? I know you had an affair, all those years ago.' I took another swig and whiskey dribbled down my cheek. Wiping it off with the back of my hand I prayed the meth would finally leave my system. I'd had enough.

'What happened?' He got straight to the point. 'Anyone I know?'

'Probably not. Emery Wade and some fuck-stick called Craig Murdoch, head of the Red Devils bikie gang. They got together in prison and decided to kill two birds with one stone. They're still after me, my family and even my friends.

Most of us are going into hiding. Except my stupid mother, who refuses to leave her bloody yoga retreat.'

'Which prison?' he asked.

'Port Phillip. What does it matter? Listen. I've got to go to hospital and get some sedatives. The drugs aren't wearing off.'

'What drugs?'

'It's a long story. Sorry, but I've got to go.' I hung up.

•

After almost a week in lockdown with Chloe, Curtis and the unnamed baby in a suburban brick veneer, I'd just about had it. The baby wouldn't stop crying, Chloe and Curtis argued constantly and dramatically, and I was seriously coming down from my ice-capade, near-death experience and the toe-curling way I'd finally destroyed any relationship with Alex and Sean. I was about to chuck it all in and take my chances with Craig Murdoch's hitmen out on the streets when Caroline Swift showed up with a copy of *The Age*.

'Check it out.' She threw it on the seventies smoked-glass coffee table and I snatched it up and read the front page.

> *Two inmates found dead in maximum security prison*
>
> Port Phillip Prison is in lockdown after the death of two inmates.
>
> The bodies of Emery Saxon Wade, aged 55, and Craig Alan Murdoch, 38, were found hanging in Wade's cell last night.
>
> A prison spokesman confirmed that officers from the Homicide Squad, Police Corrections Inspectorate and the State Coroner's Office were investigating.
>
> Wade, a former criminal lawyer, was awaiting trial on three charges of murder and the attempted murder of Melbourne private investigator Simone Kirsch in March last year.

Murdoch, president of the Red Devils motorcycle gang, was serving a six-year sentence for the serious assault of Michael Riccardo, head of rival gang the Assassins, which left Riccardo brain-damaged. Murdoch was also convicted of firearms offences and masterminding the fire-bombing of the Assassins' Melbourne clubhouse eighteen months ago.

It is understood both men were being investigated by the Homicide Squad over the slaying of author Isabella Bishop as well as facing blackmail, kidnapping and drugs charges.

When asked about the possibility of a murder–suicide, a police spokeswoman said it was too early to comment. The police investigation is continuing.

A note at the foot of the article directed readers to related coverage a few pages on.

Lethal lies

Action writer Rod Thurlow, recently refused bail after being charged with attempted murder and conspiracy, is now at the centre of a literary scandal. His agent, Brendan Reed, has confessed the ex-army officer didn't pen the best-selling Chase Macallister novels—it was Reed himself.

'We thought naming Rod as the author would boost sales,' Reed revealed. 'He's got the look, the background and readers love authenticity—I mean, look at Andy McNab.' Reed said he decided to come clean because he was tired of the deception and wanted to finally receive the recognition and profit share he deserved.

epilogue

I was out the front of what used to be my office, sweating in the heat, wearing my cut-off shorts and 'Damn Right I'm a Cowgirl' t-shirt. A bandana restrained my re-dyed dark brown hair and I hoped I didn't look too much like Axl Rose.

Orthodox Jews, junkies and old ladies with shopping trolleys glanced at me as they strolled by, and the shorts got a few whistles from rev-heads in passing cars. I sneered. Although the threat to my life had been, to use military euphemism, neutralised, it wasn't a happy day. It hadn't been a happy month. The bonus Liz had slung me after rescuing her brother was long gone, and I was injured, dumped, unemployed and about to become homeless. I'd heard nothing about having my licence reinstated and had finally decided to scrape the *Simone Kirsch Investigations* sign off the glass. About time Chloe recouped some money from renting out the shopfront.

'Hey.'

I turned and nearly dropped the scraper. A part-Maori guy wearing dark sunglasses slouched against the wall like he was starring in a Hugo Boss campaign—even though it was obvious he hadn't been to bed all night. He was six foot, with mussed-up black hair and a pouty mouth, designer jeans hanging off slender hips. It was my younger brother, Jasper. I stood on tiptoe to hug him, smelled sweat, smoke and expensive cologne.

'The hell are you doing here?'

'Expected a *slightly* warmer welcome after two years . . .'

'Sorry.'

'What you up to?' He nodded to the door, where all that was left of my name was a cursive *irsch*.

'Shutting up shop.'

He pushed his sunnies up on his head, revealing the soulful brown eyes that earned him more in a year than my moot could make in a lifetime. An old lady clocked him and nearly walked straight into a power pole.

'Stop it.' He grabbed the paint scraper. 'You'll only need to get it done again.'

'Doubtful.' I cricked my neck and rolled my shoulders. My back had been giving me hell since the helicopter crash and I should have seen a physio, but couldn't afford it. Cheaper to pop the occasional painkiller. 'You been to bed yet?'

'Bed yes, sleep no.'

'You're a worse slut than me.'

'Don't you mean a better one?'

Bada-bing. Just like when we were kids in the car, only filthier.

'I want to go up to the old house for a while,' he said. 'Maybe study something, definitely take a break, stop partying.'

'Up north?'

'Uh-huh. Mum and I were up around Byron for New Year's, and when we weren't sequestered at the cop shop because of you, we went to look at the old place. Even stayed one night but it was more like camping. I'm thinking of spending at least a month fixing the place up, getting the electricity connected and the phone back on. We could go swimming in the creek, revive the old kitchen garden. We could buy chickens!'

'We?'

'You're not doing anything. Why don't you come and help?'

'You've got to be joking.'

Jasper looked over my shoulder and slipped his sunnies back on. 'Shit,' he said. 'It's the cops.'

'Don't be a dick.'

'I mean it.'

I glanced at the road behind me. A marked police car had pulled up. I put my hands on my hips. What now?

The passenger door opened and Dianne Talbot stepped out wearing pants, heels and a shell top. She carried a clipboard and when she spotted Jasper she smoothed her brown bob and pulled her shoulders back. I hoped Chloe didn't come downstairs; she'd probably start humping Jasper's leg.

'This is my brother.' I introduced him to Talbot.

'Great to meet you, ma'am.' He shook her hand and gave her his thousand-watt grin.

'You need another statement?' I asked. They always needed another statement.

'No. I was on my way to the St Kilda station and thought I'd stop by to tell you that my friend in licensing has agreed to reinstate a provisional inquiry licence effective—'

'Immediately?'

She checked a piece of paper in her folder. 'The fifteenth of March. And only if you keep your nose clean and stay out of those bloody strip clubs.'

'I was broke.'

'Word gets around,' she said.

I was so happy I felt like punching the air, but kept it in check, acted cool.

'What the hell am I supposed to do for the next six weeks?'

Jasper looked at me and grinned.

acknowledgements

Thanks to:

Michael Lynch and the rest of my family: Thea and Bruce, Tony and Kelly, Stella, Jean, Jesse, Kate, Jasmine and Julian, Grandma and Oma and Opa.

My encouraging girlfriends: Dotti, Juliet, Helena, Donna B and Donna T.

Everyone at Allen & Unwin, in particular: Annette Barlow, Clara Finlay and Catherine Milne. Jo Jarrah, world's greatest editor.

Trish Weekes and Dan Edwards, for lending me your house to write in.

All the great people from the Broken Hill Weekend of Crime: Amelia Veale, Sarah McConnell, Marvis Sofield, Dr Steve Flecknoe-Brown and Detective Senior Constable Ian West.

The wonderful writers I've met, who were the inspiration for this book: Jared Thomas, Miles Merrill, Katherine Howell, Jarad Henry, Shane Maloney and Peter Temple.

My Sisters in Crime: Carmel Shute, Lindy Cameron, Sue Turnbull, Katrina Beard, Vivienne Colmer, Phyllis King, Michelle Cooper, Cathy Martin, Tanya King and Robin Bowles.

Christine Cremen for the scurrilous literary gossip.

Jason from Castlemaine Cycles for suggesting a pub for Simone and an address for David Geddes.

And to Doug Mansfield. Thank you for the songs.

NOW READ THE FIRST BOOK IN THE SERIES

peepshow

Simone Kirsch, aka Vivien Leigh, is intelligent, sexy and funny.

And she needs it all as she goes undercover at The Red Room to find out who killed the sleazy owner, Francesco 'Frank' Parisi. It's the only way to get her best friend Chloe back from Frank's underworld brother Sal, who says he'll kill her unless Simone comes up with the real murderer, pronto.

Always resourceful, Simone has a few tricks up her sleeve . . . and she's never been afraid of getting herself into sticky situations. But now she's tangling with the city's most corrupt cop, some crazy strippers and a rockabilly band called Las Vegas Grind.

A criminally witty romp on the sexy side of the mean streets.

chapterone

I was lying on my back in the peepshow at the Shaft Cinema, legs in the air, wearing a peekaboo nightie and no knickers.

Two of the six booths were occupied, and every time one of the guys put a coin in I heard a buzz, the glass went from opaque to clear, and a small orange light came on above the window.

It cost them two dollars for forty-five seconds, and I got a dollar of that. The booths were dark and the men's faces shadowy, unless they pressed them right up against the glass. Not a good idea.

They kept putting coins in so I writhed around on the thin mattress, got on all fours, flipped my long dark hair around in faux orgasmic throes and pretended to play with myself. A portable stereo blasted out Madonna and the small room was lit with coloured disco lights. Mirrors on the walls and ceiling reflected each other and there were thousands of me, stretching out into eternity.

The peep's door opened and my best friend, Chloe, pulled across the tatty red curtain.

'Simone!' Her blonde hair was in rollers and she popped out of a small pink bikini top.

'You're keen.' I glanced at the clock. It was three forty-five in the afternoon. 'I've still got fifteen minutes.'

'He's dead.' She was clutching the pm edition of the *Herald Sun*. 'That fat bastard's been murdered.'

'What fat bastard?' I lay on one side and lifted my leg up, Jane Fonda style.

'Strip club slaying,' Chloe read from the front page. 'The body of a man discovered floating near St Kilda beach this morning has been identified as strip club boss Francesco (Frank) Parisi, thirty-eight. Police have confirmed Mr Parisi, proprietor of Flinders Street table dancing venue the Red Room, was brutally hacked to death before being dumped in the bay.' Chloe worked at the Shaft during the day and moonlighted at the Red on Friday and Saturday nights.

I bent over in front of the windows and gave everyone a flash. 'Did you knock him off?' I joked.

Chloe wasn't laughing. She hugged the paper tightly to her chest and chewed her bottom lip. 'I think we'd better go for a drink,' she said.

•

We crossed Swanston Street, dodging trams and Silver-top taxis, and headed to the Black Opal. It was a pokies place with cheap drinks and the men were too busy willing their machines to pay out to bother cracking onto a couple of off-duty strippers. Maxine was covering for us in the peeps. She should have retired back in the mid eighties but that was another story.

I bought bourbon and Coke for Chloe and champagne for myself and we sat at a high table at the back of the bar, the newspaper between us.

I sipped my drink and waited for her to fill me in. She lit a ciggie and looked around the bar with big scared eyes. Drama queen. I slid the paper over and read my horoscope. It worked.

'I never told you what happened on Saturday night,' she blurted out. 'I should've, but I was embarrassed.'

When she paused for effect I flipped through to the employment section. She lasted five seconds.

'It was early in the shift and Frank called me into his office to do a line of coke. You know, kickstart the night.'

I knew, even though I hadn't done any drugs for a year.

'I'd been alone with him before and nothing ever happened. But this time, after we'd done a couple, he gets up and comes over to where I'm sitting and unzips his pants. Gets his cock out and tells me to suck it. Mate, I just fucking laughed at him, thought it was a joke, right? Then he tries to push my head down, like, hard, and somehow I manage to wriggle out of his hands and I bolt back into the club.'

Shit like that made me really mad. If Frank wasn't already dead I would have had to kill him myself. 'Why didn't you tell me?' I asked.

Chloe took another slug of bourbon and rubbed her face with her hands. 'I shouldn't have got myself into that situation. You wouldn't have.'

It was true Chloe flirted and appeared promiscuous and up for anything. But that was no excuse.

'It wasn't your fault,' I said.

She shrugged. 'So there I am at the bar and I'm like, coking off my head but I'm also in shock and a couple of the girls are asking me what's the matter when Frank comes out of his office and tells me to clean out my locker, I'm fired.

'And I say, well that's OK 'cause I quit anyway and where's the two hundred you owe me from the night before? And he says he's not giving it to me. Fuck, mate, I just went ballistic.

I earned that money. I worked fucking hard for every cent of it. I went off at him, called him every name under the sun and told him I was going to report him to the cops, charge him with sexual assault, drugs, you name it.'

I raised my eyebrows. Chloe groaned. 'I know, not the smartest thing to say to a prick like that. So he goes, you don't know who you're dealing with, bitch, you want to wind up dead? And I say, you don't fucking scare me, you better watch your back motherfucker 'cause I know people. And then Flame, she's kind of like his girlfriend, hands me the stuff from my locker and the bouncers drag me out.'

'Do you really know people?' I asked.

'No, that bit was bullshit.'

The card machines sang electronic songs and Chloe lit another Winnie off the butt of the first. I wanted one too but I'd given up a few months before.

'Tell me what I should do,' she said.

I'd finished my investigative services certificate in October and gained an inquiry agent's licence soon after. Since then the girls at work considered me the last word on all matters of law and order. They asked me about custody disputes and apprehended violence orders, taxation and drug busts. No matter that I hadn't found a job and my training covered following people and pissing into a funnel.

'How many people heard you threaten Frank?' I asked.

''Bout fifty.'

'You should go to the cop shop now and tell them about Saturday night. Makes you look innocent.'

'I am innocent!'

I drained my champagne. It had given me a nice buzz and I was tonguing for another.

'Come on, I'll take you.'

•

We caught the number 16 tram and rattled down Swanston Street. The top end where it intersected Lonsdale was home to the Shaft and a bunch of sex shops and as we moved towards the river we passed takeaway stores, discount clothing outlets and shops with spruikers out front flogging perfume rip-offs and cheap sunglasses. The Flinders Street station end had all the druggies. Junkies in bad tracksuits hung around the fast food joints and the alcoholics congregated on benches outside St Paul's Cathedral. Swanston was the street they never showed you in the tourist brochures. I knew it well.

We passed the Queen Victoria Gardens and the Domain and got off at the St Kilda Road Police Complex. I led Chloe straight up to the reception desk.

'We're here about the Parisi murder,' I told a young cop. 'My friend worked for him and she'd like to speak to someone.'

'I didn't kill him,' Chloe exclaimed.

The uniform grinned. 'That's what they all say.'

Chloe smiled back. She was wearing a low-cut top with 'Pornbabe' written across the chest.

I was good at flirting but Chloe was better. She could flirt for Australia. They stared at each other, smiling, while he picked up the phone and spoke to someone.

'Detective Talbot will be down in a moment,' he said.

I sat in the corner and left them to it. Just as she asked to see his gun a door opened and a female detective with bobbed auburn hair stuck her head out a door. 'Chloe?'

She followed the D and I settled back to wait. Crimestopper's posters adorned the walls and cops went in and out the automatic doors. I watched them and couldn't help wondering what they had that I didn't. I'd tried to join the police force a year before and hadn't got past the application stage. They'd rejected me when I told the truth about my work history.

Either I didn't have the moral credentials to be a girl in blue or the Victoria Police had enough scandal without dropping a stripper into the mix.

It was a weird career to aspire to after growing up in a hippy community where the kids were taught to hate the 'pigs' and our parents lived in fear of the choppers that buzzed the hills around harvest time. But aspire to it I did, partly from rebellion and partly because of something that happened when I was thirteen.

My mum had hooked up with a man named Russell, an ex-bikie, straggly but good looking in his own way. He'd come to our town to buy dope to sell in the city, but liked it so much he decided to stay. My younger brother Jasper and I weren't too happy when he first moved in, but he brought us round with jumbo packs of M&Ms and hand-held, battery-operated computer games. He even hooked up a small black and white TV to a car battery so we could watch *Countdown.*

The trouble was he had a problem with alcohol, and heroin, and when he was really drunk, or couldn't score, he'd lose the plot. Anything would set him off and his arguments with my mum escalated from yelling to pushing, to slapping her in the face.

We wondered why she didn't just leave him. She'd been a women's libber in the seventies and had worked at a battered women's shelter, but Russell seemed to have her under some sort of spell. He could go from frightening to charming, and after one of his outbursts he'd be extra sorry and romantic, and promise never to do it again.

He'd been living with us for three months when Jasper and I were woken by shouting. We peered down from the attic loft where we slept. In the light of the kerosene lamps we saw Russell looming over our mum, hand raised, face twisted with rage. Jasper, who was only eight, started sniffling.

'I've called the police,' she said, but this got him angrier.

'Are you fucked in the head, woman? I've got ten pounds drying in the shed. You have got to be the stupidest fucking unit I have ever met.' He was pacing back and forth on the faded oriental rug, a bottle of bourbon in his hand. All of a sudden he dropped the bottle and punched her in the face. She staggered back, crashing into the unlit potbelly stove and knocking out the flue.

I half climbed, half slid down the ladder and ran at him as he raised his fist again, jumped up and hung off his arm. He swung it back and I flew off onto the floor.

My brother's cry was now a high-pitched wail. Mum was cowering in the corner, Russell advancing on her, when the front door crashed in.

'Police!'

Two uniformed officers stood there, one male and one female. Russell grabbed a poker from beside the stove and wielded it like a baseball bat. 'Come on,' he yelled. 'I'll have ya!'

The woman had her hand on the butt of her gun. The male approached Russell with his hands out, talking in low tones, calling him mate. Russell swung at him and the cop leaned back and grabbed the poker, pulling him off balance, so he fell face first to the floor. It was the coolest move I'd ever seen. The female officer leapt into action, wrenching Russell's hands behind his back and digging her knee in as she cuffed him tight.

They made sure we were all right and took Russell away. It turned out there were a number of warrants out for his arrest, and we never saw him again. And since that day I'd wanted to be a cop. But the cops didn't want me. So I'd done the PI course; it had seemed like the next best thing.

When I'd graduated, one of my lecturers said he might

have a bit of surveillance work coming up. Tony Torcasio was an ex undercover officer who had his own agency, a good guy, but so far nothing had eventuated. There were ads in the paper for investigators from time to time but if you didn't have experience or weren't an ex-cop you didn't have a hope in hell.

I loved dancing but after three years it was time to quit. I'd turned twenty-eight two days earlier and although I could pass for twenty-three, I felt old. Maxine was a well-preserved forty-five but that didn't stop the younger guys yelling, 'Get grandma off stage.'

'All done.' Chloe stood in front of me, wiggling her hips.

'They're not going to throw your arse in jail?'

'Nuh.' She skipped off to the front counter, whispered something to the constable and handed him one of her cards. I could have sworn I heard 'bring your handcuffs'.

•

Ten days later, November thirteen, I was sitting on my balcony in Elwood among palms and potted herbs. My first floor unit was in a block of sixteen and although the building was ugly brown brick the one bedroom flats were renovated and the street, Broadway, was full of oak trees. Dean Martin was on the stereo and I had a glass of cask wine and half a pack of individually wrapped cheese singles in front of me. I love plastic cheese. It was Thursday evening, still light because of daylight saving, and I felt the itch to go out. It was a toss-up between seeing a band and getting so pissed I ended up pashing some grungy rocker, or going to the Godard version of *Breathless* at the Astor. Decisions, decisions. The wine flowed through my limbs, relaxing them, and a breeze that smelled of saltwater came in off the bay.

The phone rang. It was my mum.

'You're home, I don't believe it. How's work?'

'Great, fantastic,' I lied.

'I worry about you, you know. Not so much the peepshows but the bucks' parties. What if the guys get out of hand? What if it turns violent?'

'It's really not dangerous. There's always heaps of security. And the bucks are more scared of us than we are of them. Just last weekend—'

'It irks me. It just does.' She actually said irk. I wondered if I'd heard anyone say it in conversation before and decided I hadn't.

'I know.' I started craving a cigarette.

'And apart from your physical safety I worry about your psyche.'

'My psyche?' I would have killed for a cigarette. And something a bit stronger than wine. I leaned back in the canvas director's chair and put my bare feet up on the balcony railing.

'It's got to affect you, pandering to men, reinforcing ridiculous stereotypes about women, buying into the whole madonna/whore thing—'

'I don't buy into—'

'I know *you* don't but by working in that industry you perpetuate the myth. And to think I named you after Simone de Beauvoir.'

My mum was an old school feminist who lectured in women's studies and I couldn't win an argument with her. I turned into a petulant fifteen-year-old every time I tried.

'It's an art form, Mum, like . . . like Josephine Baker or Gypsy Rose Lee.'

'Did Josephine Baker do "floor work" and show the world what she had for breakfast? I think not.'

I picked at an ingrown hair on my leg and didn't say anything until she changed the subject: 'I heard from Jasper.'

'What's he up to?'

'He's doing really well, said to say hi. He's in New York doing some stuff for *GQ*, then he's off to Canada for fashion week in Montreal.'

My brother had scooped the family gene pool and worked as a model. I considered asking my mother if she didn't think modelling was similar to stripping but restrained myself.

'How's Steve?' I asked instead. Steve was my mother's 'partner'. They met a few years after the Russell episode and had been together ever since, eventually moving to Sydney where my mum became an academic. Steve ran courses in mud-brick housing and solar power at the College of Adult Education.

'He's great, really busy though, organising a rally against the government's stance on greenhouse gas emissions.'

'I've got my inquiry agent's licence,' I said. 'There might be some work coming up.'

'Why don't you finish your degree? You've only got one semester to go and you could finish it in Melbourne. I've looked into it.'

'I'm a bit busy at the moment.'

'You could study part time. A qualification would get you out of the sex industry.'

'I dunno about that, heaps of strippers have arts degrees.'

There was a beep on the line. Call waiting. Hallelujah.

'Mum? I've got another call, I have to go . . .

'Hello?'

'Simone,' Chloe sounded out of breath, 'you've got to come quick. Someone's trying to kill me.'